INTO DARKNESS
BY
JASON R. DAVIS

BREAKING FATE PUBLISHING

Published by
Breaking Fate Publishing
5 Loomis Circle
Suite #2
Madison, WI 53704

Please visit us online at http://breakingfatepublishing.com
Jason Davis' website can be found at http://jasonrdavis.com

Edited by: Kim Young, Kim's Fiction Proofreading & Editing Services
Cover Illustration by: Jason R. Davis
Copyright 2017

For Patty
Thank you for keeping me writing.

INTO DARKNESS
Book 2 of The Guardian
A novel by Jason R. Davis

When his life was ruined, his family killed, his farm destroyed, Job knelt down on the ground and yelled up to the heavens, 'Why god? Why me?' and the thundering voice of God answered, 'There's just something about you that pisses me off.'

-Stephen King (Storm of the Century)

PROLOGUE

Chief Winston sat in his squad car on the outskirts of town. As he often did on most weeknights, he had tucked himself back amongst the trees, hidden from the road. He'd rather be asleep than pulling over speeders or harassing any of the local kids for whatever shenanigans they'd get into. Not that he expected too much on a Tuesday night, what with school having started back last month. Most kids would be home working on homework, but there were still the rambunctious few who wanted to burn off that summer energy before fall really kicked in.

There were always going to be the troubled teens. The kids who wouldn't be at home doing homework. He knew those were the ones he should be harassing. He hated to profile, but that was the way it was. They would be the ones who vandalized houses, egged the squad car, or even slashed his tires. They were his problem children. Many nights, he would just keep a watchful eye on them, letting them have their occasional night of fun. It usually never went too far. When it did, well... He'd put a stop to it. He'd been in town long enough, nearly fifteen years, that when things escalated, he knew which parents to call. He also knew who would care and who wouldn't. It sometimes just came down to who was worth the extra effort. Some kids just needed a swift kick in the butt.

So far, tonight had been an easy night. There was a cool breeze blowing through his window, which felt good. He was parked just off the road where the old highway ended. A person either drove into the cornfield at the end of the road or they turned toward town. It wasn't a place to catch speeders, although he would occasionally see someone run the stop sign. Sometimes, he would pull them over, especially if he saw an out-of-state plate. Most times, though, he'd just watch them. As long as they weren't driving recklessly, he would let them go.

Parked down the driveway of a private property, it was hard for anyone to see him from the road. It was owned by one of the local churches. Not one of the large Catholic congregations, but a smaller Pentecostal operating out of a little storefront on Main Street. They bought the property nearly five years ago and had been raising money so they could build themselves a nice church. Why? He didn't know, but maybe it had something to do with how often they were broken into and vandalized. However, the church still hadn't been built. In fact, there was nothing out there except the driveway leading back into the long rows of pine trees. It was such a great hiding spot, he could just sit, nod off a little, and let the night pass around him.

It was a peaceful place. Standard, Illinois, was that little town, the one that most people just drove through and barely saw. It had a little police force, but wasn't large enough to have a full-time officer during the day. It consisted of himself, he worked from four p.m. to four a.m. during the week, and the weekend warrior who did the same shift Friday and Saturday. If anyone had any problems during the day, it could wait. At least that was how it used to be.

Ever since he brought on Rob Alletto as his weekend warrior, he felt sorry for the former Chicago cop, working in a bonus for him to be on call during the day. That didn't mean much more than a hundred extra dollars in the paycheck. For the most part, it was nothing more than the occasional call to get a cat out of a tree. Rob was a good guy, so Dan wished he could do more for him. He hoped the rumors he heard about the man's house about to go into foreclosure were just that. He would hate to lose him.

Dan closed his eyes, leaning his head back against the headrest. Another cool gust came in through the window, the sweet scent of pine coming with it. In the distance, he heard cars passing on the freeway. It was a soothing, rhythmic sound, like the white noise tapes he had used back when he'd been trying to quit smoking. All they did was help him sleep. Damned things hadn't done crap to help him quit smoking. Served him right, though. That was what he got for allowing himself to get roped into one of those late-night infomercials.

He felt his skin prickle, the breeze dancing along the hairs on his arm. It was reminiscent of camping and lying under the stars. There was a time he had no cares in the world. He was just another kid camping with his folks. Some nights, when things were quiet and the campground was nearly empty, he would lay on a picnic table, enjoying the cool night air. His parents would find him there in the morning, fresh dew covering his body, but it was worth it just to enjoy that little breeze.

He felt himself slipping away. He knew he should try to push it off, not letting himself drift into the darkness of sleep. It was still early, and if he were ever caught sleeping, it would probably be his job. A night officer who didn't stay awake at night wasn't serving and protecting. He would never get caught, though. Not by anyone who cared enough to do anything. Most people already knew he occasionally napped on his shift, but nobody ever said anything.

His head bobbed, sleep being a thief trying to steal him away. With a jerk, he came to full attention again. He wanted to just doze off and drift away. It had been a long day. The mayor now felt Dan needed to be in town meetings with him, so time he would have used for sleep had been spent in a stuffy room listening to town officials drone on endlessly. So sleeping tonight would be justified. It was the mayor's fault he was exhausted.

Too bad he just wasn't wired that way. It wasn't in his nature. When he did take naps, it was never due to a desire to get out of his work, but because he had worked too much.

Then there was also the part of him that just refused to let him do it. Not because of a work ethic, but because his body sensed he was not in his bed. He would start fading away, giving in to the abyss, when...*BAM*...his eyes would fly open and he would sit rigid in the driver's seat. Tonight, he was tired enough not to care about his work ethic, but not tired enough that his body was ready to ignore the lack of a bed. As much as he wanted to drift away, his body wouldn't let him.

He felt sleep try to take him again, his head becoming heavy and slowly slipping forward. His chin rested on his chest, body slumping forward, going slack. He could feel his butt slipping in the seat.

And then he jerked his head up, the whole world jolting back into place. His eyes opened and the fog of exhaustion faded away. He wasn't sure, but it felt like the car had moved when he jumped.

That was it. He had tried to will himself to take a nap, but it just wasn't happening. The best he had done was a little five-second power nap. He needed something to keep him awake.

It was funny how that little jerk out of a nap was enough to fuel a change in attitude. Where he was ready to just fade away a few minutes ago, he now had energy to get through the rest of the night. Of course, if he didn't get moving, that would change in a few minutes.

He wasn't going to catch anyone running that stop sign anyway, and had trespassed on the church's property long enough.

They haven't even made any effort to clear out the landscape. Yeah, that church is never going to get built.

5

* * * *

Minutes later, he drove down Main Street, the windows of his patrol car still down. It was just too nice a night not to enjoy the crisp air.

The town was so quiet and serene. This was the time of night he liked his job. Well, that wasn't entirely true. There was never really a time he didn't like his job. He felt like it would always be his calling to be the chief in a small town, and Standard had long since become his home. Yes, there were kids who caused him problems, slashing the tires on the squad car and his personal car, damaging his property. He'd been upset at the time, but it was all to be expected. People always blamed someone else for their mistakes, and being the chief made him an easy target.

However, this was the time of night everything just faded into a memory. Yesterday's problems slid back into the forgotten realms of confused thoughts, and tomorrow's misfortunes were yet to be conceived. This was that time where reality seemed to slip into a lost void, everyone holding their breath for it to come back.

It was also the time when it was easy to believe there was no one else in town. That he was the last survivor of some horrendous apocalypse. That all life had been snuffed out. He could just sit and watch the rest of the world fade away. This was the quiet time.

He looked at the dashboard clock. Just past two a.m. He only had two hours left, knowing he would probably end up parking just outside the Casey's to listen to the drone of the distant highway. Although he went off duty at four, he often stuck around until the opening cashier came at five.

Nancy was an elderly woman who shouldn't be opening the store by herself, so he enjoyed making sure she got in safely. To repay him, she'd fire up the coffee machine before doing any of her other morning procedures, and he would enjoy the first freshly brewed cup of the day. On the house, of course, since the little gas station wouldn't open until six and she would spend the next hour getting the cash ready for the registers.

He pulled into the lot and slipped past the dark gas pumps. They were old and not well maintained, making him question the last time they had been inspected. He guessed it couldn't have been too long ago. There had to be regulations on pumps, the older ones being inspected more often, right? He had his suspicions they had barely passed. The things needed to be upgraded, maybe getting the ones that accepted credit cards.

God help how every damn thing nowadays had to be digital. Digital card readers, and now, according to the news, they had to have those little chips in the card to make us more safe.

Yeah, then how the hell did hackers get my info from the damn hardware store? Whole damn world is getting techsized, but it's all going to hell for it.

With the gas station being so far away from the interstate, the business had been downsized to the point they barely stayed open, most people just getting the fresh morning donuts and the excellent pizza. He wasn't sure if that was going to be enough to keep it competitive with the nice new truck stop out by the interstate. It seemed like the little gas station's days were numbered.

He hoped not. The town was quiet, but the few calls he did get often came from trouble out at the truck stop. Hell, if those damn cashiers would stop doing God knows what with the truckers out there, his life would be simpler. But with the truck stop came updated pumps, fast food, and a little larger grocery area for the people who didn't want to drive fifteen miles to the closest full-sized store.

His town had started changing, but he wasn't sure he wanted to get up to speed with where it was headed.

He eased the squad car into his normal spot by the front door, facing the road. He could see the little field across the street that gave way to the woods and the large

7

mound of shale left from when the town had been a coal mining community. That was long before his and many of the residents' time. That hill at the outer portion of town was a remnant of a long-ago era. It was a mound that would probably equate three blocks wide and six blocks long, rising high into the sky and covered in trees. People were forbidden from going to it, which meant everyone did. They happily ignored the No Trespassing signs so often, there were well-worn trails through the woods leading up to it and a wide path that twirled around the little mountain leading to the top.

Military remnants sat on top. He wasn't sure what had been up there at one time, but he'd heard something about a military radio tower. He'd never looked into it. Whatever it had been, a partial wall of one building and a cement slab of another still remained. He assumed that were the reason for the winding path to the top, although most kids liked using the direct paths up the sides because they were quicker, more direct, and more challenging. If he were still young and didn't have the early signs of arthritis creeping into his knees, he might have enjoyed the climb.

He looked up at the large, dark shape. It was a mountain of black blotting out the deep blue of the night sky. It was so dominant and so much a signature of what would otherwise be a non-descript small town in the Midwest, he doubted anyone would have thought twice about the little town without it.

He paused, squinting, noticing something that shouldn't be there.

There was a light at the top. An orange flicker bright enough to be seen through the trees and tall enough to rise above them. It swayed with the small gusts of wind, dancing its own hypnotic dance. He sat watching it. Someone was up there.

Well, there went his peaceful night. *Crap.*

He pulled out of the lot and quickly made his way around to the other side of the street, parking at the entrance of the long path. It was time for him to put his climbing skills to the test. He knew it would be so much fun doing this crap in the dark. He'd make it easier by taking the longer, winding path. It would be less likely he'd sprain his ankle or something. Flashlight or not, there were roots that were sometimes hard to see.

He put the car in park, reached for the radio, and called it in. When he set the radio down and got out of the car, he didn't realize it would be the last time anyone ever heard from him again.

PART I

In the beginning, God created Light and saw that it was good. In this light, he created the heavens and the earth. Hell came later, but was still a part of what was created. Before the light, before God, Darkness was all that was known. It was from then, the creature came into existence.

Time was unknown, not yet a part of days. The dark was not split amongst the light, and everything continued as an endless night. The creature was used to this darkness.

It flourished in this moment outside time. It devoured others and took them to be a part of it.

Others lived in this time and thrived on each other. Some lived off misery, some off life essence. It was a savage time. Worlds hadn't existed and these creatures lived without form...pieces of the dark, but not a part of it. They had their own sentience and did not rely on the dark. They only existed upon it.

Then the light came. Time came. Days started and ended with the darkness now splitting the light. The things of before had to remove themselves to a pocket of nonexistence outside of time, but those who could not had to find the shadows.

One such creature hid deep in this new rock that flowed of the dark earth across its surface. It burrowed itself deeply, finding solitude a comfort as time moved on away from him. As light and dark, night and day fought for domination in a new existence, the creature hibernated, hiding from it all.

CHAPTER 1

Walking out, the screen door slammed behind him with a satisfying *whack,* making Bobby smile, knowing just how much his grandmother hated it. Sure enough, not long afterward, there she was, standing in the doorway. He didn't have to look around to know the short, squat-looking woman, who usually always had a warm smile for anyone, would not have that smile now.

"Robert Evan Taylor, you know better than to let that screen door slam behind you," she called after him.

He turned and saw a glare and frown on her face, just as he pictured. It wouldn't last, though, and he knew it. She loved him too much. All he had to do was flash a grin at her and watch as the hardened face softened. It wasn't in her nature to stay upset, her usual, heartwarming smile quickly reemerging.

"I'm sorry, Grandma," he said, jumping down the few cement steps to the front sidewalk.

"Okay, well, make sure to have your mom call me when you get home. I want to know if she still intends to go garage saleing with me tomorrow and if so, she better get here early."

Bobby knew his grandma could call his mom. No, the reason for him to tell his mom to call was her little subtle way of checking to make sure he got home safely. He was ten. He didn't need them to constantly check up on him. For half the kids in town, their parents never knew where they were. He was so annoyed that they always kept a watchful eye on him.

Okay, he knew why, but it still wasn't fair. It happened over a year ago. They should move on already. He had.

"I will."

Bobby walked toward the end of the sidewalk. He'd turn left and go through what his grandmother called the "Fool's Woods". It was a dark spot of town, the little mini-forest surrounding the large coal dump. Of course, neither she nor his mother allowed him to go through there, but if he didn't, he would have to walk downtown and get harassed by the older kids who hung out up there. The coal dump path was a straight shot home. It was stupid to go around it every night.

"Bobby, where's your bike?"

He turned back toward his grandmother. Yeah, he wasn't happy he didn't have his bike, either. He didn't want to tell her he had bent the rim yesterday by jumping off one of the little cliffs around the coal dump. Well, he hadn't bent it by jumping off. It had been the landing. He had gotten some really good speed. So much so, he realized he was going too fast. His survival instinct kicked in and he had bailed off his bike right before the cliff's edge. In the end, he walked away with scratched knees. His bike hadn't been so lucky.

He planned to go to some of the garage sales by himself tomorrow to see if he had enough allowance to get some other crappy bike. It wouldn't be as nice as the sixteen-speed mountain bike he had now, but it didn't have to be. He hoped to find a granny rider or a banana special he could tool around with, maybe salvage some of the parts from. It wouldn't be the first time he had done it, their second garage starting to look like a bicycle graveyard.

"Oh, it had a flat tire before school this morning, so I just walked." He rushed through the lie as he stepped onto the uneven asphalt of the road.

The gravel crunched beneath his sneakers as he jogged the short distance to the streetlight at the end of the block. When he heard the screen door ease shut behind him, he slowed to a walk, happy he was no longer being watched.

He knew she would be back inside, already changing the TV channel as she sat at her kitchen table. It was how she always was without him there. The TV would be on some game show or a lame country music station. Something no one under the ancient age of fifty would enjoy.

At least she didn't force him to watch any of that boring crap. When school let out and he had to go to his grandma's so she could watch him until his mom got off work, he would come in the door, drop his backpack, and quickly grab the remote. It was his time to watch what he wanted.

He would sometimes come in through the back door and sneak up behind her. She never heard him, so he would give her a quick hug from behind. She would jump and give a shout every time. Then he would say sorry and grab the remote. After all, he had just given her a hug.

He stood under the glow of the next streetlight. With the fall chill, night had started coming earlier and it was already dark. It wasn't chilly enough for him to wear a jacket, not that he would. He liked to avoid it until he was forced to, wearing shorts and t-shirts until it was a command from his overbearing mother. "Wear this." "Wear that." "Don't be out too late riding your bike."

If she found out he was going through the Fool's Woods tonight, she'd nag him about that, too.

He walked past the streetlight, keeping his eyes focused on the next one, the gravel crunching under his shoes. There were no sidewalks on this street. Normally, he would ride his bike down the side of the road, but he now let his feet follow where his tires would cruise.

Mrs. Brady's house was up on the right side of the road. All the lights were on, the curtains wide open.

Outside, she had orange Halloween lights, which looked like Christmas lights someone had pooped on, running along the edges. Halloween was only a couple weeks away, and she was one of those town nuts who loved to overdo it. However, her version wasn't haunted or creepy. She seemed to think Halloween was like Christmas with lights and inflatables of smiling skeletons. What fun was that? It was too childish. Come on. These weren't any kind of decorations for Halloween. Where was the scary?

From light, it seemed like he went to completely pitch black as none of the houses on the next block were lit up. He knew people lived in the first house, but only because he would sometimes see cars parked in the driveway. Bobby didn't know them, but whoever lived there never really cared to socialize anyway. The streetlight gave off the only light on the block until he reached the alley and Tina Limpquist's house, which was right along Main Street.

Tina was annoying, and Bobby would often pick on her at school. He found it hard not to as she was such a snot. One grade behind him, she still found ways to tattle. It seemed getting him in trouble was her personal mission. When he pushed her down at school, she always ran to Mrs. Sanchez. Then he would have to sit out another recess, writing those stupid sentences up on the blackboard until the underside of his hand hurt.

Once school was over, Tina waited to see if he would go into the Fool's Woods. Then she would call his mom or grandmother and get him in trouble again. What was it with little girls knowing his mom and calling her? There were others who gave little reports to his mom, but Tina was the worst.

At least he knew she didn't watch for him at night. She didn't know of all his night trips through the woods. Tina was afraid of the dark...*Ooh, boohoo. Little girl afraid of the dark*...which meant she wouldn't be out or even looking out her window. Little girls were always afraid of monsters. Besides, unless he was under the streetlight, she wouldn't even be able to tell it was him.

Bobby made it past her house and to Main Street, which actually had a sidewalk. When he had his bike, he would fly down it, not caring if the cops caught him. He'd been stopped a few times, the cops telling him it was illegal, threatening to give him a fine. He still rode his bike on the sidewalk, not caring if they liked it or not. He felt safer there than on the street. People who walked, well… They needed to get out of his way. He was the bike rider, the midnight flyer, and on his bike, he was the king. Everyone should know to get out of his way or get run over.

But he had no bike tonight, so he was forced to be one of the walkers, *yuck*, and he wasn't happy about it. He wasn't going to go along the street, though. His goal was to cross it and into the open grass area, then into the woods. His grandma would call him a fool. She always warned him of all the hobos in the woods at night, telling him they liked to steal little kids and run off with them.

Like a hobo is really going to grab me.

Even if he didn't have his bike, he could still run pretty fast. And when had he ever seen a hobo in Standard? It's *Standard*. There were no big towns nearby, nothing close that would be considered a city. He had only ever seen one creepy guy. Bobby guessed he could have been considered a hobo. He had heard he lived in the alley behind Main Street. Everyone knew he didn't have a regular job, doing odd jobs and stuff liked that. Sure, he could be in the coal dump, but everyone said he slept in the alley. Why would he leave back there to stay in the woods?

Besides, if anything happened to Bobby, that guy would be the first one questioned. He didn't know if it would be like in those cop shows where they put him in a room and sat him down, waiting it out, maybe even beating the guy up for a confession. If it were, he kind of wished he could be there to watch it. That would be so cool.

Huh. Just where did they question their perps anyway? Bobby wondered.

He had seen inside the little police headquarters in town when he had to go up there when Mikey had disappeared. He saw the little office all the kids called the "Cop Shop". It was so small, barely having room for a desk and a file cabinet. Where did the cops take the people they needed to question? Did they have some other jail hidden somewhere?

He walked across the street, not hurrying because there were no cars. While it was still relatively early, it was a school night. It seemed like most kids just didn't stay out as late anymore. Their loss. They should be out enjoying this. Who cared about what the adults said? They should be out running through the alleys and having fun. Maybe it was just a fluke that most people wanted to spend the night at home, but it had been like this all week. Where were his friends? Why weren't they playing tag in the coal dump when it was dark and harder to find each other?

He made his way across the street, turning to look at downtown two blocks away. Sure enough, it was pretty much what he would have expected. There were three cars parked in front of Doc's Sweet Shop, four or five older kids sitting on the steps. It was too far away to know who, but he could make a guess. It would be the normal ones, Springer being one of them.

Springer, the one he was really trying to avoid. The rest of them weren't that bad, but there was just something about Springer that dug deep into Bobby's chest and gripped his heart. It had been a long-standing feeling that traced back to even before Springer began picking on him. Bobby didn't know why, but the kid had it out for him. When they were in the same school, Springer would push him into lockers. He once chased him down and slammed Bobby into a fence just because he had looked at him. Springer would snicker and make up cruel nicknames for Bobby whenever he was near.

Bobby would much rather face whatever was in the Fool's Woods than go uptown. There was no way he wanted to face Springer, not with all his friends standing around. Instead, Bobby rushed down the gravel maintenance vehicle entry until he came to the edge of the path and the yellow bar blocking it. From there, he could see the small path running along the south edge of the large mound. He didn't know why his mom called it the coal dump, or the surrounding woods the Fool's Woods. Both seemed like strange names, but especially the coal dump because the rock mountain was covered in small, thin red rocks, which looked nothing like the coal he had seen. It was just another one of those weird things he didn't think he would ever understand. And why call it the Fool's Woods? At least the whole town called it the coal dump. As far as Bobby knew, only his grandma and mom had a name for the wooded area around it. He had called it that to Emily once and she just looked at him funny.

He stood at the barrier. Of course, no one ever let the bar stop them. Walkers just stepped over it, and those who rode their bikes just went around. There was a well-worn path around the side where bike tires had long since stripped the grass. It was a good symbol for how everyone felt about the coal dump. The adults said to not go there, but everyone did. No one cared.

He let his knees rest against the bar as he looked down the long path. A cool breeze rustled the remaining leaves in the trees. He closed his eyes and listened as the night talked to him. The wind pushed against him, as if telling him to turn back around. Bobby chuckled.

His overactive imagination often talked to him. Whether riding his bike or running, he felt like people were in the trees, watching. Sometimes, they were spies and he was a secret agent making his daring escape. Other times, they were ghosts. He was always much more afraid of the ghosts because they would scream at him as he rode by, their howls piercing the night, crying out that they knew what he had done.

Tonight was different. He really felt like he was being watched, and not just because of his imagination. The night had an edge to it. He knew Tina wasn't watching him, but it still felt like it. He knew the older kids weren't anywhere near him, but it felt like they were right there, breathing down his neck. He wasn't alone. Something *was* watching him. Even in the open, he felt like there was something just out of sight, hiding in the darkness.

Come on. Don't be a dork.

Bobby laughed and put his foot up on the bar. The muscles in his leg flexed as he pushed himself up, then it was off to the races. He could sometimes see a little light from the streetlight just past where the path twisted, but not tonight. He landed hard on the other side of the bar and took off running.

The night came to life around him. The wind picked up, hammering into him, as if warning Bobby he was running into danger. It howled around him, screaming, piercing. He tried not to focus on it because it was hard enough to see where he was going. The moon was bright overhead, but as he went deeper, more and more trees took away the light.

He knew the path well, but he was usually riding his bike. It all felt different when he ran. His feet didn't land right because of the ruts. There were times he slipped or snagged a foot on a root.

Shadows moved, twisting and turning around him. Their dance slithered amongst the light. When it seemed like Bobby could see where he stepped, the light changed and his foot fell into darkness, making him trip on the uneven, rocky ground.

Taking a breath got harder, the air around him growing thick. He hadn't noticed it at first. He thought it was because of his running, but now it felt like syrup as he fought to breathe. His head grew fuzzy, the world around

19

him turning gray. No, it wasn't the world going gray. It was his head. It was heavy, like he had to struggle to think. He couldn't remember where he was going.

His shoes felt like weights, slowing him down. The roots he had to step over seemed to have grown, making him fight to get over them. He finally misjudged. Before he knew what was happening, he fell.

The ground came up quickly. His arms plunged into the thorn bushes running along the edge of the path, cutting his skin. His knees hit hard, the sharp pain making him turn his body as he skidded along the red shale rock. He had fallen off his bike enough times to know how it felt when skin got scraped away. Somewhere in his mind, he heard his mother yelling at him about his long-sleeved shirt being in his backpack.

Home. He wasn't that far. Being so close was somehow important.

His body was sore, his chest feeling like a hammer had slammed into it. He reached out to push himself up, his palms burning, his knees screaming as he knelt. Glancing up, he could see the streetlight at the end of the path. He was almost there. Almost out of there and away from…

Something. There's something in here.

Bobby could feel it. It wasn't his imagination. There was something hiding in the shadows, reaching out for him. When he had fallen, the pain pushed back some of the fog and he could breathe again. He knew there was a presence watching him.

He couldn't believe it. His grandmother was right. There was something in the woods, and it was coming after him. He had to get out of there. He had to run and go and get the hell away before it got him. He could see the shadows dancing again, circling him.

A chill came over him, but he couldn't shiver. His body wasn't his to control anymore. Bobby's mind started to spasm. He couldn't escape the cold or shake it away as it overtook him. The fog came back, the weight on his chest getting heavier. It felt like waves slammed over him, pulling him deeper into exhaustion.

Bobby knew he had to get out of there before whatever it was completely took him. There had to be a way for him to break free. He'd been on that path a thousand times. It was his home away from home. When he'd ride his bike through there, he'd hit speeds where it felt like he was outrunning the devil. Well, the devil was back. He had to get away.

How do you beat the devil?

He wasn't the most religious, not after *him*. His parents weren't churchgoers. His grandma went a few times a year, usually when he would go along. What had the pastor always said?

Please, there has to be some prayer.

There had to be something he could do or say. Something that would get him out of there. Bobby needed to remember, but thinking was just so hard at the moment. The harder he tried, the thicker the fog grew.

From somewhere, the words came to him. A ray of light shown through the clouds as the words formed. He recognized the bedtime prayer. As he visualized it in his head, his mouth formed the words.

"Now I lay me down to sleep," he gasped. The words tried to choke him, but with a watery cry, he forced them out. "I pray the Lord my soul to keep. And if I die before I wake..." *I don't want to die. God, don't let me die.* He forced in more air, the weight on his chest lightening. The next few words came out in a rush. "I pray the Lord my soul to take."

The fog receded as a shiver rocked through him. Bobby could move again. Before it even registered, he jumped up and ran. His feet pounded on the ground, pushing him. *Go, go, go. Faster.* The devil was back there, and it wanted him. If he stopped again, he didn't think he'd get another chance. He had to win. He had to get to the light.

21

The bar at the end of the path got closer. Bobby saw the yellow paint, which caught the light of the streetlight. He had to reach it. He'd be safe then.

His legs pumped harder. New pain coursed through him, but he fought to keep himself moving. *Run faster*. The fog was there, but he felt like he was running through it. It seemed like the faster he ran, the more it drifted behind him. It lifted more and more out of his mind.

I...just...have...to...run...fast...enough...

Then he was there. Holding his breath, he leapt high over the bar, his heart pounding. It would have been easier for him to just run around, but he was sure that whatever was behind him would have caught him if he did. He had never cleared it before, but he needed to now. If he tripped… If he were to get caught on it, he would fall just short of the glow of the streetlight and it would get him.

Bobby landed with a whoosh of air. He swore he heard the night around him come alive with cheering. Crowds roared and applauded. He reacted by standing, raising his arms, and jumping around, doing an end zone dance as he worked his way into the round circle of light.

"And the crowd goes wild!" Bobby cheered, his hands held high. He jumped up and down a few times before the burning in his lungs forced him to bend over, coughing, fighting to take in deep breaths. He didn't care. He had made it to the light. He was safe. If he stood up and looked, he would see his house just across the empty lot.

"And the crowd goes wild," he said again, looking at the asphalt of the road. He had won. He stood and looked over to where his house was…

It wasn't there. Nothing was there. All he could see was black. He turned to look in the direction he had just come from.

Nothing, just blackness.

"No! No! No!" Bobby cried out, spinning around. As fast as he turned, he could only see glimpses of the world around him, the darkness cutting him off. Then it drew closer, the circle of light shrinking around him. Above him, the dark moved across the light, Bobby's world disappearing.

If anyone had come down the street, they would have seen what looked like a circle of nothing, not much larger than a ten-year-old child.

If a person was really close, they could even hear the muffled cries, screams of a child calling for help.

Then the ball of blackness shrank in upon itself until the glow from the streetlight above illuminated the area once again.

Bobby was gone.

CHAPTER 2

Rob knew she was going to kill him, but not because of how late he was. She was getting used to that, even though she didn't like it. She understood it was only temporary and she had accepted it. After the second week of him coming home to a dinner that had been sitting for three hours, she'd learned not to cook too early. That fight had already happened. He thought she was okay with that part of the job.

No. She was going to kill him because not only was he coming home tonight smelling like sewage, but his clothes were covered in it, he was covered in it, the towel on the car seat was covered in it. He didn't want to think about how their only car was covered in it. His sense of smell had long since evaporated after the second hour of being coated in the stuff, so he wasn't sure how bad it was. He would find out soon enough. Robyn would probably take him right into their back yard and hose him down before he was even allowed in the house.

Her house, *yeah*, and if he just walked in like he was now, he would immediately be pushed back out of her house. In the cool night air, he would be forced to clean up with the garden hose. Maybe he should just go into the back right when he got home. Just walk around to the side of the house and spray himself down. Rob had already done it once tonight while still at the sewage plant, but there was only so much he could do without getting undressed. Much of the chemicals still covered him, and there was no hope for his clothes. He would have had to strip naked at the plant, and that wasn't happening.

The smell just had to come home with him. Each day, he thought he left it at work. According to Robyn, though, he still smelled like sewage when he got home.

Thank goodness the job was only temporary. Rob Alleto, town deputy and overall nice guy, did not see himself working there for long. It was just a nice bit of additional income to get them ready for the winter. The job wasn't him, but it was what they needed to do to get by right now.

When Rob left Chicago, he had been a beat cop for over fifteen years. When he left to become a small-town deputy, he didn't know how much less he would make. He was used to being a full-time cop. He came to Standard assuming the job was full-time. He didn't expect to only be working weekends, the chief giving him the occasional weekday out of pity.

He didn't know if he could say he loved being a cop. He loved his wife and son. His career as a police officer was different. He was a protector, a guardian. Being a cop was so intertwined with his being, he wouldn't be himself, the man he was happy to be, without it.

That had been put to the test just over a year ago when he was caught in the mess down in Hammond. He still wasn't over that, but he had moved on as best as he could. He had saved some, but not everyone. On one level, he knew that would have to be enough, but there were so many more people he should have been able to save. He should have rescued them.

He took a long, deep breath. *It's all behind me. It has to be.*

He took another breath, tasting the smell hanging in the small space of the car. Rob hauled sewage from the plant to the fields. It was a seasonal job, just until the end of October. He worked during the week so as not to

25

interfere with his police duties. It also paid well enough that not only was the mortgage finally up to date, but there was extra. It was enough to get Jake clothes and supplies for school. They also put money away to actually pay the power bill on time this winter. The job allowed him to provide for his family once again.

He sometimes worried someone would say something about how being a town deputy and a truck driver might be a conflict of interest. Maybe it was. He knew working every single day pushed the hours of service laws, but he walked the fine line of harvest field exception laws for farmers. He had to walk it, even though it meant he wouldn't be able to spend much time with his wife and son.

Dan had tried to help him. He knew how much they were hurting. When the chief had to reduce Rob's time on duty and cut the weekly day bonus due to cutbacks of what the town considered unnecessary police spending, Rob's life started to get increasingly more difficult. They had been three months behind on the mortgage, the power was about to get turned off, and their house in Chicago wasn't selling.

Dan told him about a farm outside of town that needed a driver. Bruce, a friend of Rob's, had been happy to help him get his CDL. He couldn't afford to get his commercial driver's license through a school. He knew there were programs out there, but he couldn't leave the part-time job he had now for a chance at making a little more.

Without Bruce, he never would have managed it. At first, Bruce was nervous. Rob was the only officer who knew about his second log book, and he had to constantly reassure his friend he wouldn't turn him in for it. Of course, that deal came with conditions. He looked the other way, but Rob had been adamant about the real reason he stayed cool with the second log book. Bruce was a decent guy who didn't do drugs. When he used the second log book, he just stretched the law a little bit to get by. If he stayed safe, stayed responsible, Rob didn't have a problem with it.

Then there were the guys he worked with from the plant. At first, they were wary about being around a cop all day. Drivers had a history of not trusting law enforcement, and he could understand why. From their perspective, the DOT was always out to get them. They thought officers were around every corner. As if to justify the belief, Bruce had told him about some of the things he'd seen out on the road. Rob had a hard time believing it, but he understood why the guys would be as wary around him as they were.

It had taken some time, but he had worked his way into their good graces. He had even adopted the CB handle "Da Bear".

Not too many drivers went by anything other than their names, but none of them called him by his. He was "Da Bear" and he liked it. At home, his son used to call him "Daddy Bear", and he knew truckers called cops "Smokey Bears". So he was "Da Bear", and he took pride in it. It warmed his heart when they called him on the CB. Of course, it didn't have anything to do with an old SNL skit and Rob actually being from Chicago.

Yeah, and Ditka is not a god. Daaa Bears.

Rob smirked. *Da Bear is going to be dead once the mommy bear gets her hands on him.*

He pulled the car into the driveway, not wanting to go in. This wasn't going to be pretty. His shitty job had led to a shitty day, which would probably lead to a shitty night. Oh, where was the justice in the world? The second he opened that door, she would drag him out to the hose. He knew it was coming. It was inevitable. He might as well just go right over to the hose and do it himself.

As he walked up to the door, the cool breeze rustled the trees. Weeks earlier, the leaves had turned yellow, many of them now scattered on his lawn. The few remaining in the tree caught in the wind, gliding down amongst that brisk fall air to land on his windshield. The

27

air blowing through his hair, he imagined it turning to freezing when the water slammed into him.

It was going to be a long night. All he had to look forward too was the hot shower to come.

CHAPTER 3

The sound of frying grease and the pleasant scent of bacon floated in the haze filling the kitchen. It smelled good, distracting her from the long day. Mr. Sydney, who always screamed, and Sarah, the other R.N., always disappeared when Ms. Finch had one of her fits. In a way, Wendy was glad Bobby wasn't home yet because it allowed her some peace. Five minutes after he got home, she knew she'd have to swat his hands from the already cooked slices, then rush after him.

But tonight's dinner was simple. BLTs. It would only take her a few minutes to slice the tomatoes and pull apart the lettuce. Bobby could toast his own bread. He was old enough. It should not be on her to do everything for him. His hands weren't broken.

She pushed the bacon around in the pan, feeling the little tingles as grease popped and splattered against her forearms. It wasn't anything she hadn't felt before. She had other, much larger scars on the inside of her arm. Round ones that were suspiciously the same size as cigarette burns. She always wore long sleeves to keep them covered up, but those were now pushed up high on her arms.

None of those scars were recent. The visible ones had long since faded to just annoying reminders. It was the unseen wounds that still caused her problems.

She looked up from the pan, glancing over her shoulder at the window above the sink. It had gotten darker the last half-hour. When she started cooking, there was still a slim ray of light hovering over the horizon.

Bobby should have been home by now. He knew better than to stay out this late. That damned woman. She was going to have to have a word with her about keeping her grandson over there so late. There was no reason for it. She knew Wendy got home early enough now that he didn't need to go over there anymore. It was different when things were still awkward, but it was better now. *He* wasn't here anymore.

Wendy took a quick glance around the kitchen, looking for her cell phone. It wasn't on the counter. She had knocked it off too many times cooking, no longer making that mistake. She didn't see it on the little television nook they had in the far corner, and the table was covered with a mass of unopened bills and flyers.

Dammit!

She must have left it in the front room when she walked in. It wasn't a big deal. She'd grab it to call her mom after she finished. She quickly placed the last few pieces of bacon on a plate and put a paper towel over it.

It really is getting late. Bobby has never been this late from leaving mom's. That damn woman knows I hate him out this late, Wendy fumed as she walked into the front hallway and saw her phone sitting next to her car keys and purse. *She'd better be planning on driving Bobby home. There is no way I want him walking home. It is way too late.*

"Hello?" her mother said a moment later.

"Hey. So when are you bringing Bobby home?" Wendy said in the cheeriest tone she could fake.

There was a pause. "You mean he's not home already?"

"No… He's not still there? How long ago did he leave?" *That little asshole,* she wanted to add, but she wasn't ready to give her mom a reprieve just yet. *If he had*

31

left already, she should have called and let me know. What the hell was she thinking?

"It was a while ago. Before I started cooking supper and before Pat Robertson came on."

"So where is he?"

"I don't know. He's not home? Have you checked his room just to make sure?"

Like I wouldn't have seen him come in and walk past me. Damn, why does the woman always have to push my damn buttons?

"No. I'll check now," she said, working to keep from saying it through gritted teeth. She walked to Bobby's room, looking in. "He's not here."

"Then where is he?"

"That's why I called. How long ago did he leave?"

"It had to be over an hour ago. It was before it got too dark. He should have been home by now."

"Okay," Wendy said, her mind racing. Maybe he ran into a friend or went to someone's house to play video games. There was no reason for her to worry yet.

Where is he?

If he had come home the way he was supposed to, it was well-lit and there were plenty of people who would have seen him. That wasn't much to base hope on, but it was all she had at the moment.

But what if he came home the way he *wasn't* supposed to? Would he have gone through the coal dump? He was continually told not to go through there. Would he dare, especially at night? Especially with what happened to his brother?

She couldn't see him doing that. There were just too many bad things there. *He had to have gone the other way. There were always all those boys up there sitting in front of the sweet shop... Maybe some of them gave Bobby trouble.* She wouldn't know unless she went up there herself.

Should she drive? What if Bobby came home while she was gone? Her best bet would be to walk, maybe running into him in the process.

She reached into the closet, grabbing a flashlight off the shelf. Then, thinking it was probably chilly, grabbed her coat, as well.

When Wendy found Bobby, she was going to tan that boy's ass until he couldn't sit down for a week. Of course, that would be after spending about an hour hugging the life out of the little son of a bitch.

She quickly hurried into the darkness of the night, turning on the flashlight, lighting up her path. She strode up the sidewalk, hoping to find her son.

* * * *

David felt the sensation as ice-cold vanilla-flavored soda run through him, the fizz dancing on his tongue. It was a heavenly taste, a nectar from the gods, and one that he so desired after a day from hell. A day he had to struggle just to get through.

It was a turd of a day, one he seemed to enjoy making worse by standing at the only local hangout the small town had with two people he liked the least. Yes, he lived in a craphole of a town. Yes, he had nothing to do. Yes, he was grounded, so even if he went home, he couldn't even play Xbox or watch TV. Yet he continued to subject himself to more torture by standing up there with Tina and Singer.

It wasn't even a warm night, so why the hell was he standing there? Why?

Because there was nothing else to do in Standard. There was the coal dump, but it was dangerous to go there at night. If you weren't prepared, you could fall into a hole or off the little cliffs. Then there was the main drag, which consisted of about six blocks. People would sometimes

33

drive up and down, wasting away hours just horsing around. If you didn't want to risk breaking a leg or wasting your gas, there was always the sweet shop.

David didn't know how the sweet shop had come to be the hangout for older kids in the evening. When he was younger, it had been the previous older kids, and now that he was part of that age group, he found himself there. And it wasn't like the business wanted them standing there. They did their best to dissuade the kids from loitering, calling the cops when they actually stood in front of the building. But the paint store next door had no problem with the kids standing in their little entryway.

It was *so exciting* to stand up there, watch who stopped by, talk to everyone they had just seen at school that afternoon. He needed to get out of this small joke of a town. Every day was the same as the day before. Being banned from his Xbox made it that much more painful.

Was he seriously there with people he couldn't stand to see if other kids he could barely tolerate would come up, then they might talk about something other than who got drunk here or who tore through which farmer's field?

Kim came out of the sweet shop, holding her soda in one hand, Singer's soda in the other. She wasn't as short as Tina, her blonde hair pulled back into a ponytail that poked out the back of her baseball hat. David avoided looking into those round, cute, and innocent brown eyes. She was nice, even to him, and he couldn't help but feel something for her.

"Hey, thanks," Singer said, taking the offered Coke. David shook his head as he took another long pull off his fountain soda. Last year, Singer was banned from going into the sweet shop after getting into an altercation with the owner. He always wondered what the hell they had fought over. No one knew, but the owner was still adamant about him not being allowed in. The woman even called the cops if Singer walked too close to the front door. If anyone got caught bringing out sodas to him, they'd be banned for a week and given a stern warning not to do it again.

Yes, Singer was an asshole, but even David couldn't imagine what he had done to bring on that much hatred.

"Any word on what's going on this weekend?" Kim asked, looking briefly at David before turning around to sit on the stoop.

"Lukas is talking about having a party out at his barn. His parents will be out of town. He thinks he'll be able to get a couple of kegs from over in Streator."

"Really? That sounds promising."

David tuned out their conversation. It didn't matter. He knew he would never go, even though there was a part of him that wanted to. His penis screamed, *Hey, don't be a loser. Do the party and get laid*! There was always a chance he would find some girl to "knock boots" with, as his dad would say, but that just wasn't him.

Besides, he had Ally. He shouldn't even be looking at other girls. If he ever did hook up with a girl at a party, she would be extremely hurt. If one of their friends in town didn't rat him out, he knew he wouldn't be able to look her in the eye. Even with all the miles separating them, he still thought of her. Just thinking of those tear-filled eyes sent a tinge of regret through his chest. Damn, he hadn't even done anything, but still felt terrible.

What were they now? They were best friends, growing up only a few houses apart. When they got older, they kissed and played around until, one night, it went further.

Had they ever officially been a couple? They had always been together. With her being gone, it felt like he were missing a part of himself.

He looked back at Kim's short, petite frame, which was similar to Allison's. She was cute, but he knew nearly nothing about her. What if he said something to her and they had nothing in common?

Why did all this have to be so complicated?

He looked away from Kim, trying to find something else to focus on. The town was deader than usual. Other than the distant hum of the interstate, it seemed like the rest of the world had slipped away. There hadn't been any cars driving down Main Street, no people walking dogs, nothing. The sweet shop was quiet, the four of them providing the night's only business. The town was deadsville. Come to Standard, the last dead town on earth.

There is a fifth dimension beyond that which is known to man. It is a dimension as vast as space and as timeless as... Suddenly, he had *The Twilight Zone* theme stuck in his head. *Na na, Na na, NAAA.*

And he had just hit a new level a boredom. The boredom of the sixth dimension. *You have traveled here from the small little town of Standard, the last town on earth. Only four people remain, and there is nothing to do. They are stranded there and...*

David's eyes narrowed. *Who's that?*

Someone walked up the side road across the street. He watched her as she approached the streetlight, recognizing her. She looked different than her daughter, but he sometimes wondered if that had to do with the rough life she had endured. He knew she was much younger than she looked, but he could easily recognize Ally's mom.

Ms. Taylor stood on the other side of the street, visibly agitated, looking around before settling her gaze on him.

* * * *

There was still no sign of Bobby. Wendy wasn't sure how long it had been since she left her house. It couldn't have been too long, but she just wanted to hurry home and check to see if he were there. What if she missed him? She could be out there for hours, and he could be home playing video games.

She had walked out of her house and strode to the neighbor's, asking Mr. Rawslon if he could keep a lookout for Bobby. Now she couldn't remember if she have given him her number. He had the landline, but did he have her cell? She was always so reluctant to give that out to anyone, but she thought she had written it down for him. Part of her wanted to turn around, go back and double check, but she had already gone around the block and was halfway to Main Street. It wasn't all that far, but she thought she remembered writing it down on the little notepad by the television.

All of this was just too much for her. She shouldn't have to be doing any of this…not again…not after last year…not after Mikey. She should be able to just go home, walk into his room, and find him playing video games. This wouldn't be like last time. This couldn't be like Mikey…

A mother should never have to deal with that. One missing child was enough, but to have two children taken less than a year apart…

When she reached Main Street, she scanned the direction he should have come from. Nothing. So he hadn't snuck off with his friends to the park. She hadn't thought he had. He knew he needed to come home. It was that or she'd tan his hide, and she was pretty sure he had gotten most of the coming home late garbage out of his system by now. He knew better.

So which way to go? Bobby was supposed to walk down Main Street. After a couple blocks, she would turn down the side street and be at her mom's. If he had gone that way, she would have seen him by now. He had to have taken a different way home or gone to a friend's. He had so few of friends, though, and she didn't know their phone numbers. *Dang it.* Why didn't she know where any of them even lived? They always played outside. By the time she'd get home from work on weekends, he would already be home. She never had to go to any of their houses.

He was never this late. *Never.*

She hoped he had just gone to the park with a couple friends. Otherwise, she could walk around all night and never come across him.

She looked over at the sweet shop. Kids always hung out there. Sometimes there were decent ones, but it was usually the hooligans who harassed her Bobby. Good-for-nothings who just liked to cause trouble. She'd heard stories about people's houses and barns getting vandalized. Not that anyone talked about it too loud or told the chief because that would just get their tires slashed. A bunch of young miscreants she was determined to keep her angel from.

Bobby wouldn't have gone near them. He always kept his distance. He hadn't said too much to her about them, but she still heard it. It broke her heart when she was just a few cars away and heard them yelling at him, pushing him around. If she got involved, he'd never be able to stand up for himself. She couldn't always protect him.

That tall kid was the worst of them. He never gave an inch, was always the first one to make a comment. She didn't know his name, but he was the ringleader of it all.

Then she noticed David. What was he doing up there with them? He was a good kid. But maybe it was good that he was there. If Bobby walked by, he would have seen him. Maybe he knew where he went.

* * * *

Maybe she was thirsty. That wasn't too much of a stretch. There had been many times Ally and he had gone to get a Coke and she had asked them to bring her back one. She always got the same thing—vanilla Coke, extra vanilla, topped with marshmallow. David hated the combination because the marshmallow always made the

Coke leak through the top of the plastic lid, and either Ally or he would have to lick it off their fingers.

As David looked closer, he saw she looked upset. Glancing around, she approached him. The closer she got, he saw she was shaking. He shivered, the memories of last year creeping back. Memories he tried not to think about.

He remembered where he had been when Allison had gotten the word her youngest brother was missing. It had been a beautiful summer day, so they went for a drive, ending up lost. He kind of knew where they were and knew he could find his way back. The whole purpose of the drive had been to get out of there and be together.

It had been a long day. Her parents had been fighting and so had his. They both needed to just get away. Like most times when it seemed the world around them was nothing but shit, they left to find their own private spot. It usually lead to just a long night of joking and goofing around, but this time, Ally had been really upset, worried about her brothers.

She usually worried about them, but she was more concerned this time as Kurt, her step-father, was drunk again. David wasn't sure, but he thought Ally was afraid he might hurt them while she was away.

They had driven, driven, driven. When they finally pulled down a long dirt road to a cemetery, they really didn't know where they were. It didn't matter, though. The sun had started to set, so they watched as it lowered past the tombstones, the red fire of the day fading into the purple flowing cloud flowers of the dusk. It felt like it belonged in a painting aged to beautiful museum perfection. They just held each other in silence until the day slipped away.

She tucked herself into him, placing her head on his chest. With how often others looked at him as the fat kid who was picked on more than talked to, he felt like her protector, felt like he was good for something.

He had no idea how long they sat there. Time lost itself, and dark had long since settled when her cell phone buzzed. When she didn't reach for it the first time, it immediately started to buzz again. With a sigh, she uncurled herself from his arms and took the phone from her little clutch purse.

After she hung up, he saw the devastation on her face, the worry lines forming on her brow. He had tried to pull her back to him, asking what was wrong, but she pushed him away, saying she needed to get home.

For weeks, he tried to visit her, help find her youngest brother, Mikey. He had talked to Ms. Taylor more than Allison. Allison was always busy, always fighting with her step-dad. He watched from a distance as she screamed and blamed Kurt. When David would come to the door, Wendy answered it, telling him there was no news and they appreciated his help.

Understandably, the family had fallen apart. He had no idea how it felt to lose a child, to never know what happened. It had to be the hardest thing for a parent to live though.

She continued to push him away. Before he knew it, it was the night before she left for college.

He hadn't talked to Wendy since Allison left. Growing up, she was like a second mother to him, but now that Ally wasn't around, he had no reason to go over there. Even when they talked, there was a strange awkwardness between them. It didn't matter how close they had been before. Now all they gave each other was a passing "hey".

Then there was the pain whenever he talked to her, reminding him how much he missed Ally. He knew Ally no longer blamed him. They talked on the phone. The camaraderie that had once been there had started coming back, but she wasn't here. He missed actually being able to touch her, look into her eyes. He wanted to tell her he loved her and needed to be with her.

Wendy hurried up to him, out of breath. "Dave."

The other kids stiffened. Tina slinked back into the shadows, while Singer seemed to step forward, like he wanted to confront Wendy. David didn't think he would. He was probably just posturing. Wendy didn't pay any attention to him.

"Is something wrong? Is Ally okay?" David felt a huge weight on his chest, moistness forming in the corner of his eyes.

Wendy blinked, as if he had asked something that wasn't processing. She blinked a few more times, then shook her head, pushing away the noise of useless thoughts.

"No, no, no. Bobby… Have you seen him?"

"Bobby? No. He hasn't been around." David talked slowly, double-checking his memory. He was pretty sure he hadn't seen the kid. The more he thought about it, the more it seemed kinda strange. Now that Ally wasn't home to watch him, he knew Bobby went to his grandma's after school. He should have walked by there…unless he went through the coal dump.

Wendy was talking, but he had lost part of it. He heard her say Bobby hadn't come home yet. Because it was dark, David understood why she would be worried about him.

"Can you help me look for him?" He heard the plea in her voice.

David nodded. He remembered Bobby. A prankster, he would always bother Ally and him while they were in her room. But just because he couldn't stand the little turd didn't mean he wouldn't help look for him.

"Of course. Have you looked through the coal dump yet?"

Wendy shook her head. "No, he wouldn't have gone through there, not after his brother."

David wanted to agree with her, but he'd seen Bobby up there quite a few times since Mikey. However, he didn't think now was the time to tell his mom that.

"Yeah, you're probably right, but I'll double-check anyway."

"We'll help. We'll drive around, see what we can find."

David turned, surprised to see Singer pulling his truck keys from his pocket. Was that actual concern he saw on his face? Maybe he wasn't so cold-hearted after all. Still, David wondered how Bobby would react if Singer, a guy who bullied him, were the one to find him. They needed everyone they could get, though.

And if this were one of Bobby's little pranks, maybe it would do the little turd nugget some good if Singer found him. The little snot would never live it down.

"Okay." David didn't know why, but he felt himself taking control. He turned back to Wendy. "You need to go back home and stay by the phone. I'll call if we find anything. If he's not home when you get there, call the police. The chief should be on duty, right? He can help look."

Wendy nodded, a fresh rush of tears coming to her. "Thank you. Thank you," she kept repeating. He almost pulled her into a hug to tell her it would be okay. She felt so much like a mother to him, it hurt to see her like this.

"Come on. I'll drive you home," Kim said, gently pulling Wendy with her. Good. David didn't like the idea of her walking back home. In her condition, she'd probably walk down the center of the street.

Bobby was missing. With Mikey still fresh in his memory, all of this just felt way too familiar. Why was this happening to the family again?

He could imagine how Ally would take the news her other brother was now missing. He had to find him. He couldn't let her go through that again.

He looked at the dark shadow looming in the distance, a large shape rising up. Somehow, even at night, the coal dump was darker, visible only because of how black it was.

He had been up there many times, but something about it now, how it looked so ominous, sent goosebumps along his arm. In the pit of his stomach, he felt lead forming, a little voice in the back of his mind telling him not to go up there.

He watched as Singer and Tina climbed into his large, jacked-up Chevy truck, Wendy and Kim slinking down into her little Grand Prix.

The world around him suddenly seemed to be a much darker place. It had to be his imagination, but even the stars seemed to fade away as he stared up at the sky, saying a little prayer before he took a step forward, committing to searching the coal dump.

CHAPTER 4

Rob looked down the long barrel in apprehension.
It was aimed right at him. At any second, it would fire,
giving him little hope he would survive it. Just the thought
sent a shiver through him, his bones getting chilled.

"Are you ready?"

He could hear the playfulness in the female voice.
In the little glow from the back porch light, he saw her
smile as she held the hose steady. She was enjoying this.
He had just a second to think he might have married a
sadist before he felt the water hit him.

He howled. It was cold. The breeze picked up,
making him feel like ice, sending tingles across his skin.
Hot damn, he thought, shivering as he spun.

Then the water stopped. His shoulders slumped,
his shaking growing worse. He was going to get
pneumonia and have to call in sick. Then what would they
do for money?

As he took a step toward the door, Robyn called
out to him.

"Oh no, you're not done yet. Strip."

He turned around to glare at her. He was no
longer happy with this game, and he felt a heat rise up in
him. His anger burned at he got ready to snap something
back at her.

Growing up, he had anger issues. He would be
quick to get into a fight, but that wasn't necessarily a bad
thing, especially if you grew up on the streets of Chicago.

In an Italian neighborhood, anger always ran hot, fights were often, and you either adapted or you got hurt. When he got into high school, he started to realize how fighting would only get him into more trouble. More and more kids in the neighborhood started going to juvie. Others got pulled into the outer fringes of the local mob family. Crime called for many of his friends, but he didn't want to be part of it. Not when he came from a family of cops.

Rob's mother had always told him to calm his temper. Somewhere along the line, he had. It wasn't easy, and it took a lot of self-control. He had to have a reason to keep calm. Robyn was usually it.

Although, right now, Robyn was not "enhancing that calm", as she often joked. She was doing the opposite.

"Hey now, pretty boy. I said to strip. Come on. Dance for me."

He lifted the bottom of his sweater and pulled it over his head. However, the white undershirt clung to the growing bulge of his stomach. Because of the more sedentary working conditions, his stomach had increasingly gotten bigger, his shirts becoming tighter. Struggling to pull it free, he gave a loud grunt, pulled it over his head, and tossed it on top of the sweater.

As he fumbled with the button on his pants, he heard her giggling.

"Come on, 'Da Bear'. When did bears start having issues tearing their way out of their clothes?"

Rob looked up at her as he pushed his pants down and let out a guttural growl. Robyn laughed harder. He pulled his pants off and tossed them on the pile. He looked around, thankful that the high wooden fence hid the surrounding houses' view.

"No striptease?"

He was so glad she was enjoying this. He shivered, maybe even showing the first signs of hypothermia, but she just made jokes. He wanted to curse her in response, but his teeth chattered so hard, he didn't think he could get the words out. Could she not hear them? They sounded like a Led Zeppelin drum solo in his mouth. The woman was crazy. That was all there was to it.

"You might want to take that off." Robyn pointed to his cross, the one dangling around his neck, the one his grandmother had given him. He wore it every day, feeling the comfort of it against his skin.

Rob undid the clasp as she held her hand out. He lowered it gently into her palm. She closed her hand around it, then reached out for his arm, pulling him to her. He wasn't expecting it and stumbled forward into her awaiting kiss.

Her tongue quickly made it into his mouth, and he could feel her warmth. Her arms went around him, pulling him closer. He could smell the familiar scent of her shampoo, a fragrance he had come to associate with her over the years.

"You're shivering. Let me warm you up," she whispered against his lips.

And she did. Her presence filled him with an inner warmth. He did everything he could to pull her closer, wishing to feel all of her in his arms.

"You already have." His shivering relaxed, his teeth no longer chattering.

"Why didn't you tell me you were so cold?"

"What do you mean cold? It's a warm summer's day. How about we light a fire and toast some marshmallows."

"Don't be such an jerk." Robyn vigorously rubbed her hands along his arms, the friction barely generating any kind of heat. "We should get you inside so you can take a hot shower."

"You going to join me?"

"Maybe after you wash off your stink." She pulled away, waving her hand in front of her nose. She turned, picking up his soiled clothes and tossing them to the back steps.

"I think you should. After all, you'll need to get out of those wet clothes."

She spun around to see the hose pointed at her.

"You wouldn't." Judging from Rob's smile, she knew he most definitely would. "Don't you dare." Robyn took a step back, not taking her eye off the hose. "You pull that trigger and you'll be sleeping on the couch, mister."

Rob took a step forward, measuring her distance to the door. He still had plenty of time to soak her.

"Oh, I think I will."

"You'd better not."

He let the hose respond for him. The water flowed out, catching her in the chest, drenching the knitted fabric of her sweater.

"Ahh! Stop! I mean it, Rob."

He took another step forward, but she turned, moving out of the path of the water. When the spray hit against the back door, he turned. He saw her moving in the shadows, getting around him.

Rob would be the first to admit that, over the last year-and-a-half, he had let himself go. He used to hit the gym a couple times a week, keeping pretty fit for an officer in the Chicago PD. Since the fire and his hospital stay, he didn't work out as much. When he did, it was working through sore muscles, trying to get back his flexibility. He still wasn't quick, couldn't turn fast enough to keep up with her. Before he knew it, Robyn was behind him. He heard the valve turn, then felt the hose in his hands grow slack.

"Can't keep it up?"

"Oh, how you know better."

When he turned to face her, mud hit his face. He felt it up his nose and tasted it in his mouth. He stumbled away, but the grass was slick. Before he knew it, he felt himself falling to the ground amidst laughter.

"I warned you," the giggling woman standing over him said. He tried to wipe the mud away, but his

47

hands were just as wet and dirty. It felt like he was just spreading it. As much as he wanted to openly glare at her, he couldn't.

Rob heard the back door open, more giggling coming from behind him. Jake. It frustrated him that he couldn't turn around and look up, the mud forcing him to keep his eyes closed.

"Go ahead and laugh you two. Just wait. I'll get my revenge."

The laughing behind him stopped momentarily, then came again in small bursts.

"Sorry, Dad," Jake said between chuckles.

"Did you get it in your eyes?" the woman asked, laughter dying away, genuine concern replacing it.

Rob wanted to bite out a response. Instead, he took a deep, steadying breath. "Yeah, I got it in my eyes." Okay, there might have been a little more sarcasm in there than he wanted.

"Oh, hun..."

Then he felt her arms slip under his and around his chest from behind. Robyn pulled him close.

"On three, I'll get you inside and we can wash your face in the sink."

He didn't know if she could see his nod, but she counted. When he felt her pull, he was quick to push with his feet. Rob stood and let her guide him inside. He was frustrated, covered in muck, smelled like sewage, and was cold. Right then, though, he just focused on her perfume and the warmth of her against him.

* * * *

As warm as the water felt, Rob didn't believe it would ever get warm enough. The shivering had stopped, but no matter how long he stood under the stream, steam filling the bathroom, it just could not penetrate into him. The chill was there, and felt like it would always be there.

It just wasn't hot enough. He was sure that if he went any hotter with the water, he would burn himself. He was tempted, though. If it meant getting rid of this chill, Rob was more than happy to have some first-degree burns. It would just add to the scars from his third-degree ones.

That fire had been so hot, he smelled the burning flesh around him. He had watched as writhing bodies got consumed in a fire that leapt at him the moment he entered. Fire burning from…

Rob closed his eyes and lowered his head into the water, letting the stream sluice over him and take away the memories. He tried to save them. His memories sometimes tried to show him differently, but deep in his soul, he knew he had done all he could, even if a part of him wouldn't accept it.

But why did that part have to be the one in control of his nightmares?

"Knock, knock." Robyn stepped into the bathroom, waving her hand in front of her face. "Geez. Enough steam in here? It feels like a sauna."

He pulled his head out from under the water, pulling the shower curtain back to look at her. "Still cold." The steam was so thick, Rob couldn't even see the door.

"Well, supper is ready. Jake already grabbed and went. I guess he's got some gaming about to start."

"You didn't make him eat at the table?"

"He got me. He was so sweet and innocent when he asked, then volunteered to take out the garbage."

"Really?"

"Yep, although him taking it out meant he just opened the back door and threw the bag of garbage in the *proximity* of the garbage can before running off to his room."

He sighed. "Robbie..."

"Yeah, I know, but it's Call of Dangerous, or Danger… I don't know, but it's some big tournament."

Rob felt the chill, wanting to close the curtain and get back to the warmth of his shower. It started getting colder in there. She must have left the door open, letting all the warm air out.

He shook his head. "Well, you can deal with him when he's a teenager and you can't get him out of the house because he's playing video games all day."

"Oh no. You'll be too busy teaching him how to drive."

"Yeah, right," he said, hearing her close the door. thankful she was finally trapping the steam back in. He closed the curtain, soap threatening to get into his eye. "I'm not teaching him to drive. You ever watch him mow down people in that Grand Theft City. Oh no, driving duties are all on you, my dear."

"Nope. Can't hear you. Try telling me when you're not in the shower."

"Uh-huh. What'll be your excuse then?"

"Don't know. I'll come up with something."

Rob chuckled. "Sure."

"Hey, hun, are you working this weekend?"

"You know I am."

"Okay."

He could hear the disappointment. It didn't take a rocket scientist to know something was on her mind. Sure, he had never been a detective, but he wasn't dumb, either. Rob had been around detectives enough to pick up on the subtleties. This wasn't even subtle. She wasn't happy, and she wanted him to know.

"Okay what?"

"Well, you work every weekend."

"That's the job."

"Yeah, I know, but, well... I hoped we could make the trip down and visit my parents one weekend. It's been awhile since we have, and it would be nice to get away for a couple days. They can take Jake and hang out, and we can find our own fun things to do."

He heard the plea in her voice, knowing what she was trying to do. It wasn't just about taking the time off to visit her parents, but about getting away from other things. Ever since they moved to the small town, strange little things seemed to happen, making him more and more detached from them. Worst yet, Rob could feel himself getting more distant, caught up in something that kept pulling at him. He knew it was happening, but was helpless to do anything about it.

No, there isn't anything going on. We're just caught in a rut.

Yeah, and that voice in his head always told him not to worry. The inner whisper kept telling him everything was fine, but was it? He wasn't even sure anymore, so a weekend away did sound like a great idea. Maybe the chief would switch shifts with him and let him take a weekend off.

"Okay. It was just a thought."

Rob heard her disappointment, pulling him out of his thoughts. He'd been standing in the shower, not speaking.

"Hun?" he said, pulling back the curtain so he could look at her.

She stood there in the steam. The beautiful woman he had married so long ago. As the mist swirled around her, he was reminded just how breathtaking she really was.

Robyn was a little shorter than he was, her pale skin never tanning. It would just redden in the sun, freckles appearing. She was a beauty with short dark brown hair, and when she smiled, he saw those kissable lips.

Those lips were now pouting, but not in that way she used when she playfully manipulated him. These were genuine sad lips, ones that were hard to watch as she looked toward the sink.

She had changed out of her wet clothes and had put on what she called her PJ's—a black tank top and sweatpants that clung to her curves, making her look like heaven. He would sometimes slip up behind her, putting his arms around her and pulling her into him. They'd even dance to their own song as they held each other like that.

God, please let her always remember how much I love her.

* * * *

Robyn wasn't sure if they were safer since moving from Chicago. She thought they would be, but it seemed like something always happened. None of it was like the small town she had grown up in. Maybe it was because the world was changing, or because she was now an adult in a world in which she had once been a child. She had lost her childhood innocence long ago.

"Hey, do you want to join me?"

Robyn blinked, not realizing she had just been standing there. "Aren't you almost done?"

"I can stay in a little longer and enjoy the view. I'll wash your back."

"Down, boy. Jake's in his room playing Xbox. Don't need him hearing us." She came closer as he held the curtain open. "Besides, the water will start getting cold."

"You'll warm it up."

"You are laying it on thick today." He blew her a kiss, making her smile. "We'll see about later."

* * * *

Rob watched as she left the bathroom, the mist swirling in her wake. As soon as she left, the mist closed back in and turned dark. Really dark. It blocked out the light, surrounding him. The water in the shower grew so hot, it felt like it burned his skin.

Shapes appeared in the haze, walking toward him. He couldn't see their faces, but knew they were the ones he couldn't save. The room disappeared and he was alone in the dark.

Breathe, Rob. Come on. Breathe.

He couldn't, though. As he tried to pull in air, the steam burned his lungs. The water got hotter. Fire flickered and writhed around him, touching his skin and turning it red.

Not able to see the shower wall, he reached out. He ran his fingers along it, but it was like touching ice, making him recoil. He reached out again, feeling the knob for the water and pushing it.

The rushing fire pulsing at him died away, a sudden rush of air assaulting his lungs. He was able to take another breath, then another. The water no longer running, the mist dissipated, the room reemerging around him.

He knew the room hadn't gone anywhere, but he wasn't sure whether or not *he* had. It wouldn't be the first time he had found himself somewhere else.

That had been then, but things were good now.

Get dressed, go downstairs, and eat that nice, warm supper made for you by that amazing wife of yours. Everything is just fine.

He stepped out of the shower, quickly drying with the towel. In the fading mist, he saw a glint of metal on the vanity and reached out to grab his cross. The glistening steel was cool to the touch, comforting. He felt relaxed as he placed it around his neck, taking a deep breath, smiling.

Bacon. Damn, that woman is truly amazing.

* * * *

"…and I pray the Lord my soul to keep. Amen," Rob said, listening as Jake, who knelt to his left, spoke in unison. He looked over and saw his son nodding in agreement.

53

"And you brushed your teeth? I don't need to go in there and check the toothbrush?"

Jake stood, frowning. "Dad..."

Rob laughed. "Okay. Give me a hug and get some sleep." Rob also stood, although he needed to rely on the bed, then the dresser. His leg felt better, but he was used to using support whenever he could.

Jake, his growing boy. Rob was always amazed at how big he was getting. Already up to Rob's chest, he'd probably be as tall as he was within a year. How was his son able to grow so fast? It should be a law that boys couldn't grow up until the parents were ready.

And where did his attitude come from? Where did his sweet little baby go, and how did he get replaced with the know-it-all who seemed to begrudge anything his father asked him? It seemed like Rob had to pull Jake's teeth out to get a hug. Was it really that much to ask? He didn't think it was, but he watched his son slump his shoulders and walk over. He wrapped one arm around Rob, barely making it around his growing stomach. The other arm dangled, Jake not using the energy needed to lift it. It was a quick hug, then he walked to his bed and pulled back the covers, getting ready to climb in.

"Good night. Love you," Rob said as he reached the door.

"Love you, too."

Was it Rob's imagination or was there no real show of emotion? It was just a catchphrase with no meaning behind it. Rob sighed as he turned off the light and closed the door just until there was just a slight gap in the doorway.

He went downstairs, hearing Robyn washing the dishes.

"I told you to leave those to me," he said, walking into the kitchen. The smell of burned hamburger still hung in the air, and the haze that had set the smoke alarm off still clung to the ceiling. He moved up behind her and slid his hands around waist, moving in for a gentle kiss on her neck.

"Yeah, but I wanted them done tonight, not sometime next week."

"I would have done it."

"Yeah, I'm sure." He knew she was mocking him. "Ooh, you still smell like that crap. Do I need to take you outside and hose you down again?"

Rob pulled her in tighter, feeling the warmth of her body as a shiver tremored through him. He thought about that cold water sure he would never be warm again.

"Nah, I'm good. Unless someone wants to join me this time."

"Yeah? Do you need someone to wash you down?"

"Maybe later."

"Maybe after you get another shower."

"Maybe."

An annoying tone screamed from somewhere in the other room. Rob groaned as he closed his eyes and rested his head against hers.

"Or maybe not," he mumbled.

"Sounds like somebody's calling. Either Dan needs you to go in early or Chief Winston is calling in sick."

"Yeah."

He opened his eyes to see Robyn's lips coming up to meet his. It was a brief peck, but it lingered just a second longer than normal. When she pulled away, she pulled his bottom lip just a little bit. A shock went through him, his heart skipping a beat as she let go.

His arms itched to reach out and grab her, but the phone in the other room had quit ringing for only a brief moment before it started again.

He stepped into the living room and listened, trying to remember where he had set it down when he came home. He found it in his duffel bag among malodorous clothes. He wrinkled his nose as he flipped the phone open.

"Yeah."

"Officer...Alletto?" The voice on the other end had paused for a brief moment, as if looking up his name. It was a female voice he didn't recognize. It was odd to get a call from a stranger when he wasn't the deputy on call. By now, most people in town had a certain amount of familiarity with him.

"Yes. How can I help you?"

"This is Officer Cantrall at County. We have been trying to get in touch with Chief Winston, but have been unable to do so. Will you be able to respond to a missing person call?"

"I can. The chief should be on duty now. Have you tried his cell, as well as the radio?"

"Yes, Officer. He has not responded to either. The last we heard from him was when he called in that he was going to check a strange light in an abandoned area this morning. He never radioed back in and never reported going off duty this morning."

"Wait," Rob said. The little bit of happiness he had moments ago evaporated as concern crept into his voice. "You said he called in this morning and said he was going to check something out, but no one followed up on it?"

"Officer Alletto, there are many times you locals forget to call in when you are going off shift. It is a large county. We don't have time to check in when someone just forgets to sign off. It is not the first time Chief Winston has not called in."

The woman had gone on the defensive, and Rob understood her point. If not for the chief not answering when they called about the missing person, he wouldn't have thought anything about it, either. When he did those long shifts, getting off at six in the morning, it was hard for him to remember to sign off. If the county police came to his house to check on him just because he forgot, he wouldn't live that down for a while.

"Okay. Give me the details and I'll check in with the missing person. Keep trying the chief. Where was his last position?"

"GPS has him reporting in at an abandoned field on the northeast side of town across from the school."

Rob had to think for a moment about what abandoned field she could be talking about. There wasn't a field over there. There was the coal dump, and south of that was a field. That field wasn't even close to the school, though. If the squad car were parked there, he would have seen it on his way home. There hadn't been anything parked there. He was certain of it.

But if the woman had an aerial view, he guessed the coal dump could look like a field. She was probably using some kind of satellite program.

"Okay. Give me the address of the missing person and I'll check them both out."

He wrote down the details as she rattled them off. In the back of his mind, he realized his long day had just turned into a long night.

CHAPTER 5

The dark sky gave way to the early light blue hue of dawn. The darkness fought to stay, but the sun was stronger. Its alarm was set. Although feeling like it was too early, it knew it was time. If the sun didn't come out now, who knew if it would come the next day or the day after that. Then the world would be lost in eternal nothingness.

Rob could barely focus as he looked out the kitchen window. He smelled the coffee, hearing the percolating of a fresh pot being brewed. That helped keep his eyes open, but it didn't help the exhaustion invading his senses.

He had been up all night, but where had it gotten him? He could barely recall driving up and down the streets of town, walking down some of the alleys along the way the boy would have taken home, having to use his flashlight to scan the darker areas.

He still hadn't heard anything about the chief and hadn't gone to find the squad car. He was surprised no one had followed up on it. When he called county back, they said the GPS had died and they were no longer able to track it. He would have to worry about it later, although it weighed heavily on his mind.

Two missing people within a day of each other. Could they be related? Both had possibly been around the coal dump when they disappeared. Why was the chief there? And the boy had been told to never go near the area.

"Here you go."

He looked down to see the slender, shaking hands of Wendy Taylor handing him the cup of coffee. When he had first showed up, she had been worse, but giving her something to do, talking to her, seemed to bring her back a little.

"Thank you," he said, nodding, turning to sit at the table. His eyelids felt like they had started to sag. His whole face, what he felt of it, was numb, and his head felt heavy. He wasn't sure how much longer he could stay awake.

Looking at the clock, he saw it was nearly five. He had now been up for twenty-four hours. He could go for a little longer. He had done it before. They had to find the boy.

"You don't think he went to the coal dump? You're sure of that?" he asked, enjoying the bitter taste of the coffee. It was hot and strong enough to shock him awake. He hoped the cobwebs stayed away a little longer this time so he could think this through.

"He knew not to go through there. We told him about the hobos that live up there and the mineshafts he could fall into. He's a smart kid. He wouldn't have gone up there. Not at night," the boy's grandma said. She looked so much like her daughter, her eyes piercing into him. She blamed him for not finding her grandson. The disappointment was evident in that glare.

"Okay, but we haven't found him anywhere else," Rob said. "Could he be there?"

Wendy looked at him, her lip quivering. The tears started flowing as she nodded. Her mother moved to put a hand on her shoulder. Wendy reached up, grasping it.

"He might have. I have caught him going through there before. He always complained that, if he went the other way, the big kids picked on him."

59

"If he was being picked on, why didn't you pick him up…" He looked at the older woman, "or you bring him home?"

Rob knew his voice had grown cold. He tried to keep the edge out of it, but it was hard. The tired cop in him came out and he knew why. It dug at the back of his thoughts, pushing this line of reasoning. He didn't want to face the ugly truth. There was a strong chance this could be a domestic kidnapping, an abduction, or other more terrifying possibilities. They might not be looking for a missing boy. They might be looking for a body.

"He liked to ride his bike home," Wendy said.

"But he walked last night."

"He's grounded from his bike."

"Could he have run away?" Rob was grasping at anything.

Wendy shook her head emphatically. "No. We called all his friends, and there's nowhere else to go. His dad… His dad couldn't care two shits about him. He's gone, not even paying the child support."

Rob nodded, looking down at his notes. He had asked them most of this earlier, but wanted to go back over it, checking for any inconsistencies.

He had searched most of the town last night. The county planned to send out an officer to help with the search, but Rob still hadn't seen him. He was getting agitated. Last time he had talked to county, they just said he was on his way. No ETA, no other information. Where was he coming from? Mars?

Rob was so glad to know that if he had been shot or was in danger, county could be counted on to get there quickly to back him up.

That's being too harsh. There have been many times when I've needed them and they were right there. When I pulled over speeders or was in pursuit, they were always there to give backup. I have no idea what's

60

causing his delay. That doesn't change the fact he should have been here five hours ago.

He took another long pull on his coffee and felt an odd sensation, as though his face were sliding down. It wasn't getting any better.

Looking into the front room, he saw a young man sitting in there, dozing. When there was a knock on the door, the teen jerked awake. Rob had seen the boy walking the streets a few times and figured him to be a friend of the family or a relative. It was hard to tell in the small town. It seemed like everybody knew each other or were related. It was often hard for Rob to keep up with everyone.

The kid was quick out of the chair and to the door. Outside, the early morning light touched the tall figure taking up most of the doorway. Rob heard the two women behind him shift to look at the door, feeling their disappointment when it wasn't Bobby. For Rob, seeing the county officer standing out on the front porch was a relief.

He couldn't help himself as he thought, *Good. Maybe I can go home and get some sleep.* In truth, he doubted he'd be able to. Not until the boy and the chief were found. However, if he did go home, Jake would be up soon. He could ask him if he knew Bobby, maybe find out more about him and the family. Rob had noticed the scars on Wendy's arm. There had to be more to the story than what he was told.

"Officer Alletto?" the newcomer asked.

Rob walked over and held his out his hand, amazed at how tall the man was. He towered over Rob's six feet. He motioned for him to come in. When the officer removed his hat, Rob wasn't surprised to see the buzz haircut.

"That's me," he said, trying to imagine how he must look to the officer. Rob could feel the roughness of his unshaven face, and with his habit of running his hands through his hair when stressed, it had to be a mess.

"Sorry for the delay. There was a pileup over in Ottawa. A semi jackknifed on 80, causing a backup for five miles. Two dead, five rushed to St. Margaret's, one airlifted to St. Francis."

Rob nodded, figuring there had to have been a reason. Why the hell someone didn't tell him, though, he didn't know. If he had the squad car, he would have heard it on the radio. None of that made a bit of difference. Their main focus was finding Bobby.

With the officer finally here, it meant an Amber Alert could be put out for the missing boy. As just a local officer, Rob didn't have the authority. He had to wait on county to do it, which meant they had wasted half the night before they could let anyone outside town know. If the boy were indeed taken by someone, they could be in the next state by now.

The man pulled his notebook from his chest pocket, then nodded to the mother and grandmother.

"I am sorry I couldn't get here earlier. We'll find your son." He turned back to Rob. "You want to fill me in, then get your day officer to check in with me."

Rob smiled sadly. The day on-call officer used to be him until budget cuts made the chief have to take those responsibilities, as well as patrolling weeknights. Sure, Rob was the backup, but that was the problem. He had worked yesterday, been up all night, and now the officer assumed there was someone available to come in and relieve him. There wasn't. Rob's backup was a full-time Peoria officer who helped out when someone needed the night off. Rob was it. There was no one else.

"There's no day officer. I'm it."

The county officer looked at him, his eyebrow raised slightly. "You? You look like you've been up all night and are about to fall over."

"Yeah, well, we can't find our chief, and my backup is a full-time officer elsewhere."

"Well, you need to get some sleep. Give me what you got, then get some rest."

Rob nodded and started going over his notes.

* * * *

Rob stepped into the cool morning air, enjoying the breeze as it trickled across his skin. Eyes closed, he leaned his head back and let a brief smile cross his lips. He wasn't happy, but the chill creeping in allowed him to wake up a little bit and push some of the grogginess away.

Hurrying down the porch steps, he walked toward his car. His bed was calling. It wouldn't be a long sleep, not like the kind he'd normally get after working all night, but he was exhausted enough to salvage as much as he could.

He made it to the car before he stopped and looked toward the mound of trees and shale that looked like a black hole in the early morning.

The coal dump really wasn't that far from the house. If he crossed the yard of the neighbor behind the house, he would be right where the exit was for the side path. It really was more convenient for Bobby to take that as his way home rather than walking uptown and working his way back.

If he were a kid, Rob knew he wouldn't have gone around. He would have gone straight through. He wouldn't have listened to what his mom and grandmother said about the dangers, thinking it would have been safe to go through there.

And where was all this insight when I talked to Jake lately. Seems like I can never get into the boy's head. He has just become so distant lately, always playing those damn games on his tablet thingy.

Bobby would have gone through there. Rob was sure of it. They probably wouldn't find him until there

63

was more light. There wouldn't be any point in him going there to look around, but he still felt like he should check it out. They had searched everywhere else.

"Hey, Officer?"

Rob turned to see the kid hurrying up to him.

"Yeah?" Rob hoped he didn't sound as tired as he felt. To him, his words sounded like a slurred garble, similar to that of a drunk.

"Hey, I'm David. I'm a friend of the family and well.. " David looked uncomfortable, and Rob understood. This was hard for all of them. Tragedy always was that bind that brought people together, but somehow made it hard for people to talk to one another. "Do you think he's up there?" David asked, nodding toward the coal dump. He must have seen Rob looking at it.

"Might be. Once it gets light out, we'll search."

"I went up there…" David paused, letting his voice trail off.

"You went up there looking for him?" David nodded. "Probably not too smart. You know, I can give you a ticket for trespassing."

"Yeah, but I was looking for Bobby."

"I know. Don't sweat it."

David nodded again. Rob was certain the kid was hiding something.

"Got something to tell me?"

"I..I saw something up there. At least, I *think* I saw something." The kid got a faraway look, his eyes getting glassy. Then he blinked rapidly, quickly changing the subject. "And I found a car up there. It was parked on the other side on the maintenance path."

"A car? Wait… What else did you see?"

"It was nothing."

Rob grabbed David's arm. "Show me."

* * * *

They entered the woods around the coal dump. The sun had started rising, making it easier to follow David as he quickly lead him to a fallen tree off to the side of the path.

"It's over here," David said, climbing over the tree. Rob turned in the direction he pointed.

He tried to follow as best he could. The faster they moved, the more his back felt like it was going to lock up on him. It wouldn't be the first time he tried to push himself, the pain nearly paralyzing him.

"Hey, kid, slow down," he called, not thinking he could take much more. His right side felt like there were little needles stabbing down his leg. He had to slow down.

"It's just over here, past those trees." David looked back, seeing how far Rob had fallen back.

"Yeah, well, another minute longer won't make it magically disappear." *That is, if it was there to begin with.* For all Rob knew, maybe the kid liked dragging him around on a wild goose chase. It wouldn't be the first time the kids in town played games with an officer. He remembered they had played a little game of tag with him a few times, driving around after curfew, then hiding when they knew they had gotten his attention.

Rob followed David around a group of trees, then stopped.

The squad car. David hurried over to it, but Rob had to stop. He felt his leg threatening to give out from under him. Damn, he had pushed himself too hard. Thankfully, he had just passed a tree, so he reached out, leaning onto it.

David turned back around to look at him. "Are you okay?"

Rob nodded. He couldn't really speak. He was winded. It felt like something had ahold of him, like a hand grabbing his insides and squeezing. He fought against it, forcing himself to pull in deep breaths.

65

David ran around to the driver's side of the car. "The door's open. Battery's probably dead."

Rob pushed himself away from the tree and limped his way over. That was probably why the GPS didn't work. The door being open meant what? That the chief had been taken? If he had a heart attack or something like that, David would see him there.

No, the open door meant someone had to have pulled him out of the car.

He needed to call this in. They weren't just looking for a missing boy now. It was official. The chief was also missing. If somebody had taken him, it made sense that they had taken the boy, as well. Maybe Bobby had seen somebody attacking the chief. If that were the case, it didn't bode well for either one of them still being alive.

They needed to get county out there in force. They needed forensics and more officers. This was about to get very messy.

And it looked like he wasn't going to get sleep anytime soon.

CHAPTER 6

"We have two more officers coming in. Have you reached your other guy to help with the search?" the county officer asked as he walked up to Rob, who leaned against one of the trees closest to the police tape. Although Rob had already been near the car, he wanted to keep his distance until the lab guys were done.

It was strange to be doing this type of investigation here because so much was different from when he had been Chicago PD. There, local CSI would process the scene. They didn't have an in-house lab, but it was close enough to the various precincts that worked with them. Everything was at the detectives' fingertips, information could be called upon, and labs worked with each other.

Here, it was just him. When there was a crime that actually needed investigating, he had to call the county. They then called lab techs other counties shared. Thankfully, they were in an area where the three counties were large enough that it was only the three. Still, it was a process to get them there, wasting most of the morning just arranging it.

Just before eleven, the first lab tech had arrived, actually beating the person who had been at the lab when they called. However, he didn't have any equipment with him, so they still had to wait. In the meantime, the tech told them how he wanted the scene closed down and how much of it cordoned off. Rob had closed off half the coal dump, which frustrated many of the townspeople who had come to walk the woods, looking for the missing boy.

"Yeah, finally got ahold of him. He's getting with his dispatcher now to get off duty there and come here."

"Good." The officer nodded, continuing to look at Rob. "You need sleep. You look like a zombie."

Rob winced, not liking the memory. If this officer only knew what a real zombie looked like, he wouldn't joke about it. Rob had seen many of them, and continues to in his nightmares.

"I'm fine." And it was the truth. The sun was up. He didn't think he could get more than an hour's sleep if he tried anyway.

The officer nodded and turned back to the scene. There really wasn't anything exciting happening right now. One tech was going over the car, dusting for prints. Getting the car washed would be hell, but the town council could worry about that. The other tech studied the ground in the area, looking at the dirt, tree limbs, and leaves. Amazed at what these guys could do, Rob realized he'd never want their job. There was too much that could be overlooked, especially out in the middle of the woods. Would they be this thorough if it weren't another officer missing? He didn't know if they knew the chief. One of the techs was a younger woman who didn't look like she had been at the job too long, but maybe the older man with silver hair knew the chief.

"Have you checked on the search for the boy?" the officer asked, nodding toward the sound of yelling they could both hear in the distance.

Ten people had arrived, David calling his friends, who brought their parents. With how red David's eyes were and how he seemed to twitch, Rob wasn't going to ask what he had taken. He just hoped it was an energy drink and not something like Adderall. All they needed was for the kid to OD on them.

69

None of them were worried about school or work, for which Rob was glad. He was certain the school would understand. Once word spread, there would probably be kids and parents all over the place.

They couldn't all search the coal dump, though. It was not that large an area. They would have to start searching the rest of the town, then work their way out to the cornfields. Most of the corn and beans were being harvested, so there was activity out there. It was going to be difficult to coordinate a search out there. He hoped it didn't get that far.

Maybe he was the only one obsessed with the coal dump now that the chief's car had been found there. They hadn't been good friends, barely knowing each other outside work. He had remembered Jake's birthday, but had gotten the age wrong, getting him a little stuffed toy.

He guessed they knew each other without really knowing one another, but when Rob had needed a job, Dan gave it to him. When he needed to make extra money on the side, even though it was sure to be against some rules and regulations, Dan had looked the other way. He had given Rob a chance. Now it was up to him to repay that.

"Not in the last half-hour. I'm about to go check in with them." He hadn't really planned on it, but knew he should.

"Yeah. Why don't you go do that."

Rob nodded and turned away, feeling his hip pop. It had been doing that a bit more since last night, and his lower back kept up a constant stream of uneasy reminders telling him he couldn't run like that anymore. He chose to ignore it as he limped toward the voices.

* * * *

"Sam, have you walked through here yet?"

"Yeah, Dean. Why don't you try over there."

Rob recognized the voices right away. He knew he was coming upon the little dump area some residents liked to drop off garbage. It was illegal and came with a heavy fine, but some still did it. He never understood why. Garbage was picked up from the curb regularly, so there was no reason to risk the fine.

He walked to the little cliff overlooking the dump. Sam Bradley and Dean Tanden were down there, each holding a long pole they pushed into the gaps. Rob saw two refrigerators, the doors pried open.

Rob worked his way down the steep embankment. He leaned up against a tree, enjoying the momentary relief. "Find anything," he asked.

"Well, Sammy here found his winter wardrobe, but nothing else."

"Hey, watch it, smart ass."

The two men were both in their late thirties and had been long-time drinking buddies Rob had to separate on more than one occasion. Most times, he was called in to stop them from beating up some of the younger guys. Those two were like brothers, often fighting, but having each other's backs at the same time. From what Rob had heard, it had been that way since grade school.

They were also good hunters. The good thing was they knew how to track. The bad thing was the open carry law. Both had their guns strapped to their waists like an old western. There was not much Rob could do about it, but having them out there with loaded firearms made him uneasy. Everyone was already too worked up. An accident seemed inevitable. Civilians with firearms always made him antsy.

Rob sighed as Dean started poking Sam with the long stick, Sam trying to pull it away. These two were a prime example that men didn't grow up. Their toys just got more expensive.

"Anything useful?" Rob asked, fighting to keep from saying it through clenched teeth.

71

"Not yet. We're going to keep working here for another few minutes, but I don't think there's anything to find," Sam said, holding the end of the stick, keeping Dean from poking him.

"Okay. Where's the main search moved to?"

"I think they're taking a break over by Main Street. That one kid looked pretty rough, then some girl-"

"Suzie," Dean interrupted.

"Yeah, Suzie. She almost fell into a hole and sprained her ankle. Someone ran to get some ice to put on it."

"She's okay?" Rob asked.

Sam nodded. "Yeah. She caught herself. Could have been much worse. Looks like an old mineshaft."

"Nah, can't be. They filled those in when they were done in the area," Dean said.

"Yeah, well, they could have missed one. They seemed in a rush to get out of town. No one ever knew why. They just up and started filling in holes. Before a bat could bat an eye, they were gone."

"How the hell does a bat bat an eye?" Dean raised his eyebrow.

"Shut up. You know what I mean."

Rob rolled his eyes, stepping away from the pair before he'd have to get involved. He headed toward Main Street, briefly wondering how long it would take the two to realize he had walked away. When he got back to his car, he could call county. While he wasn't holding his breath for anything to come back on the Amber Alert, there was always a chance. Maybe they had been able to track down the father, see if the kid was over there.

He quickly dismissed that idea. If that had happened, he was sure they would have found a way to get word to him. He had to leave his cell phone in his car to charge, but there were plenty of other people around who would have told him. His little flip phone was probably as ignored as he had been for the last hour.

If he could just go home and get a few hours' sleep, maybe he would come back and be more useful. No one would probably even notice he was gone.

He didn't have time to think too much about it, hearing voices as he neared the cars.

"And, by the wrath of God, the sinful will be punished..."

That's the last thing we need right now, he thought, rolling his eyes as he emerged through the last of the thorn bushes and onto the path. He saw a crowd of people, easily making out the man talking.

John Amery... Pastor John to some, Pastor Amery to others. It didn't matter too much as Rob had dealt with the man a handful of times, none of them pleasant. He was very strong in his beliefs and stubborn as a mule. Pastor John also felt that anyone who didn't believe the way he did was someone with a touch of the devil in them and was headed straight to hell. It wasn't a surprise that was how he felt about Rob, who didn't put up with the man's mouth.

He wished he could just sock him in the mouth a few times and shut him the hell up. For a man of faith, the pastor was a major pain in his ass. With all the exhaustion Rob had pushed out of his mind, much of it suddenly crept its way back.

"This boy was cursed, and has been cursed. He was a demon seed that the Lord has felt the need to take him up and save his soul before he could be corrupted even more by this vile and evil place. He has been saved from the depravity that grips this town. The evil that can be found in the fortresses of sin that is on every street corner. Look around and see. Count how many of those immoral havens can be found, then count how many good places there are to worship. There are nine bars, seven houses of false gods, and only one true church. This boy has been saved, and we should look to see who else will be saved."

Rob's steps quickened. The pastor stood in the bed of truck as he spoke to those gathered around him. Some of them swayed back and forth, their hands raised, punctuating the end of every one of his sentences with an "Amen". The other half of the group looked like they were getting ready to do something. Timmy Doyle, a kid who was David's age, had his fists clenched and was moving to come up behind the pastor. Rob cut him off, shaking his head.

"We shouldn't be out here searching, walking through the devil's playground. We should all be revisiting our love for God and scripture. The rapture is here. The children will be taken, but all are not forgiven. We need to be reborn in the-"

"That's enough!" Rob yelled, his own voice loud enough to shut him up and have him take notice of the limping man walking forward. The pastor's eyes focused on his own, Rob swearing he could see madness storming behind them. Maybe it was just because of how wide the man's eyes were. He swore he could see the whites as they bore down on him.

Don't shoot until you see the whites of their eyes.

Wasn't that the old Civil War philosophy, or did it predate that? Well, he wouldn't have to be far away to see the glare trained on him.

"How *dare* you interrupt me. I am only helping these poor people find the road to salvation."

"You're only helping to piss people off and interrupt them as they try to find a missing boy."

"That is your belief and you will serve your time in damnation's flames once the rapture has taken the Lord's servants home."

The man had an odd accent for the area. It wasn't the first time Rob wondered where he was from. His English was more pronounced, more clear. Maybe from some upscale northeastern city? It was possible it came from his religious training, but anyone could call themselves a man of God and start a church nowadays. The pastor at Rob's own church didn't sound that way. He was pretty good at keeping things simple, which felt natural for the area.

"You can stay and help search if you'd like. I won't stop you from that. But if you're just going to cause trouble, I want you out of here."

"We have every right to be here. We are a peaceful gathering here to spread the true faith to the unenlightened. This is when they need us the most. To understand their loss."

Rob stopped at the back of the truck. "I told you once. You can help or you can go. Get down out of that truck before I *make* you get down."

"You would not *dare* touch a servant of the Lord," the man scoffed. Rob smiled in response. He felt like cracking his knuckles, but that would send the wrong signal. He wasn't going to hit the guy, but he had no problem climbing up there and knocking the man down a peg or two, then taking him away in handcuffs. In fact, he was kind of looking forward to it. He needed to work out some frustration.

When Pastor Amery reached out, Rob grabbed his hand to help down the tall, dark man he guessed to be in his early thirties. He stepped down in a long stride, then stood there, trying to use his height to tower over and cower Rob. However, he stood his ground, his glare matching the pastor's.

"I am only spreading the word of God."

"You are antagonizing and disturbing the peace."

"How am I disturbing the peace?"

"By pissing me off."

Rob pulled out the handcuffs tucked into the back of his utility belt. Before the man had a chance to react, Rob spun him around and pushed him against the bed of the truck.

"Hey, you can't do that," one of the pastor's followers yelled. "You heathen!"

Rob didn't even turn to see who it was. He reached out and grabbed the pastor's other arm and pulled it behind his back, keeping his body pressed against him so he couldn't twist away. It had been a while since Rob had to handcuff someone this way, but he'd responded to enough domestic violence calls to deal with an uncooperative asshole.

He was careful not to press too hard against the man or shove him into the truck. With so many witnesses, he knew that whatever he did would be closely scrutinized. It was hard, though, as he just wanted to pound the man, slam his face against the metal. That had to be the exhaustion, the voice in his head telling him to let out some of the frustration.

He heard the click as the second handcuff closed around the pastor's wrists. As he pulled the man away from the truck, he felt wetness hit his cheek, then more on the back of his neck. He turned in time for another one to catch him in the eye.

They're spitting *on me?*

Rob pulled the pastor in front of him, walking him toward his car. It wasn't his squad car, but it would work.

"You are going to lose your badge for this. This is harassment. You are preventing me from exercising my religious freedom and my right to assemble."

Rob opened the door and forced him into the back seat. "Stay," he ordered, then slammed the door, feeling the car vibrate. The window shook, making him remember the crack that was starting to form. If he did that too hard, he was liable to make it worse. The last thing he wanted was to have to replace it.

When he heard the faint little chirp of his cell phone, he opened the front door and grabbed it, looking at the display. Ten voicemails. Most mornings, he would wonder who had called him so many times. With everything that morning, though, he was actually surprised there weren't more.

He flipped the phone open and saw most of them were from one number. *Shit. Sewage. I was supposed to be in the truck this morning. Damn. This isn't going to be good.*

He listened to the first voicemail, hearing the angry voice on the other end asking him where the hell he was and why his boss was getting phone calls about needing to get a driver out there for the truck. That had come in at seven.

Before he could listen to the rest of the messages, the phone rang. He saw Mark's number again.

He clicked TALK, but before he could say anything, the person on the other end started talking.

"Rob? You there?"

"Yeah."

"Okay. Are you involved with the search?" It wasn't the angry voice he expected. Mark must have heard about what was going on.

"Yeah. Been here all night."

"Okay. I got another driver to cover your shift, but I'll need you back tomorrow. Get some sleep."

Before he could respond, the line went dead. Rob just shook his head, which had started to get heavy again. He needed to get some sleep. He didn't think he could go much longer before he fell over.

He climbed into the driver's seat. As much as he wanted to just go home, he had to take care of something first. He looked in the rearview mirror, glaring at the man in the back seat. The pastor returned it.

* * * *

"How can you live with yourself?"

"What's that?" Rob asked, taking a quick glance at the pastor in the rearview mirror. They were barely a block away from the coal dump and Rob had been thankful the man had stayed quiet. He hoped it would stay that way for the whole drive back to the man's church.

"I said how can you live with yourself, living your life of gluttony and sin."

Rob couldn't help himself. He broke out laughing. "Gluttony? Sin? You don't even know me."

"You drive around this town, you go into those filth-ridden places, you fornicate with the devil's servants and lie in their beds, smothering yourself in their depravity."

"What?" Sputtering, Rob couldn't think of anything else to say. His mouth opened and closed, but no words emerged. He tried to laugh it away, but it was forced, his smile stretched.

"Each night, I see you go into those bars."

"Sir... Father... Whatever you want to call yourself... I go into a bar when I am called there to break up a fight."

"You live your life in sin and you will continue to be lead to burn in the devil's playground, feeling his fires until your skin is torched."

Rob's smile vanished. He pulled off the road in one of the many available parking spaces so he could turn around and stare into the man's eyes. "You'd better shut up before I shut you up. I've been amongst those fires you've seen. I have watched good men and women die, whose only sin was to be a slave to it. I have seen a whole town caught up in a fiery blast, nearly dying as the whole complex burned down around me. I have faced the flames of your hell, and you know what, you self-righteous son of a bitch?" Rob waited for the pastor to say something, but the man was smart enough to keep his mouth shut. "I'm still here. You can take that back to your God or whatever devil you worship. I'm still here, and I am not going anywhere."

Rob pulled the car back onto the street. He was thankful it was such a small town, only taking a few minutes to pull into the lot next to the man's parish. Rob found it harder and harder to think of him as a man of faith. He seemed to only be content with spewing vile words, not converting followers to believe in God.

Rob was glad to be getting rid of this scum. He opened his door, then the back one, pulling the man out of the car, twisting him so he could remove the handcuffs.

"If I catch you back over there, I *will* arrest you."

"What about my car?"

"You can send one of your followers over to get it after 6 p.m. If you need it before then, too bad. Walk."

The pastor nodded, continuing to glare. Rob turned his back on him, moving to climb into the car.

"The boy is lost. You will never find him."

Rob stopped and pulled himself back up to stare into the dark pits of the pastor's eyes.

"What do you mean by that? Do you know something we don't?"

"I know his soul, if he ever had one, was lost long ago. He is lost to the darkness, and there will be no return."

Rob just shook his head, frustrated that he allowed this man to pull him into more of his bullshit. He should have just let well enough alone and took off.

"There is an evil coming to this town, Deputy. An evil you are blind to. You must open your eyes and see. The darkness is coming."

Rob climbed into his car, not hiding the smirk as he looked back up at the pastor.

"Pastor John… Why would evil waste time on such a small, pissant town like this? I think the devil has better things to do with his time."

The pastor reached out and grabbed the door. Rob looked at the hand, then back at the man. "Let go."

"Evil is in the heart of every man. The devil wastes no one. He is greed incarnate, desiring every soul."

"Love is in the heart, as well. Evil is what happens when people like you get into their heads."

"Love," the pastor scoffs. "Love is just a chemical imbalance of the weak mind. The only true love is that for God."

"Some say that about religious zealots, too. That you're all chemically imbalanced."

"All those born in sin are lost to the darkness as the sinners get what they deserve."

When Rob pulled on the door, the pastor let go, allowing Rob to slam it closed.

He drove away, his chest burning. He really needed to get some sleep. He couldn't stay awake much longer, his breathing starting to come in short bursts. This had to be over soon.

CHAPTER 7

"Hey, Allison, will you be there tonight?"

She turned, seeing the girl rushing to catch up with her. Allison forced a smile as she looked down at the shorter woman.

"Hey, Leannette. I'm not sure. I just got out of Chem lab and have to study tonight. Ms. Mazur is a beast, and tomorrow I have that Calculus exam."

"Well, that's why you should come."

Allison knew she was right. After all, the point of a study group was to do just that. Allison wasn't used to it, though. She still thought of David and his study groups, which usually consisted of more kissing and less studying than what had probably been good for her.

Sure, they hadn't really needed the extra studying. It had just been their time together, something to make their parents think they were doing something productive. They both got good enough grades, so their parents believed them.

Now, she was away at school and study groups had to be just that. Every time someone asked her to join them, she felt that little flutter in her chest, yearning to hear David's voice.

She knew she should call him. He would soon be leaving to join the military and she may never get the chance to see him again. Would she be okay with that? She wasn't sure.

"Earth to Allison... Anyone home?"

Allison blinked and looked back at the cute, short black woman. They had first met in their dorm. Allison wasn't quite sure how, but they just started talking to each other. Leannette had come up to her and stuck her hand out, introducing herself, not giving Allison the choice as to whether or not they were going to get to know each other. That had probably been good because Allison was homesick, seriously contemplating about going home. As much as she hated to be back there and couldn't stand the idea of moving back in with her mom, she had been crying herself to sleep every night. Her roommate hadn't been any help because she had barely said more than three words to Allison since she had moved in. Her head was always in a book. When she did look up, she would say hi, then seem lost in the pages again.

She was glad Leannette had forced her way into her life, but there were times Allison just wanted to be by herself. Leannette seemed determined to never give her that space.

"Yeah, I'm okay. Just got a lot on my mind."

"Yeah. I said study group, and your vagina started crying out David's name."

Leannette was also extremely blunt.

"Hey now," The laugh that broke free lifted the weight Allison didn't know she had been carrying.

"You know I'm right, girl. Hey, it's cool and he sounds like a good guy, but girl, I'm not going to give you the college speech sayin' he's back home and your here. I *am* going to say that just because you go to a study group, it does not mean you have to make out with anyone. There's nothing *against* it…" Allison glanced around the common area they were walking through, her cheeks turning a bright shade of red, "but it's not a requirement."

Allison was thankful it was just after lunch, most everybody already in class. This was normally her time to chill in a comfortable lounge chair in the area, enjoying her time alone. She wished Leannette wouldn't blather about Allison's private life. What if someone had been in there?

As if reading her thoughts, Leannette snorted. "Hey now, it wouldn't matter. You've been here almost two months. Everyone already knows. Haven't you learned you can't keep secrets in a dorm?"

Allison nodded. It had embarrassed the hell out of her when Scott brought her a box of dark chocolate when she was on her period. Her *period!* What was wrong with these people? Even though he was awesome, and the first openly gay man she had come to know, how could he do that to her? And why was it everyone's business?

Although the dark chocolate had been a godsend.

"So will you be there? We are going to go over Chem. Rodney and Scott both want your help."

Allison snorted. "Are you sure they're going to listen? Last time, they made out nearly the whole time."

"That was early. The semester had just started and it was still all the easy stuff. Rodney nearly failed that last lab. He's freaked out. That's why he had Scott go out and get you chocolate. They're trying to bribe you."

Sure, that was the reason. She wasn't sure how much she believed that.

She plopped her large carry-all purse, which she used as a makeshift book bag, down on the far end of one of the couches, then fell into the other end of the plush cushion.

"Ahh," Allison sighed, letting her head fall back against the cushion. Why hadn't she planned her schedule so she had afternoon classes? She knew she wasn't a morning person. What made her think an eight a.m. class would be okay? And what kind of a sadist schedules a class that early? Didn't the professor have a life outside his own classroom?

Leannette dropped down into the chair across the small round coffee table, putting her bag on it. "Late night?"

"No, well… Yeah. I was up late last night. Couldn't sleep, so I was reading."

"Ooh, the excitement. No wonder you didn't try to join a sorority. You are just too much for them to handle."

Allison lifted her head up, looking at her, raising her brow. Leannette wasn't even paying attention. Her head was in her bag and she was sifting through, trying to find something. She must have found it as she leaned back with her phone in her hand and was already quickly punching in her passcode, having to shift it in her hand to deal with her long nails.

Amazed, Allison had to ask. "How do you do that with those things?"

"Practice."

"I bet."

Leannette looked up and smiled before she looked back at her phone, positioning it so she could see herself in the screen, using the camera as a mirror.

Smirking, Allison shook her head at her friend. Why couldn't she just be alone, close her eyes, and let the minutes tick by until her next class? She had no problem with drifting off on the comfortable couch. It was better than going all the way across campus to her dorm.

As much as she wanted to do just that, she had to check on David. She hadn't heard from him last night. He always sent her a "good night" text, a quick text about whatever he saw on TV, or they just talked about books they read. But he hadn't sent anything. This morning, she had turned her phone off on her way to class. Maybe he had sent her something and she missed it.

Yeah, they were supposed to be over, not that they were officially ever together. She wasn't sure either one of them really believed they wouldn't be together. It was the a lie they both told themselves.

Oh, we're not together. You can totally see other people. Go and enjoy it. It's college. Take in that full college experience. No, we're not long-distance dating, so you can have fun.

So why did she constantly miss him, feeling like they were together now more than ever?

She pulled her phone out and turned it on before setting it on the table. It would take a few minutes to start up and connect, so she might as well get a drink of water while she waited.

"Want anything?" she asked Leannette as she stood, pulling out her wallet.

"Nah, I'm good."

Allison nodded. She would normally have her own water bottle with her, but she had completely forgotten it. She really didn't know what was with her lately. Up late last night, got up late this morning, tired all through class. That really wasn't like her.

She walked up to the vending machine, made a selection, then watched as her water slid down the shoot to the side.

"Damn, girl. Your phone's lighting up over here."

Allison grabbed her water, looking across the room. Leannette had already reached over and grabbed her phone off the table.

"Oh yeah?" she said, walking over. She could hear the vibrations as more and more notifications came in.

Her smile fading, Leannette looked up at her. She had been reading the little snippets of the messages as they came in. Before she handed the phone over, she stood and wrapped her arms around Allison.

"Oh, girl..."

Allison pulled herself away, concerned. "What?"

Leannette handed her the phone, the color draining from her face. "I'm sorry."

Allison looked at the phone, not taking the time to unlock it. She didn't need to see the full messages. The snippets were enough to let her know what was going on.

No, no no no no. This couldn't be happening
again. Bobby had … No, this *couldn't* be happening
again. She had already lost one younger brother, *no not
again*. No, this just wasn't possible.

She collapsed, missing the couch, the world going
black as she fainted..

* * * *

The pounding started again. It had been regular
until the sun had come up, then he had relief for a little
while when his body had become confused, his internal
clock resetting. Well, the clock had figured it out. He was
tired, the pounding behind his temple screaming for him
to find a bed, a floor… Hell, even the street looked
inviting. Just somewhere he could crash and get some
sleep. If he were lucky, he wouldn't be behind the wheel
when it happened.

He felt the vibration in his pocket and let out a
soft groan as he pulled to the side of the road. The little
flip phone squawked at him. He winced as he put it to his
ear.

"Yeah?" he said, his voice sounding alien and far
away.

"Officer Alletto?" came a young female voice that
sounded way too chipper, making him want to strangle
whoever was calling him. He wasn't in the mood for
happy.

"Yeah."

"Officer Sims wanted me to call and give you an
update. The search party has pretty much gone over all
they could of the woods. That's not to say forensics won't
be expanding their search later, but the townspeople who
were looking for the boy are starting to disperse."

"No sign of him?"

"No." Her voice lost some of the happiness,
sounding concerned.

"Any ideas?"

87

"Officer Sims is having a few more patrols come to the area, and they want to coordinate with those who want to help search through some of the fields. With it being harvest season, though, they are concerned it may not be safe."

He nodded, having thought the same thing earlier. Realizing she couldn't see the motion, he cleared his throat. "Yeah, okay."

"They will continue through the rest of the day, scheduling additional patrols in town."

"Okay."

"When you come back later, just call in from the squad car, as usual. County will patrol the streets until then. And, sir?"

"Yeah?"

"Get some sleep."

He closed the phone and tossed it on the passenger seat before resting his head on the hard plastic of the steering wheel.

Just what the hell was he supposed to do? Was he really going to go back to his house? Did he honestly think he would be able to lay down and sleep?

He probably could. He could probably sleep right there in his car. Even with the steering wheel pushing into his forehead, he felt how much his body wanted it. He just wanted to give in.

Maybe sleep was a good idea.

* * * *

Robyn lifted up the pile of dirty clothes sitting to the left of the washer. Her hands were still a little wet from just having taken the whites out of the washer and putting them in the dryer. They felt a little clammy as she continued to grab at the assortment of jeans. Of course, Rob's "work jeans" were off to the side. They would need to be washed, rewashed, and maybe washed again. She just hoped that whatever chemicals they used in that crap...*Ha! Crap*...wouldn't ruin her washer/dryer.

Her washer and dryer were still semi new to them, and she was thankful she no longer had to drag baskets of clothes to the laundromat. She was now in her own home, not some back room of a bar. *Really? How could the only laundromat in town be in a bar?* While she was always happy Rob joined her, she felt it had more to do with him not liking her going there alone. He often commented on how often he was called to break up fights there. Still, it was sweet he came, showing that he worried about her. *The dumb brute.*

She thought Christmas had come early when she saw the washer/dryer listed on Freecycle. She'd found others on the local community board, but these were just like new. Why would anyone give them away? It was just dumb luck. Although, if she really thought about it, much of how life treated them since they moved to town was pretty lucky.

Rob might not feel that way. He had to be the one who rented the dolly and found a way to get them both out of the elderly couple's basement, then they almost didn't have a way to get the units across town. Rob had to call his truck driver friend, Bruce, and ask him to bring over his truck, but he didn't help Rob do any of the lifting. With Rob's back after the accident, it probably wasn't the best idea for him to do it all. By the time they took the units out of the truck, Rob had started limping and rubbing his back.

Once he got them home, she hooked them up. Rob wanted her to wait until he could do it for her, but she didn't want to. Plus, he needed to take it easy, and there was also the hard truth that when it came down to it, Rob was not the most mechanical. Don't even ask him to put together a bookcase unless you wanted it to look like an imitation of the Leaning Tower of Pisa.

She loved him, but he was not a man she would trust with a hammer. She wondered if that had anything to do with his big city upbringing. He grew up there. She had moved there for college, but grew up in a little town. Her father taught her how to change her own oil, fix the toilet, clear a drain. So, letting Rob rest, she hooked up the washer and dryer so their basement wouldn't flood every time she did laundry.

She loved her washer and dryer because they were hers. It had nothing to do with the little bit of serenity she found in the basement and away from all the other rooms in their large country home that was not the easiest place to keep clean. No. It had nothing to do with any of that.

Robyn jumped a little when she heard the door slam upstairs. The last few pairs of jeans she had been holding slipped out of her grip. She tried to catch them, losing the battle as more of the jeans slipped through her arms, coming down in a tangle of Levi's. *Dammit!*

"Hello?" she yelled up the stairs as she grabbed the clothes she had dropped, flinging them into the washer. She could hear footsteps on the hardwood floor in their entryway.

"Hello?" she said again, hurrying up the stairs, frustrated that someone had just walked right into her house. Who just walks into someone's home? Well, her mom did when she came to visit, then there was Aunt Cindy, who felt like she could. And Father William seemed to just walk right in when he visited, but he would usually stand in the entryway and call out for them.

Could it really be her mom again? She had just visited last month, and she should have called if she were coming over. The house was in no shape to have her mom nitpicking over everything.

She reached the top of the stairs, stopping when she saw Rob sitting on the little wooden chair by the front door. It looked like he had started taking off his shoes, then placed his head in his hands and drifted off to sleep.

"Hey, hun, you okay?" She knelt down next to him as he lifted his head. His eyes were sunken, dark rings around them, and it looked like he had aged ten years since she had last seen him. His skin seemed so pale, rough, and wrinkled. He hadn't shaved that morning, and the stubble came in with sporadic patches of white. "What's wrong?

When his head dropped back into his hands, she tried to pull him to her. He straightened, shaking his head, sniffling back the pain that had broken through the mask. She knew the man she married and how he cared so deeply about people, but he never showed it much. She loved his strength, but she sometimes just wished he would let it out.

"I'm going to go get some sleep. I'll probably have to go back out in a few hours, but I just need to get some rest."

"You said it. You look like shit."

A small smirk creased the corner of his lips as he pushed out of the chair to stand. He wobbled, leaning against the wall. She reached out to give him a hug, holding him up as he tried to support himself. She felt his body tremor. His leg must really be bothering him.

"The chief and a little boy are missing."

She stepped back, eyes wide. "What!? How long?"

"Sometime last night."

"You've been out all last night and this morning looking, but you didn't think to call me to let me know what was going on? Where have they looked? Do they have any ideas?"

"We searched the slag pile."

"They call it the coal dump."

"I know. We searched it once it got light out, finding the chief's car."

"I could have helped."

"I know, hun, but we didn't find anything. We still don't have any leads."

"Oh, hun."

She pulled him to her. She felt his warmth, finding her little nook within his arms, her head against his chest as she listened to his heart.

"What if it had been Jake?" she felt him say, the words vibrating through her. It took her a moment to really comprehend what he had said. When she did, she felt her heart quicken.

What would she do if Jake were missing? Her baby, the little creature who had tormented her for over nine months. He had been born late, and she had fought to bring him into this world.

What if he just disappeared? What would she do. How would she handle it?

"Maybe I should go to the school and bring him home," she whispered and pulled back, looking at Rob, his sadness matching her own.

They had moved to the small town to get away from Chicago, away from the violence. This town was supposed to be safer. Nothing was ever supposed to happen here.

Chicago... Jake's school had a shooting, and there were more just down the street from their house. It was supposed to be a safe neighborhood, but more and more violence had started moving in, swarming them. She couldn't go a day without reading a story about another shooting nearby.

They came to Standard so Jake could be safe, play out in the street, run around a neighborhood without them worrying about him getting shot. They wanted him to be a normal kid, be able to enjoy his childhood.

But it seemed like the violence had followed them. It was all happening again. She needed him here. She needed to know he was safe.

He needed to be home.

"No. He'll be fine at school. I'm going to get some rest. We'll find them. Okay? Everything will be okay."

Robyn nodded, not really believing him. It was hard to believe someone when you knew, deep down, they didn't believe it themselves. She probably should go get Jake and keep him close to her.

Rob worked his way up the stairs. She watched as he stumbled near the top.

"Please, God," she whispered. "Please let him get some rest without all the nightmares."

CHAPTER 8

Ally looked up at the house she had grown up in, glancing at all the cars in the driveway and lined up along the street. It didn't take long before it turned into a parking lot of vehicles. There were so many people. She didn't want to deal with any of them, wanting to deal with her mom even less. With how Ally left for school, she wasn't sure she could.

It had been over a month since she had talked to her mom. Whenever Wendy called her, Ally was quick to send it to voicemail. If it hadn't been for David's texts about what was going on, she wouldn't have even listened to any of the messages. They would have just been deleted like the rest.

She wasn't ready to return home. Her chest threatened to close in upon itself, tears lingering on the fringe. It was so much easier to just close off the pain.

"Seems like a lot of people here."

Ally looked over at Leannette, who had given her a ride. She really didn't think she could have driven herself from Chicago. Not with how lightheaded she felt. All it would have taken was someone running across the street or a red light when she wasn't paying attention.

"Yeah. They're probably all out looking for Bobby," Ally whispered.

"So you don't think they've found him yet?"

Allison pulled her phone out and looked at the dark display. She tapped the little button on the side and the screen lit up, displaying the time, but no new notifications. She shook her head as she looked back over at her friend.

"We'll find him," Leannette said, reaching out to place her hand on Allison's arm. Allison gave her a brief smile and a nod. "Do you think your dad's here?"

Allison quickly turned her head and scanned the cars. For a brief moment, her heart leapt into her throat.

She sighed. "It doesn't look like it."

"Okay, well, we'd better go in, don't you think?"

Allison nodded. They got out of the car and moved slowly to the front door. Allison paused. This didn't feel like her home anymore. Should she just walk in or knock? She paused, uncertainty taking over.

She took a deep breath, closed her eyes, and opened the door, ready to walk into chaos. To her surprise, it was quiet. Even though there were cars outside, the house was nearly empty. She heard a chiming, like a little bell, coming from the kitchen. Knowing there were no bells in the house, and considering the fact she smelled freshly brewed coffee, she guessed someone was stirring a cup of coffee.

Then she heard a sniffle. "Allison?"

She turned and saw her mom lying on the couch. It was dark, all the lights off, but the filtered sunlight showed her how rough her mom looked. Her hair was a mess, her eyes dark and puffy, her face flushed. She tried to sit up, despite her apparent tiredness.

"Allison, you're home."

Her mom made no move to stand, holding her arms out, but Allison didn't go near her. That sickness she often felt toward her mother was overwhelming. How could she be so weak? Why was she lying on the couch and not out looking for Bobby?

95

She watched the glow of her arrival fade from her mother's eyes as she looked past Allison, her arms lowering.

"Who's this?" Wendy asked, appraising the black woman behind her.

"My friend."

"Hi. I'm Leannette. I live in the same dorm as Allison." She stepped into the living room, holding her hand out to Wendy. She looked at it for a moment, then slowly reached out, shaking it gently. Wendy looked past her at the television and the DVD player, as if checking to see if they were still there.

"It's nice to meet you."

"David around?" Allison felt the blood rushing to her face, barely able to stop her teeth from grinding together.

"I think he went home for a while. He was out all night looking for Bobby. They don't know where he is." Wendy sniffled as she reached for more Kleenex. The floor was covered in the discarded remnants.

"Allison!"

She turned just in time to see arms pull her into a hug before she even saw the white-haired older woman.

"Hey, Grandma," Allison said. For the first time, she felt a little happiness at returning home. She felt the hard exterior, which came so easily when she was around her mom, soften as she returned the embrace. She enjoyed the warmth and felt safe in those arms. They offered her protection. Now, she really was home.

"Thank you," her grandmother whispered into her ear. Then she pulled back, studying the woman standing behind her. "And you must be Allison's friend."

"Yes, ma'am," Leannette said, unsure of herself after the cold greeting she had just gotten from Ally's mom.

"Well, the more the merrier." She reached out and pulled her into a hug. Allison had to fight to keep from laughing at the surprised look on Leannette's face as she was engulfed by the woman. "Here. Come into the kitchen. I just brewed up some coffee."

Leannette allowed herself to be led by the older woman, and Allison suddenly found herself alone with her mom.

"Why is she here?"

Ally glared at her. "Who? Leanette? She offered to give me a ride home. Probably not a good idea for me to drive myself."

"Yeah, but her?"

Allison crossed her arms. "What don't you like about her? She's my friend and she gave me a ride."

"But now I gotta worry about things going missing."

"Why? Because she's black?"

"Because she's a stranger."

"Whatever." She wanted to get out of there. Maybe there would be a little peace in the kitchen. She turned away from her mom.

"Hey, Ally?" she called. Ally sighed, turning back around. "How is school?"

"Fine. How's Kurt?" Allison asked, taking a little pleasure in watching the brief reflection of pain in her face. Her mom looked down, suddenly studying her hands. "Has he been around?"

"Kurt? No. The police found him. I guess he's over in Ottawa. There were no signs he came for him. I think he's just happy not to have to worry about 'those bastards' anymore."

"He can't even come home to help find his son? What... Lose one son and just take off. Who cares if the other one comes up missing? What the fuck is *wrong* with this family!?"

"Kurt was never their father..or yours."

It was said so quietly, Allison almost missed it.

"Wait... What?"

Shocked, her knees went weak. She dropped into the closest chair.

Wendy shook her head, biting her lip as a fresh wave of tears trickled down her face.

"Then who's our dad?"

"*Your* dad was a great man. I wish you could have met him. He would have done anything for anyone. Henry was my high school sweetheart. He died in a car crash a few days after you were born."

"Woah... Wait, wait. Then who-"

Wendy continued. "When I met Kurt, he was a nice man. He would always come to work and make sure I made it home safely. But he liked to drink, and when he did, he would get into fights. I thought if we got married, maybe he would calm down. He really acted like he loved me. He didn't run away when he found out I had you. You were only a year old when we got married."

"So how is he not their father?"

"Kurt can't have kids."

"*Wait*. You were *cheating* on him? You were cheating on him, and so every time he got drunk and called you a lying, cheating whore, you actually *were* sleeping around?"

Wendy tried to answer, giving up as a fresh round of tears formed.

"Do you know who the dad is? Could he have taken them? Do they even have the same dad?"

"They do, but he would never claim them. He's a soulless bastard who I hope rots in the hell he has created."

"Who is he?"

"Don't worry about it."

"Mom!"

"No!"

Allison jumped to her feet, towering over her mother. "Who...is...it?" She saw her react, pulling into that ball she would go into whenever she expected to get hit. Allison realized she hovered over her mom like Kurt used to, suddenly feeling like something inside her died.

Something in her chest collapsed, the world around her seeming to dull into numbness.

Allison fought against it and turned away from her mom in disgust. She had to get out of there. She couldn't stand to look at this person anymore. How could she ever have shared genetics with this woman? She brushed past her grandmother and Leannette, who had come out of the kitchen.

"Allison?"

She didn't look back as she slammed the front door closed.

Why did she even come home? Bobby had always been a nuisance. She didn't really want to find him, did she? Yes, he was her brother, but the little bastard was just that. She couldn't think of a time they ever got along. Mikey had been the good one. The one she would have gone to the ends of the earth to try and find. So why had she come back?

She could only think of one reason. David. She really wanted to see him again, not realizing how much she had missed him. Right now, she needed him.

* * * *

"When the darkness comes, how will ye find the light?" Pastor Amery said to the dark room. Then, with a twist, the light bulb illuminated, flooding the little pantry with light. He wobbled as he stood on the little stool.

"There we go," he said, slowly stepping down.

"Oh, Pastor Amery, you should have asked me to change that. You don't need to be climbing up on ladders. You're likely to hurt yourself."

He turned to see a younger woman in her mid-twenties standing just outside the door to the pantry. Olivia, a regular at his parish, had been walking by when she had seen him. She held a large sheet pan in her hands, the smell of freshly baked cookies wafting from it.

99

"Everyone must face time in the dark; otherwise, they don't appreciate the light when they find it," he said, wiping his hands, which were now dusty from the bulb, on his pants. She gave him a distasteful look, but knew she wasn't going to say anything about it. He nodded at the pan. "What are those for?"

"I thought I would cook up something nice for the bible study tonight. That way, we'll have something more than just those little finger sandwiches Linda always makes."

"Ahh… Well, they smell good. Did you make plenty? I'm expecting a big group tonight."

"Really? I'd think people would be out searching."

"Heathens. No. I think that when people realize those boys were evil devil spawns, taken by their lost nature, they will turn to the one true God and come to study in his words."

"Shouldn't everyone be able to find God?"

"Some will never find the light, no matter how much they are shown."

They entered the little kitchenette. Olivia quickly made her way around, pulling out a platter for the cookies.

"Why didn't you put them on a platter at home?"

"They needed to cool, and I wanted to join in the search."

The pastor shook his head. "Olive, don't search out evil. Evil tries hard enough to get into our souls. We don't need to seek it out."

She continued putting the cookies on the platter. Her light fingers moved quickly, the cookies peeling from the pan. Olivia made sure all of them were in a neat, circular pattern before looking up at him.

"Pastor, he's just a boy. Then there's the police chief. They are people."

"Sin to sin. One is just a person. Everyone is a vessel for the soul."

"I understand. I'm sorry, but Robert is a friend of my daughter's. I can't just *not* look for him."

"I will pray that the darkness does not touch you."

She reached out and put her hand on his arm. "Thank you."

Giving her a weak smile, the pastor put his hand over hers, then brought it to his lips for a brief kiss.

"I will pray."

* * * *

John watched Olivia walk out the back door and into the afternoon sun. She was a good woman, and he always liked to watch the round shape of her tight ass, especially when she came to the church dressed in tight spandex right after her afternoon jog. It was hard not to admire what a form of beauty she was.

He bit down on one of the cookies, grimacing. As good as she looked, she was never going to win any baking awards. It was probably another one of those vegan recipes. No meat, no dairy. How could anyone ever live off such a diet?

Turning away, he reached to close the pantry door, stopping. The light was out again? He'd just changed it. How was it already burnt out?

He stepped into the darkness. Suddenly, it was all around him. Even the daylight outside had disappeared. Everything was just black...

He saw a shape in the darkness. It was faint, looking farther away than where he knew the wall was. He could see it, but couldn't quite make it out.

Then he was gone, the pantry empty, the light overhead pushing back the shadows.

101

PART II

The creature's sleep was interrupted. It had no knowledge of how long it had slumbered. It was well beneath the earth, civilization growing while it slept. Time had passed and it had not been a part of it. What had happened while it was dormant? Had the darkness returned? Was it able to be a part of it again?

It didn't know. It was barely awake, not fully extending beyond its tiny cave. It wanted to stretch out and see what was above, but it could wait until later. The creature was still tired. It wasn't ready to leave its isolation. Maybe it would just fade back to sleep.

It had only been awake for a few moments, like that brief moment in the middle of the night. You wake, get up, and dress, but then realize it is the middle of the night and your bed just looks too comfortable to leave. You nestle back in and, within seconds, fall back to sleep.

The creature would have returned to its hibernation, but it realized it was not alone. There was something else down there, calling out, crying. The creature moved toward the voice. It had to burrow through dirt that had long since collapsed on the entrance. As it did, the voice continued.

The creature had not heard a voice before. It had never met any of the things living in the light. It was not of the light and shied away from these things.

He came to where he found the little creature. It was pale and lying in the dirt. It wore torn rags, a red substance flowing from it and into the dirt. When the creature smelled this, he felt a hunger he had not felt since before...

The creature wanted to sleep, but found it needed sustenance to do so. It was so hungry, it doubted this little thing would be enough. Maybe if he devoured slowly, taking more of it to be a part of itself, it could stave off the hunger while it drifted off again.

It pulled itself to the thing, surrounding it. As the creature did, it heard a sobbing noise, a word the thing cried out. It did not know the meaning yet, but understood it was a word. As the darkness folded around it, the thing cried out, "Mommy!"

CHAPTER 9

An hour of sleep was all he got before he had to go out on another call. Maybe that was why the chief disappeared. He knew today would be the day from hell. The old man had decided he was done dealing with all this crap.

Knowing he shouldn't think that, Rob grimaced as he climbed out of the squad car. He hadn't taken the time to get into uniform. At least the county had done what they'd promised and parked the squad car in his driveway when they were done with it. He kind of wished they hadn't. It was just another reminder that the man who had given him a chance here was nowhere to be found.

The sun burned his eyes, but he didn't feel it was bad enough to keep his glasses on. He placed them on the dash and looked at the flower shop on the corner, Flowery Dreams. He hadn't been in there before because it was new to town, although he heard it was supposed to open soon. Since he had gotten the phone call saying there was some kind of disturbance, they must have finally opened.

He walked in, a small bell over the door chiming. His first reaction was to wince, as every high-pitched sound felt like screaming banshees inside his head. He was sure while the bell alerted the owner, it was also there to give a feeling of nostalgia. He noticed it fit well with the shop. The owner made good use of the windows on both sides of the building, the sun seeming to dance in little mirrors placed throughout the store, making it feel bright while not overpowering the senses. Prisms mingled with the light, rainbows sparkling on the reflections and on little puffs of mist around some of the flowers.

The air was sweet with the aroma of freshly cut blossoms. Was that jasmine? He wasn't quite sure because there were other scents hanging in the air, tickling his nose.

He closed his eyes momentarily to bask in it. His head cleared of the grogginess he hadn't even realized he had been carrying with him. His senses seemed to sharpen.

"Hello. Can I help you?"

He opened his eyes and looked at the woman behind the counter. She was tall and thin, her long black hair falling around her shoulders. She had full lips, small nose, and her bespectacled eyes were blue and cheerful. He felt like he could swim in those eyes for the rest of his life. All he wanted to do was stay lost in watching them.

"Yes, I..." He couldn't remember why he was there. "Yes. I got a call. Some kind of disturbance?" It felt as if he were stumbling over himself. He looked around, trying to find something out of place. The flower shop was picturesque in its pristine and calming façade.

He looked at a deep blue flower in full bloom. The blue petals swayed, dancing on the breeze. He was lost in its intoxication.

"Yes." Her voice seemed to be barely above a whisper, but he could hear her as though she were speaking into his ear. He could almost feel her moist breath on his neck and her lips brushing his cheek as she continued. "Are you the police chief?"

Rob felt himself shaken back to reality. He blinked and looked at the woman...who still stood behind the counter across the room.

"No, I'm a deputy. The chief is unavailable."

She seemed perplexed by that, then nodded. "Okay. I want to file a complaint about that...that crazy person next door."

107

Rob hadn't noticed her heavy European accent before. He wasn't quite sure what it was, but guessed it to be either German or Polish.

"What? Who?"

Her hands on her hips, she pushed her chest out, which he noticed was pretty pronounced compared to her thin waist, stretching the fabric of her shirt. He caught himself and pulled his eyes back to hers. He wasn't sure, but he thought he saw a faint smile on her face before it disappeared, her annoyed glare returning.

"That woman next door. She came here twenty minutes ago, carrying new baby and screaming at me. She told customer to get out, then yelled at me for stealing money out... No, wait. For stealing food out of her baby's mouth. Said I had no right to have shop. Said that me being open takes money from her. She can't feed daughter."

Rob nodded and reached for the little notebook he kept in his uniform chest pocket, growing frustrated when he remembered he wasn't in uniform.

"Okay. What lady from next door?"

"I don't know her. You are town constable. She has flower shop next door."

Now it made sense. Even in Rob's tired mind, the picture started to form. It was one thing to be an outsider, but to open a business that competed with a local was sure to aggravate some people, especially when you opened it right next door.

As he took another look around the cozy little shop, he was thankful he didn't see any property damage.

"Did she break anything? Hurt anyone?"

"She drove away customers!"

"Yes, but she didn't break anything, did she?" She shook her head. He nodded. "Okay. I'll go talk to her. Right now, I don't think it would be a good idea to do much more."

"That is all you going to do?"

"Yes, for right now." He lowered his head, thinking about some of the things happening in town. "It doesn't pay to be upset. You will both probably be getting a lot of business in the next couple of days."

"Missing boy?"

"Yeah."

She nodded. "Customer she ran out getting flowers for family."

"Oh yeah?" It was kind of early for someone to get them flowers. "Who was that?"

"Said he was neighbor." She shrugged.

"Okay. Like I said, I'll go talk to her. Just don't fight back. Let's not escalate this."

She pouted a little, but nodded in agreement.

He turned to leave, but the blue flowers stopped him again. The fluid petals seemed to race faster, the whole flower spinning in a blur and flashing red, then white, then back to blue again.

When he blinked, it was back to normal. Just a blue flower sitting in a vase.

He nodded to her and left, then walked next door. This time, there was no little bell, and while the small shop had the same physical dimensions as the other, it seemed smaller. The place was not as bright or as vibrant, either. In fact, the store was a harsh contrast to what had made him smile and feel welcome in the other one.

Where Flowery Dreams was bright, warm, and homey, Sweet Essence had no natural lighting. The front windows were covered in curtains, letting the unflattering, fluorescent light give even the whitest flower a withered, partial green hue to it. There weren't many flowers on display, the open room leading to the small counter holding an old-style cash register. He wondered if it even worked to ring up a sale.

Unlike what the name implied, the essence of the store was far from sweet. There was a slight odor of something, like mold had seeped under all that tacky, faded, flowered wallpaper. Rob saw a curtained doorway

109

leading to somewhere in the back of the store. The curtain was dark and dingy. Now a tan color, he hoped it hadn't been white at one time.

No one stood behind the counter, but he could hear the sounds of a baby crying and a television playing behind the curtain. It was too familiar, memories of crack dens during his Chicago PD days surrounding him. Those were times he never wanted to recall with too much clarity. He had to work with child services to go into homes where the smell of drugs, shit, and decay overwhelmed him. Images of stoned mothers and screaming babies were not ones he wanted to remember when he went home at night. It was something he still worked to put behind him.

"Hello?" he said, knocking on the counter.

He listened, hearing someone moving around.

"You quiet down!" a woman yelled. The crying stopped. Moments later, a large woman came from the back room, the pattern of her shirt containing massive, bright flowers, a gaudy arrangement of them overlapping each other. It was hard to look at, but hard to turn away from, as well. He tried to focus on the baby on her hip as she did a little hip shake to calm her.

"How can I help you? Flowers for the wife? Mistress?" She winked at him as she stepped to the cash register and grabbed a pen, ready to take down his order on a little notepad.

"Did you go harass the woman next door, today, running out one of her customers?"

The woman dropped the pen back down on the counter, glaring at him.

"Who the hell are you? Her boyfriend?"

"I'm the town const...deputy." He caught himself before he called himself a "constable". "She called in a complaint."

"Yeah, well, where the hell's Danny?"

"Unavailable. Did you do it?"

"Listen, why the hell is there some foreign chick opening up a flower store in a town that I've lived in all my life. She has no right to be here. Is it even legal for her to open that store? Have you checked all her paperwork? Is *she* even legal? You know, if she's not legal, you gotta deport her."

"So you did it."

"Hell yes! I went over and told her she has no business being here."

"She's got every right to be here."

"Look, I don't know who the hell you are, but you don't go telling me how to run my business."

"If you don't cause any trouble, then I won't have to come over here. If I find out that you have been harassing any more of her customers, or if you disrupt her business in any way, I'll be forced to come back."

"Get the hell out of my store."

"Did you hear what I just said?"

Her lips pursed and she stood there, continuing to glare at him. Her daughter had gone quiet and just bounced there as she rocked, not paying any attention.

"I told you to leave. Tell that bitch she best not be stealing any of my customers."

"If I find out you have threatened her or any of her customers, I *will* be back."

He left the store, the door barely closing before he heard the notepad slam against it. He could have written up a report and fined her for a misdemeanor, just to let her know he meant business, but he didn't want to push his luck right now. Maybe if he played it down, it would all go away.

He looked back at Flowery Dreams and wondered if he should go in and let her know he talked to the other business owner. It would also be nice to get some flowers for Robyn. She might appreciate it, then she could get angry for him wasting money on flowers when they didn't know how much longer he would have a steady paycheck.

Best to just leave it alone for now. His bed was calling him anyway. He wanted to get a little more sleep before he had to go on duty in a few hours.

* * * *

Robyn was worried. At one time, her worry was just about Rob getting shot or killed while on patrol. In those days, she was still new to Chicago. She was from a small town, so just living in the city scared her, but to hear some of the stories her husband and his friends told terrified her.

Things were just so much more complicated now. What had happened a year ago? He had been gone for months. When he came home, the nightmares got worse. She had spent many nights with him, having to hold him when he woke up screaming. That was on the nights he slept, but there were very few of those. Most nights, he stayed up until he passed out on the couch, exhaustion finally pulling him deeper than the nightmares. She would find him there and have to help him to bed.

At most, he was living on four hours' sleep a night.

He now got less than that and it was taking its toll. Had he even realized all the weight he had gained? She used to love to wrap her arms around him, nuzzling herself into the nape of his neck. He was her teddy bear, and the extra padding was just more for her to love.

Now, she could barely get her arms around him, his eyes seeming to sink deeper into his face. And she knew she was part of the problem. She didn't say anything, joking and laughing with him like it was nothing. She could have said something when he came home last night, but it had turned into a nice night. He'd been able to relax more than he had in a long time. She had hoped he might even be able to get some sleep. He was in such a good mood, it was like something had changed. Then the phone call came in and he wasn't home again until this morning.

He had a good reason to be out, but he needed his sleep.

She heard buzzing down in the basement, knowing the load of laundry was done. Instead of going downstairs, she made her way to the kitchen and looked out the back window. They lived on the edge of town, woods just past their large back yard. It gave Jake plenty of room to play, but what if there were someone in the woods? What if someone came and took Jake while she wasn't watching? He was ten. It wasn't like she could watch him all the time, but there were all these stories nowadays about kidnappings. Trafficking of kids was happening everywhere. Just last month, she had heard of three kids being taken in Ottawa, which was only twenty miles away. It worried her to think of how much evil was in the world, but what could she do about it?

Robyn wanted to call Sarah. They were good friends in college, taking a series of psychology classes together. Robyn found them interesting, but didn't take them as far as Sarah did. She was now a psychiatrist in Chicago. Sarah's specialty was in corporate work, dealing with the rich and their problems, but she still talked to her old dormmate. Life had taken them down different roads, but they still shared a bond.

Sarah had already given her advice, which wasn't going to change. She would still say Rob needed to get help. There was no way around it. His problems were just too deep for there to be anything Robyn could do for him.

When a tear fell into the sink, she wiped her eyes, not even realizing she had started crying. She just couldn't help herself anymore.

She looked back at the woods, watching as the morning sun shifted the shadows and the trees danced in the wind. They had already lost many of their leaves, the branches looking like skeleton hands stretching across the grass, moving closer. They reached out for her, coming to

113

take her. There was something there. It was dark, angry, and…afraid? Was it afraid of her? No. It was afraid of Rob. The dark was coming for him, but it couldn't get him, could it?

It needed to take her. It was hungry for her…and her baby.

Robyn blinked and took a step back from the sink, instinctively reaching for her stomach. When she looked at the woods again, she could see the shadows, see normal reflections of the shifting trees.

Had she really felt that? Was it really after her, or was Rob not the only one losing himself?

Maybe she should go to church and talk to Pastor Thomas. She wasn't sure what he could do, but just being around him sometimes really helped calm her down.

But that anger… She had felt something. How did it know about the little one inside her? She had only tested positive a few days ago, and hadn't even been able to tell Rob yet. It just wasn't a good time. It seemed like it would never be a good time.

I need to talk to Rob.

It had to have been her imagination, but she could still feel it. It wasn't the same as before, but it was still an evil, cold hunger.

Maybe she was going crazy, but she couldn't take her eyes off the shadows, now paying more attention to the shadows in the house. Something, some voice whispering in the back of her mind, told her not to trust the shadows.

Deep breaths. Just keep taking deep breaths, she thought, walking down the hall and grabbing the keys from the bowl by the door. She was glad Rob had the squad car so she could drive herself to the church. She didn't want to walk down the street, next to the woods, on her way to see the pastor.

CHAPTER 10

"Hey, kid!"

Emily spun around to see the school janitor rushing toward her. She had to get out of there before she was caught.

"You say a word and you're dead," she shot back to Todd, the scrawny kid she had been kicking just seconds ago. Then she took off down the hallway and away from the old man.

"Kid!" he yelled.

She didn't look back, hearing him running behind her, his breathing loud as he got closer. When she saw the door, she sped up slightly. She could hear him falling farther behind. Shoving open the door, she escaped into the sunlight.

Emily didn't stop, hurrying across the gravel asphalt behind the school and over to the bus shed. She wasn't going to go in, though. She didn't know if any of the bus drivers or even a teacher were in there. School would get out in about an hour, so someone might be getting ready. She never knew if Sarah's mom, one of the bus drivers, was in there. She'd definitely recognize her.

Instead, Emily veered behind it. She had just made it out of sight when she heard the distant crash of the school fire door slamming open and shut. She hoped she had made it back there before he saw her. Maybe he would see the shed and think she had gone in. Or maybe he'd think she had gone to the playground. Those did seem like the most obvious places…if she planned to go back into school. She had already decided to take the rest of the day off.

She had caught Todd as he came out of the locker room. He was always running late, making him an easy target. Emily had seen him hurrying, trying to get to class before the second bell, but he wasn't fast enough. She slammed him down to the ground. When he said he didn't have any money, she decided it was time to teach him it was better off for him to *always* have money. He needed to be taught a good lesson.

How was she supposed to go up to the sweet shop and buy a Coke now? She didn't have enough, and that damn janitor had stopped her before she had a chance to search the little puke's pockets.

If Emily went up there now, her sister would probably show up soon. The high school got dismissed before the junior high, which wasn't fair. Why should they get out early?

Either way, if she went up there, her big sis would probably be there around the same time. Lisa might even get her a Coke if Em played the nice, sweet little sister. Emily didn't like playing nice and sweet, but for her sis and a free Coke, she would.

She made her way to the other side of the shed and glanced around it. Quickly, she pulled her head back when she saw a bus pulling into the parking lot. She didn't look too closely, but knew there were kids on it who had gone on a field trip. They would all go into the school from the side door, so there was no way she could get around the school that way.

What was she going to do? She couldn't go back the way she had come, and she couldn't go around the school. The janitor would quickly figure out she wasn't in the shed. Emily was trapped.

She looked around. This was not going how she had planned. All she wanted to do was get the hell out of there. Mrs. Hemsworth was boring as hell, and she didn't want to sit through another long lecture about some damn history thing she couldn't care less about. It was all such a drag. Who wanted to just sit there and listen to her drone on about some old guys who died long ago? Like she was ever going to do anything with that information. It was all so pointless, usually putting her to sleep. She knew if she fell asleep again, it would mean another after-school detention.

She looked at the woods behind the shed. It wasn't very far, then she would be hidden among the trees. She could then run down to where no one could see the road and cross over to the other side. The woods over there ran along the side of the school and past it. She just had to cross another road, but she could do that.

Would the janitor follow her? She didn't think so. She should be lost in the multi-colored leaves before he even got back there.

Hadn't Bobby come up missing in the woods last night? She had heard he was gone. *Hey, maybe I can find his body.* How cool would it be to see his rotted corpse? Maybe there might even be some maggots already eating out his eyes.

She liked Bobby and all, even found him cute, but if he were dead, well... When would be the next time she would ever see a dead body? There was no way she was going to pass that up.

She'd been in the coal dump plenty of times, so there was nothing to worry about.

* * * *

It hadn't taken her long before she was in the woods past the school. She had played hide-and-seek there enough times she knew where all the paths were. The afternoon shadows flickered through the trees and danced around her. Thoughts of a free Coke quickly forgotten, she thought about Bobby.

She couldn't believe he was really missing. Would Emily be the one to find him? There were so many people in town looking, wouldn't they find him first?

But the grown-ups didn't play in the woods, did they? She was sure they had when they were younger, but soon lost that sense of fun. They did adult things. None of them knew the little paths and tunnels, so how would they find Bobby if he were down there?

Could he have fallen into one of them? Or maybe there was a cave-in. She remembered when Mikey disappeared last year. Bobby and she were supposed to be looking for him, but they hadn't. They had mostly run around, tickling each other. Everyone else was furiously looking for that little "brat", as Bobby had called him, but they were just having fun. Thankfully, no one caught them.

Making sure there were no cars, she hurried across the second street. The road led out of town, but there was hardly anyone around. The town did seem a little "deader" than usual. She thought more people would probably be around the coal dump, so she'd have to be careful not to get caught.

Once she crossed the road, she made her way over to a smaller footpath. While the main path swirled around the coal dump, this was a smaller path going directly up the side. It was a shortcut she liked to take when she wanted to feel on top of the world.

Emily only went halfway up to a spot where the footpath crossed the main path of red stone before she split off. She had a rough idea where she wanted to look for Bobby. It was a place they had gone a few times. She knew she shouldn't sneak off with boys. According to her dad, that was how babies got made. While she knew it took more than that, knowing it involved sex, she got the hint.

119

Would Bobby be the first boy she had sex with? Probably, but there was no way she was ready for that. When she was, Bobby was definitely the one. For now, though, she was happy with just kissing him and letting him play with her. He was a really good tickler.

She found the place Bobby had brought her a few times. She had started to call out to him when everything deflated. He wasn't there. She hadn't realized she had actually pictured him sitting there, waiting. Where else could he be? This was their place. It was a nice little area hidden away from the path, surrounded by bushes, two stumps they had rolled there sitting in the middle. They had placed them in front of a large metal grate covering a hole.

Bobby loved to spit down into that hole. Sometimes, he would even jump on the grate, laughing at Emily for being afraid to join him. He didn't see how the metal bounced on the ground. It moved as he jumped up and down, one edge inching closer to the hole. He would fall through one day, then she would have to tell his mom about how Bobby disappeared and fell through to China. She didn't know if the hole were that deep, but whenever they threw things down there, they never heard them land.

She walked over to the grate and looked down into it. She couldn't see anything. Beneath the grate was only black. The sun didn't even shine on the sides of it.

She sat down on one of the stumps, her shoulders sagging. She didn't really want to wander around the woods. Besides, if she were caught, what would she say? How would she explain it? She was supposed to be in school. The only reason she left was to get away from that nasty janitor chasing her. Well, she guessed she wouldn't have to mention that.

In fact, she could tell whomever she saw that she was worried about her friend and left to come help find him. That was true, wasn't it? Well, kind of. He was her friend, and she did want to try and find him, but she would have been happy with just finding his body. She had never seen a body before. Yeah, it would be sad that it was Bobby, but still cool.

She looked up and watched the branches dance above her. When the sun shone through them, she saw the finger-like shadows move around her. The branch hands looked to be reaching out to her. Jumping when she felt something brush against her leg, she chuckled. It was probably just a bush.

If she closed her eyes, maybe she could feel Bobby there with her so she wouldn't be alone. If he were dead, she really *was* alone. She couldn't stand her parents. They usually just ignored her and Lisa. Emily hung out more uptown than she did at home. Lisa was usually either off at her boyfriend's or over at Tammy's. She was never home, so it really was just Emily there.

Most of the other kids were afraid of her, which was how she liked it. She was taller and stockier, having a wide face and nose that looked nearly flat. Kids used to call her "boy face" because they said she looked like a boy, then she started beating them up. Now everyone, except Bobby, just ignored her. He was her friend, and they both picked on all the little dirtbags.

Feeling the chill, she ran her hands up and down her arms. Her legs were especially cold, even though she wore jeans.

She looked down, blinking, not sure what she saw. That wasn't right. She had to be seeing it wrong. It just...

Below her was nothing, blackness, as if the darkness under the grate had worked its way out and was now around her. The sun did nothing to penetrate the shadows. They spread slowly, tentacle-like strands expanding over the ground.

Her legs were in it, but she knew she had to get free. It didn't matter what it was or if it were in her mind. It wasn't right. It was so cold. She felt its touch as it slithered up her.

121

She couldn't let it take her. She tried to pull her legs free, but couldn't. Something gripped her. As she pulled hard on her legs, it held tight. Something was in the darkness. It almost felt like a hand had grasped both her ankles, but that just wasn't possible. There was nothing there.

She opened her mouth to scream, but as she did, the world around her went dark. She whipped her head around to see the blackness had formed a dome. It wasn't thick, but was enough to block out the brightness of the sun, seeping away any color.

She looked at her arms to see they looked even whiter than normal, her pale skin looking ghostly.

"Please, help me!" she screamed, hoping there were some searchers nearby.

The darkness became thicker. Through her jeans, she could feel the cold touch of whatever was in the black. She didn't need to see it to know what it was, though. It was a monster. Not like the monsters Bobby's mom always told him about…the hobos she said lived up there. Unlike those, this monster was real, and it had her.

She could think of only one way to get away from it. She had to break out of its grasp. To do that, she had to fall.

She thought maybe if she fell back, whatever had her would have to either support all her weight or release her, letting her fall back to the ground. It would hurt, and she figured there was no way she wasn't going to clip the stump. She could deal with the pain later. She had to focus on escaping.

With her eyes closed, she let herself fall back. She pushed off with her legs, expecting to be propelled backwards.

Instead of feeling herself break free, the grip strengthened. The darkness was nearly as high as her stomach, tingling against her bare skin. Something rigid and slimy moved across her, but she couldn't see anything past the endless black cloud engulfing the dome.

Her chest heaved as she struggled to pull herself free. The darkness held her up, so maybe there was something to push against. When she thrust her hands down into it, they disappeared into the solid black mist and were held by its icy grip.

This wasn't going to get her. No, she was strong. She was not going to go down like this. She had pounded little kids, knew how to fight back. This was not going to take her. There was no way she was going to lose.

"Help me!"

She pulled her arms, shaking viciously to get them free. The grip that held them was unrelenting, but if she could wiggle enough, maybe they would start to give. Then she could just work her way free. There was still the dome, but she knew she could break through that.

But the dark force didn't release her. It rose up slowly, closing over her neck. It rose faster, taking away more and more of her movement. She could barely move her head. Nearly everything was now completely black around her.

She tried one last time to call out. This time, someone had to hear her, had to come save her. There wasn't any way she wasn't getting out of this. As she opened her mouth to scream, the darkness covered it, smothering her, as if she screamed into a pillow. When she tried to pull in more air for another scream, it covered her nose. She couldn't breathe. Her lungs burned. Her head swam as the world disappeared around her.

When the darkness covered her eyes, everything was gone.

CHAPTER 11

The void was endless, the darkness enveloping every part of his being, allowing for the sense that there was nothing beyond his own self. It made the feeling of being alone push on him, surround him, pull him into its grip. The despair of it put weight on his soul and dragged him into something he had felt before, but it had only gingerly touched him then. Now it flooded into him. It was anger. It was hate. It was everything he had always felt wrong with the world. All the moral depravity pushed through every barrier he had ever put up, reaching far into his core. He could feel as it went for his very being.

He had been a cop for so long, seen so many evils, but he had always kept it at arm's length, never letting any of it get to him. He would get depressed now and then, but only because of what he saw. He had always been the one who was able to keep his sanity.

Now, it felt like the darkness had gotten its grips into him and he could no longer push it away. Rob was surrounded by darkness. He couldn't tell if his eyes were closed or open, if he were awake or sleeping, alive or dead. Everything was gone, except the black nothing around him.

But when he took a step forward, his bare foot fell on solid ground. It was cool and smooth, like marble or glass. He crouched down to see what it was, but no matter how he moved or where he looked, there was nothing.

"Hello?" His voice echoed. He thought he closed his eyes, but wasn't sure. Everything was wrong and he was lost inside himself. He could only feel his hatred building, his breathing quickening. He wanted to hit something, to pound it into submission.

A child giggled. He heard it all around him as he spun, trying to see and feel where the sound came from. At first, he thought it had been behind him, but when he turned, it stayed behind him. It echoed, everywhere...and nowhere. The soft sounds were a tease of something there as it shadowed him. His anger caught in his chest as his breath turned cold and frightened.

How had Rob gotten there? What was the last thing he remembered?

What was his name? Rob Alletto. He was a beat cop in Chicago. No, he wasn't in Chicago anymore. Why? Because he felt it was too dangerous for his... Who?

Jake... Remember Jake? Yes, I remember. I have a son and a wife, Wendy. No. My wife is Robyn. We are Rob and Robyn. Everyone likes to make a joke about our names.

So who is Wendy?

The giggling intensified around him, now feeling like a needle trying to slowly push into his temple. He could feel a tear at the corner of his eye, threatening to fall. It tried to get into his mind like it had his body. It wanted to take him, like...like...like someone had fought for his mind before. He remembered he had to fight with someone else, some*thing* else. Something wanted to take control of him. Was the giggling trying to control him?

No. It wanted something, but he couldn't quite place it.

How had I fought it before? How did I beat it?

He thought of Jake and Robyn and remembered that moment. It was amazing. It was the first time he had held Jake in his arms. Robyn was a new mother, he was a new father, and the nurse had handed him this small

125

bundle of joy, his eyes not even open yet, his mouth moving as he received his first taste of the world.

He felt the giggling fade a little, the pressure against him easing. His eyes fluttered open. He hadn't even realized he had closed them. The world around him was still black, but now he saw a boy standing in front of him. He wore a torn and dirty white shirt and cut off jeans that were barely held together. His skin was pale, but he could still recognize him from the picture. It was the boy he was looking for. What was his name?

Name... Name... Come on. What's his name?

"Hey!" Rob called out to him.

The boy looked at him, surprised and scared. Feeling his foot move, Rob took a step toward him.

The boy took a step back, then another. Rob continued to move forward, but he couldn't get any closer. The boy always stayed just out of reach.

When the boy realized this, a wide smile stretched across his pale face and he laughed again. This time, it was deep and menacing, somehow having the force to echo around him. The sound cascaded off the unseen walls, growing in volume. More laughter joined the hideous sound, growing louder and louder. Rob thought he was going to faint as, even in the darkness of the place, colors danced in his vision. The pain pushed at him again. He was losing it. He was going to give in. Everything shifted and he started to fall...

* * * *

As his eyes fluttered open, the afternoon sun blinded him. His body ached as he tried to roll over. When his spine locked, he stayed lying on his back. He had a momentary sense he was still asleep, trapped in another nightmare. He strained to listen for the screams of dying victims, the fire tearing away at the house around him. He didn't hear any of it. The only thing he heard was the quiet sound of a child's laughter. He vaguely remembered dreaming about a child, but this sounded nothing like what pulled at his memory. He recognized this sound. It pushed away some of the grogginess as he smiled.

He had to lift his leg so he could pull himself up. It was a nagging reminder that he wasn't a young cop anymore. That officer had died in the fire, a grizzled, old man replacing him.

Walking slowly to the window, he looked out, seeing his son playing with his friend, Chris. Rob was happy when Chris came over because the two got along so well. He watched as they both ran around the yard, their arms outstretched like they were flying.

It was good to see them playing, although Rob often regretted they never had enough extra money for Jake to have the game consoles other kids had. Unless he went over to a friend's house, he never got to play all the games he saw on television. Jake never let it bother him, though. Rob watched the two boys, realizing it wasn't all that different from how Rob and his friends would have played at that age.

Jake would always be a good boy, always be Rob's little angel.

He stepped away from the window, hearing Robyn downstairs. She had told him she was going to be running errands for much of the afternoon. Either she had gotten done early or it was later than he thought. He wasn't ready to look at the clock to see just what time it was.

Rob looked at his uniform draped over the back of a chair. He hadn't worn it last night and didn't relish putting it on now. Every day, it felt harder to find the energy to put it on. It seemed like it had become his prison. What was he being sentenced for?

He guessed the better question was when did he start feeling this way? He used to love being a cop and helping people. When had that changed? When they had

127

moved? Being in the smaller town, he thought he would feel more like he was helping people. He didn't.

Shaking his head, he walked to the bedroom door. He knew the time would come when he'd need to go on duty again, but he wasn't ready yet.

With a deep breath and a sigh, he stomped down the stairs, his heavy steps his sign of reluctance.

"You up already?"

"Hey, hun," he said, walking into the kitchen. Robyn was putting away groceries, breaking up the chicken breasts into individual Ziploc bags.

"You want to help me separate breasts?"

"I'll gladly help you *play* with your breasts." He stepped up behind her and made a playful grab for her chest.

"Down boy." She shimmied away, laughing.

He watched her, pouting playfully, then grabbed one of the apples from the bowl on the table. He took a large bite as he leaned back on the counter.

"Any messages?" he asked as he chewed.

"Pastor Thomas called. He said it wasn't important, but just wanted to check to make sure you're okay and see if there's anything he can do. He also *kindly* reminded me that I had promised to make some of my cinnamon twists for the potluck dinner this Sunday night."

Robyn didn't want to tell Rob she had actually gone to see the kindly young minister. Rob liked him, but knew he felt she spent too much time at the church lately. She couldn't explain it, even to herself. In the last couple years, considering everything that had happened, going there made her feel better. She wasn't sure it explained anything, but it helped quell some of the fears she had.

When she had spoken to the pastor, he had expressed concern about Rob, saying he wasn't the only one who was worried. One of the local priests had also expressed his concerns to Pastor Thomas.

"Didn't know you had offered."

She broke herself out of her thoughts and smiled as she met Rob's gaze. "I guess I got volunteered."

"Okay." His mood darkened as he watched her put the bags of chicken together in a larger bag before she put it in the freezer. "Well, I guess I'd better call county to see if they found anything."

Robyn walked over and put her arms around him, placing her head on his chest. He held her tightly.

"You'll find them," she whispered.

He ran his hand through her hair, enjoying the feeling of her against him.

Jake came crashing through the door. "Hey, Mom! Can me and Chris head over to the park?"

"Whoa," Rob said, quickly pulling away from her warmth, already missing it, as he looked at the two tornadoes barreling through the kitchen. "I'm not sure that's—"

"Chris and I…," Robyn said, talking over him.

Rob knew they should be on top of his grammar, but he couldn't help it. He had heard "go" and "park", already planning his rejection. Right now, he couldn't stand the thought of Jake being away from home. Not when Rob had to go out on patrol. Not when he wouldn't be there to know that he was safe.

He looked at Jake, whose face fell as he turned to go back outside. He knew they'd play for a little longer, but if Jake couldn't go with him, Chris would probably leave. That would leave Jake alone when his friend took off to play with the others. Chris had grown up there. While he played with Jake, his son didn't really hang around with anybody else. He was still the outsider. Chris was Jake's connection to those other kids.

"Wait," Robyn said, catching the boys before they walked out the door. She turned and looked up at Rob, silently asking for his approval. He closed his eyes, fighting back the tears. "Rob, it's just to the park, and Chris will be with him. I'm sure there will be other kids there, too. *And...,*" she said loudly so Jake could hear her, "I will be there in an hour to pick him up before it gets dark. He will be there and *nowhere else* when I get there." She turned away from Rob, who grimaced, knowing he was losing this battle. She stared down at Jake. "You understand me?"

He nodded and, smiling broadly, he and Chris ran out the door.

Rob wrapped his arms around her again, pulling her to him.

"He'll be okay," she reassured him.

"I know."

They stood there holding each other, swaying back and forth, letting the minute linger. These moments came less and less often. When they did, he never wanted to break it. He knew he had to, though.

"I better check in with county, make sure there's no good news. If I'm working tonight, I'd better get moving. I need to check with Ms. Taylor to make sure they're okay, maybe see if she came up with anything else that could help."

Robyn pulled away and nodded. "Okay." She sniffed back a tear, Rob feeling the wetness on his t-shirt. He hadn't even realized she had been crying. She was just as worried about Jake going to the park as he was. She was just better at hiding it. He kissed her forehead, then headed to the living room to find his phone.

* * * *

Rob waited for a car to pull out of the driveway before he pulled in behind a late-model SUV he thought he recognized. The glowing orb of the sun had started to creep behind the trees. It had been a long day, and with his nap, even as short as it was and split into segmented parts of tortured nightmares, it felt like days since the last time he had been at this house. He wished he were coming here with news. Even the worst news would be some kind of closure, although no one ever wanted to hear they had outlived their child.

He knew it was too soon to think that way. The child had only been missing since yesterday. The last thing he wanted to do was go in the house thinking the boy was dead. He had to stay positive so Wendy stayed positive. There was always hope.

As he reached the door, even he could smell the bullshit of which he was trying to convince himself. Yes, he knew the numbers were in their favor...out of the nine hundred thousand juveniles who came up missing each year, typically only a hundred were murdered...but that didn't change the fact only sixty-two percent were recovered alive. The first three hours a child was missing were the most crucial.

He hadn't even been called within the first three hours. They had been trying to find the chief during that time. Could he really believe the two weren't related? They had to be. Had the chief tried to stop something and been killed? Had the boy seen it? Maybe he had gotten away and was hiding.

Oh God, please let that be the case. Let the boy be okay and just hiding somewhere. The last thing I want to deal with is coming across the little boy's body. A boy Jake knows and goes to school with.

He knocked on the front door. It didn't take long before a young black woman opened the door.

"Hello. Is Wendy Taylor available?"

The woman opened the screen door, then stood there, arms crossed. She scowled at him.

"You the town bumpkin who's not finding her son?"

Rob's mouth dropped open, taken aback by the hostility. "Excuse me?"

"You heard me."

"Hey, who is it?" he heard someone call from inside. Another young woman came up and stood behind her friend. Her eyes were puffy, but not wet. The girl must

131

have gotten past some of her grief, although Rob knew it was only a calm spot in the storm.

"Hello. I'm Rob Alletto. I'm the deputy in town."

"Lea, let him in. He may have some news." The black woman stood aside, allowing Rob to enter. "Do you? Have you heard anything about my brother?"

"Not yet. I just checked in with county. They questioned your father and searched his residence. He-"

The young woman started toward the living room. "That was a waste of time. That piece of shit wouldn't have had anything to do with Bobby."

"Well, its best to search rather than assume he had nothing to do with it."

She nodded as they stopped.

"Who is it?" Rob heard Wendy call from the other room. He saw her lying on the couch, a blanket covering her. Tissues covered the floor, and it looked like she hadn't moved recently. He guessed she had been up all night, which must have taken its toll. It could not be easy to go through the loss of a child.

"It's the deputy," the woman called, then turned back to Rob. "I'm Allison, Bobby's sister." He nodded, shaking her hand. "So you don't have any news for us then?"

"Not yet. If it's all right, I wanted to talk to your mom. Ask a few more questions, see if there is anything else she might be able to tell me about where Robert liked to go. There might be somewhere we haven't looked yet."

Allison rolled her eyes. "I doubt it. She's graduated from drinking amaretto to whiskey. She'll be passed out in about an hour."

"Do you really think you'll find him *now*? You've had twenty-four hours. Aren't those the most important?" Leannette asked, her tone openly hostile.

"The first three hours are the most important, but I hadn't been called in yet. I'm doing everything I can."

"Obviously, it's not enough."

Rob tried not to show his frustration with the truth in her statement, but his gaze dropped, finding it hard to meet her glare. He avoided looking at her as he turned toward Allison.

"May I speak to your mother? We have to hope that maybe your brother is just hiding somewhere. There is also the chance he is hurt and is in need of medical attention. At this point, we can't rule anything out."

Arms wrapped around her waist, as if to keep herself warm, Allison stepped back, letting Rob walk into the room.

As he eased himself into the chair next to the couch, he heard Allison tell Leannette she should head back to the city before it got too late. The door opened and closed quietly.

"Hello, Ms. Taylor."

Her eyes opened slowly. She pulled herself up and reached for another tissue.

"Have you found him?" Her voice was shaky.

"Not yet. I wanted to ask you some more questions."

"I had a dream you found him and he was sleeping in his room."

"Hopefully soon."

She smiled as she blew into the tissue, then placed it on the pile on the table. "Okay."

"Is there anywhere your son might go to hide from someone?"

"Bobby? He would always go to his grandmother's."

"Anywhere else? Anywhere he would go to play with other kids or whenever he was in trouble? Just somewhere he would run off to?"

"Not really. Whenever his dad yelled at him, he would go to his room to play Xbox."

Rob opened his mouth, trying to ask the same question another way, when the radio on his shoulder crackled.

133

"Officer Alletto, copy?"

He keyed the mic. "Yeah. Go ahead."

He stood and nodded his apology to Wendy, who grimaced and lay back down as he stepped away.

"Officer Alletto, we have another missing person. A John Amery. His wife said he was at his parish, but is no longer there. Can you take the report and follow-up, or do we need to dispatch another officer?"

"I can check it out," he said into the radio.

"That asshole can go straight to fucking hell."

Rob turned to see Wendy sitting straight up, looking at him vehemently.

"Ma'am?"

"That son of a bitch Amery can burn in hell. That lying, cheating asshole had better *stay* missing."

Rob nodded. She must have heard about the earlier incident involving the pastor. He would probably be pretty upset himself if it had been said about Jake. The good pastor would probably have a big ol' fat lip, as well as a few bruises.

"I'll keep looking for Bobby, ma'am. You try and get some rest."

She nodded and reached for the bottle of dark liquid on the floor. He walked to the door. Allison opened it for him.

"Bobby liked to play up at the coal dump." Rob looked at her. "Mom always told him not to go there, but he never listened to anyone."

"Well, we've already searched most of it. I can't imagine there is anywhere up there we haven't looked."

"He had a special spot. It was close to the top and hidden from the trail. I had to go get him a few times and bring him home."

His heart sped up at the possiblity. "I have to take this report, but is there any way you can show me as soon as I'm done with Amery's wife?"

"Sure." She quickly wrote down her phone number and handed it to him. "Call me when you're ready and I'll walk over there."

Rob nodded and left. He stepped off the porch and walked down the stairs, the shadow of the house seeming to follow him, keeping him in its darkness as he walked toward his car.

He shook his head. *Shadows reaching for me...* He really did need to get more sleep.

CHAPTER 12

"I really don't think we should. If my mom comes to pick me up and I'm not here, I'm dead," Jake said. Chris stood right next to him, as if they were conspiring some secret plan. There were other kids around who could hear them, but it was more that there could be adults who would hear. Just because Jake and Chris didn't see them didn't mean they weren't there.

"Come on. We're gonna go as a group. We'll head to the dump and just walk around. What's the harm in that? Maybe we'll find Bobby. You want to find him, don't ya?"

Not really. He knew Bobby and didn't really care if they found him. Bobby always pushed him around at school, and Jake had to take back hallways instead of main stairs just to avoid running into him. The thought of finally not having to worry about him made Jake not dread going to school. Sure, there were the other kids in Bobby's group, but without him, they weren't as bad. Most were actually decent kids. It was only when Bobby was around that they were all jerks.

If he helped find Bobby, though, maybe he would lay off. Then perhaps Jake would be part of their group. It would be nice to have a few kids he could hang out with. Chris was all right, but the others... They were the cool kids, the tough ones. The ones who stood up to the teachers. They didn't even call on them in class. The teachers always picked on him, asking him questions, making him solve problems and write on the whiteboard. It was like they had it out for him.

If he went off with the cool kids, maybe they would accept him. Maybe they would ask him to hang out with them more often, teach him how to be cool.

Jake looked past Chris at the group of four kids, all of them taller than either of them. Two were supposed to be in the next grade, but had been held back. They were all intimidating compared to Jake. He was taller than Chris, but not by much.

"I guess. We'd better not get into trouble, though."

"We are just going up there to check it out. Then we'll be back down before it gets dark. Your mom won't even know."

Jake nodded. They'd just rush to the coal dump and check it out, then come right back. They would be quick. What trouble could they get into? They were only trying to help find a kid from school.

He looked at the sun. There was another hour before it started to set, then they still had time before it really got dark. It was only a short bike ride there. So why did he tell himself it was a good idea, but still not believe it?

Chris led him back over to the group of kids.

"Yeah. We'll come with you guys."

"Cool. Alletto, you lookin' a little pale. You're not scared to go up there, are ya?" Joel, a thin, rough-looking kid, one who had been held back a grade, stood with his elbow on top of another kid's head.

"No, I'm fine."

"Really? It looks like a cat is trying to scratch its way out of your stomach," John said, frowning, pushing Joel's elbow off his head.

"That's a good one," Joel laughed as John pushed him away. "You never know what might happen up there. There are ghosts, ya know. You might go up there and never come back down."

"If that were the case, you wouldn't be going up there, either," Chris said.

"Nah. I'm not afraid of no ghosts. They won't bother me."

"Yeah. He's too ugly for them," John teased. Joel tried to push him, but John dodged, the others giggling.

"Like you're any better," said Julie.

"At least my nose doesn't take up half my face."

"Guys, he said he would come. Just leave him alone," Chris said, finally coming to Jake's defense.

"Yeah? What you going to do about it? Get your dad to beat all of us up?"

Jake smirked. He had met Chris' dad and the man was a monster. He reminded him of those old black-and-white *Frankenstein* movies where the man towered over everyone else. Chris wasn't that tall yet, but everyone knew he'd eventually be huge. It was just taking a long time to happen.

"Come on. Let's just go," Danny said, pulling his bike from the rack. Julie had already pulled hers out of the other side, scowling at them for not moving quicker.

"So where are we going to go?" Jake asked as he picked his bike up. He hadn't had the chance to rack it because they had just gotten to the park when they saw the other kids getting ready to leave. He had just dropped it, knowing his dad would complain about him not taking care of it.

Joel glared at him. He opened his mouth, but Julie cut him off.

"There's a spot up there near the top. Bobby would go there."

"Don't you think the cops know about it already?" Jake asked.

Danny shook his head. "Doubt it. It's kinda hard to find and looks like it's covered in thorn bushes." He pushed off on his bike, done waiting.

"Shouldn't we tell the police?" Jake asked as he turned and pedaled to catch up. Joel was quick to ride up next to him.

"What? You wanna run and tell your daddy?" he sneared.

"I'm just saying we should tell them. They're looking for him."

"You can do what you want, but you won't find it without us." Joel pedaled himself into the lead.

"Yeah." John took his position next to Joel. They both shook their heads. Jake sensed they were mocking him.

He knew there was no use arguing with them. If he went with, he could tell his dad where it was later. What if they found Bobby? Either way, Jake would be in trouble, but at least he had CPR and first-aid training. If Bobby were hurt, he could help.

The kids around him probably went hunting and fishing with their dads and had all kinds of survival training, though. He was still the "kid from Chicago" who everyone thought was some kind of thief. No one expected him to know anything about the woods. He had joined the Boy Scouts, but was still that kid who didn't know how to tie knots or use a fishing pole. He was amazed to see that it wasn't like in the movies...swinging the fishing pole back and forth, instantly catching a fish. It was much more boring. You just flung it out there once, then sat there and watched your floaty thing. That was something else he got made fun of for. Always forgetting it was called a "bobber".

"No, I'm coming with you guys."

"Cool," Julie said as she caught up, giving him a little smile and a nod. He felt his heart flutter a little, his face heating. Had she really just smiled at him?

He gave her a brief one, quickly turning back to watch the road as they all rode toward the large, wooded mountain all the way across town. It was nowhere close to where he was supposed to be.

He was definitely going to get caught. This time, he was certain his mom would deliver on her promise of an ass whipping so hard, he wouldn't be able to sit down for a week.

But he was with the cool kids. They were laughing, making him feel like a part of them. He actually got to be there. All of that made whatever his mom did to him a fair price to pay.

* * * *

Rob closed the door and took a long, deep breath. He shut his eyes, not wanting the setting sun to blind him as he took another deep breath. In and out, trying to slow his racing heart and quell the migraine pushing at his temple.

For the last thirty minutes, he talked to the pastor's wife, having to listen about how he was a heavenly man who was taken by some evil that was loose in this godforsaken town. The sinners, the whores, the corruption, and the police were responsible for the man going missing.

The woman, having heard about what happened between Rob and her husband, wasn't happy he was there to take the report. She almost accused him of taking the man. He sensed it was on the tip of her tongue, and he was certain she truly believed it. In her eyes, he was part of the evil because he allowed the sinners to propagate the town, allowed the vileness to spread.

Rob wasn't sure, but he felt like that had been the longest thirty minutes of his life. He was convinced it had been longer, but his phone confirmed it had only been a half-hour.

It must have had something to do with all the yelling. He never understood why people thought yelling and accusing him of something was going to get him motivated to do what they wanted. Out of the three people missing, the pastor was not one he was eager to find. Something about the man made Rob wonder if he acted like a godly man in public, then screwed a bunch of mistresses in private. He would never voice that opinion to anyone, but every time he saw the crazy look in his eyes, it struck him as cunning.

What was more alarming was that he now had a third missing person, one Rob had seen only a few hours ago. None of this made any sense. Either there was some psychopath out killing people and hiding bodies, or the pastor was just using the missing kid and the chief for his own ends. Maybe he wanted to get some sympathy from the community after Rob had mistreated him this morning.

He wouldn't put it past the man.

Rob was just glad to be back in the squad car, looking over the notes he had taken from the woman. He would have to call county in a minute, get the word out so a larger search could be set up.

Mrs. Amery said he had gone missing from the church shortly after Rob had dropped him off. When she arrived to prepare for the bible group tonight, he wasn't there.

Normally, she wouldn't have been suspicious of this. He could have just run out for a moment, but what made her uneasy was when she had arrived, the back door was wide open. When she went inside, she found the pantry door open, a stepladder sitting in the middle. She called out for her husband, then walked around the church, finding his wallet in his office. The man never liked to keep it in his pants, hating to sit on it, so he always placed it in his desk drawer. She called his cell, the ring echoing. Following the sound, she noticed his suit coat still there, hanging on the back of his office door, his cell phone in the pocket. She hadn't thought about it earlier, but walked back outside, seeing his car parked right next to where she had pulled in.

She was so sure the man should still be there, she waited another hour before calling the authorities. Oh how her face went red when Rob walked in. She really did believe he had something to do with his disappearance. As soon as he left, she probably rushed to call county to accuse him of not taking appropriate notes. He would get a call in the next hour or so, letting him know she had lodged a complaint.

His cell vibrated in his pocket. He looked at the screen, seeing a local number, but not one he recognized.

"Hello?"

"This the town deputy?"

"Yes. Can I help you?" Maybe someone was calling in a tip. Maybe the day would get better.

"Yeah. Find my damn daughter. She's missing."

Rob felt his chest tighten. "Who is this?"

"Name's Jake Bloom. I got your number from Henry."

Rob wasn't sure who Henry was, but he must be someone he had dealt with before. He wasn't accustomed to how many people said they had his number. It led to some odd calls in the middle of the night. He wasn't sure how he felt about so many people knowing his personal contact information.

"Okay. Give me your address and I'll be right over. Can I get a general description of her and a list of her friends so I can start the report?"

"How the fuck do I know? She's ten, short blonde hair. She used to run around with that damn Taylor kid. The one who's gone missing. Fucking school let her run off. They should have been fucking watching her."

"Okay, and you're sure she didn't go somewhere after school?"

"No. She was gone the last half of the day, but the assholes never called. They said they did, but I never got no fucking calls. Fuckers. I got home from work and she wasn't home. Called the school and they said they tried to call. Like I'm that fucking hard to get ahold of."

"Okay, calm down. I'll be there to get a picture and take a full report. Is there a particular place she and Bobby Taylor liked to go?"

"How the fuck am I supposed to know that? I'm her father, not her fucking keeper. She came and went as she pleased."

Rob nodded, then realized the man couldn't see it. That was probably a good thing, considering the disapproving scowl he knew was on his face. *What kind of father just let his kid come and go?* Well, it was more common in the smaller town. Even he found it easier and easier just to let Jake run off and play. The town felt safe, so why not?

He knew exactly why not. He had known it back in Chicago. *Today is exactly why not. When you don't stay up on where your kids go, making sure they keep in touch with you, things like today happen. You come home to find your only child gone. After that, what kind of world would you see?*

"Okay. Give me your address and I'll be right there." He took the information and hung up.

He blew out a breath. There were now four missing people, and he was still only one man. If it kept going like this, the county would declare some kind of emergency, maybe even involve the state. He would lose the case to them, which would probably finish his career.

He had to admit, though, he liked the idea of the state taking over. He didn't know if he were ready for something like this again. It was still too soon. It seemed like his world had been turned upside down not too long ago.

Could Rob really just walk away from it? There was no way he could ever live with himself if he just gave up the case. Right now, it felt like it would be easy to just walk away, but the moment he finally got enough sleep, the weight of that decision would crash down on him.

143

That wasn't the man he thought himself to be, and wasn't the example he wanted to set for his son. They might try to take the case away from him, but there was no way he wouldn't fight to be a part of it. He would still search, trying to find out what happened.

He wished he could just call Brad and have him patrol. It would be nice to have at least a few hours of normal sleep. Then he could wake up tomorrow and feel refreshed. Maybe he'd even be able to figure out what the four had in common.

He could believe the chief had been trying to stop something, the boy saw something he wasn't supposed to, and they were both missing because of that. But the two new people squashed that theory, so there had to be something else connecting them.

He knew he couldn't call Brad in. He lived an hour away, working as a night officer in Peoria. He'd already be on shift. When he helped them out, it was only the occasional weekend. There was no way Rob could bring him in on a weeknight.

It wouldn't do any good anyway. Rob couldn't go home and get any rest because he'd continue thinking about the case. He might as well stay on duty and work at it.

He shifted the car into gear. As he watched the falling ball of light, he knew that everything would only get worse in the night. There was something wrong, something hanging in the air and collecting among the shadows. He didn't know how he felt it. Maybe it was because of all that happened before. Or maybe he had started to get a sixth sense about evil. It did seem like it had a way of finding him. It felt like something was growing. Something was in the darkness…and he had no idea what it was.

CHAPTER 13

When David left the search, he nearly had to be dragged away. He made it home and collapsed on the couch, drifting into a deep sleep. Those last few hours, as he walked the woods on one of the more lesser-known paths, he felt his body lose control. His shoulders slumped. His eyes were open, but he was in more of a trance than actually walking. At one point, he stopped in the middle of a thorn bush, cuts along his arms, no idea how he got there.

He had to keep going. He wasn't going to stop until they found Bobby. He had to be somewhere. There wasn't anywhere else in town he could be.

That wasn't true. There were many other places Bobby could be. What if someone had taken him? He could be dead, his body hidden somewhere. Then there was the grim possibility he had been taken by one of those sick pedophiles who did nasty things to little kids, keeping them locked away in a hidden dungeon for years.

"David, you need to go home," someone had said.

He had looked up. Somehow, he had drifted onto another path and Mr. Cranston stood there, supporting his body. He wasn't sure when he had fallen into the man's arms, but he could now smell his breath, David's nose wrinkling. Why did the man's breath always have to reek of onions?

David looked around and saw he was being led down the north side of the coal dump on the often unused direct path. He felt the warmth of the man's arm around him, but he could also feel his sweat through his coat. He wanted to pull away. This man was disgusting. How had kids ever made it through middle school with him teaching?

David didn't have enough strength left to pull away, so he let the man guide him. He had him in a vice grip against his chest as he took him to his car, placed him in the passenger seat, and drove him home.

Even though he had only been home a few hours, it felt like it had done him some good, but as he started to wake, he felt his nightmare lingering. He didn't know if Mr. Cranston had been real or part of the glimmers of dark pushing into his dreams. It was all jumbled in the fog of his brain. While his body tried to pull him back to sleep, he knew he was done with it. His mind was too far gone, racing like a horse down a track, a million thoughts competing for his attention.

Shakily, he pushed himself off the couch. He briefly wondered why he wasn't in his room, then he looked down, contemplating where his shirt had disappeared to. Finding it under couch, he pulled it on, not having the energy to run upstairs for a fresh one.

Now that he was up, he noticed the house felt unusually quiet. Where was everyone?

He had no idea if his father was at work or at the bar, but it didn't matter. It was better when the man wasn't around anyway. If he had been, he would have probably complained about David not coming home last night…if his dad even noticed he wasn't there.

Yeah, that's a great thought. Just how long could I have stayed away before my dad noticed? I'm not even sure I want to know the answer.

He grabbed his cell phone from the table, happy to see he had brought it home. Nothing that morning was easy to remember, so his phone could have been anywhere. Seeing it sitting on the coffee table was a huge

147

relief. He had a lot of missed calls and multiple voicemails, but he had slept through them all.

He saw one number that made him raise his brows. Allison had called him? Ally? Could she be back in town? Would she really have come back for Bobby?

The phone rang, her name popping up on the caller ID. He didn't realize just how badly he wanted to see her until he felt a little flutter in his chest, a smile spreading across his face. He really shouldn't be smiling, there wasn't anything to smile about, but he couldn't help it.

"Hey," he answered, his voice quiet, throat dry.

"David?"

"Hey, Ally. How's school?"

"I'm home."

"Really?"

"Trying to be. Wendy said you looked for Bobby all night."

He didn't know when Ally started calling her mom by her first name, but he figured it was the moment she no longer lived under the same roof. That last fight she and her mom had was one that would take Ally a while to get over.

"Yeah. I'm about to go back to look some more…unless you've heard something. Have they found him?"

She blew out a breath. "No. I'm supposed to take that town cop, the one who works weekends, up to the coal dump. You remember him? He's the one who busted us for curfew last year."

"Yeah. He's the one I helped this morning."

"Oh?" She paused. "Did you show him Bobby's spot?"

David had to think. He couldn't remember a special spot Bobby had, although he wasn't the one who always went looking for him. Ally would know more about where Bobby would go, seeing as she had to find him a few times to drag him home.

"No. I didn't know he had a spot."

He felt like he could feel her nod through the phone. She was always like that. The person who would talk with her hands, not realizing the other person wouldn't be able to see it. The image brought another smile, and he felt the corner of his eyes mist.

"Okay. So, yeah, I'll show the cop." There was silence. He found himself looking around the living room for his car keys. He was determined to wait for her to continue. "David, can you come pick me up? I need to get out of here. She's drunk. I can't be here when she wakes up. We've been fighting since I got here."

He grabbed his keys. "Yeah. I'll be right over."

"Thank you."

* * * *

Rob stepped out of the man's house, his jaw hurting from how much he clenched it. His knuckles were white, his nails digging into the palm of his hand. His inner rage was not so inner at the moment, and he was doing everything in his power not to turn around and beat the man. Rob wanted to let loose, but he knew if he did, he would no longer have his job or his morality. If he did, this guy would win. It didn't matter that the man was a piece of shit.

"Yeah, you fucking son of a bitch. I know you ain't gonna do shit!" The insult was followed by a beer can flying past Rob's head, barely missing him, hitting the squad car. He could still feel little drips of liquid that had landed on his shoulder, smelling the acrid stench of hops.

He kept walking. If he turned back now, he didn't know what he would do. He didn't trust himself. The day was bad enough. There was so much frustration boiling up inside him, he felt the strong pull to let it out. The temptation was there. He sure as hell didn't need to put up with this asshole. Rob understood the man was upset about his missing daughter, but he sensed he barely gave a shit about her. The asshole was more upset she wasn't there to cook his damn supper. Rob also suspected he was fearful CPS might step in. The man had hinted he was afraid he might report to them as part of a scheme to take her away from him.

Like Rob really needed another nut with a conspiracy theory. The town had enough of those.

"You should fucking go back to Chicago, you damned nigga lovin' homo!"

Rob felt his body twitch, wanting to turn around, but stopped himself and kept walking. He reached his car and got behind the wheel, making sure the door was closed and locked before he called in his report.

"County Dispatch, this is Standard Unit 1, filing missing person report at 1034 Walnut Street."

"Roger, Unit 1. This for the missing boy?"

"Negative. Missing girl."

"Missing girl, Unit 1? Clarify. How many people are missing there?"

"As of now, four."

"Sounds like something is going on."

"Yes, ma'am," he said to the concerned voice over the radio.

"How long has the girl been missing?"

"Since earlier today. She got in trouble at school and ran away. No one's seen her since."

"Oh."

He heard the woman's voice change, probably suspecting the girl was just hiding. He supposed that could be true, but his gut told him it wasn't. It just didn't seem probable, not unless Bobby was hiding with her. That was the most optimistic scenario, and the one he grasped onto. His gut told him that wasn't the case, but he ignored it.

"The father is sure she should be home by now, and is growing hostile that she isn't. I suspect child abuse."

"Anything proven?"

"Not at this time."

"Copy that. Okay, Deputy. Go ahead with your report and description, then we'll get out the Amber."

Rob gave the woman the details. It had been hard even getting that much information out of the father with all the cursing, but he had many years dealing with all kinds of witnesses. Sometimes a little bullying was needed and sometimes kindness, but it was usually a little of both. It always took that right touch to coax information out of someone.

He had barely finished with the county dispatcher when he heard the *kachung* against the sidewalk. The father had thrown another beer can at the car, but this one had fallen way short, the remaining beer soaking into the dirt. Rob was surprised the man would waste any amount of alcohol. He must have really pissed him off.

Rob should arrest the man, but his daughter was missing. He would be pissed if some cop came into his house and accused him of doing things to his child, too. Maybe he had gone a little too far, but Rob was tired and hadn't handled it well. He tried to justify it, telling himself he had to gauge the man's reaction. He was now pretty sure that, even though he was an alcoholic asshole, Rob highly doubted he was molesting the child. It still didn't mean he didn't beat her.

His phone rang. He looked at it, seeing another local number he didn't recognize. Dread running through his body, he answered.

"Hello?"

"Is this Deputy Alletto?"

He could hear the woman sniffling. Just how many devastated families would he have to deal with by the end of the day?

"Yes, ma'am?"

"My baby… He's missing."

He knew he sat there longer than he should have, just staring silently out the windshield. This had started spiraling out of control. How could so many people just vanish? This was a small town. There wasn't an area for all these people to be disappearing to. It just wasn't possible.

"Are you there, Deputy?"

"Yes, ma'am. Was your baby taken out of his crib? Did someone break into your home?"

"No... No. My boy, he's ten, but he's my baby. He's my only one, and I don't know what I'd do without him."

"Okay..." When his phone beeped, he looked at it. Another local number.

Then he heard ringing on the other end of the phone. He listened as the woman answered another phone. Probably her landline.

"Hello?" he heard her say. "No, Danny's not here, Denise. Joel's missing. He isn't at any of his friends' houses, and Roger said he isn't over at your place, either... He was supposed to be home an hour ago. I told him I didn't want him going out tonight. He should be here. He was supposed to be here when I got home."

She cried as she spoke, the words coming out in a barely understandable rush. He felt like an intruder as he listened to the woman's unimaginable pain.

The voice grew louder. "Deputy?"

"Yes, ma'am?"

"It's not just Joel."

"I heard. What's your address? I'll be right there. Have the woman you were just talking to meet us. We'll try to find out what's going on. More than likely, they all ran off and are playing somewhere."

"Not Joel. I told him to be home. Something's happened to him." Her voice rose in volume with every word. He had to pull the phone away from his ear as she spoke.

"Okay, okay. Just hold tight. I'm on my wa-"

His phone beeped, interrupting. He looked at the display and saw Robyn's number. He hated doing it to her, but he tapped the icon to send it to voicemail.

"I'm on my way, ma'am." He quickly wrote down the address and got off the phone. It immediately rang again. Robyn.

What was so important that she needed to call him? She knew he was busy. He was about to send her to voicemail again, but answered instead, wanting to hurry up and get her off the phone.

"Hey, hun. I can't really talk right now. Ther-"

"Rob, Jake's missing!" she screamed.

CHAPTER 14

After putting down the phone, Samantha...never Sam, even to her closest friends...fidgeted. She couldn't help herself. Every part of her wanted to move, to tap her feet and run at the same time. If she could run in a thousand different directions, she would.

Her baby boy was missing.

Why had Roger let Joel go out? He knew better. Samantha never let him go out on a school night unless she knew where he was, but Roger had just let him go. Men never asked details. If they truly ruled the world, no one would ever know anything.

Her mother used to say, "Now, when two women talk, both know everything going on and all the details before the conversation is over. When two men talk, as long as there is no blood and no jail time, the story lasts two minutes. They just don't ask details."

Just like men never notice when kids go out without their coats or shoes on. She could never trust Roger to take care of their baby when she wasn't home, which was why she hated working afternoon shift at the diner. She was never home when her baby needed her.

Thankfully, she had done a mid-shift today and had come home early. If she hadn't, who knew how long it would have been before Roger figured out Joel was missing. He was watching some damn sports crap on television and hadn't even noticed…or the fact the dog had crapped on the floor beside him.

Damn the man. Damn him, damn him, damn him.

Her fingers tapped on the surface of the table, her legs bouncing to their own worried song. So much pent-up energy inside her, bubbling up, wanting to escape. What was she supposed to do? Just sit there?

That was what the deputy told her to do. He asked if she called all Joel's friends just to make sure none of them had seen him. Like she hadn't already done that. Did the officer think she was completely dumb? Just because she had a slight southern accent, it didn't make her ignorant. When she was nervous, the accent became more pronounced, but she had lived in the north for over ten years.

She guessed she could call all his friends again. She didn't have to call Denise because Danny was also missing. Could he be with Joel? Probably. Those two were nearly inseparable most days. Maybe they had just run off and lost track of time.

God, she hoped so.

If Danny and Joel were together, maybe a few of his friends were with them. When she had called everybody before, she had only asked if they had seen Joel. Could other parents be worrying about their missing children, as well? If they were in a group, maybe they were all out somewhere. Nothing could happen to them if they were in a group, right? There was safety in numbers. Maybe she should call all the parents back.

But what if the kids were missing, like that Bobby kid?

At first, they had barely said anything about it, but by noon, it was the hot dish. It had somehow become bigger than politics. All her normal customers had gone out in the morning to search for him, walking through the woods and the slag pile. Tammy had told her one of the

155

pastors had fought with the deputy, and that the police chief had been murdered.

Dean, a local knucklehead who came in nearly daily just to tick her off and pinch her butt, said the kid was murdered, too. He and that other guy she always saw with him…she forgot his name…had seen what looked like a boy's arm at the dump. Tammy had cried bullshit at that and told him to stop telling stories. Samantha also figured he was full of it. If they'd found anything like that, people would have heard, the state police taking things over.

She remembered the days after Christina Locke's body had been found just outside of town. Some kids discovered her car submerged in Big Sandy when they had snuck onto the property to go fishing. Big Sandy was one of the creeks outside of town that kids liked to sneak to and do various things they shouldn't. Christina was found inside the car. It looked like an accident until the state troopers came in and ruled it homicide. Sure enough, they found out the boyfriend had strangled her and pushed the car into the water.

So she was sure if the boy's body were found, the state police would be all over town. Right now, it was still just the town deputy, who seemed nice enough over the phone. She had no idea what he like in person, though, and had never seen him around town. At least, she didn't think she had. He might have come into the diner on his days off, but he wouldn't be in uniform.

She needed to focus, but it was hard with so much going through her head. She tried to think about anything and everything to stay away from considering the possibilities of what had happened to her little baby. Her little noel. Her Christmas joy whom she needed home.

She picked up the phone and started dialing. She actually wanted to hear about more missing kids because if there were more, they had to all be together. If they were together, they had to be safe. They just had to be…

She looked out the window at the street. Nothing moved. The town she had come to think of as home was so quiet, so unnerving. Her gaze focused on the cracks crisscrossing in their own uneven patchwork. In a town that now felt alien to her, she looked at those cracks. Were they spreading? Because the world around her was certainly falling apart.

* * * *

Jake glared at Joel as he held his arm to his chest. It was bleeding and stung like hell. The multiple little punctures had torn into his flesh, the dark red crimson now dripping down to the pale dirt below. The soil darkened and the blood seeped away. Jake's glare did not. Joel had purposely swung the thorn bush branch at him.

Joel continued to smile, although it was more of a smirk, as he turned away, hurrying after Danny.

"Why did you do that?!" Jake called after him. He was not about to let it go. So far, things had gone pretty good with the others. He thought he might have finally started to fit in. Danny had even joked around with him about the new *Call of Duty*, asking Jake if he had an Xbox or PlayStation.

Jake had lied, of course. Knowing Danny liked the PS, he had said he was an Xbox player. He could add Danny to his friends on Xbox, but they wouldn't be able to play together. He had created a Microsoft account long ago to let others think he really had one.

He had gotten used to the lie. Since most of the kids were all on PlayStation, nobody would catch on. Most didn't have the money to have both systems, so he claimed to have the one no one else did. He was always worried someone would either eventually get an Xbox and he would get busted or would want to come over and play his.

157

"What, man? You can't keep up," Joel called back, not even looking over his shoulder.

"You know what I mean. You did that on purpose."

"No pain, no gain."

Obviously, Joel hadn't liked Jake getting so chummy with Danny. The thorn bush was just the latest, but there had been other little taunts here and there. Joel wanted to make it clear that Jake was still an outsider.

"You try getting hit by a thorn branch and see how you like it."

"You going to cry home to Mommy and Daddy? Going to have Daddy arrest me?"

"A-hole."

"What was that, twerp?" Joel said, whirling around to look down at Jake. Joel towered over him, his chin inches away from Jake's nose.

"You heard me."

"You know, no one can hear you if you cry out up here. You might want to watch your mouth."

"You gonna beat me up?"

"That's enough, Joel." Chris stepped in between the two boys, pushing Joel back a step. Joel looked at him, his face red, his breathing deep. They were both pissed, and Jake had never wanted to punch another kid so much in his life. He was raised to turn the other cheek and walk away, but he didn't want to hold back this time. He wanted to take a swing at Joel, his mother be damned.

Breathe. Remember what dad told you.

His dad said many things…"Be a good worker." "Always treat women right." Those were the ones he said often, but there were others. There was one that didn't help with his anger, but helped explain why. "If you can explain it, you can fight it." However, when his dad had said that to him, he had lost that particular fight.

Jake loved spending time with him. Some of his favorite memories were helping his dad work on the car.

He'd usually grab the tools while his dad was under the hood. One time, he even had to remind his dad to put the oil plug back in before putting in the oil. He had joked it would have been a mess. Jake had saved the day.

As with anything, there were good days and bad. It was sometimes the bad days that gave the best life lessons. It always seemed like they led to those "this is how you should live" talks. The one time his dad smacked his head on the hood had definitely been one of the bad days. Jake had asked him if he was okay, which seemed to infuriate his dad even more. He had turned, yelling at Jake for disrupting him. Somehow, hitting his head had become Jake's fault. He had handed him the wrong tool, which wasn't true, and that made him hit the hood.

Jake had run to his room, crying, believing his dad was really mad at him. He flung himself on his bed and buried his face to the pillow, the tears soaking it.

About a half-hour later, his dad had come in to apologize. He told him that when a person hurt themselves, they sometimes had a surge of adrenaline, often saying things they didn't mean.

Jake knew the anger he felt now must have been what his dad meant. He actually felt the adrenaline. He wanted to hit Joel more than he had ever wanted to hit a person. He had to fight to slow his breathing, his eyes unfocused. It didn't matter if Joel was bigger. Jake wanted to make him pay for hurting him.

Joel studied Chris, then glared back at Jake, who stood with his fists balled, ready to fight. He scoffed at him and turned around.

"Let's just keep looking. The spot is up here past another bunch of thorn bushes. Don't get yourself cut on these, ya pansy ass. You got me?" Joel said to Jake as he stepped around the rest of the group and took the lead. Danny fell in quickly behind him.

"Thanks," Jake said to Chris, feeling the anger edge away.

"Don't let Joel bother you. He's used to being the bully. He's going to have a lot to learn next year because he's not going to be the big dog anymore."

Jake nodded as they turned to follow the others. "Do you think we'll find anything?" he asked.

"Nah. Your dad had people up here searching all morning, right? I can't see how that many people could have missed anything. It's not like the woods are that big. But what else we got to do? I was kinda getting bored of playing Superman."

"You weren't Superman. You were Robin."

"But Robin doesn't fly."

"Yours did."

"No. We were both Superman."

"Okay, but I was the good Superman. You were red kryptonite Superman."

"No way."

"Yeah. I'm too good to be bad."

"That's bull," Chris laughed.

"And I'm too pretty." Jake smiled wide and made some waving motions in the air, then took a bow.

"What the hell are you guys doing back there?" Julie asked. Jake looked up to see her looking at him funny.

"We we're playing Superman before you guys dragged us along."

"No one made you come with."

"How were you playing Superman?" John asked.

"It's right over here," Joel growled as he pushed through more thorn bushes, not even looking back or holding any of the branches out of the way for them. He just rushed forward, the branches completely enveloping him.

Jake looked around the woods. The sun had started to set, the long shadows of the trees dancing around them as the wind picked up. He had a jacket on, his mom wouldn't ever let him go out without one, but it suddenly didn't feel warm enough.

"Hey, man, you okay in there?" Danny eased into the thick bushes, tentatively pulling the branches aside. Jake guessed he didn't come up there as much.

"Come on. Hurry up," they heard Joel yell from deep in the bushes. "I need someone to help me lift this grate."

Jake hurried up behind Danny, grabbing at the branches before they fell. If they did, it would hurt, but he could deal with it. When he heard a branch snap behind him, he looked back to see Chris right behind him. John and Julie seemed happy to stay on the path.

He felt a sting when he missed a branch. New spots on his arm started to ooze. He wanted to scratch at the burning sensation.

Danny pushed past the largest bush, disappearing. The branches threatened to spring back at Jake, but he reached out to catch them, moving past.

He stepped into a clearing. There were two stumps in the center, as if to sit on, but what really drew Jake's attention was the object both Danny and Joel studied. It was a large, rusted metal grate. Most the slots were filled in with nasty dirt and grime that looked like it had been worn in over a long period of time.

Jake glanced around, taking in more details as he heard Chris cursing the thorn branches. He must have let go and gotten cut. It was hard not to. The thorn patches were thick and it was hard to push through all of them. But once inside the clearing, it was as if no life grew. There was no grass on the ground, the tree branches didn't hang over. There was nothing like what he would expect this far in the woods. It was as if the thorn bushes guarded this place, keeping any unwanted visitors at bay.

This was the hidden place the kids always tried to find. That secret garden only they could see in their imaginations. The wondrous place to hide from parents and bullies, to disappear from everything for a while. It was where adventures happened, journeys to other planets possible.

161

Staring up, he saw the first couple stars in the darkening sky. This was the place to come to start his journey into space. While he sat on the stump, he could see himself flying on a spaceship among those stars. This place was…

Wrong.

It slammed into him. There was something else there with them, all around them. He felt the hairs on the back of his neck lifting, goosebumps forming along his arm. It watched them, and it was hungry.

The wind picked up again. This time, it wasn't just cool. It was cold and bitter. It rushed through the trees and thorn bushes, making him take a step back to keep his balance. It felt like a hand trying to push them away. They had disturbed something otherwordly and it was making its presence known. It wanted them out.

When he turned to watch the lingering shadows, he saw the dancing army. Shapes surrounded them, dark forms slipping among the thorns.

Jake looked back at Chris, who had made his way clear of the thorns and didn't seem to notice the wind. He was focused on the grate, just like Danny and Joel.

"Get your ass over here, momma's boy," Joel grunted as he and Danny fought to lift the metal. It didn't look like it should be that heavy, but both of them strained, the grate not budging. Chris hurried over to Danny's side, but even the three of them couldn't get it to move.

As Jake grabbed the side closest to him, he looked down into the hole. It was so dark down there, like the pit fell into nothingness.

He shivered, but not from the cold. There was something down there. He put a face to it, a face from his own childhood nightmares. A dark blue face with fangs and large round, orange eyes. He saw that face in his mind's eye as he stared down into the black. Any time now, he knew it was going to come at him. It would shoot a hand out, reach through the grate, and pull him through it.

"What the hell are you waiting for? A written invitation?"

Jake snapped his head up to see they waited for him to grab his end. He hadn't realized he had pulled back, unconditionally afraid of what was going to come after them. He breathed deeply, finding courage as he reached for it, sure something was going to attack his fingers as he wrapped them around the cold steel.

"Come on, man. Lift," Danny grunted.

Jake adjusted his stance and pulled, joining in the struggle with the other three boys.

The grate just wouldn't budge. For a second, it felt like it was moving, then it pulled against them and became firm again. It were as if someone held it from the other side.

Jake pulled harder, his arms hurting from the strain. The metal bit into his hands. His back and legs burned with the pressure. He put everything he had into pulling on the grate, knowing Chris, Joel, and Danny did the same.

The ground shook, but he didn't know if the tremors were actually in the ground or his own legs. He could hear the wind rustling through the trees, whipping around him. The woods had come alive, protesting them being there. The little bit of light faded. It should be a full moon tonight, but he didn't see any light coming into the clearing. Everything had gotten dark way too fast.

Was it even darker by the grate? Jake knew it would be, but it seemed like there was something more to the darkness. A fog seemed to rise above the rusted metal and hover there. He could see…

No, that can't be right. It looked like the fog had taken the shape of hands gripping onto the grate.

Jake looked around to see if anyone else saw it. The other three were focused on lifting the grate, not noticing anything happening around them. He must be imagining things.

"Come on. Put your backs into it. This shouldn't be that heavy," Joel said, the exhaustion showing on his face.

"I am," Chris barked. Jake could see the muscles in his arms. He knew he worked out sometimes and it showed.

Then Jake saw it. The dark fog seemed to let go and fade back into the grate. It gave up, if it had even really been there. The wind quieted down. Everything went back to normal, making him question if he had really seen any of it.

When the grate finally lifted, they eased it up and over onto the side, moving quickly to get out of the way. They didn't look to see what was below. Moving the grate was more just to see if they could rather than actually wanting to know what was below it.

Then he heard the scream. He spun to see Julie standing in the clearing, covering her mouth and pointing. He looked to see what she was pointing at.

A hand *had* been holding the grate. When they lifted it, it had dropped to the side. It was pale and lifeless, but Jake recognized the wedding band. He knew that ring. It belonged to his dad's boss. It belonged to the chief.

CHAPTER 15

That familiar feeling in his chest was back. His heart pounding so hard, he thought it would explode out of him. The lump forming in his throat. The dryness in his mouth preventing him from talking. His head playing a drum that felt like it belonged in a marching band. The world around him blurring.

He recognized the symptoms, closing his eyes to cut off the outside stimuli. Oh yes, he recognized the panic trying to overtake him. These attacks had become more common after surviving the meth lab explosion, then the incident last year.

The world spun, on the verge of slipping away. Was he fainting? It had never gone that far, but there was always a first time. Somewhere in the background, he heard Robin's voice. It seemed so far away.

"Rob! Rob!" she screamed.

Was he in the dream again? Many times, when he was in his own nightmares, surrounded and lost in the flames, he would hear her and know he would never see her again.

"Rob!"

He heard something heavy fall to the floor and her voice became muffled.

You dropped your phone. Come on, man. Pull yourself together. You were talking to Robyn and dropped your phone. She's not somewhere far off. Come on. Pull yourself out of it and breathe.

He felt himself moving against the tide. His consciousness started pulling itself back, the thickness inside his brain clearing. Overhead, the light from the streetlight caught him in the eye. What the hell? Had he actually just fainted?

He pulled in a deep breath, the pressure of an anvil crushing against his chest. Stars swirled through his vision. He couldn't think, finding it impossible to focus.

"Robyn?" he asked, his tongue thick and speech slurred.

"Rob!"

"Hey, hun, I'll call you back."

"Are you okay?"

Her voice still sounded far off. He looked around, moving slowly to keep his breakfast, lunch, or whatever had been his last meal down. He couldn't see his phone on the floor. He must have hit the speaker phone before he had dropped it. At least she could still hear him.

"I have to call county. I need to get more officers out here to look for these kids, look for Ja..." He couldn't say it...not yet. It was too soon to list him among the missing. Even just saying it caused a tidal wave to wash over him again. "I'll call you right back."

"Okay." Her voice sounded subdued. He didn't have to see her to know she sat at their kitchen table, tears streaming down her cheeks.

Then he heard the beeps and knew she had disconnected. He tried to focus on that so he could find his phone.

He leaned over and reached below the seat, feeling around. His head wanted to loll to the side, but if it did, he wasn't sure he'd have the strength to straighten it. The steering wheel called to him. Its hard surface would work as a pillow. In his time as a small-town cop, it wouldn't have been the first time. He was just so tired. His fingers seemed to scratch against something sharp, then he felt a pinch. The pain was minimal, but helped keep him awake.

His heart pounded, but he could feel it slowing. The fog finally cleared enough that he was able to think again. If he opened the door and got out, he could crouch down and look under the seat to find his phone. It would be easier.

He pushed it open, a sudden rush of cool air flowing across his skin. His head further cleared, the pounding becoming a throb that just hovered at the corner. It stayed as a slight ghostly presence, but did not leave. As long as he didn't have to move too quickly, he might not even notice it.

It didn't take him long before he saw his phone, grabbing it. He saw a text from his wife, the three sweet words making him smile. He swiped right and dialed the number for county.

As it started to ring, he texted her back with one finger. He didn't know how people texted so quickly on these damn things.

I love you, too.

He managed to hit SEND before the county dispatcher answered.

He should have just used his radio. Maybe his mind wasn't as clear as he had thought. It really made no sense for him to call. He knew it would take longer to get a response that way, although they had picked up rather quickly.

"Livingston County Sheriff. How may I direct your call?" said the flat voice. Rob swore no one in the county office ever sounded anything other than bored or hostile. He never enjoyed working with any of them.

"Deputy Alletto, Standard Township, calling in another Amber, requesting some more patrols in the area."

"Didn't I just talk to you on the radio, Deputy?"

"There have been more since then." His voice sounded so dead to his ears, like he was on autopilot and he had no control.

"What's going on over there, Deputy? You need to get a handle on your town."

"Ma'am, now is not the time to start with me," he ground out, trying to rein in his temper.

"We don't have the resources to dedicate a full-time patrol because—"

"Ma'am—"

"Son, don't get smart with me. Towns have runaways every day. They've probably all just run off and are playing a joke on you all."

"Ma'am," he repeated, grinding his teeth together to keep from yelling. She must have caught his change in voice because she remained silent. He was at the point where he seemed calm, but his anger threatened to boil over. "One of the missing children is my son. I can assure you that he did *not* run away."

He heard her gasp. "I'm sorry. I will get another unit there within the hour. I'll see if I can get some more people there ASAP."

He closed his eyes, barely able to thank her as the world tried to spin around him again. Struggling to push the feelings back down, he disconnected the call and looked around. He still had to go to that woman's house and take down her information. Jake was just one of many kids missing.

But none of them mattered. He could lie to himself and say they were all equal, but that would be a lie. His son was the only one who mattered right now. The boy he promised to take ice fishing this winter. The boy who prayed with him each night before slipping off the sleep. The boy whom he fought so hard to come home to every night, making sure he stayed safe. The boy they changed their lives for. The boy they had left Chicago for so they could raise him somewhere safer.

The boy Rob may never see again.

169

He didn't try to stop the tear falling down his cheek. He knew there wasn't going to be a tidal wave of them this time. This was the one tear he knew he could afford right now.

He put the car into gear. His mind still wasn't one hundred percent clear, but he didn't think it could be with Jake missing. He felt like he could focus enough not to kill anyone while driving, though. That was easier in the small town where people actually waited for traffic to stop rather than rushing across, not caring about the oncoming car or truck.

He turned left onto Main Street and saw the two floral shops at the end of the block. He didn't know why in the hell a small town needed two. He knew there were plenty of flower shops in the city, but they would have been boutiques. He was sure there was some competition between businesses, especially if they were family-owned. Even so, it was hard to imagine an owner walking into another shop, a baby on her hip, to curse them out.

That new shopkeeper had been cute, though. He couldn't stop himself as his mind wandered to the smile she had flashed him. She had a beautiful mouth, her teeth glistening in the little light of the shop. Her eyes danced in excitement as she welcomed him into her. She cried out in pleasure as he pulled her close.

He blinked and shook his head. *What the hell was that?*

He had to fight to keep from looking over at the little shop. If he did, maybe he'd see her looking out the window and could get a glimpse of her.

The car drifted to the side of the road and he caught himself slowing, preparing to park along the shoulder. It was wide there to allow semis the ability to pull off and line up for the grain silo across the street. He could park and walk over to see how she was doing. After all, that other shop owner had harassed her. She might have done something else, or maybe she just needed someone to talk to. After all, she was new in town.

170

He shook his head again, jerking his car back onto the street. *Really, Rob. What the fuck is wrong with you?* Jake was missing, but his mind slipped into those kind of thoughts. Just what would Robyn think if she knew he thought about another woman?

She had often joked it was okay to look, as long as he knew where his bed was at night. He typically never let his mind wander that way, but this had been more than just wandering thoughts. He had actually seen himself taking her, pulling her to him as he entered her, his hands on her firm breasts.

His breathing quickened as he adjusted himself. The sudden erection was painful as it pushed against his pants.

Really. What the hell would Robyn think if she found out?

But if he was having those thoughts, was there a reason for it? Had their sex life really started to fade away? Should he start thinking about what was next in his life? What would Jake think if Robyn and he got a divorce?

Jake is missing! Concentrate on that, you asshole!

Their boy… The one he held in his arms at the hospital. The one who had come early and with so many complications. Robyn would never be able to have another child, not with what she went through to bring him into the world. Jake would always be their one and only.

Their little boy… Who, when he was younger, could never say the name of his favorite fast food place, so they would always take him to "Kids Donalds". Who would always come home and cry whenever someone pushed him down at school, but he never fought back. Who listened to his dad when he said the bigger man always walked away from the fight. Who never got into trouble, other than not getting his homework done or not taking a shower every night like his mom demanded.

Their little boy… Who, when an evil had infected the town, trying to take over Rob's mind, had kept him

171

sane. Back then, Rob had felt himself letting go, losing himself to the insanity taking everyone, feeling the rage that drove men to kill. He had wanted to submit to it and be just like the others, but then he saw Jake, his little boy, and it had brought him back.

His Jake, his boy, his baby boy...

Jake had only been missing a half-hour, but Rob was already thinking of not only leaving Robyn, the woman he knew he still loved, but screwing around with another woman. What the hell was wrong with him? It sure as hell didn't make any sense.

The squad car seemed to just crawl down the street, not even going close to the speed limit. Thankfully, there wasn't anyone behind him. That was probably a really good thing as he felt tears flooding down his face. His eyes and cheeks were wet, but so was the front of his uniform. His nose ran and he sniffed, trying to stifle some of the flow. It didn't feel like it would stop anytime soon.

He felt like he was pulling from a deep well of pain, more than he knew he had been holding in. It opened up, a torrent of raw emotion spilling out. He didn't know whether it stemmed from the sleep deprivation or the bottled up feelings he held in tight. The more it flowed, the more he saw his son at the corner of his eyes.

He pulled onto the little access road that lead to a path into the woods off to the side of the coal dump. The glow of the streetlight washed over him, then faded away as he disappeared into the darkness. It was quiet back there. He couldn't help but think about the other side of the little hill. That morning, he had stepped onto that little path and had found the squad car, no trace of the owner. It was a good place to be alone, but he couldn't help but wonder where his boss had gone. A little chill ran down his spine as he killed the engine and turned off the lights. He wanted to be away from everyone because he knew his control, the tight bundle of emotions he held inside, had started to unravel.

Yes, that woman, the one with her own son missing, was waiting on him. He had to go there and take her report. It would have to wait, though. Right now, he couldn't go through with it.

How long? One hour? Two? With Jake missing, can I really go and take a report about somebody else's missing child?

He didn't think he would be able to go there at all tonight. He would probably wait until the county officer showed up, then have him go take the report. That would be best. He just didn't think he had any more left in him. He was done giving a shit about everyone else.

But Jake is missing. You have to care. You can't just give up.

Even though they told him not to, Rob knew there were times Jake and Chris came up to the coal dump. It wasn't too often, but he had seen them walking away from there a few times. That probably meant they had gone there more times than he knew about.

So it was back to the coal dump again. There had to be more places these children could go. The coal dump was a large, tree-covered slag pile that took up approximately six blocks. It was a small part of town, but in comparison to the surrounding area, it was a large piece of property. They had spent much of their time exhausting themselves walking these woods.

He looked at the looming shape in front of him. From his angle, he had to lean forward to see the top. It was a black shape, barely visible against the dark blue of the night sky. The large mound of slag and trees seemed to just disappear into the sky, all melding together in one dark lump.

Where else could they all be if they aren't there?

Jake said he and Chris were going to the park. That was across town. Maybe that was where all the kids went. Maybe there was something around the park…

No, not something. Someone. He had done enough of this "something" crap. All of this had to come back to someone. Someone had to be luring and taking all of these kids, and it was perfectly reasonable that they lived right by the park.

It would be too dark to search there now, but they had lights they used for baseball games in the spring. If need be, someone from town maintenance could come and turn them on. Maybe he would find something from one of the missing kids. An article of clothing, a backpack, something. One of the kids had to have struggled…unless they knew the person taking them.

He looked around the dark interior of the squad car, finally finding what he was looking for. He never would have left it in there, but no one else would be using the car. Even if they did find the chief, Rob doubted he would return to work right away, so there was no one to complain about the grease-soaked bag containing his evening supper. He grabbed it and pulled out a napkin only slightly covered in grease.

It felt stiff, smelling of old french fries as he used it to wipe away the moisture from his cheeks. It wouldn't work to wipe away all of it, but he should be fine. What did it matter? The last thing he cared about right now was what everyone else thought. With so many people missing, his appearance *should* be disheveled. There was no reason he should look better than how he felt.

He adjusted the mirror and checked himself in it. Yeah, he would be fine.

He adjusted the mirror back into place so he could see the streetlight shining behind him. He put the car into reverse, focusing on that light.

The park… Jake has to be there. Maybe Rob would get lucky and find something.

"Dad!"

I want to believe so badly, I'm hearing his voice in my head now?

"Dad!"

I'm losing it.

Something slammed against the driver's door. The car jerked as he jumped, his foot slamming down on the gas, then the brake.

He looked at the window as he quickly turned on the headlights, illuminating the figure standing there. Others stepped out of the darkness, too, but Rob could only focus on one.

Jake. His face was pale, his eyes wide and scared, his breathing coming in gasps. When he saw his dad noticed him, he dropped his hands to his knees, bending over.

Rob couldn't get the car back in park fast enough. He grabbed for the door, fighting not to trip over himself. The tears were back.

He tried to talk, but nothing came out. He rushed to his son, grabbed him, and pulled him into a hug like nothing either had ever felt before. "Jake... Thank God."

CHAPTER 16

Lights flashed, the world glowing in swirling colors, everything shifting between red and blue. It made stars flash behind his eyes. The teenagers called them the "blueberries and cherries", but he had never thought of them as anything other than the reassuring lights of safety. It *was* safe and he was safe in their glow.

Rob felt it. The flashing lights slammed into his retinas and danced off the trees around them. He had his son, some of the other missing children also found. That should make him feel happy. It was a huge win. He should take the win, but as the lights flashed, he knew they would follow him into his nightmares.

You're not safe. None of us are safe.

He knew it was true as much as he knew those lights would haunt his nightmares. Chicago had been a nightmare. The last year had been a nightmare. His life was full of nightmares. They kept building with each passing horror he survived, keeping him from ever getting a restful night sleep. Even with all those tortured dreams, his life was a challenge to fight against the cruelties that surrounded and lived in the world. He had not been ready for what he had found. What his son had led him to.

He felt the little hand in his, the warm body tight against him. Now he would have to worry about what nightmares he was passing on to his son. Rob always hoped he'd be able to keep the things he had seen, what he had been through, away from Jake, sheltering him from the nastiness out there. That was his number one job as a parent. He was a shield from the evil, a protecting sword in the fight against it. He did what needed to be done to keep Jake safe and innocent, but it was too late now. His son had seen what hid just beyond the dark.

Would his son be able to go back to being that innocent child he had been that morning? His life had been so bright and positive. Would he still be that way tomorrow? Or would the image of seeing the chief's body keep him awake and screaming?

Rob had heard children were resilient. That they could handle a lot of bad things without it affecting them. If that were true, if Jake was able to move past this, he'd have a new admiration for his son. Rob wasn't sure he could be as strong. He'd already imagined the fresh nightmares that would surface, dreading the time he would finally sleep.

He couldn't stop seeing all of it as it replayed through his thoughts. When Rob had tried to talk to Jake and the other kids, they had all started screaming and crying, talking over each other. From what Rob could understand, they had found a body under a grate up there. Or had they found two bodies? No, it was one body, but in pieces. No, it was an army of elves... They were kids, and they were scared. None of them really knew what they had come across, except for Jake, who had been silent. When he did speak, he was just above a whisper.

"Dad, the chief is up there."

The other kids continued to talk over each other, but Rob had focused on his son. The boy was solemn, his face blank, his eyes sad. He looked like he was in shock. Rob nodded at him, then pulled him into another hug so tight, he could almost hear his bones protesting.

"Dad...," came the muffled response. Rob let go. Jake glanced at the kids around them. Chris looked down. The rest kept talking, oblivious, trying to get Rob to follow them so they could show him what they found. He wanted to, but he needed to call their parents.

He called Robyn first, who showed up within minutes. She immediately wrapped Jake in her arms as Rob called the other parents. He was more comfortable with her there, keeping track of Jake. It wasn't as though he was going to go missing again if Rob took his eyes off him, but that didn't stop the man from worrying. He wasn't sure he would ever be able to stop worrying again

Even before Rob finished with all the calls, cars started to show up. After Robyn, he had called Samantha, who set the phone lines ablaze. As Rob got down to the bottom of the list of parents, he found they were already on their way. It didn't take long for him to start getting phone calls from other people with missing loved ones, knowing some kids had been found. Even with all the excitement around him, those were hard to get through, having to tell people he hadn't yet found their child.

After he hung up with the last person, he knew he had to do something he should never ask of any child. No one should be forced to relive their nightmares.

He sat sideways in the front seat of his squad car, then called Jake over. Reluctantly, he left the protection of his mom's arms. The look Robyn gave him was one that should have told him he was already on thin ice. He couldn't meet her eyes for too long. Every time he did, his vision filled with the florist, her ripe breasts thrusting into his face. If he hadn't done anything wrong, why did he feel so odd around his own wife? Why was that damn woman inside his head? How many times could he make her orgasm?

Get out of my head!

When Jake stood in front of him, he pulled his son into another hug. He wasn't sure he could ever get enough hugs again.

Rob pulled away, holding Jake's arms. "What happened?" he asked, looking into his son's innocent eyes.

178

They held him, the large orbs reflecting the red and blue lights.

His son sniffed, tears forming. "We were looking for Bobby. The other kids thought they might know a place he would hide, so they wanted to see if he was there."

"Okay."

"Well, we went to this place, and there was a metal grate. It was really heavy, and it took almost all of us to lift it."

Jake fell silent. His eyes lost focus as he looked away. Rob figured he was trying to remember something difficult, making him feel like the world's worst dad for making his son go through this. Would other parents do it? They would probably be there to protect their kids. If he were talking to any of the other children, their parents would probably scream at him, telling him their child has been through enough.

They had seen something. Rob was certain of it. They all said different things, their stories all so wild, Rob was quick to believe there was something up there.

"What did you see once you lifted it?" Rob prodded.

"There was a hand holding the grate. Just the hand. We all ran after that," Jake whispered.

"But you said you thought it was the chief."

"The ring." Rob looked at Jake, cocking his head, trying to figure out what he meant. "I saw the wedding ring on the hand."

Rob nodded, the pieces clicking together. He knew the ring. It was a man's wedding ring, a single silver band, but he was sure if he looked around town, he would find a half-dozen men with rings just like it. Seeing it on a severed hand didn't necessarily mean it was the chief. He had to wonder how Jake was so sure. There weren't too many other missing people, but it just wasn't enough to go on.

"Jake, I need you to show me where."

"Rob!"

He looked up to see the fury on his wife's face.
"Robyn, hun, I have to see—"

"Don't you dare."

"Robyn, please." He stood from the squad car. "I don't know where the kids saw what they did. I need him to show me."

"Like hell you do! He's already seen enough."

"Robyn..."

"No, Rob. I'm taking him home."

"I'll show you," one of the other kids said. It was a taller boy. He wasn't sure of the name, but he thought he was Samantha's son.

Rob looked at him. He didn't want to subject any of the kids to it again. "It's Joel, right?"

The boy nodded. Rob looked at his wife. He didn't want to take any of them up there, but he would feel more comfortable if it was Jake. Taking someone else's kid up there felt irresponsible.

But someone needed to show him. If it weren't so dark, he'd be able to take them as a group, but it was pitch black, neither the moon nor the stars visible. All he'd have was the long barrel flashlight in the squad car.

Robyn looked away from him, holding in her own shame. Did she know he needed at least one of these kids to go back up there?

She had to understand that, didn't she?

"Okay, Joel. You think you can help me find the spot?" The kid nodded, his eyes wide as he smiled enthusiastically. Rob returned the nod and reached into the car, pulling out the flashlight.

A van pulled up, its headlights trapping Rob, making him feel like a deer. The doors flung open.

"Joel!"

"John!"

A dark shape rushed by him, another one hurrying through the headlight's illumination. Two women ran toward the group of kids.

John was quick to go to his mom, giving her a brief hug. Joel was more reluctant, playing it cool, as his mom looked over his body, asking if he was okay.

"Yeah, I'm fine. We were just looking for Bobby when we found a dead body."

It didn't matter now much Joel tried to play it cool. Once he said that, his mom gasped and pulled him into her arms again. He fought it, his mother ignoring his protests. Embarrassed, his face was nearly as red as the lights flashing over them.

"Oh, my god. Well, it will be okay. We'll get you home. I'll call Dr. Sherman in the morning and make an appointment."

Joel rolled his eyes. "I don't need therapy."

"Yes, you do."

"It might be a good idea," Robyn said. "Ms.... I'm sorry. I don't know your name."

"Ms. Jordon," Samantha said, glancing over her shoulder at Robyn before turning back to Joel. She wasn't going to let him out of her sight until she was sure there wasn't a scratch on him.

"Ms. Jordon, would you be willing to share your therapist's number? It might be a good idea for all of them, and it would be nice to be able to give out the information when the rest of the parents arrive."

"I guess I could."

"I'm about to take Deputy Alletto up to show him the body," Joel said, the enthusiasm bubbling out from the boy.

"What?!"

Rob walked up, wanting to justify what he knew was a mistake. "Joel offer-"

"Deputy, if you think I am letting you expose my child to any more atrocities, you had better start looking for a new town with new children to terrorize."

"You are *not* taking our children back up there," the other woman said, pulling her son closer.

"Miss, I need to see where they found the body."

181

"Well, you go right ahead. I'm sure they've told you whatever you needed to know, Deputy. You go right on up there, but you won't be taking any of our children. What kind of monster would do that?"

Joel's face fell. "Ma-"

"Don't. I don't care, Joel. Did he do anything? Make you say anything you didn't want to say?"

She crouched down, looking Joel in the eyes. The eagerness he had earlier was gone. The kid looked disappointed. She acted like he *wanted* to take the kid up there. If just telling him where they had found the body would help, he would never have asked. None of these people seemed to understand that. Over the last twenty-four hours, the search party had been all over these woods and slag pile, and no one had found anything until these kids came across this grate. They obviously knew of an area nobody else did. How was he supposed to find it on his own?

"Ma'am..."

The roaring engine of a truck cut him off as it sped past the minivan and came to a screeching stop, barely missing them. The truck was raised high in the air, so Rob could see through the large gap underneath as the driver hopped down from the other side.

Unconsciously, Rob pulled Jake behind him, then looked at Robyn, who watched a man walk around the truck, the headlights making his shadow stretch into the woods. He could see she had the same apprehension he did. Rob wondered if she had met him before.

Why is she so afraid of him? She's sleeping with him. She's allowing him to noodle her while you're away at work.

No, there was no way that was possible, but the images kept flexing themselves. Rob had already recognized the truck, remembering cans being thrown at him as he walked past it. It had made an impression, the large Confederate flag waving in the faint wind, the duel chrome exhaust pipes rising up behind the cab. He had seen the man drink enough earlier to constitute Rob giving him a DUI right there. Even though the thought was tempting, he wanted as little conflict as possible at the moment.

Mr. Bloom, Emily's father, stalked toward him, anger in his eyes. "Where the hell is my daughter?"

Stepping away from his family, Rob walked to meet him. The man was a monster, so he was not about to let him get any closer to his wife and child. Rob didn't want to touch him, but he put his arm around his shoulders to lead him away from everybody. Mr. Bloom wasn't having it, pulling out of Rob's grip.

"I said where's my daughter?" he growled.

Rob held up his hands, hoping to pacify the man. "I don't know."

"What the hell do you mean you don't know? You found these little assholes. My daughter ain't good enough for you to look for? You find these little shits out fuckin' in the woods, but can't find mine?"

"Don't you dare!" Samantha had her hands over Joel's ears.

Rob glanced at her and looked at the rest of the kids, then turned back to the angry parent.

"I haven't found her yet. I'm about to go see what the kids *did* find."

The man's eyes hardened as he looked at the group of kids again, then turned to look back at Rob. "Where is she?"

"I don't know."

Rob didn't register the blow until he felt the cold steel of the squad car, the front of his uniform constricting around his neck. The man had grabbed the front of his shirt and was twisting, forcing him back onto his car.

"Get...off...me....," Rob strangled out.

He saw a pair of arms around the man's neck, knowing it was probably Robyn trying to pull him off. The man wasn't strong, but he was big, his girth heavy as

183

it forced Rob down. There was no moving him. That beer gut just kept pushing, and he could smell alcohol and the junk food from the gas station on the man's breath.

"Let him go!" Robyn screamed.

When the man released him, Rob gasped for air, coughing. His knees went weak and he slipped to the ground, stars fading out of his vision.

"I'm...going...up...there," he whispered, speaking around the shards of glass in his throat.

The man paced, his hands clenching and unclenching. Rob watched him, wondering when he would come back for round two. He wasn't going to let the man get in the first hit again. He had just caught Rob off guard.

He squared himself up, standing a little straighter than he had before. Rob had to deal with many drunks in town. Some of them stood a head taller, but he had never let any of them intimidate him. He had too many years on the Chicago PD. Too many drug dealers, pimps, and random scum he had to take down for any of these assholes in town to come close to taking him. This man had just gotten lucky. Next time, Rob planned to have him on the ground in cuffs.

The man looked Rob up and down, seeming to take stock of him. What Rob initially took for a snarl had been chewing tobacco. Mr. Bloom spat out a brown glob of it near Rob's boot.

"Where the fuck's my daughter?"

"I don't know."

Jake came up to stand behind his father. Rob took a chance to take his eyes off Bloom, sure the moment he showed any sign of distraction, the man would pounce on him. He reached out and put his arm in front of his son.

"I see your own little pissant is here. Was he with her? He do something to her, asking you all to cover it up?" No one answered as they continued to watch him cautiously. The man was feral. Who knew where he would focus next. "Who gives a shit about some white trash's kid, right?"

Bloom took a step forward. Rob forced himself to stand a little straighter. He could smell the sour mint from the man's chew as he looked deep into those eyes. They were sore and red, but the pupils had a yellow tint. Rob guessed he was on meth.

"Or are you some kind of sick bastard. You put her away somewhere? You want her tight little ass?"

Rob didn't turn away. He forced himself to stay calm, keeping tight control over his breathing while concentrating on counting his heartbeats. Rob didn't have to look down to see the clenched fists at the man's sides. As soon as Rob showed any weakness, that fist would come toward him.

"Where...is...my...daughter?" Bloom pushed his chest out and stepped forward, forcing Rob to step back. He felt the warmth of his son behind him. He never took his eyes away as he brought his leg back as a brace, not allowing the man to push him any farther.

"I'll find her," Rob said. The reins on his self-control had started ebbing away. He had the urge to push the man away or, better yet, just slam his fist into that large jaw. He wanted it to shatter. He wanted to hear the man scream in pain. He wanted to beat him down and put him in his place.

Do you really *want that?*

It wasn't him, but there was another part of him, some caged animal buried inside, that screamed to attack.

"I can take you up there," Jake said from behind him.

Bloom finally blinked, as though coming out of a trance, and looked down at the little boy tucked behind his father.

"My daughter up there?"

Rob turned and looked at his son, who shook his head.

"Are you sure?"

"I didn't see her, but we didn't look too hard. We pretty much ran."

They ran because they had seen a hand. There was still a chance the whole body wasn't there. They had done what all ten-year-olds would have. They ran away, screaming. Rob knew some kids would have poked it with a stick. He was proud his son didn't do that. They must have done something right in raising him.

Another set of headlights washed over them, more red and blue lights dancing around the area. Bloom looked over quickly. Rob followed his gaze to see another squad car had arrived.

Finally.

Rob took notice to the kids and adults standing around, their eyes wide, the adults having a protective arm around their child. All of them watched Rob and Bloom as if it were some kind of freak show, not sure how to react.

He should have been watching the man in front of him. Caught off guard again, he felt a blow to the chest. He tried to step back to keep himself from falling, but Jake was too close. The boy tried to move, but wasn't fast enough, getting slammed between the squad car and his dad.

When Rob steadied himself, he looked and saw Jake on his hands and knees, crawling away, sniffling. That was it. Rob quickly stood, his fist balled as he swung, wide and hard. It wasn't a move to take down a perp. This was pure fury put into a hammer blow of a punch. It took Bloom completely by surprise, the man staggering back. It didn't stun him for long, though. When he hit his truck, he used that little bounce to propel himself back at Rob.

Rob was ready. When the punch came, he grabbed the man's wrist, spun him, used the momentum behind the punch, and smashed him down on the hood of the car. Bloom cried out in frustration. Seconds later, the cry of anger turned into pain as Rob pulled the man's arm tighter behind his back. There was an audible pop, Bloom's screams growing louder.

"You have the right to remain silent. Anything you say can and will be used against you in a court of law." Rob didn't care if this man has a missing kid anymore. He had lost that pity when Rob's son had gotten in the middle of it. "You have the right to an attorney." Rob whipped out the cuffs from his belt and handcuffed the man's wrist, making sure to give his injured arm another tug. "If you cannot afford an attorney, one will be appointed to you." He clicked the last cuff into place, then shoved the man against the hood of the car before he released his weight and stepped back.

"Hey, Deputy. Trouble?" A woman stepped from behind her squad car.

"Just a parent getting rough. Maybe a night locked up will help clear his head."

She nodded as she stepped over to them. She was short, her head barely coming up to his chest. She reached out and took the man, pulling him up hard.

"I'll put him in the squad. These the missing kids?"

"Yeah."

"And they found a body in the woods?"

"Yeah. My son was just about to show me where."

"Okay."

"We'll make it quick. I'll make sure to leave markers for forensics to find their way."

She nodded, narrowing her eyes. "Just don't contaminate anything. Step carefully, then come back out in your own footprints."

"Yes, ma'am. I know."

She cocked her head. She may think he was being an asshole, but he really didn't care. He was ready to get this night over with. If they found something up there, maybe it would lead them to the rest of the missing. Then he could go home and get some sleep. It would never again be good sleep, but maybe the nightmares would be quiet for a while.

"Come on, Jake."

CHAPTER 17

What the hell had he just done? Damn, he'd probably just lost his job. Just what had he been thinking? Hitting that guy, dislocating his shoulder, allowing him to get under his skin... How many times had a suspect tried to provoke him? He had never allowed himself to make a young, dumbass rookie move like that?

A large bush slapped against him, bringing him out of his musings. The shape in front of him continued walking, and Rob worked to keep the beam of the flashlight focused on him. He had a hard time keeping up, his son finding his way through the dark better than his old man could with the flashlight. Much of that probably had to do with Rob worrying about not having a job in the morning. When you didn't pay attention to where you were going, it was easy to trip over your own feet.

I'm a parent. What would any parent have done?

He didn't think anybody would have acted any differently. So what if he might be out of a job? As much as he replayed it in his mind, he knew he wouldn't have changed anything.

What was he going to do for a new job, though? He still had the seasonal driving thing, but could he see himself being a truck driver the rest of his life? Could he really walk away from being a cop? It was his life, his heritage, and everything he knew.

He would never be able to walk away from it, but none of the small towns around them would want him after they heard about what happened. It wasn't like in Chicago were he could hide in obscurity, moving from one district to another. There, unless it made the news, it would just get overlooked. However, nowadays, everything seemed to make it into the media and everyone had to have a damned Facebook.

"How much farther, Jake?"

Because of the meth lab explosion in Chicago, a drug bust gone bad, his back wasn't the greatest and he sometimes had a nasty limp, his right leg not always working the way it should. But, thinking about it, when was the last time the limp had been anything but psychological? When was the last time his back hurt so badly, he couldn't get out of bed? It had been nearly six months, hadn't it?

"Just on the other side," Jake said.

His son disappeared into the darkness. He had been there one minute, gone the next, Rob's flashlight not penetrating the rippling inkwell of blackness. He tentatively reached out, remembering Jake saying something about some thorn bushes. He felt a flash of pain, quickly pulling his hand back. Sure enough, he saw a dark splotch of blood dripping down his hand. Rob looked back into the darkness, taking a deep breath as he stepped forward.

"Jake, you okay?" he called out, fighting the irrational fear that he just lost his son again, panicking after losing sight of him.

"Yeah, Dad."

He emerged into the clearing, feeling the tearing of flesh from unseen thorns. He ignored it as he looked around for Jake. Stepping over, he pulled his son into a hug.

"You did good today. I'm proud of you."

"You are?"

"Of course. You hung in there when all this happened, then found me. Yeah, you did good."

"I thought you'd be mad at me."

Rob pushed him back a little so he could stare down at his son, seeing his tears. "Why?"

"We left the park."

"Oh." Rob nodded. "Yeah, well, you're grounded, that's for sure. But I'm pretty sure your mom is going to lock you inside until all this is figured out anyway, so don't feel too bad."

Jake nodded, smiling slightly. Rob pulled him into another hug, never wanting to let go.

"You going to be okay while I go check out the body?" Rob felt Jake nod against him. "Okay. I'll be right back. If you get scared, just call out for me. I'll be right there, no further."

"Okay."

Rob let him go, then scanned the clearing. He saw the signs that kids did, in fact, frequent the area. There wasn't any grass, candy wrappers and Coke bottles littered the ground, and there were two tree stumps they used as chairs. The clearing looked more like a local make out

spot than an actual party area. He'd have to take note to check there when he patrolled, just to make sure no one was getting down and doing the nasty.

When the light of his flashlight came across the top of the grate, he saw the hand holding it. It was thin, gaunt, and looked like it belonged to a much older man. The ring reflected off the beam of light. It did, indeed, match the chief's.

He bent forward, focusing on the large opening. He kept his distance, not wanting to contaminate anything or fall in. He didn't have to lean very far before he saw the glint of the chief's dead eyes looking up at him.

They now had a murder investigation. The state would step in and assist county, taking it out of his hands. It was common in small towns, most local cops hating to be pushed out. Rob thought he would actually appreciate it. One, he did not have the resources to investigate this, and two, he had never been a detective. He was a beat cop. They weren't meant to do the thinking. Beat cops were just there to do the doing, being the physical hands of justice as they chased down and arrested those the detectives had identified as the perps.

Rob tried to look into the pit below the chief. All he could see was endless darkness.

Take another step, maybe two, and you can join that darkness. It's right there. You wouldn't have to worry about losing your job tomorrow. You wouldn't have to deal with the pain of Jake going off to school. All you have to do is take another step forward, then everything will be fine. You will be okay, and it will go on forever. Darkness always went on forever.

He would be lost.

He shook his head and took a step back. There it was again. That voice getting into his head. He kept hearing it, that urging trying to pull him in, but it was stronger this time, more distinct. He had felt it, and...

And he wanted it. He had wanted to give in. Just step forward and he would be a part of it. This was all getting insane, none of it making sense.

He took another step back, then another, before he turned away and started walking through the thorns.

Jake, confused, watched as his dad walked away. He didn't acknowledge him, but just walked like a zombie back through the thorns.

"Dad!" Jake called as he rushed to catch up.

CHAPTER 18

How many hours had it been since she'd lost him? How long had she thought she would never see her little angel again? Too long, and she never wanted to feel that way again. She was never going to let her baby out of her sight. He would never be allowed to go anywhere without a chaperone.

"I'm going to my room," Joel said when he walked through the door. He announced it so loud, Samantha wasn't sure if he were telling her or his father, who was God knows where in the house. With how she yelled at him earlier, he was probably in the garage working on his roadster, getting it ready for the weekend.

"You need to eat first."

"Mom..." The sound of him whining her name, as though he were still a five-year-old, was uncalled for. It wasn't like she would tell him he couldn't go to his room. He just needed to eat first.

"How about I make you some corn dogs and mac n' cheese?"

"Fine."

"It'll just take a minute."

"Okay, but I'm going to wait in my room."

"You go do that." She really wished he would stay with her as she cooked, but she figured he should be fine in his room.

* * * *

Joel walked in and closed the door. Turning on his television, he flopped onto his bed. Why did he have to have such an embarrassment for a mother? She hugged him in front of his friends. How could she do that to him? She even did it in front of that little brat. Now he'd have to pound it out of their memories tomorrow morning before they got it into their heads that he was soft.

Joel was not now nor would he ever be a pussy. Tomorrow, he would get that Alletto kid alone and kick his ass. Everyone would know he wasn't soft after that. Did he think he could just hang out with them and talk to his best friend? He acted like they gave a shit about him. Well, that wasn't going to last. Alletto would soon realize he was shit after Joel wiped him from the bottom of his shoe.

"We're out of corn dogs, but we have hot dogs. Would those be okay?" his mother called from outside his door.

"I'm not hungry."

"You have to eat."

"Fine."

"So hot dogs will be okay?"

"Sure."

"Okay. Dinner will be ready in a few minutes. Why don't you come out and spend some time with us while it cooks."

Joel didn't answer. He grabbed his iPad and put on a large pair of headphones, white skulls over the earpieces. They muffled the sounds of the outside world. He hit PLAY and let the world fade around him, closing his eyes to lose himself in the beat.

The music soothed him and he felt himself go, the rhythm pushing and pulling, the air dancing.

Who the hell were all these people who thought they could make me feel like crap? Why had she hugged me?

None of it mattered as the beat continued to throb, his heart moving in time.

"*Mama, ma-ma-ma-mama, just killed a man…*"

The song, a remix of some crap song his dad listened to, cried out to him as he mouthed the words. This was his world. They all just served him, and he was now gone.

"*Killed, killed, killed, killed, killed a man…*"

The song kept repeating, the beat getting louder. At first, it seemed so natural. Even though he had heard the song a thousand times before, he never noticed the repetition. He listened to it as it continued to crescendo. When it grew painfully loud, he was dragged back to this world, realizing there must be a glitch in the track. He knew it never went on this long, just repeating itself, screaming "killed" over and over.

He pulled the headphones off, opening his eyes to the dim light of the room. He felt the headache as soon as he sat up against his headboard. He must have drifted off. He hadn't even realized he had been that tired. Sure, he had a long day, and it wasn't every day that one of your friends came up missing.

Yeah, Bobby was an ass, but he had also been part of the crew. It would have been like if Danny or John came up missing. He'd be upset, even though he knew they were both dickwads. He'd be more upset if Danny came up missing because they'd been friends since they learned how to walk. John, on the other hand, was a tool who took up the mantle of being a douchenozzle like his old man. He'd miss him, but he could do without him.

Bobby, though, was someone Joel could relate to. Sure, he was a grade above Joel and ruled the eighth grade, but they still occasionally hung out, roughing up a few kids. It was never that much, but he knew him and Em, the girl he was always with. They made a good team and didn't take crap from anyone. They took some lunch money, and Joel might have been around on occasion.

Those days, they'd let him sit in and throw a few punches, even sharing the spoils.

Bobby especially liked to beat the holy jesus out of his younger brother, and Joel was always inclined to help. Mikey was the same age as Joel, but was a lot smaller. Maybe that was why Bobby allowed Joel to be around. He was often mistaken for being older.

He looked back at the headphones in his hands. He could hear the increasingly loud chant. *Killed* echoed through his thoughts, working into his body. The voice was distinct, not like the vocals he had been listening to. It had grown deeper and distorted.

"Piece of junk," he muttered, hitting the STOP button on the iPad. The chanting continued. The large round button clicked as he pressed again and again, worried he would break the damn thing. He became frantic, suddenly not caring if he broke it. He slammed his thumb on the button repeatedly. He felt himself start chanting along with the voice.

"Killed, killed, killed," he cried, tears stinging his eyes as he focused both hands on getting the iPad to stop. When it wouldn't, he pulled the cord of the headphones, then tossed the device across the room. However, the hollow voice continued from the little speakers of the earpieces.

"Stop it!"

He threw the headphones and grabbed his blankets. He balled them up and threw them over the headphones, but he could still hear it. In fact, it had gotten louder, becoming more distorted. He could almost feel the voice pounding into him.

They were cheap plastic, which was breakable. He should know. He'd broken many, and how did he break them? He stomped on them.

He brought his foot crashing down, hearing the loud crunch of the plastic as it snapped. Thankful for the blankets, it didn't hurt as much as he thought. He brought his foot down again and again, pounding the piece of possessed demonware to the deepest pits of hell. He didn't normally believe in that crap, but those things were clearly messed up.

The room shook with his continued assault, but he wasn't going to let up. He wanted to smash them into pieces. It became rhythmic. His foot came down, the rattle of glass in the pictures on the dresser, a slight pause, then his foot came down again. It was almost like music, and he slammed his foot down in time to the beat.

He chanted, "Killed, killed, killed."

He stopped, his chest heaving with the exertion, the room spinning a little as he caught his breath. It didn't matter, though, because the chanting continued. He heard that lost voice, then himself. They spoke in tandem. As he tried to focus on stopping himself, his own voice grew louder.

Something was wrong. Why hadn't his mom or dad come to see if he was okay? Normally, all he had to do was step heavily in his room and he'd hear a knock. Where were they? His mother had said she would be back in a couple minutes with something to eat. It had to have been at least that. Why hadn't she knocked on his door? This was all very wrong.

He looked around the room. It was quiet. Nothing had fallen over, which was strange, considering his stomping earlier. The family picture his mother insisted he keep on his dresser still stood in its frame. That should have fallen and been in pieces on the floor.

"Mom?!" He wanted to scream for her, but he couldn't stop himself from chanting long enough. His mouth kept moving, Joel having no control over it.

He walked to the door and pulled it open. He had to find her. If she saw him, she'd call a doctor, maybe even a priest to give him one of those exo…exo… Whatever it was that got rid of demons. Yeah, he needed one of those. She'd call the priest and he could come take care of him.

He stopped in the open doorway, afraid to take another step. It was really dark in the house. Really, really dark. Like he couldn't see anything beyond his room kind of dark.

"Mom?"

Why couldn't he see the television? His dad would usually watch TV, Joel being able to see the glow of it from his room. His dad always watched the news this time of night.

But he saw nothing.

"Mom, how's supper coming?"

Was that his voice cracking? He wasn't scared. Not him. So why did he take a step back into his room, slowly easing the door closed as he did?

His room felt colder. He hadn't noticed it at first, but there was a definite chill.

He hadn't closed the door all the way. He was trying not to, holding out hope that he would see the flicker of the lights or the TV returning from some technical difficulty. In the back of his mind, he knew this wasn't some technical issue and the power hadn't gone out. Something wasn't right, and he needed to get out of there.

A shape appeared just outside his door. It looked like a person, but even though he saw arms and legs, his gut told him not to trust it. In those old horror movies, those body snatcher things looked like people, too. He had stayed up many times past when his parents went to bed and watched all those old flicks. This could be one of those things, coming out of the dark. It would reach out and take him.

He waited, expecting the eyes to start glowing red. They were going to, right? This thing was an alien, there to take him up to its spaceship. That was what these things did. Maybe that was what happened to Bobby. Holy crap, it really was aliens.

It was too dark to really see much of the figure's details. Maybe if he got closer... Instead, he took another step back, letting go of the door. That was a mistake. He should have closed it. He had a moment to debate with himself before it came closer and he took another step back.

He had started to shiver, the room feeling like ice. He looked around, trying to see what had made it so cold. Had a window been opened? His mother might have earlier, although that wasn't like her.

Suddenly, he wasn't in his room anymore. Everything around him was black. That wasn't right. He had been lying on his bed, walked past the dresser to open the door, blankets on the floor. All of it was gone.

He looked back at the shape as it got closer. Joel could now see it was shorter than he was. Something about the way it walked told him it was a boy, one he vaguely recognized.

"Killed, killed, killed."

He knew he had stopped chanting for a while, but realized the moment he started again. Each time he said the words, a tentacle of the darkness wrapped around him. First, it took his legs, rooting him in place, then his arms. He was held there, not able to see what had him or where he was. He watched, helpless, as the shape approached.

Then he recognized the figure. He tried to scream, but the chant continued.

"Killed, killed, killed."

* * * *

Samantha finished in the kitchen and walked past the waste of life sitting in his easy chair, watching some damned news broadcast. He had emerged from the garage shortly after they returned and had gone straight to the La-Z-Boy. He would be glued to the TV until his stomach screamed for supper, then he would wonder where his meal was. It wasn't uncommon for her to cook multiple meals because no one wanted to eat what someone else was having. She was sure her husband would have issues with what she made Joel. She didn't try to make enough for two people anymore. What was the point?

So she let him be. He could just eat his supper when he was ready for it. She continued past him and knocked on Joel's door.

"Honey, supper's ready."

No answer. She put her ear to the door, trying to hear Joel inside. It was quiet, so she wondered if he had drifted off to sleep. He had a long day, and she was certain he was tired. She wasn't sure what she should do. He needed his sleep, he was a growing boy, but he also needed to eat.

She knocked again, louder this time.

"Honey?"

Her husband growled. "For crying out loud. He's probably taking a nap. Either go in there and wake him up or leave the boy alone."

She turned to glare at the man, but he had already turned back to the TV. What was so damn important? Why did he pay more attention to it than her or their son?

He was right, though. If she wanted Joel to eat, she had to go in and wake him up.

She opened the door, quietly stepping in. Everything was gone. No room, no Joel, nothing. Just...black.

"Joel?"

Tentacles of darkness shot out, swirling around her arms and legs, quickly grabbing her. She opened her mouth to scream, a piece of it slipping in and into her lungs. Her eyes widened as it lifted her off the ground. She watched as it slithered out of the room and into the hall, stretching like vines across the walls.

The TV cut out, the sound of boiling water in the kitchen quieted, and the lights flickered off. Nothing remained as everything faded to black.

201

CHAPTER 19

"From darkness comes light. Without the light, you would never know the dark. Two sides, Alpha and Omega, beginning and end. If there is not one, the other cannot exist. So what is living in life and walking that enlightened path unless you know how to avoid the darkness?"

No... No, that isn't right.

Father William looked around the large cathedral, then down at the empty pews. There was a peaceful serenity to the church when it was only him and God. He often found this was when he wrote some of his best sermons. Tonight was one of the exceptions. He seemed off this week. He knew why, but he shouldn't let it bother him. It wasn't anything he had to deal with, being actually forbidden to do anything directly. That didn't keep him from *in*directly pushing. A soft whisper from an invisible voice to help nudge a wavering decision was often his best tools to fight evil. While he bellowed in his sermons, his whimper contained all the power. If only he could do more.

This should be different. This wasn't like what he was put there to do.

He wasn't sure if he truly believed that, though. What made this different than last year or the year before that? In many ways, it was all the same. The world was the same, and there really wasn't much point to any of it.

It hurt him to play by the rules. He was not one to do so, always walking that fine line between interference and guidance. He had felt the earliest pieces of the awakening years ago, finding a guardian he could guide to be here when it happened. He had hoped he would be able to prepare him more. He befriended Rob when they had moved to town, but Alletto was not strong in the path of God.

Why Father likes to pick those not strong in their convictions as his most needed warriors has always confounded me, but I'm not one to question.

"Remember now thy Creator in the days of thy youth. While the evil days come not, nor the years draw nigh, when thou shalt say, 'I have no pleasure in them.' While the sun, or the light, or the moon, or the stars be not darkened, nor the clouds return after the rain."

In the empty room, he felt the echo reverberate deep in his essence.

His eyes closed and he let his chin fall to his chest. It really was all coming to an end. Everything he had witnessed. The beauty that had come and gone and come again. These people who bustled around him, living their busy lives. The babies who came and grew into parents, continuing the cycle he watched again and again, enjoying it each time.

Why should he prepare for a service this weekend? If it was all going to just fall apart, what was the point? The faithful part of him told him it was to give hope, but how could he give what he did not possess? Was that true? Had he lost his faith? Would he, who had seen so much, lived so much, finally be brought down?

The darkness worked its way into him. That had to be it. He had felt it when it first woke, both cursing and celebrating its awakening. At first, he hadn't known what had reemerged from such a slumber, but had felt the celestial stirrings, the energy being pulled around him. His initial feeling had been hope. He knew what was coming, hoping maybe he had found an ally for the pending fight.

203

When he heard a pounding on the church door, he opened his eyes and looked toward the back of the room. Father William didn't need to look to know who was out there. He had felt its awakening, its growing presence, and knew it was getting stronger. Although the night came, he knew there was more than just the earthly dark descending on the sleepy little community.

It was just another demon, society's fictional monster, on the doorstep. What society had created in its stories. There were no true demons, not in the sense people thought. There were many different things only seen in fiction, as the true world hid deep in the shadows. In one form or another, many of them were what was once known as angels, like himself.

Time was a funny thing. Many people wanted it to go on forever. Father William thought that had to be based on the fear of death because if people actually knew what living forever entailed, they would never seek it out. It did things to the creatures that were eternal. Some minds warped as things were forgotten. Some just got bored, found a hidden shadow, and rested until they were disturbed. Others dabbled as much as was allowed, but didn't interfere because interference brought punishment.

The creature outside, the one he had once called brother, had slept peacefully until something had changed. What happened to spawn this madness outside these doors?

Why had he awoken now?

Father William was nearly alone. Just one angel with one guardian who had not fully accepted his nature. It brought back memories of David. He hadn't thought of him in ages, and what he did remember didn't feel real. With time, there was always that haze, desire amplifying what you had versus what was wanted.

David had been one of the good ones. Maybe Rob would be one of the good ones, too. He had a good heart and his family meant a lot to him.

He heard the pounding on the door again. He stood just inside it, his hand inches away from the thick mahogany that strengthened the gates into this house of God. Through the door, he felt what had become of his brother. It didn't matter what shape or body he took. He recognized that inner presence. It wasn't like what people referred to as a soul. For them, it was something more. A piece of the celestial universe connecting them to the plane beyond. It was also another piece of their prison that kept them as a part of this place.

Father William's hand hovered, not wanting to touch it. He could feel the rotting presence trying to seep into the wood. He felt the light slipping away, tentacles reaching out, trying to swirl around him.

Did his brother think he could take him like he had taken the others? Did he not recognize him? Or had his madness grown that deep?

Of course he was mad. They had all grown into their own madness, this world having not been what any of them ever expected. The question is in what form their madness manifested.

And what does that say about me?

He opened the door and stared out into the night, not seeing his brother. Instead, there was an older couple walking by, smiling at him and waving as they continued along the sidewalk. A car drove by, and he could hear more on Main Street just a block away. The night was serene and peaceful, not the menace and chaos he had felt just a moment before.

Is my madness that of imaging my brother's awakening? Are there even missing children, or is that also in my head?

He closed the door, then fell into the nearest pew, bowing his head in prayer.

"Dear Heavenly Father, guide me so I may help them."

205

As always, there was no answer. Father never answered directly anymore. His answers consisted of action, not words.

"He doesn't listen. Not anymore. He's left us."

Father William jumped, raising his head to see a little boy standing in the aisle. Those dark tentacles swayed in the air around him. The boy was one Father William recognized, but not the one he thought he would see standing there. He was young, his hair so caked with dirt, it was hard to tell what color it once was. His skin was pale, his tattered clothes hanging from him. His coal-black eyes stared off into space, occasionally glancing at the stained glass windows lining the church.

"Who are you?" the angelic priest asked, realizing this wasn't one of his brothers. This was some other creature, one he didn't recognize. There was pure evil behind those eyes. For the first time since his creation, he was frightened. It brought question to everything he thought he knew.

His Father was the Alpha and Omega, so where had this evil come from if not from him?

A tentacle of darkness shot toward him, striking him in the chest. He felt the intense cold and hate trying to darken him, just as it was the whole town.

He had seen that, hadn't he? How this darkness seeped into everything, corrupting all it touched. This town was slowly descending into the dark. He saw the fights escalating, the rising of evil and sin. Even the strongest in the faith gave in to pride and boastfulness.

He felt how they all stemmed from this beast, how it wanted them all. The hunger was immense, starving for their sin. It wanted him, too, but was confused at how he seemed different. It reached for him like it reached out and touched the couple Father William had seen outside. It wasn't pulling them in yet. He could watch as it withered at the good inside them. By the end of the block, that couple, who had warmly greeted him, screamed at each other, blaming one another for infidelities that never happened. This beast had pushed at something inside them. Later tonight, if they didn't find themselves, one would probably kill the other.

He knew it was forbidden, but the priest pushed gently at a memory they shared—the two of them at church when their son had been baptized. Hoping that would be enough, he focused his attention back on the creature in the child skin before him.

"Get out!" the priest bellowed, shaking the walls around him. He stood to tower over the boy, the child-like face looking at him, confused, as the black tentacle was forced away, a light shining around Father William. "I said *get...out!*"

The child was gone, the church empty. The priest closed his eyes, not able to restrain the tears.

"Father, how are we ever going to save this world?"

He sat back down in the pew, waiting for an answer he knew would not come.

CHAPTER 20

"So why are we heading out here?" Ally looked at David as he pulled onto the little hidden back road. It was four miles out of town and tucked away, not able to be seen from the road. Everyone from the area knew about it. In the light of day, it looked more like an abandoned driveway than a road.

It was one of the many popular make out spots outside of town, right along a stretch of creek that most people just called Little Sandy.

"Well, it was somewhere away from everything."

"Oh, not for some other reason."

He looked over at her, seeing a little smile that he couldn't help but return, and shook his head.

"No, just to talk. Although..." He stretched it out as he said it, knowing he was being coy.

This was the kind of playful banter they had known most of their lives. As a young boy and girl, their banter had been innocent. Getting older, it had changed and became boy against girl because girls had cooties. Years later, mix in teenage hormones raging, and that closeness brought on something else. They were friends, knew everything about one another, so when they had both gotten drunk at a party, barely able to drive down the two-lane road, the inevitable happened.

David might have had a little bit of a concussion. He wasn't sure. Some asshole had nailed him with an empty beer bottle when he snuck off to take a piss in a cornfield. He never saw who threw it and everyone had laughed. It hadn't mattered as he had been three sheets to the wind by then.

So he had been drunk and she was tipsy. They drove under thirty miles per hour down a highway that most people would have been going ninety on. David kept slowing down, the road becoming harder to focus on. Eventually, the car rolled into a ditch, neither of them feeling like trying to get it out. Instead, a longing had started. They were out there alone, and after what seemed like an eternity along the side of the road, he pulled her into his arms.

From that moment on, they had played coy. Neither of them remembered what really happened. They might have gone all the way, but it didn't matter. It was the beginning of changing how they acted around each other. The chemistry was there, they knew that, and the friendship was there. What more did they need?

She pulled him out of his thoughts by giving him a playful thump on the shoulder. He rocked back, his smile deepening as he rubbed the spot she hit him. She was never one to hold back on her punches.

Damn, that stung.

"Cool it. I thought we came out here to talk."

"We did." His smile disappearing, he looked back to the road as he eased around another curve. The area was covered in trees for another couple feet, making it pitch black around them.

David slammed on the brakes, both of them thrown forward in their seats. A car, its lights off, blocked the road. The brakes locked on the gravel, pebbles flying as he turned the wheel back and forth, trying to keep control as the car slid toward the other vehicle. Having been going too fast, not expecting something to block his path, he didn't know if he could stop in time.

"Dammit," he cursed under his breath, his teeth grinding as he watched the other car getting closer. He should have known better. This was a party spot. He should have figured somebody else would be out here.

Thankfully, with just a few feet to spare, the car stopped.

David looked over to see Ally glaring, those fiery eyes burning into him. How those eyes could always make his breath catch when he was caught in their gaze.

"Well, I guess we won't be alone out here," he said as he eased the car off to the side of the road, watching out for the tree stump he knew was there somewhere. When the canopy of trees above them thinned, the moonlight filtered through, making it possible to see the stump farther down.

"Yeah, who would have thought."

He turned off the lights, and couldn't help but chuckle a little as he looked at the car. "Looks like we interrupted something hot and heavy."

It was obvious by its steamed windows. They could see two shapes moving around inside, quickly working to separate themselves.

He looked over at Ally and saw she was chuckling, as well.

"You know, they probably think we're cops. You *did* pull up with your lights on."

"Crap."

He had forgotten. It had been so long since he'd come out there with anyone. The unsaid rule was you turned off your lights once you left the main road. Only the chief kept his lights on. All the other police had never known about the area, seeing as none of them were local and it was way off the beaten path. David thought the new officer, the one he'd talked to last night, had tried to find it. He wasn't sure if he ever did.

A door opened in the other car and someone tried to climb out, falling forward onto the gravel.

David winced. "Ooh, that's gotta hurt."

Ally nodded. "Yep."

"I should probably get out and let them know-"

"You think that's going to go over well?"

"Not really, but they're going to see we're not a squad car, probably coming back here anyway."

"True."

David pushed open his door and climbed out.

He saw the shape trying to scramble up, his back to them. It was kind of funny to watch because his legs were still in the car as he fought to pull them free. He caught glimpses of clothes quickly being slipped on while the guy rushed to get around into the front seat. Both of them moved frantically, not looking back at David's car at all.

The man slammed the door as David approached. Then lights flashed, the red brake lights glowing as the car started. David got pelted with rocks as the driver slammed down on the accelerator. The car fishtailed, more rocks flying back, the sound like hail hitting a metal roof, the *ping, ping, ping* as they shot from beneath the tire and hitting David's car.

The car flew out of there before David even had a chance to say anything.

Instead, he stood there, watching as the car went around the curve a half-mile down the gravel road, then flew off the road into the nearest cornfield. They were gone. Running because they thought David and Ally were cops. They had probably been drinking, too.

David shook his head and got back into the car.

"You know, when they find out it was just us, they're going to be pissed," Ally said, looking at him.

"Yep."

"You should have turned off your lights."

"Well, I wasn't expecting anyone to be out here. Hell, most the town's out looking for your brother. I thought this would be a safe place to just come and get away from it all." He looked over at her and saw her frown. "I've got a lot on my mind."

Her face softened a little as she nodded, looking away. It seemed a little brighter out there, the full moon

211

shining down and casting everything around them in a light blue glow.

"How are you doing?" David asked, breaking the silence that had crept in on them.

"I'm okay."

"That's good. How's school."

"It's fine. You still graduating early?"

He nodded. "Yeah."

"You don't have any idea what you're going to do, do you?"

"Yeah, I do."

Ally looked at him, an eyebrow raised. He couldn't help but turn up the corner of his lip in what he felt was his best smile.

"What?"

"I'm going to sleep in my bed and eat my parents' food."

She chuckled a little. "Yeah. Your dad's going to convert your room into a music studio the morning after you've graduated, and all your comic books are going to be out on the porch."

"Yeah, well, he won't know I'll be living in the garage."

"Um, he might when he gets his motorcycle out in the spring."

"Nah. I'll be on the other side of all the junk. There's so much shit, I could live for a decade in there and nobody would notice."

"You're probably right."

"I know it."

When she caught his eyes, he saw it. That genuine smile he had hoped to see. There was his friend.

He reached out and eased his arm around her shoulders, pulling her close. She took off the seat belt and slid toward him. He sat sideways and kicked his legs out along the floor, letting her lay back against his chest. He pulled her closer, enjoying the familiar sensation of her warmth.

They both looked out at the woods. David could feel her chest rise and fall with each breath. He closed his eyes and leaned his cheek against the top of Ally's head, feeling the fluff of hair, that little tickle in his nose from the loose strands.

"I can't stand her."

She said it so quietly, he had to strain to hear. "Your mom?"

"Yeah."

"I know. Could be worse, though. Your dad could still be there."

Ally laughed humorlessly, sitting up and looking at him. "You know what bomb she dropped on me tonight? What she has known all these years and hasn't said anything?"

"What?"

"That bastard wasn't even my dad. He wasn't Mike's or Bobby's dad, either. Hell, I don't even know why she was with that damn loser. She seems to go through guys like cigarettes."

David wanted to defend Ally's mom, but he wasn't there to argue. It wasn't something he really believed anyway. He knew the rumors of all the guys she'd been with. He had heard the stories, always making sure he never said anything when he was around Ally. There were just some things you never told your best friend. Besides, it wasn't like he knew any of the stories to be true. He had never actually seen any of it, but if enough people said it, it was probably true. Where there was smoke, there was often fire.

His dad had once made a comment about it when he had seen her, which wasn't often. David's dad and Ally's mom didn't like to be around each other. It kind of felt like they had once had a thing. His dad would glance at her strangely, almost sad, then look away. When he'd look back, David would see the hard mask his father showed the world.

213

There was one time his dad was drunk, which wasn't uncommon, and he saw bruises on Wendy's arm...almost looking like a handprint.

"So sad what's happened to her."

"What?"

It had caught David by surprise. At the time, his dad was climbing into the driver's seat of the car, David on the passenger side. His dad took his eyes off Wendy to look at him. They had just been to Ally's dance recital, Wendy waiting outside for her to come out.

"Nothing."

David should have just let it go. It was one of those rare nights they had gotten along, almost bonding. There wasn't any fighting and, for a short time, David felt comfortable around his dad. Maybe that was what gave him the courage to ask his next question.

"What was she like before?"

David had only ever known the mother Ally couldn't stand to be around. He had spent many nights hanging out with Ally in her room, listening to her mom and dad screaming back and forth. David couldn't help but wonder what she was like before she had turned into a mean and bitter bitch.

His dad was silent. Not looking at him, he started the car and put it into gear, driving out of the parking lot, the only sound being the music that spilled out the gym doors whenever they were opened, blasting them with some god-awful pop song. He figured his dad wasn't going to answer him.

It wasn't until they had passed the last stop sign and were cruising on the back road that his dad spoke. Maybe it had taken him all that time to pull up the memories, to get past all the images of what Wendy had become.

"Wendy was a really good girl growing up. She went to church every week, even though her family didn't.

214

When that new pastor came to town, she got all fucked up."

David looked into Ally's eyes. He had always wondered what his dad had meant. There were always rumors she was with so many different men around town, especially when Ally's dad worked second shift. If even half the rumors were true, he was sure Mrs. Taylor had caused many failed marriages.

He wondered what Ally had finally learned. Did some dark secrets come out?

"So who's your dad?" he finally asked.

"I don't know." She closed her eyes, wrapping her arms around her stomach, trying to hold herself together.

"But she said it wasn't him?"

"She said he can't have kids. Never could. Some birth defect. When he found out, he left her."

"I thought she kicked him out."

She shrugged. "Who knows. They both hated each other."

She looked out at the dark sky, her thoughts floating among the clouds.

"So that means Bobby and Mikey weren't his, either?" David asked.

"Nope."

"Damn."

"Yeah."

"And she wouldn't say who your dad is?"

Ally shook her head, still looking up at those stars.

"Ally?" He reached out, placing his hand on her shoulder. She wouldn't turn, but she cocked her head to the side, her cheek resting on the back of his hand. The warmth felt good. "Do you think maybe he came back and did something Bobby?"

She sniffed as she shook her head. "No, he's gone. The police tracked him down. He's been out of the state for the last month. There's no way he could have come back and taken Bobby."

215

"Okay."

David didn't know what to say, so he left it to sit there, hovering. Outside, the breeze bristled through the trees, and he felt the chill starting to creep in. The windows began to fog, their bodies too warm for the cool fall air.

"Thank you, David," she said as she leaned back into him.

He raised his brows. "For what?"

"For being here."

"Where else would I be?"

"Well, you didn't have to pick me up."

"Yeah, I did."

She smirked. "Whatever."

"I wasn't going to let you go through this alone."

"I know."

"So why even make a big deal out of it."

Ally sighed. "I don't know."

The silence hung between them. What did she really want? Was there something she was trying to say, or was he reading too much into it?

Oh, how he missed her. David had a hard time keeping that thought to himself as he shifted in order to not poke her in the back. Damn, why did his body have to betray him now? He couldn't just be the friend he had always been. She needed him to listen, not be a guy.

But it was hard to push the images from his mind. The pale flesh he would like to feel. Her hair smelled like peaches, and he just wanted to breathe it in as he kissed along her neck.

He closed his eyes and took deep breaths, knowing the windows were fogging that much faster as he fought with his own desires. If this went on too much longer, he felt like he would have to take a quick swim in the cold water of Little Sandy. That cold water was sure to calm any hot thoughts rattling their way through his thick skull.

"I guess we should be getting back," Ally said.

"Yeah," he croaked. He was barely able to say it, and it came out as a muffled whisper. Any louder and it would have betrayed how his voice floundered. David wanted to do several things, but driving back was not one. He wanted to turn her around and pull her in so their lips locked, allowing his tongue to meet hers.

"Okay then."

"Yeah."

She still hadn't pulled away from him. Was she waiting for him to do something? Did she want something more?

No, he wasn't going to go there, not when her brother was missing and her life was such a mess. She wasn't in any condition to think about that right now.

When she pulled away, he turned himself in his seat and reached for the keys. The moment, whatever it was, had been shattered. It was time to get back.

CHAPTER 21

Wendy didn't know where she was. Everything around her was dark. There was a flashing light somewhere in the distance, and she could hear a faint buzz and a ticking, like tapping on metal. She didn't recognize any of it, and it didn't make any sense.

Wait... I'm awake, but something's wrong. What is it? It doesn't matter. I'm okay. I'm safe. Right?

Something about that didn't feel right. Yes, she was alone and it was dark, but she was still safe. So why was that wrong? Where was she and why was it so dark?

Because you haven't opened your eyes, Wendy. You're not fully awake yet, she thought.

She started to move, feeling the softness of the blanket around her. Her mother's comforter clung to her, not wanting to let her go. She didn't want to leave its warmth, either, but she had to get up. Someone needed her...

No, there wasn't anyone who needed her anymore. Bobby was gone. Her mother was gone. Ally was gone. They were all gone. Her mother and Ally had both fought with her and left, but Bobby was missing. She needed to find him. He still needed her.

She opened her eyes and tried to sit up. She had fallen asleep on the couch. She could feel the metal bar that stretched across the center pushing into her body, making her back stiff. Damn, why did they have such an old couch? She should have tried to get a more comfortable used one. This one had been so old and uncomfortable when that son of a bitch found it on the curb ten years ago. The cushions were so faded and worn, you couldn't tell what the original color had been.

There was a sharp pain in her back as she tried to roll to one side. It made her right leg tremble as she fought to hold down a scream.

How in the hell had that bastard slept on this damn thing? There was just no way he could do it and walk the next morning.

That bastard. Just how the fuck could he up and go. It didn't matter what she had told him. It didn't matter that he already knew most of it. He knew that as much as she yelled at him to go, she still needed him.

No, you don't. You are stronger than that. You popped out two sons and a daughter, raising them alone. He was never truly there for them. Don't start doing the pity party thing now. You don't need him to get you through this.

There was that little voice again. The one that was always her cheerleader, telling her she could do it. There wasn't any other choice. She had to.

But what if they never found Bobby? They never found Michael. Could the same thing have happened to Bobby?

She sniffled back the tears, raising her head. It felt so much heavier than it should be, and the fog that had stayed away while she lay there came flooding back. The world spun, and she quickly reached out to the arm of the couch, trying to keep it from slipping out from under her.

"Oh god," she whispered. Her eyes tried to focus, but kept drifting to the flashing light across the room. It was blue, seeming so bright in the dark room. Why was it so dark in there?

She vaguely remembered talking to Ally earlier. The sun had been out then. They had fought again. It seemed like they always fought nowadays.

219

Wendy reached down, her hand knocking against something hard. She felt it move, then heard it thump to the floor.

The whiskey bottle. The pain and fog in her head seemed to make a little more sense as she tried to push herself up again, taking it a little slower this time to keep down the rising tide of nausea trying to force its way out. The couch felt like it was moving, even though the cushions were solid under her.

At least she hadn't taken any pills while she had been drinking this time. She doubted she would have woken up if she'd taken any of her meds. She must be learning from some of her mistakes. One trip to the hospital and a suicide watch must have made her wise up a bit.

What had she and Ally been talking about? It had been about her father, hadn't it? Not the bastard, but her biological father. Wendy didn't think she had mentioned who it was, Ally didn't need to know, although she did vaguely remember saying it wasn't the bastard.

A click came from the kitchen, making her realize she had been listening to the hum of the refrigerator. It was the only sound in the house. As the hum faded away, the silence was almost unbearable.

She looked over at the flashing light. *What is that*? Squinting, she could see her phone. Someone must have left a voicemail. She wished she had changed that damn setting. It really was annoying when it flashed in the middle of the night.

Wait... Someone had left her a voicemail? Had they found Bobby?

She pushed herself up, past the waves of nausea flooding around her, and forced herself to stand. It almost worked. She made it up, but as she stood straight, everything spun faster. Her legs gave out and she came crashing back down onto the couch, the cushion giving out a large rush of air in protest.

There was no control. She hadn't even felt it rising up in her, but she could feel herself heave, the contents of her stomach releasing. The world around her was so blurry, she didn't even know if she were sitting up. She could feel the retched stuff spilling out of her and was probably covered in it. Did she even care? How did she ever get this bad?

A fresh wave of tears came back. Was this really her life now?

She wished Kurt were there. She needed someone to hold onto so she could feel like she wasn't alone. But they had all left her. They were all gone, leaving her alone. Well, they could all just go and die, the bastards. Why did Ally have to leave her alone, though? She could at least have stayed and helped her mother get through this?

She knew her mom would come if she asked her to. They had fought earlier, but she would still come back. Yeah, but then she'd have to deal with the old nag telling her how much of a loser she was, always screwing up her life. The last thing Wendy needed right now was a reminder of just how much she had thrown away. Always marrying the wrong man, always doing the wrong thing. Why couldn't she have stayed a good Christian woman instead of having kids out of wedlock?

Yeah, she wasn't going to call her mother anytime soon. And Kurt leaving was a blessing. It had been a long time coming. She was certain he suspected the kids weren't his for a while. Hell, half the town probably knew with how these prudes liked to talk. Yeah, he had to have known, choosing to ignore it until she finally had enough. They had been in one of their heated, drunken, throwing things at each other fights when she had finally let him have it. Let him know he wasn't even man enough to spawn their kids. That his little kiddies didn't like to flow down the chute.

He hadn't taken it well, and neither had their dining room table when he flipped it. Damn bastard could have at least bought her a new one, but she knew he never would.

He had to have known. How could he not? Mikey and Bobby looked nothing like him, and Ally had been born six months after they started dating. Truthfully, that was the only reason she had started dating Kurt, she needed a baby daddy, but had he never done the math? She knew he wasn't the sharpest tool in the shed, but he had to have suspected something.

She wasn't sure if he cared enough about the kids to come back for them. He had raised them, had always been there for them. Sure, he'd been drunk and abusive most of the time, but he had been there.

She needed someone. There was just no way she could make it through this without someone by her side. Her babies were gone. There wasn't going to be anyone to take care of her. She was all alone.

A shiver ran down her spine, the temperature in the room feeling like it had dropped. She sniffled back some of the tears, trying to wipe away the crust around her eyes. That pulsing in her head had come back. At least the pain pushed away some of the fogginess.

She looked down to see she was sitting up, the front of her robe covered in vomit. She could feel it on her skin, wrinkling her nose at the stench. That smell would never come out. She would have to burn the robe tomorrow.

That clicking sound… Probably the refrigerator going into defrost or whatever it did in the middle of the night. She could hear the rumble coming from the kitchen, but it sounded different. There was a shimmer and a dullness to the sound. She could hear it, but it was muffled.

It made her head swim again. She reached out for the end of the couch, using it to steady herself. It was coming. She couldn't stop it. Another wave hit as she sat forward, the regurgitated alcohol splattering onto the floor. Wave after wave hit her. God, would it ever stop?

When it did, her stomach felt like it pulled in on itself. There wasn't much left in her, and now her insides were trying to leave. Just like everything else, even her own body wanted to abandon her.

"Oh God. Why?"

She didn't expect an answer. No one was there to hear her. Only the dark, empty house listened. Everyone else was gone.

"There is no God."

Wendy looked up, her head spinning as she looked around the dark room. She had heard it. Someone had just said something. It sounded like… No, it couldn't be, but it sounded like her baby. She looked. The house was dark, no one there.

"Hello?" she said, her voice shaking.

The clicking of the refrigerator faded away, the room getting quiet. Too quiet. Unnaturally quiet. It just felt wrong, darker somehow.

She still had her hand on the side of the couch, deciding to use it to try and stand. It probably wasn't her best idea, but she felt like she needed to be on her feet. She had heard it…him. He was there. She just needed to look for him. He must be hiding somewhere. Maybe behind the chair on the other side of the living room. That ungodly large chair she had always said needed to be thrown out. He was there. He had to be.

She took a deep breath in, swallowing the gag from smelling her own vomit. She closed her eyes and leaned forward, her legs wobbling as she pushed up. *Deep breath. Keep going. Don't focus on the smell.* Finally, she was up. She could feel the room spinning around her, but it had already started to slow. She was up and wouldn't fall back down this time. Not in front of Bobby. He would never see her that drunk again.

"Hun?"

Her head cleared a little as she took a small step forward. Before she could lose her balance, she took another, then another. When the room threatened to swirl around her again, she had to stop. The chair seemed so far away, it was hard to see. She had been walking toward it, but where did it go?

She could feel her balance shifting again and shuffled her foot back to steady herself before she fell.

"Baby, come out from behind that chair."

Nothing. Only the uneasy silence answered her.

"Get out here right now before I have to come back there and pull you out."

When she saw something move, her face flushed with warmth. Her baby... She was going to see her baby again. He hadn't left her. She knew he would come back to her.

"Come on." She took another slow step toward the chair. "You can come out, hun. Mommy's here. It's safe."

She made it to the chair, reaching out when she stumbled. Her stomach threatened to empty again, but she was sure there wasn't anything left. Instead, it twitched, as if a worm were inside her, occasionally shaking violently. She shook off the feeling and walked behind the chair. Empty.

"It's not nice to hide from Mommy," she said, holding back tears. "Come on. I need you. Come back to me." The room stayed quiet, her voice sounding like it disappeared as soon as she spoke. "Please, come back to me." Her voice was barely above a whisper.

"Tag. You're it," came a voice, but she couldn't tell from where. It sounded so much like her son's, but it was all around her and there was something...wrong with it. It was like there was an echo, but not. It was hollow.

She spun around, trying to see where the voice came from, but there was nothing. She couldn't see anyone. Wait... Where were the couch, the coffee table, the TV stand? There was nothing in the room. Everything around her was gone.

She turned back to look at the chair. Gone. She was alone, standing in an endless sea of black.

"I missed you, Mommy."

She heard the voice, knowing it was her son, but she never got the chance to turn around before she felt herself start to fall.

And then she screamed.

* * * *

Brady never felt like he had fit in to the Standard way of living. In fact, that had always been his credo. His life wasn't cut out to be Standard material. He was meant for more than this. He had grown up in this little town, only leaving for short trips, such as his daily commute to the community college fifteen miles north.

This town just wasn't him. Sure, he looked like nearly everyone else. He was just under six feet tall; had a few extra pounds around the middle that, no matter how much he starved himself, always felt like there was more there than the day before; his blond hair never lay right, so no matter how much effort he put into it, it was always a mess; and no matter how hard he tried, he could never grow a beard, his baby face always confusing people about his age. Not that he was into drinking, but whenever he did try to buy the occasional beer, he was always carded, probably thinking his ID was fake.

Maybe that was just his insecurities. When your name is Brady…and yes, it was because his parents had been big fans of the show…you were always on edge. He was a joke just waiting to happen. His parents were great, but were also always there. He still lived with them, still enjoying the comforts of living in his room in the basement.

Yet his life felt like it was stuck there. He was twenty-one, working on the four-year plan of junior college, and worked in a grocery store less than ten minutes away from town. He wasn't even sure how it stayed open, considering the high prices. Was this really all he had to look forward to in life?

It could get even better. Once he got out of junior college, he could always work at one of the local factories for a few bucks more an hour and still be living at home, like a loser.

With a heavy sigh, Brady set the large wooden box on the grass. At least his parents lived on the edge of town so there weren't as many houses nearby.

"Hey, now, be careful with that," he heard his dad say.

Brady turned to see the taller, thinner man lumbering down the back stairs. His dad had started going bald just a year before. Rather than watch the rest of it go, he began shaving his head. It was weird, but he had to admit his dad looked younger without all the white hair. Now he just needed to do away with the beard. It reminded Brady too much of Santa Clause and just looked wrong on him.

"I am."

"Good. It cost me an arm and a leg to have the lens fixed last time. I've had that telescope since I was your age, and it will be yours to use with your own kid someday."

Brady shook his head. *Yeah, I need to meet a girl who finds me the least bit interesting first.* "Like that'll ever happen."

"It will," his dad said as he squatted down and unlatched the first of the four sides of the box. As he finished with the last latch, there was an audible release of the pressure, allowing his dad to lift the top, revealing a telescope that still amazed Brady. For fifteen years, his dad and he had used it to look up at the moon.

He still remembered the first time. He had to have been five years old, as that had been when they moved into the new house. His father had brought him outside, set up the long lens, then motioned Brady over. He told him, "Don't touch anything. Just look." And Brady had…seeing the moon. He could see the craters, which was mind-blowing to his five-year-old eyes. His dad had told him it was filled with cheese and the astronauts went up there to bring it back. He then told him it was blue cheese and, just between the two of them, it tasted like puke.

"You want to set it up tonight?" his dad asked as he set the lid down on the freshly mowed grass.

"Sure. I'm not sure we're going to see much, though. Look at all those clouds." Brady looked up at the sky.

"Yeah, I know, but we can always try."

Brady was sure there was another reason they were trying tonight. His dad had made it a tradition to come out every full moon. The only times they had missed were in the bitter cold and during storms. They would still try on a cloudy night, although they usually gave up on finding the moon and started looking for other things. It was sometimes just a brief glimpse of the neighbors, although Brady still blushed when his dad poked fun at him for catching Mr. and Mrs. Sanderson naked in their bedroom. He hadn't been trying to see that. In fact, he wished he hadn't seen it and never wanted to see anything like it again.

But most cloudy nights, they wouldn't find anything to watch. It was more about spending time together. Brady had figured that out years ago. During his teenage years, he had been a real pain in his dad's ass about it, just wanting to be watching his favorite shows inside.

Brady quickly went to work setting up the telescope. The ground was soft, but the spikes at the bottom of the legs dug into the dirt for sturdy supports. The tripod they used was thick, wooden, and something Brady was certain his dad or grandfather had made long ago. He was used to the strange mechanism that operated the crank of the lens and, within minutes, he had it up and tilted toward the sky.

"Ready," he said, stepping back. His dad always did the fine tuning.

He started working at the controls. There were ones that would focus on the moon, while others adjusted it from side to side to zero in on the rotation. His dad did his thing, then stepped back, looking confused. He looked at Brady, then back at the telescope.

"That's odd."

"What?"

"I can't see anything."

"I told you it was too cloudy."

"No. I mean, I can't see *anything*. Not even the clouds."

"What do you mean?"

Brady stepped up to the side lens and bent down so his eye was close to it, but didn't touch. He had years to practice. He closed his left eye, focusing his dominant eye to stare through the cascading lens that magnified the stars…

Nothing.

"Huh," Brady said, stepping back.

He adjusted the telescope, figuring maybe there was just a really dark patch in the clouds. He noticed his dad hadn't zoomed in too much yet, so there should be enough light to make out the traces, but as he looked again, he still couldn't see anything.

"Here. Let me look again."

Brady felt his dad standing right behind him, so he moved to the side, looking up. There was nothing up there. That wasn't possible, but as he stared, he couldn't see stars or clouds. There was nothing but black above him. It wasn't the dark gray tone you usually saw. This was black, no color stretching to the horizon. There was nothing up there.

His dad scanned the sky, then stepped back. His mouth hung open as he looked at Brady, reminding him of someone who had just seen something they couldn't accept. That shock that came when you found out Santa

Clause was real, or Elvira had just appeared at your front door.

"I think maybe we should pack up and go back inside," his dad said softly.

"What's wrong?"

"I don't know." Brady started breaking down the stand and looked at his father, who still stared at the sky. "I really don't know."

"Should we call someone?"

His dad looked at him, eyebrows furrowed. "Who?"

"I don't know. NASA?"

His dad laughed. "And tell them what? The sky above our home town is missing?"

It was a nervous laugh. Brady joined in, helping to cut through the tension.

His dad gestured to the house. "But maybe we'll go in and watch the news. Maybe they're saying something."

Brady nodded as he fastened the last latch and picked up the box. He followed his dad inside, away from the pitch black sky.

PART III

Time wears on us all. It drags us down, though we may not feel it. It is the burden that adds weight to our steps, slowing them more than the pull of gravity. Time is heavier than gravity. In the end, it is time that places us beneath the earth as it eventually wins against our eternal fight against it.

The creature once thought he had won against time when he left the surface light by burrowing below. In some ways, he had beat the human concept of death by going to his own grave.

His. How had he become to think of himself with gender? Before, there had been no thought of gender. If he wanted to reproduce, it just happened.

It must be the boy, the one he had gone to devour but had somehow pulled him into its being. Before, the creature had only been partly in this world, but when he joined, he had found that part of him had been missing. In his slumbered state, he had not known. Now he was whole, hungry, but still so tired.

Sleep alluded him. He could feel something tugging at him, not allowing it. It had started with the boy, but there was now something else. It got stronger as this new thing called time passed by. He didn't know how long since the boy had come to him, but he felt it now as it passed. His hunger grew, but he just wanted to sleep.

Then the pull could no longer be avoided. A new voice called out to him, fully dragging him from his place of solitude. It pulled him up. Fully awake, he was hungry, but the boy's thoughts mixed with his own, desiring something more. The boy wanted...revenge.

231

CHAPTER 22

It had been a long time since he had slept without dreaming. Nightmares had become an evening ritual, so Rob wasn't sure how he felt about sleeping so well. Sure, it had been a long day and he had gotten no sleep the night before. He had long days and nights before, stretches of time when there was no opportunity to sleep, so last night was nothing new. He didn't think he would sleep a whole night with no interruptions again. But he had... He had come home and gone right to bed, but he now felt guilty that he had slept so well. Sure, they had found some of the kids, but there were still others missing, not to mention finding the body of the chief. He had no right to be sleeping, his son safe, when other parents didn't know where their children were.

He knew it was unfair, but as he had just come out of the peaceful slumber, he found himself not caring. His son was in his bed, his wife slept beside him, and they were all safe. Why should he care if others out there weren't as lucky? He was free of the nightmares, free of the worry.

When he had climbed into bed, he expected the nightmares. Even if there weren't new ones, he expected one or two of the old ones. He had quite the list tormenting him, like a playlist. Nightmares in a queue. Between the meth lab fire, the burning bodies, that creature, spiders, those "z" things he still refused to name, his dreams had an endless list of boogeymen it liked to pick from regularly. After the last two days, he expected something new to be added to that list. So when he woke up, the rays of light just beginning to peek through the window, he was amazed it was his bladder that had awoken him.

Robyn was still asleep next to him, which wasn't a huge shock. She'd grown accustomed to sleeping through his thrashing, and he was always surprised she still wanted to share a bed with him. He knew many other wives out there would not, and she paid the price. He'd seen bruises on her body, and while she wouldn't admit it to him, he knew she probably had been hit more than once by him fighting some internal demon. That alone should have her using the guest bedroom.

On top of that, she still hadn't forgiven him for taking their son up into the woods the previous night. When they had gotten home, she gave him the cold shoulder. He was quick to grab his pillow and head to the guest room. He had a long day. He wasn't going to waste the energy arguing or begging for forgiveness. When she saw him in the hallway, she shook her head, grabbed his pillow from him, and threw it back on their bed. He had taken the hint and climbed under the covers, quickly falling asleep.

He didn't know what he would ever do without her. She kept him sane, which wasn't easy. It seemed like all the crazy shit always seemed to happen around them. She had once told him they were blessed in a very odd way. Something to do with an angel looking out for them. He told her if they did have a guardian angel, he must have one sick sense of humor.

But that angel must help her sleep through the screaming, the kicking, the turning, the snoring. She slept through it all.

He eased himself out of bed and silently walked down the hall to the bathroom. He guessed it was probably a little past seven because the sun wasn't too high yet. The house was quiet. Too quiet. It was the kind of silence where you felt like you would wake everyone just by breathing too hard.

Yet he couldn't help himself. With all the running around, the non-stop rummaging through the woods, he felt like he was coated in some kind of grime. It didn't matter if the dirt was in his head or not. It was time for the longest shower in history. After emptying his bladder, he cranked the hot water, stepped in, and let it blast him.

* * * *

Rob stood in the bathroom, looking at his reflection in the mirror. The water had felt good. His tired muscles had ached more than he realized and the hot steam had loosened them up. Now he just had to try and stay that way. Last thing he needed was any more cramping.

The man looking back at him needed a lot less of many things. Less wrinkles creasing his face, less gray hair that seemed to multiply daily…and more hair on his receding hair line. Maybe that was why he avoided making eye contact with the man in the mirror so often. That man was getting old.

He quickly dried himself, then hurried out of the steam-filled room, his senses perking up in the hallway. Coffee. Robyn must have gotten up while he was in the shower. In a way, he was a little sad she didn't come join him, it had been a while since they'd been in the shower together, but he knew he'd be thankful for the coffee.

Had their marriage started to fall apart? Were they losing their romance, the love they had once shared with one another?

He thought of himself standing in the shower, feeling the warm bliss of the water cascading down his sore muscles. His eyes closed as it washed over his face. A hand, long, sleek, and feminine, reached around from behind, running across his chest. It went lower. He turned around, smiling, a twinkle in his eye happy for the morning visit. He stopped when he saw the woman from the flower store naked in front of him. She pushed herself forward, forcing her breasts toward him, wrapping her arms around his neck.

He blinked away the sudden desire as he stood in the upstairs hallway. His boxer shorts bulged, and he had to adjust to hide the sudden rising desire. Just what was going on with him lately?

The smell of coffee helped bring him back to the present. He could hear the squeaky springs alerting him that his son must be getting out of bed.

Rob hurried to the stairway, not wanting to see Jake on his way to the bathroom. Rob wasn't sure if his son would notice the hump in his pants, but he wasn't ready to explain it to him. It was probably a sure bet Jake already knew about the birds and the bees, but Rob wasn't ready to know about it just yet, and he didn't want to have to explain morning wood. How he had escaped talking about it for this many years was a miracle.

"Okay. I'll tell him when he gets out of the shower," he heard from the kitchen. Robyn's voice sounded cheery this morning. He wasn't sure if it was false or if she had truly started to forgive him for last night. He guessed he would find out soon enough. "Okay, bye bye now. Thank you."

He heard the beep of the phone just as he entered the kitchen. It felt ten degrees cooler than the rest of the house, his bare feet on the linoleum floor sending a cold shiver through him.

"Who was that?" he asked, looking longingly at the coffee pot on the counter behind her. She already had some in her cup. The slogan on it was easily readable, the mischievous devil smiling. *Queen B Devil woman. Approach with care.*

She glared at him over the rim of her cup, silently telling him he could go for his own cup of coffee, but he might lose a hand in the attempt.

235

"You've had quite a few phone calls this morning," she said. She stepped away from the counter and moved over to stand by the kitchen table. She wasn't going to sit, which told him there was still some tension in the air, but at least she got out of the way of the coffee machine.

He had spent way too many years around this woman and too many years as a cop to know he was probably analyzing things way too much. But he had to, right?

He nodded his gratitude at her for moving and grabbed his own cup. His usual coffee mug, *World's Greatest Dad*, seemed to be missing, so he had to grab just a standard cup.

"Oh?" he asked as he poured himself some.

The phone rang as in answer. She didn't even look at it, just hit the button and handed it to him. He set down his coffee, frustrated he hadn't had a chance to take a sip first.

"Hello?"

"Hey, Rob."

It was a soft-spoken voice he recognized, but couldn't quite place.

"Hey," he finally said, pushing past his ignorance.

"I need to talk to you. Can you meet me at the café in an hour?"

"Sure."

He didn't have to ask which café. In Standard, there was only one diner, one fast food place, and two gas stations. The gas stations were separated…one was the "truck stop" and the other was the "gas station". Rob had learned that name brands and recognition mattered little in this town, unless you were talking about bars and churches. Churches were known by denomination, but bars were important. Everyone knew the bars by name.

He never remembered whom he was talking to before he heard the click and the line went dead. He would just have to show up at the café to find out.

236

He set down the phone and started making his coffee. Now it was Robyn's turn to be curious.

"Who was that?" she asked.

Rob shrugged. "Not sure." He turned toward her. "So I have messages?"

She nodded. "Don't worry about driving sewage anymore."

"Shit!"

"Nope. Not anymore." She smirked as he looked at her, the horror of losing their primary source of income evident on his face. "Mark says he needs to find a more reliable driver. He's covering again today and he wasn't too happy about it."

"I bet."

"Also, the county guys called. You need to call them back, and Father William wants you to stop by later."

"Great. He probably wants to pray with me to help find the missing children."

He wasn't sure when she had crossed the room…until he felt the smack on the back of his head. It wasn't anything hard. Just a playful little whack that reminded him she hated when he joked about a man of God. He couldn't help but laugh as he turned and brought the coffee up to his lips.

"Robert Chase Alletto, you need to watch that tongue."

"Yes, ma'am," he said playfully.

Over the past few years, Robyn had gotten more and more religious. She had always been spiritual, but ever since the strange shit that happened, she was more into it. Rob hoped he didn't lose her to it. He just couldn't ever see himself being that devoted. Pastor Thomas was a nice guy and was friendly to Rob, but he could just never fully grasp everything in the Bible. There were too many names and, other than the story about Jesus, it was too hard to follow.

He had that flash of bare breasts in his face again.

237

His coffee spurted back up through his nose. Coughing, he bent over, the cup falling from his hand, crashing to the floor.

Robyn rushed over and started pounding on his back. "You okay?"

"Wrong tube," he gasped out, pushing down the images.

"That's not what I mean, Rob."

He cleared his throat. It still burned, but he was able to push the choking feeling away. He looked into those beautiful eyes he used to just gaze into when they were head over heels for each other. He saw her concern.

"I'm fine."

"Really?"

She didn't believe him, but that was okay. He didn't believe himself. Right now, he wasn't sure he felt anything. He should be concerned about those missing kids, and now there was a dead body. Just because Jake was found once didn't mean he would be found the next time…

He felt lightheaded, like he wasn't getting enough air. He needed to breathe, get the coffee out of his lungs. His head swam as too many thoughts flooded through him. He coughed some more, trying to expel the rest of the liquid.

Then the tears came. He pushed them away, swiping at them with his hand. It was as if the pressure he had felt before faded, none of it seeming to matter anymore. That was what he told himself anyway, but tears kept slipping from him. He wasn't sure if they were for Jake, the missing kids, or his former boss. On the surface, he felt nothing, which was the problem.

So… Maybe he wasn't okay.

Maybe it had something to do with Jake's disappearance. When Rob thought he had lost him, everything changed. He had felt something so much worse than he ever thought possible. There was a part of him that felt like it had been ripped out, and this nothingness had pulled him to want nothing more than to get his son back.

After he found him, he was so relieved, nothing else mattered. He was home with his wife and son. He never wanted any of them to ever leave again. They were home, they were safe, and he was there to protect them.

It was a dream he wished could be possible. Why did what he want always conflict with actual life's demands?

Robyn broke into his thoughts. "I got a call from Sarah."

"Oh?"

"I had asked her if there was anything I could do at home, over the phone, so I wouldn't have to drive into the city."

"She called you or you called her?"

"I called her last week."

He nodded. Sarah was an old friend of Robyn's from school. They had both gone into counseling, but Robyn had given it up years ago. The stress had gotten to her. It wasn't an easy job, listening to people who often wanted to kill themselves, dealing with people's addictions. It was a job where you had to help people deal with the worst in their lives.

It had nearly pushed Robyn down a dark path. She had started drinking. It was just a little at first. It was easy to write off drinking one glass of wine a day, but it soon got worse. The glasses got larger, then it went from one glass to two.

Jake was only two, but her hours were flexible. Then she started not going in as much, sometimes having a glass of wine to take the edge off before work. At lunch, she'd have another.

Rob had seen what was happening, but didn't say anything. He had been happy when he got that nice little pay raise that allowed her to quit. Yeah, they would never get ahead, but it was better than watching her lose herself. He had tons of respect for anyone in that field, but the last thing he wanted was his wife fighting her own demons to deal with it.

"You called her? Everything okay?" Had Robyn started drinking again and he didn't notice? When he saw her brows crease at his meaning, he wished he had been more tactful. Whether or not it stung because it was true, he wasn't sure.

"Yeah... No... It was just... " She paused, turning away to pour herself another cup of coffee, not wanting to face him. "You're not a truck driver. You can't go on doing that. You're a cop, and will always be a cop. You know the man in you won't allow you to do what they need to do to make ends meet past the season."

Rob knew what she was talking about. While the other drivers he had worked with tried to stay quiet around him, knowing he was a cop, there were others he came into contact with who didn't know what his other job was. Once the sewage contract was up, the stuff they had to do to survive was not legal. It was a small company using paper logs, which were easy to fake. Robyn knew Rob would never put himself in danger of risking the job he loved by forging a legal document.

"So I asked Sarah if there were any counseling jobs she knew about that I could do at home."

"And?"

"There's a late-night substance abuse hotline that can route the calls here. It doesn't pay much, but I would be the supervisor, listening in randomly and helping people through tough, sticky situations."

He could feel that tightening of his chest. He didn't want her doing that again. There had to be some other way.

When the phone rang, they both looked at it, neither of them moving. Finally, with an audible sigh, she leaned forward and grabbed it, holding it out to him.

"We need the money," she said softly.

"Not that badly."

"Yes, we do..."

He slowly took the phone from her and pressed to answer it, bringing it to his ear as he watched her face take on a pained expression.

"And I think you need counseling."

"Wait... What?"

She didn't answer as she turned, walking into the living room.

They needed counseling? Was their marriage hitting that point? How could he not have seen it? Or was he the reason for it? He knew she was upset with him, but that was just from last night. Sure, he shouldn't have put his son in that position, but how could she jump right to thinking they needed counseling?

Damn woman. Why did she run off? We need to talk about this shit.

"Hello?"

He heard a voice in the background.

"Hello?" he said again, plugging his other ear as he walked into the next room.

"Officer Alletto?"

"Yes. Who's this?"

"This is Trooper Jim Wieland. I'm at the crime scene and wanted to know how soon you can be here?"

"Well, I'm just getting up and moving. Is it urgent?"

"Oh, no. I just wanted to give you an update and see if you may have some other details for the investigation. I'm assuming you still want to be part of it."

"I figured the state would take over now that it's been upgraded to a homicide investigation."

"It is, but you know this town better than we do, and we would like to work with you rather than push you aside."

"No problem. I have a meeting, but can be there in a little over an hour."

"That sounds good. With any luck, we'll have an ID on the second body by then."

241

Wait… What? What second body? Had they found the missing boy? Could this all be tied up and they just needed to find the sick bastard who did it now? Strange how if they did find the boy dead, it would at least be something.

His stomach twisted in disgust at his morbid desire for any solution. He had wanted to find that boy alive, to bring him home and watch his mother gave him a bear hug that he'd feel for the rest of his life.

He heard the trooper talking to someone in the background. The man probably hadn't even noticed Rob's silence.

"Second body?" he asked.

The officer finished giving an order to someone, then came back on the phone. "Yeah. We found a second body. They are bringing it up now and will get it to the coroner. I should know more by the time you get here."

"I'll be right up."

"No, do your meeting. It'll take some time. It can wait. I had heard you had a day job, that you're only part-time, and wanted to make sure you were around."

"Yeah, no problem."

"Okay. See you in an hour."

Rob hung up, shaking his head. The state wanted to keep him in the loop and wanted his help? Yeah, that was complete bullshit. He was a suspect, which didn't surprise him. He was still relatively new to the area, he had money troubles, and he was only a part-time cop who needed a full-time paycheck. Rob admitted that he really did make a good suspect. In addition, since the trooper had done his research, he knew he was moonlighting on another job and had an excuse to get out of town. The trooper wanted to make sure Rob wouldn't be out of town so if they did find anything else, they could quickly come grab him.

That pain in his stomach got worse, feeling like the acid itched to burn its way up his throat and out of his body.

"Robyn?" he called out.

"Yeah?" she answered from her little room. It was probably meant to be a third bedroom or a home office, but they had converted it so she had her little creative nook to do her Etsy crafts.

He knocked and entered. She sat at her desk, hunched over, her hands holding tweezers as she worked on something delicate. He waited. When she finished, she eased back in the chair and looked up at him.

"You were saying something about counseling?" he asked. He had a hard time recognizing his own voice. It was soft, not the voice of authority he was used to hearing. It sounded almost delicate, like the craft she was working on.

"Yes..." She set down the tweezers. "Rob, I know you've been through a lot. I also know the symptoms. How you twitch, sometimes stare off, your nightmares, how you have to fight from going off the handle sometimes. I see you fighting with it, but it's getting worse..." She bit her lip and looked down, avoiding his eyes. "Rob...I think you have PTSD. I think you need to go to a counselor and get some help. I mean, think of everything you've been through, all the crazy stuff that has happened." She started to rush, getting it all out. "No one should ever have to see that many people die, and no one is blaming you." She reached out as she saw him falling back against the wall, his shoulders tense. "You've been through a lot. I think you need help."

He stood there, stunned, not sure if he were holding up the wall or vice versa. He just stayed there, seeming to look past her.

"Rob, are you okay?"

He blinked and seemed like he looked at her, but she still wasn't sure. His eyes looked empty.

"Yeah, I'm fine." He blinked again, seeming to pull himself together.

She wanted *him* to go see a doctor? There was something wrong with *him* and *he* needed to be fixed? *He*

243

was the problem? He didn't agree with that. He had no issue if she said they both needed counseling, but he was not going to go to some head shrink. There was nothing wrong with him.

"I'm fine. I don't need to go to a doctor."

They continued to look at each other. He looked away first, but she didn't feel like she had won. It felt more like a loss as he walked out, not saying anything more to her. When she heard the sound of the keys being lifted out of the bowl and the front door opening, she knew she had definitely not won.

Was it wrong to be worried about him? He'd been through so much. They all had. She just wished he could sleep through the night without kicking her, then there were times she'd wake up and find him just standing in the hall. He hadn't started sleepwalking before last year, but since everything happened, she'd sometimes find him standing there, a blank expression on his face.

He was going to snap if he didn't get some help soon. That had been the reason she had called Sarah in the first place. She needed to find a way to get him to someone before it was too late. The job had just happened.

The door slammed shut, startling her, rattling the windows. It had been so long after he had opened it, she knew he must have just stood in the doorway for a while.

He needed help before the anger she knew seethed just under the surface finally boiled over.

CHAPTER 23

Trooper Jim Weiland tossed his cell phone on the front seat of his squad car and looked at the police officers and forensics team working around him. He had been on the scene for more than a few hours, was already disgusted by the local swill they called coffee, and was frustrated he had to play nice with the one person he felt was his best suspect in the homicide of a police officer.

So Officer Alletto would make him wait an hour. That was fine. Maybe they would have some physical evidence by then, his questioning becoming more formal than the little dance he had to play now. Jim didn't believe the man had used his son to find the body. Maybe the kid's friends found it, and Alletto had to use his son for a cover. Convenient, although he was sure Alletto would have been happier had the body never been found.

The lead medical examiner looked over at him. Samantha Palmer was on the scene before he had gotten there and was able to get many of the pieces out of the old mineshaft, checking and tagging each one as she had. He arrived to see human body parts laid out on a long sheet, bagged, tagged, and positioned to identify the different elements. She still needed to find the right foot and the body's midsection. He had helped her find, well…the insides of the midsection. Before he had to walk away, he found some of the intestines and what looked like it had once been the victim's stomach.

That morning was the first time he had ever come close to vomiting on a crime scene. He had made it to the road before the bacon and eggs erupted onto the asphalt. When he had looked around, he saw he had not been the only one. There were various splatter marks along the side of the road.

He walked over to her, feeling for the woman. It couldn't be easy to work her way through this. This was going to stay in all their nightmares for years to come.

"Find the rest of him yet?"

"Not yet. They're probably farther down the shaft."

He nodded, finding that he was having a hard time looking at her. He kept looking off toward the woods. He couldn't shake that nagging feeling they were being watched. The gloomy day and the chill in the air didn't help.

He was sure half the town had heard by now, so there were probably gawkers in the woods watching them.

"Have you sent off the second body?"

Out of the corner of his eye, he saw her shake her head. He looked at her.

"No, we haven't gotten it up yet. The shaft isn't easy to navigate. They're setting up a lift now, so we should have it up in less than a half-hour. Hanson was just about to go down. I just wanted to make sure there wasn't anything else you needed."

"Okay. Just let me know when we have that body off and if it's one of the two missing kids."

Let me know so I can drop that on Alletto. Just what had the chief caught him doing with that kid that made him kill them both? Or had he been killing the chief and the kids saw him? Yes, I can see how that makes more sense. You finally get the permanent position by getting rid of your boss, eh, Alletto? He's old, a widower, no one will miss him. Just get rid of him and move on. The kids must have been playing around up here, saw you, and you did what with them? Did you just kill them? It's hard to

247

say what dirty thoughts went through sick minds nowadays.

He watched as she walked away. She seemed like a good kid, a good worker. She wasn't Eddie, whom he had dealt with a few times before, but that might be a good thing. Eddie never filled him with too much confidence. There hadn't been any mistakes yet, but Jim wasn't sure if the mistakes were there and nobody knew about them. He'd seen Palmer around occasionally, glad to get the chance to work with someone new.

It was also nice to admire her ass as she headed away from him. She must workout quite a bit. Her tush had a nice shape to it.

As she disappeared into the trees, he turned away, his lip curving up in that little smirk he loved to flash the ladies on a Friday night.

He really didn't have much to do until Alletto showed up. It was just a waiting game on forensics and body identification now. There were no witnesses for him to question, the closest person being interviewed when the boy had first gone missing. It wasn't so much that she claimed not to have seen anything, but according to the county deputy who talked to her, the old coot was nuts, blind as a bat, and could barely get out of the chair, let alone be outside and see something happening halfway down the block. The rest of the land around the slag pile was empty lots, so anything he would normally do at this point in the investigation would be a waste of time.

A car drove by slowly. Two kids, both teenagers, stared at him as they inched past. He watched them, then turned away when he saw they turned into the Taylor's driveway. Probably more people who wanted to give her their condolences. Jim was sure news had gotten around that they had found a body. No one knew it was the chief yet, so people probably assumed it was the boy.

Was that a good or bad thing? Which would be worse? Not knowing if your son were dead, or not knowing what happened to him or where he was? He'd never had children, so he would never know.

He decided to make his way back up to the mineshaft. He doubted there would be much physical evidence, but you never knew. Sure, Alletto was a cop from the city, so he had a decent background, but that was just it. He was a city boy, so he might have overlooked something in the woods. It would be hard to identify something in such a popular area. There was so much garbage scattered throughout the woods, tagging something that might be involved with the crime would be nearly impossible. At this point, though, it was better than nothing.

Besides, he wouldn't mind watching Palmer's ass end as she bent over to collect evidence. Since he just so happened to forget to bring any evidence bags, he'd have to ask her to pick it up for him. He'd need to make sure to find as much evidence as he could.

* * * *

Rob wasn't sure which had taken longer…the drive to the café or sitting in his car once he got there, trying to calm down. He wished the drive had been longer because he still heard Robyn's voice ringing through his ears. Just what in the hell did she even know, thinking and feeling he needed counseling?

When he was a cop in Chicago, he used to have to deal with many sick and deranged individuals. Each night, every call had its own fun story behind it. Of course, it was only fun now that they were all in the past, but at the time…

Such as when he stared down the barrel of a service revolver, the man taking it from another officer…naked. The man had been streaking when the rookie had chased him down. He was certifiable, but Rob listened as he rambled on about how his clothes had come alive and tried to eat him.

249

No, Rob didn't need counseling. Men like *that* needed it. Rob just had shit he had to deal with. There was no need for him to go to some crack just so she could tell him how messed up shit was. Besides, there was no way the doc would believe half the crap he'd been through. He'd start talking about the military cover-up, how he'd been locked away in quarantine for six weeks, or about that thing possessing people two years ago. Yeah, he'd find himself in a padded room.

His knuckles white from gripping the steering wheel, he sat for nearly fifteen minutes in the parking stall on the side street a half-block from the café. It had only taken him five minutes to drive there. When he first pulled in, he turned the car off. It had now started getting cold in the unheated vehicle.

He had to let it go.

So why couldn't he? He felt himself giving in to the frustration, wanting to just close his eyes and slam his head against the steering wheel. Instead, he found himself reaching for the handle, opening the door.

"Okay," he breathed out, trying to convince himself.

He was almost to the small café before he realized he had left the house without a jacket. He barely noticed the cold air, pushing it out of his mind. If he didn't think about it, it didn't exist.

He went into the building, the sudden rush of hot air suffocating him. He scanned the room. There were what he guessed to be the usual patrons…the older senior citizens brigade who sat at various tables. The café was what anyone would expect. It had a long counter made with that cheap fake wood and marble topper. Along the other side of the place were booths, brown leather seats with white tables. The walls were wood paneling, which had to be the cheapest option whenever anyone remodeled. It was meant to make the place look quaint, but had the opposite, trailer park feel.

The place smelled of grease. He felt like when he placed his order, it would be covered in it with more on the side. He had no regrets about never having gone in there because he didn't feel like he was missing much.

Sitting in one of the booths halfway down was a very kind-looking elderly man, gray hair covering his head, a large mustache making his mouth disappear. It seemed like something from a time long ago, and the man had somehow never changed it. He wore large, thick glasses that seemed to cover most his face and sat on top of his large nose. For all of this, the man looked like he was really short and sitting in an oversized booth, like a child sitting alone. To the side of him sat a large dog. It was a very odd site, but Rob had a feeling this was the man he was there to meet. He waved Rob over.

Rob walked up to the booth, holding out his hand. "Hi. I'm Rob Alletto."

The man stood, barely coming up past Rob's stomach. He took the offered hand, then motioned for him to sit.

"Hey. Thanks for meeting me," the man said, sitting across from him. Rob knew he recognized him from somewhere, but the man didn't introduce himself, acting like Rob should already know who he was.

"No problem. So, what's this about?"

"Well, I suppose you've heard about Chief Winston passing away."

That's putting it mildly, Rob thought, shifting in his seat.

He did not want to be in a situation where he was pressured to give out information. While the man didn't look like it, there was always the chance he was a reporter. Even if it were just for the small paper that came out once a month, him saying anything would still get out to others. If it didn't go into the local paper, a reporter could still send it up to the larger towns, getting it into their daily circulation.

"That's one way to put it," he finally responded.

251

"Well, I know it's soon and all, but we would like to offer you his job on a temporary basis."

Rob sat back, surprised. "We?"

"Me and the city council."

It suddenly clicked where Rob had seen the man. He couldn't quite remember the name, though. He tried picturing the signs he'd seen around town. He knew it started with an "A". *A...A...A.C.* He was sure those were his initials. He would have to play along, but he now knew this man was the mayor.

"Well, isn't there some sort of election?"

"There will be one, but Winston had another year on his term. We don't feel it would be a good time to try and do a special election, so we want you to take his place...for now."

Rob couldn't believe how cheery the man seemed. He was talking about someone who had just been killed. While there was a seriousness to him, the smile never truly left the corner of what Rob could see of his mouth. There was a twinkle in the man's eyes, too.

"Well, yeah, I can definitely fill the position."

"Good. Thank you."

Aidan. Aidan Coontz.

Rob didn't know why it suddenly came to him as the man looked away, staring off to look at the wall, as though he were looking past it to the town outside. It reminded Rob of the picture on the political sign. The man had this...out of place quality to him. However, his exaggerated kindness won over Rob's skeptical nature.

"Dan was a good man. He wasn't from around here and never really fit in, but I think that's what made him a good chief. Not meaning that you won't," Aidan said as he turned back to look at Rob, his cheeks flushing. "I mean, you have a family, but you're not from here... Oh, what do I mean?"

"Hey, hun. Can I get your order?"

Rob was glad for the distraction. He turned and saw the waitress was a younger woman with short dark hair and a pleasant smile. She wasn't one of those overly thin women who seemed to be everywhere, but more of a classic, homely shape. He couldn't help but return her smile.

"I'm not sure I'm staying, I have another meeting to get to in a few minutes."

"Oh, you got time," the mayor said, then looked at the waitress. "He'll just take a chicken and egg sandwich, wrapped up to go. Make sure to put it on the city's dime." He winked at Rob. He didn't want to correct him that Standard was nice, but it was barely large enough to even be considered a town, let alone a city.

When the waitress walked away, Rob realized she hadn't written anything down. Then he saw the sadness creep into the mayor's expression, the twinkle fading a little in those eyes as he turned to look at Rob.

"I'm sorry. That was Dan's usual. You know, I barely knew the man. I've only been mayor for a little under a year and had never talked to him before that. Still, he was a fixture in this town." A sad smile spread out from under the long mustache. "Be a good man, will you?"

Rob nodded, not really knowing what to say. "I try to be."

"I guess that's all we can ask."

CHAPTER 24

It felt like Rob had been in there far longer than he had, but he was glad to be back out in the cool air. There hadn't been anything wrong with it, but it just felt too cramped for him. Sure, he was used to a big city, bustling with life all around him, so cramped was a part of everyday life. But this was a different kind of cramped. People weren't crowding him. Life was. This small town he had come to hide in, to keep his family safe in, had started enveloping him, making him realize it wasn't as safe as he thought it would be.

At one point, it had felt like the walls around him were closing in and he had to take deep breaths to keep from getting up and rushing out of the restaurant. When his breakfast sandwich came, which he had never truly wanted to begin with, although he was hungry, he had hurried with his goodbyes.

Now he was back out in the cool morning air, holding the little bag the waitress had brought him. The flower shop was to his left, its open sign almost glowing in the morning gloom. It felt like his beacon in the storm. He turned, his feet taking a step in that direction, but there was still that part in him resisting going to see her.

He needed go to the slag pile. The café had been abuzz about all the police in town. The area was cordoned off as they investigated, not letting anyone up there, so everyone was full of curiosity. People had come over to their table to ask him questions; others talked so loudly, he could overhear their conversations. The slag pile was the center of attention. He should see what everyone was talking about. It wasn't like he didn't have the right to be there. The officer in charge wanted him there to ask him some questions.

He took another step, his car in the other direction. He had parked not too far from Father William's church, and he was more than a little curious as to what the priest had called him about this morning. Father William was a good man, having been there a time or two when Rob needed advice. He'd also helped him more than he would like to admit last year when all that stuff had gone on. He had been there when Rob got out of quarantine, helping him deal with the anger. He was always there for them. Rob really should repay that.

Rob knew he wasn't the easiest person to get along with. He wasn't one to be found at church on Sunday mornings, or evenings, or during the week, or any other time he could avoid it. To him, church often felt like going to the dentist. Something that was painful, something he'd like to try to avoid.

Rob didn't have anything against religion, or the Catholic faith for that matter. He had been raised on it. He had no issues with the ideals, but some of the rules seemed to be a little against what he felt was right. So while he respected the man, he felt like he would just celebrate his own beliefs in his own way. It was just a gut feeling, and he never wavered in his own feelings as to what was right.

Besides, Robyn had talked him into going to the non-denominational church on Main Street. Pastor Thomas was likeable enough, and the sermons were easier to sit through. Sometimes Rob even enjoyed it. He often felt uncomfortable going to one church while being friends with a man from another, but Father William never seemed to resent Rob for it. Oh, he made the occasional comment about how he would like to see Rob there on Sundays, but it was often said with a smile and a wink.

255

Rob hadn't realized it, but he had turned away from the flower shop when he started thinking about Father William. Hadn't even paid attention until he stood in front of the large cathedral doors to the massive gothic building. The woodwork was lavish in a way common to the faith.

Last time he had actually stepped into this building had been nearly two years ago. Since then, they only usually saw each other in passing or if the priest just randomly decided to visit their house. Last time Rob had been in there was when other people had been killed. It was strange. The only time he seemed to enter there was in times of great death. He pushed the negative thoughts away as he entered.

"Hello?" he said, listening to the echo.

"You're really going to just walk into a church and start yelling 'hello'?"

Rob spun and saw Father William standing behind him.

He was greeted with that warm smile he had come to expect on the priest's face. It radiated from his whole being. There was a twinkle that made his blue eyes sparkle, warming the room. Rob understood why so many in his congregation loved this man. He was still a newer member of the town, much like Rob, but he had been welcomed much faster. The town had embraced him, and it was hard to find anyone who could imagine the priest not being a part of the community.

Rob immediately found himself returning the younger man's smile. "I'm sorry, Father."

"You are forgiven." Father William motioned Rob over to the pew closest to them. "Besides, I called you. It was rude of me not to be sitting around, waiting. I mean, I should have just stood by the door all day, waiting for you to come in whenever you got here. How impolite for me to go outside and change the sign."

"Anything good?" Rob asked, glad for the chance to quickly get off the subject of how crass he could be.

"'Jesus was the first Avenger.'"

A smirk lifted Rob's mouth. "Really? Isn't that a little too…modern?"

"I know nothing of what you are talking about. I'm more surprised *you* know it."

"I have a son." The priest smiled as they both sat. "Every time I look out the window, I see him flying around the back yard, arms out, zooming off to fight some villain. Who knows who they all are."

"Well, it gets people into the seats."

"Thought the message was supposed to do that."

"Oh, the sermon is what gets them to leave."

"Well, someone woke up on the cynical side of the bed this morning."

"Well, we all have our dark days. When the world goes gray, it brings out the worst in us."

Rob looked around, finding it hard to keep looking into the man's eyes. He had asked him to come see him. It had better not just be about being at church on Sunday. This should have been put off until later. He really needed to get up to the coal dump.

Her luscious breasts, the round nipples, his tongue just touching the tip of one areola before he nibbled at it. He felt her heat against his, and he burned to pull her closer.

He had to shake his head. The images of her were getting stronger. He just wanted to grab and kiss her.

"Rob?"

"What?" He shook his head again, feeling as if he had to work to get his breathing back under control.

"You seemed to step away for a minute there."

"Yeah. Sorry about that."

"No problem. I called you here and there I go, babbling on again." He tapped his fingers along the back of the pew and turned so he wasn't meeting Rob's watchful eye. "I was hoping you would look into Pastor Amery's disappearance."

"What? Wait. I *did* get a call about that yesterday. There's a lot going on, but the state guys are involved, so it's being looked into."

"I understand," the priest said, letting his eyes wander. They seemed to just drift away, looking at the stained glass windows. Rob couldn't help but follow his gaze.

It was an interesting pane of glass. He was so used to the standard ones—either Jesus or Mary, bright inspirational panes, often looking up to the sky in worship. What Rob looked at now was much darker. He couldn't imagine what it would look like with the sun shining through it, but what he saw was a dark, nearly black pane at the base, varying layers of red flowing from what looked like a demon being eviscerated by an angel with a sword.

"He was a friend of mine, or I guess I should say I was his friend. He really didn't have many because he wasn't the easiest person to like."

Rob pulled his gaze away from the window to stare at the priest. He had that faraway look again to somewhere Rob couldn't see.

"He had many demons. Many, many demons in his soul. I think he might have been a good man once. I'd heard stories about how he and his childhood sweetheart were good for each other. Yes, I believe he was a good man. Once."

"Pastor Amery?"

Father William nodded and turned to look back at Rob, but he didn't look at Rob's eyes. He seemed to look at his chest.

"Do you believe in that?" He nodded at something.

Rob looked down to see the cross on his chest. This was becoming the most bizarre conversation he had ever had with the man. He was always boisterous and jolly. This melancholy man sitting in front of him, who seemed to be all over the place, bothered Rob.

"This?" Rob asked holding it up, looking at it for the first time in a while. The cross his grandmother had given him. One she had since she was a little girl. It was old, but nothing special. Just a simple cross. A cross that, even though he never went to church, he still wore.

"Yes."

"I guess so."

"You *guess* so?" the priest asked, the first sound of bitterness Rob had ever heard from the man in his voice. "That seems to be everyone's problem now, doesn't it? 'Guessing' just lets in the darkness. It grows and festers, gaining a foothold in even the most righteous of men."

Rob had not came here for a sermon, and he had been lectured at enough today. If he wanted to listen to more people badger him about what he needed, he would go back home so Robyn could drone on about how he needed counseling. He didn't need any of this…or any of them, if all they were going to do was hound him.

"I'm sorry, Father, but I really do need to be going." Rob started to stand. The man quickly reached out, putting his hand over Rob's on the back of the pew.

"Rob, do you know how to fight back the darkness, the evil?" Father William asked, finally meeting Rob's eyes. Those blue orbs glistened, burning into Rob. He sat back down.

"Belief in God?"

"'Thy rod and thy staff, they comfort me.' Do you think those words alone would stop a demon? Is it just like in *The Exorcist* where quoting scripture would push a demon from a host?"

"That never seemed to make sense to me. No, I don't see how scripture alone would. Scripture is just transcribed words from another language. How can it?"

The priest nodded. "It's not the words that have the power. It's the belief. You don't need to believe in God, but you do need to have faith and believe in the good and the power of the light. Do you understand me?"

Rob shook his head, feeling it throb a little. He wasn't able to follow what the young priest was saying, and he really wanted to get out of there, finding himself unable to move.

"Faith is an army." Father William reached out and touched Rob's cross, holding it between his fingers. "This is a symbol of faith. Believe in it, and the army of angels are with you."

"And God?"

"If you wish."

"You don't seem to put much stock in the big man. I've heard you talk more about the army of angels, but you seem to shy away from the man upstairs."

Father William let a little smile crease his lips as he let go of the cross. When it fell back to Rob's chest, it seemed to burn with a flaming cold so hot, Rob thought it was going to sear into his skin. He reached for it when he heard the priest stand.

"Belief can move mountains. Words just help us channel that belief. Remember that. Symbols and words."

Rob grabbed the cross, but it had stopped burning. He lifted it, but didn't see any marks, nor any damage to his shirt. He looked back up to see that the priest had stopped in the aisle, looking down at him.

"Have you noticed the darkness outside?" Father William asked, looking out the window again.

"It's a little gloomy. Fall's easing in."

"Really? Have you seen any clouds?"

"Well, of course there are clouds."

"Are there?"

"Well, yeah."

Father William nodded and turned away.

Rob sat there, not sure what he should do. That had to have been the oddest conversation he ever had. God, but no God...believe in faith...an army was behind him. What the hell was the man talking about? The priest wasn't making any sense.

Why didn't these religious types just come out and say what they wanted to say? Why all the damn games? He could have just said, "Hey, Rob, there's this thing going on and, well...you need to believe in this to do what you need to do."

And why did Rob even toy with the possibility that something else was going on, other than just some kids playing a prank? Why? Because it felt like things like this happened more and more in his corner of the world, and that damn priest always seemed to know something about it.

Someday, Rob was going to have to ask him about it. Someday...

"'Yea, though I walk through the valley of the shadow of death, I will fear no evil, for You are with me, Your rod and Your staff, they comfort me.'" The priest stood at the front of the church, his arms outstretched, as though giving a sermon to a full congregation. "'Who shall ascend the hill of the Lord? And who shall stand in His holy place? He who has clean hands and a pure heart, who does not lift up his soul to what is false and does not swear deceitfully. He will receive blessings from the Lord and righteousness from the God of his salvation.'" The voice boomed through the room, echoing off the walls, but the priest's eyes locked on his. For a moment, Rob couldn't look away.

Then the moment passed and Rob found himself standing back at his car. He had no memory of leaving, the time lost. There was something the priest had said, something more about what was going on, but it was lost.

It was all happening again. There was more than just a bunch of missing kids. He knew that now.

He looked up to the gray sky, but couldn't see any clouds. The dullness stretched far to the horizon without any signs of life or color.

* * * *

Father William watched Rob leave, feeling that he should have said more. He always walked that fine line, always afraid of slipping and saying more than he should. How did he know what was too much? What would violate the rules and banish him from this plane? It was a juggling act, and he felt like he was constantly on the verge of losing his balls.

He chuckled, the potty humor not escaping him, as he stepped back into the cathedral. It worried him. That thing last night hadn't been what he thought was spreading through town. When he had felt it, he felt the darkness upon it, as well as the hunger pulling at him. The thing was very old and must have slept for a long time, but what had awakened it? Why now? Why, when others plagued his thoughts, did he have to worry about this dark beast.

He didn't like it, knowing it was an unnatural distraction meant to keep him from preparing Rob. Rob was the guardian and had to be ready. Father William was sure the time was coming. He couldn't foresee it, but he could feel the powers building.

This was all wrong. What if Rob couldn't defeat this darkness? It wasn't like the other. This was darker, and he could feel how it twisted things.

Father William walked up to the bowl of water he often used to bless followers during his services. He had blessed it that morning, as he did every day, but as he neared it, he could hear the water boiling, bubbling, steaming, shaking with the ferocity of an earthquake. It rattled in its fastenings until it broke free and crashed to the floor, the water spraying out across the wood.

He watched as it darkened and slipped into the floorboards.

What did this mean? Did he have any power against this thing?

No... To think that would be questioning him, questioning his own faith. Where would they be then?

They would defeat this evil. The darkness came for them, he felt it, but they could defeat it. They had to.

But how many times do they have to fight? The dark would just keep coming for them. Its reach had touched so many, it would only take them failing once to doom them all.

He picked up the bowl, the silver ice-cold to his touch, and placed it back in the font that normally held it secure. He would have to refill it and bless it again.

The darkness was here, but what else was in their future? He feared something coming. Something that would be far more than Rob could handle alone.

CHAPTER 25

"Come on, Alletto. It's been well over an hour," Weiland grumbled, looking at his watch. The large round display kept ticking as he leaned against his squad car. Alletto wasn't there yet, and while he wanted to question the son of a bitch, he also didn't have anything new to spring on him. Palmer had been silent for the last thirty minutes, and the lab techs were still looking for evidence down in the hole. So far, nothing else had been found.

He was tired of standing around. He wanted someone to drill, to question. There was too much of this waiting around shit. It was part of the game, but this was always the hardest part. He knew there were people out there he needed to talk to, but he had to wait.

He wasn't known for being a patient man. *Calm down. You're always rushing to anger.* That was what his ex-wife would always say. That might be the case, but he believed his rush to anger was one of his best attributes. *Scare the hell out of someone because then they are afraid you're going to kick the shit out of them.* It got results when asking questions.

Well, it seemed like Alletto stood him up. Maybe the sick bastard actually ran. Weiland hadn't taken him for a runner, and he sure as hell didn't think he had showed his hand when talking to him. Maybe Alletto was just paranoid, which he probably had every right to be. Still,

Weiland kicked himself for not just driving over there to his house to talk to him.

Damn, he hated waiting.

"Palmer, anything yet?" he said into the little two-way radio he held, the grip damp from sweat, even in the cool morning.

Nothing. No reply. When had he heard from her last? A half-hour ago, he had asked her for an update, and she had sounded curt when answering. Nothing since then, but it wasn't like he would expect it.

"Palmer, you find anything down there yet, or are you just digging another hole to China?"

He started up the hill. Around him, it seemed to be getting darker, the woods growing denser. He couldn't help but shiver as the closer he moved to the opening in the ground, the more the temperature dropped.

Where were all the techs? There had been three or four of them there earlier. Not all of them were supposed to go down there. Two should have been monitoring from up above and looking for evidence. While he was sure most of the surrounding area had been picked clean, they still should have been there to monitor in case anything happened below.

"Palmer?" he asked, taking another step toward the pit.

* * * *

David was not sure what he was about to walk into, but he knew he wasn't looking forward to it. Both he and Ally had been out all night...her not wanting to go home, and him just enjoying having her back with him. He had forgotten how good it felt to be around her. He had missed her, but missing a particular feeling is an abstract. You never truly know how much you miss something until you have it back.

Her head cradled in his arms, the hours had just flown by as they sat there quietly, time just being erased

265

outside of their existence. The world had faded away, the pain they had both felt disappearing while they were together.

But when the sun came up, time woke them out of their interlocked bodies. They had both been fully clothed. There were too many emotions and too much history for anything more to happen. They had just held each other for comfort.

Neither of them wanted to go back. They had tried the night before, but couldn't bring themselves to do it. They had made it halfway back to town before she looked at him. He saw her eyes, her fresh tears, and nodded. They had turned on the next back road.

He wasn't sure how many roads they had gone down, how many twists and turns he had taken. He wasn't even sure where they were half the time. He just kept driving, thankful he had filled up earlier that day. The night just let them wander, avoiding what they didn't want to return to.

David wasn't sure at what point he had grown so tired, he needed to pull off. He didn't know where they were at the time. It wasn't until the sun was up and he looked around that he saw they were in a cemetery. At least it was one he knew and could find his way home from.

But they still didn't want to go, so he told her he'd take her to breakfast, finding a little diner in the country. Four Corners, a little auspicious place he had to guess barely stayed open as the two highways that converged there were nearly abandoned, lost to the interstate.

When they couldn't put it off anymore, he brought her home. They stood there, staring at the front door of the house. Neither of them moved to get any closer than the start of the sidewalk. She didn't want to see her mother, he didn't want to get a lecture for keeping Ally out all night. No matter what, going into the house was not going to be pleasant.

"She never called?"

Ally pulled out her phone and showed him the blank screen. "Died, no charger."

He vaguely remembered her asking him if he had a charger for it sometime during the night, but she had the latest model, and his was a couple years older. The chargers weren't the same.

That meant they had no way of knowing if there was news about her brother. If he thought about it, though, he would have guessed that if they had found him, there would be a bunch of people at the house. It was odd that there hadn't been more people out looking. All they had seen on their drive through town had been that unfamiliar cop standing at the edge of the coal dump path. Where had Officer Alletto gone? Why hadn't they seen him there?

When Ally took a step toward the house, David quickly moved to follow, staying a step behind her. He wasn't sure if she wanted to do this alone. If she did, he would stay outside, but close enough to go in if she wanted.

They reached the front door, Ally taking in a deep, long breath.

"It'll be okay," David heard himself say, knowing she wouldn't believe him. He didn't even believe it himself. Sometimes you just had to say something stupid to fill the silence. You didn't have to believe it, but the words just had the power to make it better.

She didn't turn to look back at him, but he saw the shifting of her shoulders, the almost unnoticeable drop to them. She had relaxed, even if it was just a little.

She opened the door and took a step in. David made a move to follow her, but stopped when she raised her hand, motioning for him to wait. He took a step back, feeling as though he didn't only need to wait, but to get out of the line of sight. He knew they were probably going to need some space, and Ally wanted him to stay out there until she needed him.

And he stayed there, listening, looking around. Everything seemed so quiet...until he heard Ally's scream.

* * * *

Rob's feet had a mind of their own. They carried him away, his mind lost in thought, not paying any attention to the world around him. As he walked, he couldn't help but remember what the good Father had told him. There was definitely something off about the man.

Rob had noticed it years ago when the priest had followed him into that house. Wait... Hadn't *he* been the one to suggest Rob go in there? It had, hadn't it. Rob never would have known any of that was happening. He might not have been able to stop it had Father William not come to talk to him.

So just what did the Father have to do with all of this? There had to be things Rob wasn't being told, but he didn't think the Father was behind any of it. He should be questioning the man, but there was something telling Rob to trust him.

He thought he should mention it to that state trooper when he saw him. Rob wasn't sure how long it had been since he had talked to the man, but he'd promised him an hour, knowing it was long past that.

He hurried up a couple steps and stopped at the top, his hand resting on the metal railing. Where was he? He looked around to see he stood in front of the flower shop. Next to it was the old shop, the dirty window representing how long the place had been part of the town. It was a stark contrast to the new flower shop—its window shiny, the bright pink lettering of the store's name across it, the glowing fluorescent light of the open sign.

It was odd how dark the shop was beyond the window. He hadn't remembered the place having tinted glass, but it was dark enough that he could only make out vague shapes inside the store.

What was he doing there? He should be going to see the trooper. He was waiting, and what if they had found something?

He couldn't pull his hand away from the door. He held the cool handle firmly, but didn't let go. He turned it slowly, his mind continuing to tell him he needed to get out of there. The hair on the back of his neck stood up. Something about this wasn't right. He didn't know why he was there, didn't really feel the desire to go in, but he struggled with some pull.

There was a click, the door pushing in ever so slightly.

"There is a darkness that pulls you. You need to find your way to turn from it."

He heard the priest's voice in his head. He tried to remember when Father William had told him that because he couldn't recall hearing it.

The door swung open. Inside the shop, all he could see was darkness, a void where the light from outside faded into nothing.

269

CHAPTER 26

David ran into the house, following the fading echo of Ally's scream. He didn't know what to expect or what he would find. The scream wasn't a call for help, but that of startled surprise. It was short, seeming to be cut off, but was just enough that he knew she needed him. He forced himself to move faster when he heard the next scream...one of fear.

He rushed in and stopped briefly in the front room. Something was off. He could feel it. The last he had seen her, Ally was going into the living room. He shook off the raised hairs on the back of his neck, paying little attention to the room, quickly turning to where he expected to find Ally. He stopped...

He shivered, not sure if it was because of what he saw or the sudden temperature change in the room. There was nothing there. No furniture, no light, nothing. There was the wide door frame, but past it was just nothing. It was black. There was no room, no light, the house didn't open up to the outside. There was just nothing, and in the center of it was Ally, suspended in the nothingness.

David took a step back, then another, not stopping until he bumped against the corner of the dining table, hitting it hard enough that he heard the glass centerpiece wobble, something on the other end of the table crashing to the floor. He didn't turn to look, his eyes transfixed on her.

"Ally?"

Her eyes met his. He could see her calling out to him, her mouth moving soundlessly. Her eyes were wide, the shock transparent as she dangled there. It reminded him of a marionette Ally had once given him that he hung from the blinds in his room. She was there, but as her arms swayed, it was clear she wasn't the one moving them. He could see the terror in her eyes as she tried to look to see what had her. Her head never moved, only her eyes darting back and forth, then focusing back on him.

She struggled. He could tell by the tension on her face that she was trying to move. He didn't know if she could breathe, but as he saw more in the dim light, he noticed something. There was a black mist moving around her face. Tendrils of the dark smoke flowed in and out of her mouth, and he saw them twirling around her elbows, holding her there. She looked so pale.

She looked terrified.

And he just stood there, doing nothing. What could he do? What the hell was that? How could he do something when he didn't even know what the hell that was? It was smoke. How do you fight smoke? You couldn't. You could fight the fire, but smoke was a presence that would kill quickly if you were exposed to too much.

And it just kept flowing in and out of her. Covering her mouth and nose, it gagged her, keeping her away from him.

Where there's smoke, there's fire... If he was seeing smoke, there must be a fire nearby. Maybe it was on the other side of the room, but he just couldn't see it.

There wasn't anything visible. Wait... It was getting darker, the tendrils flowing around her getting wider. They grew thicker, parts of Ally completely disappearing from sight. If he didn't know any better, he would say she was walking away from him, backing closer to the invisible fire. That didn't make any sense. He could see she wasn't moving, but she got farther away

271

from him, disappearing into that dense fog growing around her.

He gulped, forcing down the lump in his throat as he stepped away from the table.

"Ally?" His voice was so quiet, he doubted she even heard it. With how the nothingness swirled around her head, he wasn't sure she could even hear him if he had screamed at her.

She wasn't moving, had given up trying to scream. He could see it in her face. She was pleading with her eyes...and saying goodbye. She seemed to be okay. Her chest rose and fell. All he had to do was get her away from...whatever it was.

She was fine. She was going to be fine. He just had to figure this out.

So now, Mr. Smarty-pants, graduating early, brainiac who thinks he is so much better than everyone else around town, figure this out. Come on, David. You always feel like you know everything. You should know this. What is this? How do you save your girlfriend from it?

She's not my girlfriend.

Really? Whatever this is has your girlfriend, but you're going to obsess over the term 'girlfriend'?

Focus. Focus. Come on, David. Pull it together.

He took another cautious step, then another, walking to the threshold. His skin bristled with the chill. The closer he got to the room, the more he felt it. Why was the room so cold? It felt like he stood in the doorway of a walk-in freezer, the soft caress of the icy fingers running down his warm skin.

Was there really nothing there? He thought maybe, just maybe, it was that dark in the room. Maybe the room was still there, but something made it hard to see what had her. That wasn't a comforting thought, either, but at least it didn't break any laws of physics. What he saw either bent the rules of light and refraction...or opened the door to a para-dimensional universe. It would be easier if it just bent the rules of light and there was something there he just couldn't see. It would be the lesser of two evils. Because if there was a rip into another universe, it opened the door to a whole new set of horror stories, and he had watched too many horror movies growing up. Next thing they knew, some creature would come out of the abyss. The last thing he wanted to face was an "old one" coming out of the dark, like out of the pages of a Lovecraft novel.

What was going to come out of it? Something had to be there. There wasn't any way it could be nothing. And what had Ally? Why did it just hold her there? Was she bait, trying to draw him in? An image flashed. He imagined a large spider hiding in wait just beyond the threshold. Ally was caught in its web as it watched him. He held his breath, trying to listen to it scurry in the dark. He had a sudden itch, feeling as if he turned around, he'd see it looming over him.

But why would it have to stand behind or above him? He stood at the point of nothing. What would stop something from coming out of that vast emptiness to pull him into it? What would it take? How nasty a thing could he imagine?

Why even imagine it?

Part of him wanted to close his eyes to focus on pushing away the images of new and various creatures that could be lurking out there, watching him. However, he knew if he closed his eyes, he would see them clearer. The things that would tear him apart or pull him in.

The worst he could imagine would be a creature grabbing him, taking him into that darkness to cocoon him, leaving him there for their queen to come feed on. Then he would have to suffer as he waited in torment.

He couldn't help but have the image of a spider again. There were so many types out there, some where the male cocooned their victims for the female. What a hideous fate. To be that offering, waiting, watching as other victims were brought, never knowing when it would

273

be your turn to be eaten. You would be helpless, listening to their screams as their flesh was ripped away.

He thought he felt a breeze tickle the back of his neck. Maybe it was his sixth sense that there was some kind of danger behind him. If he turned, would it eat him? If he didn't turn, would it just ignore him?

He didn't turn because he couldn't take his eyes off Ally. Their gazes locked. She watched him, pleading. Those large round orbs he could lose himself in begged him to do something, called out for his help.

He wasn't worried about himself anymore. Looking into her eyes took away all concern for his own well-being. He figured if there were something behind him, he'd see it in her eyes. He would have seen the terror, perhaps even motioning for him to turn around.

He raised his foot to take a step. If the room were just extremely dark, his foot would come down on the carpet. If there were nothing, the room gone, it would just continue downward, David barely having any time to shift his weight back to keep from falling forward. If there were a creature there, waiting, his foot was now outstretched, making it easy to pull him in. His breath caught in his throat as he slowly lowered his foot...

As it crossed into the darkness, the cold became an unbearable stinging sensation. It was colder than anything David had ever felt before. Even an ice pack on bare skin had nothing on the icy touch. He started to pull his foot back, keeping his weight shifted just right so he didn't fall into the frozen depths. Suddenly, a black tendril shot out, wrapping itself around his ankle. Its cold touch burned against his skin as the darkness grabbed him.

"Fu-" he heard himself scream, his foot being pulled. His weight thrown off, he fell back. The world around him spun as he tried to turn himself, reaching out for anything to grab. Everything was in motion...or was it just him falling?

The air rushed out of him as he landed with a grunt, but he didn't have time to lay there. He felt the cold touch strengthening its grip around his ankle, pulling him toward it. Whatever was in the dark, it was ready to take him. He reached out, feeling for the only thing his searching hands could find. He touched a chair leg, grabbing onto it. It was too light. He tried to hold on, but the darkness tugged him, the chair toppling over and falling out of reach. He used his knee to push himself up, again trying to find something heavy to grasp. He reached for the leg of the heavy table, falling short when he felt another tug pull him away.

Don't turn around. Oh god. Don't turn around.

He didn't want to see it. Whatever had him had to be something from nightmares. He knew if he turned to look, what was left of his sanity would be gone. If he wanted to get away and save Allison, he couldn't look.

Instead, David lashed out with his other leg, trying to kick back at whatever it was. He kicked and kicked, not sure if he were making contact with the thing, but he was certainly making contact with himself. It was definitely going to leave bruises.

He felt the cold rising up his leg and knew he was still being pulled back.

He lifted himself up, using his hands for leverage, and brought his foot under him to push off the floor. His leg was pulled behind him as he tried to pull it away. He jerked at it wildly, but nothing helped. It felt as if his leg were caught in a vice of ice, its grip unyielding.

"Please, God, whatever you need me to do, I'll do it. Just, please, help me," he prayed, probably for the first time in his life. Having not gone to church in years, the concept of calling out to the Lord felt alien to him. Why did he feel like he should now?

Why not now? If not now, when?

It suddenly let him go. He was in such a fight to get away, he hadn't expected the release and stumbled forward into the table. He hit his shoulder hard, feeling the sting. Wincing, he turned to look behind him. He didn't want to see what climbed out of the darkness after him, but he had to know. He had to know to stay sane.

He didn't see any monsters chasing him, which almost made it worse. Where it had him just moments before, he saw a small streak of sunlight filtering in from the open front door. He looked at it, then the door. It was the first time he realized just how dark it was outside, but through that darkness in the sky, he saw a single sliver of sun. It came through the front door and fell on the nothingness in the room. The darkness seemed to part for it, allowing him to see some of the living room floor. The dark smoldered around it, recoiling...

Then the light was gone, the darkness in the sky once again blocking out the direct sun.

He blinked at how sudden it disappeared, fighting the instinct to move closer to the darkness in the other room. Instead, he pulled himself up into a sitting position and brought his knees to his chest, wrapping his arms around his legs, fighting to get his breathing under control. Stars hovered at the corner of his vision. He hadn't realized just how out of breath he was or how hard he had fought to get away from the thing. Now he had to fight off the dizziness on the fringe of his awareness.

He looked up at Ally, still held there in the other room. She looked at him, concerned. She had just watched all that he had been through and hadn't even been able to warn him. He couldn't imagine how hard that had been for her. She probably felt like a prisoner in her own mind, watching, unable to even call out to warn him.

He needed to find a way to get her out of there. There had to be something he could do, some way to channel the light. That was its weakness, right? It had pulled away from him because of the sun, kind of like it hurt.

He didn't have any other options. He had to do something. Maybe if he could find a mirror or something and shine the sunlight from outside, it would back away and let her go. It would be like an ant in a magnifying glass, right? He just needed a large enough mirror, maybe two, finding a way to mount them.

He tried to stand, leaning against the table behind him. His legs felt like rubber and he wasn't sure if they'd give out. He wobbled, eventually able to step away and move closer to the darkness. He stopped when he looked into it, seeing Ally wasn't alone anymore.

At first, he didn't recognize the boy standing just behind her. It wasn't natural how he was so much shorter than she, yet still eye level. His feet were bare, his skin an ash gray, his clothes faded and ripped into tatters hanging loosely from him. He was a ghostly apparition.

Looking closer, David gasped. It was impossible. Michael had been missing for a year. Ally's younger brother, the one Ally and he played with while they hung out. The sweetest, most innocent child David had ever met was always clean and proper, quick to obey Wendy and Ally when they told him to do something.

He barely looked anything like the kid they would both laugh with as he ran around, playing some comic book hero flying around the yard. They would take him to the pool, David teaching Mikey how to swim.

David couldn't quite place everything that was different, but he didn't have time to anyway. One minute, Mikey was there next to Ally; the next, they were both gone. Only the darkness remained.

It took a while for his eyes to adjust to no longer seeing her there. *Pop*, her brother, whom everybody thought had been dead for over a year, stood there, then *pop*, they were both gone. It was now all just black. How did one describe that absolute darkness when there was always some light?

He found the courage to take a step toward it, stopping when he saw the darkness had crept out past the edge of the door, moving steadily. It wasn't fast, but he watched it as it slithered past an old stain on the carpet, one he remembered from when Ally had pushed him on her eighth birthday, spilling his Kool-Aid.

She had always been there for him, and vice versa. Now she was gone. The nothing had taken her. If he didn't get out of there, it would take him, too.

He desperately wanted to save her, but in that moment, he made a decision, one he wasn't sure he would ever be able to live with.

He had to get out of there.

He turned and rushed to the door, but a sharp-edged tendril shot past him and into the wall, blocking the path. Three more flew past him. The door was now blocked by bars of black mist. They didn't look solid, but he wasn't going to reach out to touch them. He could already feel cold emanating from them, making him back away.

The kitchen door wasn't too far away. He only needed to back up a few more feet. He was afraid to turn and run, not knowing what the mist could sense or see. If he didn't turn, maybe it wouldn't know he worked toward an escape. He just had to make it a little bit farther. The sun wasn't as bright as it should be outside, but he could still feel himself getting closer to the slightly brighter kitchen.

When he felt the cold behind him, he stopped. He didn't want to turn around, but knew he had to, the sudden chill pushing in on him like an arctic blast.

He turned. The kitchen was gone. Just like the living room, it disappeared into nothingness at the threshold, only black remaining where the room had once been.

The pit of his stomach turned to stone and ached with sudden pain. This wasn't happening. What was he supposed to do now? The front door and window were blocked, the kitchen not there. Where was he supposed to go? There had to be a way out. He had to have missed something. People just didn't get sucked into nothing.

But that wasn't true. People went missing all the time. Ally's brothers had gone missing, and now she was, too. Then there were the thousands of people who went missing every day. He knew that, also knowing he had no way out. He wasn't in his quiet life anymore. This wasn't a movie. There wasn't going to be some hero rescuing him. He was going to die here.

Was it death, though? This thing… Was it killing them? Was everyone really dead? It was so cold… Maybe they were frozen, waiting for something to devour them.

He didn't know if the shiver running down his spine was from the cold inching closer or from thinking about everyone cocooned in some kind of dark cave.

Cave…

Why did he think they were in a cave? It would make sense, but there weren't any caves around there. There were the mineshafts up on the coal dump, but most of those were old wives' tales grandparents told kids to keep them from playing up there. "Don't play up there, you'll fall down into a mineshaft" and all that.

But isn't that exactly where Bobby had liked to hang out? By the entrance to one shaft? As far as they knew, it was the only one up there. It was also covered by that heavy grate and fastened into place. It was so heavy, no one had ever been able to lift it.

How in the hell is thinking about any of that now going to do you any good?

He knew why, though. If they were still alive, Ally was alive. He could go up there and save her.

But, David, that is a job for a hero.

Maybe it was. Maybe he would have to be a hero, and heroes lived. They found ways out of things like this.

There was a way out, and he knew exactly what it was. He was either going to run straight into the nothing, or he was going to get out of there. Somehow, he knew he was going to get out. There had to be a way. He just had to find out what it was.

Wendy's bedroom was the third door off the dining room. It was always closed because no one was ever allowed to go in there. When her ex lived there, he had been very private. There were things he never wanted anyone to know about.

So, of course, when no one was home, Ally and he had gone through it many times. There were things in there no child should ever see in their parents' room, and after they had, it could never be unseen. He felt dirty for even knowing something like that existed.

To his knowledge, Bobby and Mikey had never gone in there. It was the vault that was unopened. Even now, the door was closed.

Before he thought about it, he ran to the room. Barely turning the handle, he crashed through the door, slamming it against the wall. The window was on the other side of the room. It was closed, just a faint glow of whatever light came from outside, but he didn't pause as he ran toward it.

He hurled himself toward the glass. He felt the crushing pressure against his skull, then the sudden release as the glass broke, the painful reality crashing into him like the shards exploding around him. His world spun as he fell out of the house.

CHAPTER 27

Rob took a step forward, not sure what he was stepping into. As he did, he felt the cross under his shirt burning cold against his skin. The black mist in front of him receded as he stepped, the store no longer lost to the bleak non-existence. It was still dark, but now looked like a dimly lit room, light filtering in through the window.

He still didn't see any tint on the glass, but would he? He only had recent experience with tinting because of high school kids over-tinting their car windows. He wasn't sure he had seen much tinting of store windows, but from what he knew, even if the window were tinted, it wouldn't make the room this dark. He took another step, the darkness swirling around him, receding as he stepped in farther. Over his shoulder, he saw the open door fading, disappearing.

The darkness surrounded him, his fears confirming this wasn't right.

"Shit," he said. He could see his breath, knowing the sudden chill he felt wasn't his imagination. The room got colder as he stepped into it.

Here he was, walking into some shit again. Why in the hell did this always happen around him? It sometimes felt like he had been safer in Chicago.

Ever since they moved out of the city, he'd stepped from one supernatural thing to another. Were all small towns like this? If so, he was surprised more people didn't pack up and move to the cities. He only had to worry about getting shot there. He had no idea what he had to worry about now, but the danger felt greater than just for his life. Since they had left the city, it had become a continuous fight for his soul, demons constantly after him and his family.

Damn.

He reached to where his gun should be…if he were on duty. Of course, it wasn't there. He wasn't on duty. He was supposed to meet up with the state trooper who *was* on duty, and it would have been bad form for him to be carrying.

Again, you dipshit, you got pulled into some serious shit, and again, you do not have your sidearm.

If this continued, Rob worried he'd become one of those nuts, always afraid to be without his gun. He would have to name it. He'd call it Elvira, and it would be his mistress. He'd start sleeping with her under his pillow, and would even take a shower with her nearby. Because when something serious went down, his dumb ass was here without a gun once again.

He took another step, just barely making out a female voice coming from the back room. It was faint, although it didn't sound like she was whispering. It sounded like a yell, but muffled.

"Agnon, Desinine, Verata, I call upon the…"

The voice faded away and became harder to hear as he watched the fog thicken near the door.

The darkness continued to swirl, pulling itself into the back of the room. He felt it moving. It was impossible to see, the dark so complete, it was just a wall of nothing. He could feel it shift and move, the chill reaching out to take him, then dissipating at his presence.

It trickled over his skin, tugging at the hairs on his arm. Rob took a step toward it, following in one direction, then another. The room around him grew lighter, but it wasn't because he walked through it. All the darkness moved past him and through the door, as if sucked in by some force around the edges.

283

As he got closer, he could hear the air whistle around the door. Around him, the room grew lighter, but he kept his focus on the door. The whistling grew in intensity as the light was restored. First, a little bit of sunlight came in through the window, warming his skin. Then he could see the cooler to his right and hear the hum of the compressor working to keep the flowers inside a consistent temperature. The wall to his left became visible, and he could see the different inspirational posters, highlighting women being given flowers in various settings.

There was a squealing hiss from around the door, more air being rapidly pulled through the small space. The pitch of the whistling grew higher, and there was just a haze around the outer edges of the door as Rob stepped in front of it and placed his hand on the knob.

It was cold to the touch, like ice in his hand. Thoughts of being a child and being warned not to lick the flagpole in the winter resonated with him as the cold metal felt like it stuck to his palm.

The door wouldn't open. He put his considerable bulk into pushing on it, and as he did, it opened slowly. It was like time was warped because no matter how hard he pushed, the door moved like it was stuck in gel. The resistance always stayed equal to the pressure he applied.

As the door finally opened into the room, he saw exactly the same thing as when he opened the front door to the shop…a wall of black. At first, it appeared solid, but as he stood there, he could see shadows flying through the mist. Shapes withered, dark tendrils moving around in a quick, lashing motion. He could feel them as they whipped around him. Some reached out, trying to pull him in; others ignored him and flowed around. The tendrils were so thick, it was hard to see past them and into the room.

He stepped in, feeling like he was walking in mud. The floor before him felt slippery, not solid, and the world around him clung tightly to him. No, he wasn't walking through mud, but quicksand, and he tried to pull himself free. It shifted, those cold tentacles rubbing against him as he moved. The heavy air pushed in around him.

A gale-force wind slammed him back against the wall, just missing the open door. The force blew the air out of his lungs and he was left gasping. As hard as he tried, he could not pull any air in, even though the room was full of it whipping around. He tried to breathe in small gasps, but the pressure on his chest stayed constant.

He reached out to the wall, hunching against the wind to pull himself along. He wasn't sure when his legs got knocked out from under him. Everything seemed to be spinning. He gasped. There wasn't enough air. He couldn't breathe. He had to get out of there.

"Clatu...Sini...Definon!" he heard the woman scream. It was some kind of chant, but Rob could only hear brief segments of it as gaps in the swirling vortex came and went. "Hear me... Hear my call for power."

He finally made it to the door, not realizing he had been thrown so far away. Stars had formed on the corner of his vision. The more he gasped, the more he felt like a fish out of water. His head felt heavy. He wanted to scream out in frustration, take a deep breath to push away all the madness forcing its way into his mind. It grew harder to think through all the chaos in and around him.

Rob forced himself to look up, having to fight through the exhaustion threatening to take him. A young boy stood in the doorway, his pale skin having a luminescent quality as it glowed. He was covered in dirt, wearing what looked to have once been a blue t-shirt and jeans, but were now just pieces that clung to his frame, large holes exposing the torn flesh underneath.

Instinctively, Rob pulled back, again reaching for his gun that wasn't there. The thing before him looked like a zombie, and while he knew he wouldn't have a chance, he wasn't going to let it take him without a fight. He stayed still as the boy turned and looked at him. Rob expected the lifeless pale eyes he had seen before, surprised at the large black orbs looking at him with a hateful glare. Rob could see the malice behind them as they burned daggers into his chest. There was something unnatural about this boy...and something familiar.

He was relieved when he saw the boy turn his attention away, focusing at the swirling black mass behind Rob.

"Come...darkness to me...fill...power!"

Rob still only heard bits and pieces, but what he did hear didn't sound good. He'd stepped into another shitstorm. He really needed to start wearing cowboy boots and a hat with how often it felt like he had to ride in to save the day. At least he could justify the boots with how much shit he walked through, although Robyn would say it was for all the bullshit he liked to spread.

Robyn... Thinking of her, remembering how much of an ass he had been to her that morning, sent a sudden pang through his chest, then the floodgates opened. He didn't know why he'd been such an asshole the last couple days. She was his everything. He'd run to the end of the world and fight off the zombie horde just to be with her. However, over the last couple days, he'd been thinking of everything *but* her. No, he'd done more than that. He'd thought of that woman, thinking about how he wanted to go at her, tear her clothes off.

The sudden thought of the woman who owned the shop came back to him, but he no longer felt a lust after her flesh. He felt sick, not believing he had wanted those fantasies to be real. Just who had he been over the last few days? That had never been him. He knew who controlled his heart. He had given her the keys to that a long time ago when he said two magical words. They were the words that had empowered and completed him.. He had told her, "I do."

He shook his head, shaking away the cobwebs and focusing on the here and now. He had to do something to stop this, but he wasn't sure what. Glancing over his shoulder, he saw faint glimmers of the woman, the darkness spinning around her. From what he could make out, she wore some kind of dark robe and a red mask. It had horns protruding from the forehead and painted black tears running from the blank eyes. There was nothing for him to identify the woman, but he knew. More than just hearing the voice as it called out, he could feel that she was there. There was a connection pulling him toward her.

The boy still stood there, having taken a step into the room. He had lost that dark look, now looking worried. His eyes didn't turn away from the woman, and if Rob didn't know better, he would say the boy leaned back, like he had to shift his weight to keep from being pulled forward.

"Bring the darkness to me."

Rob heard the woman's voice as the swirling black started to fade around him. The boy seemed to fight, as whatever pulled Rob to the woman must have also been pulling him.

So if the boy was being pulled to her, and Rob was being pulled to her, what would happen when they both reached her? He wasn't sure, but he didn't think it would be good. He couldn't let her get to him, but he couldn't let her get the boy, either.

He turned to look back at her. The room started to lighten, the black tendrils streaming around them and flowing toward a long, double-edged knife. It was hard to make out much of it as the darkness flowed into the blade, only occasionally allowing him to see it had some kind of writing.

An athame...

He wasn't sure how he knew that, but he was sure that was it. The carvings on the blade, that strange language she chanted. This all had to be some kind of witchcraft.

Was he ready to believe that? When had his life become so messed up that witchcraft became something real, not just weird shit he watched in movies? Did it matter? She was there, he was there, and she was doing something to his town. She must be the one taking the kids. She had to have killed the chief. Had he seen her doing something? Had the kids?

The boy was still behind him. He could at least keep her from taking another one. He just had to find a way to stop her.

Think, think, think. Come on, Rob. What the hell are you going to do?

He hadn't realized the fog shrouding his thoughts had started lifting. The air wasn't as heavy, so why couldn't he focus? He just kept looking away from her, his eyes roaming the room. He kept seeing her, his mind filling with images of her naked body, her flesh pressed against his, her tongue invading his mouth as she pushed him against the wall.

He didn't remember her having a bust as large as the images in his head, but they continued to pummel him. He felt himself getting excited, his breath becoming rapid. He thought his mind had started to clear, but it was now cluttered with images of her, images he wanted to be free from as she continued to force her way into his mind, raping his thoughts.

"Believe. Don't let the darkness pull you in."

Father William's voice was loud in Rob's head. He didn't know why he thought of the young priest now, trying to push it away. The harder he tried, the more he focused on the young man standing at his pulpit, casting a prayer among his masses. Rob felt the air around him shifting, avoiding him, twisting around the room.

He closed his eyes. Sometimes sight just felt like it got in the way, and if not seeing allowed him to clear some of the clutter from his thoughts, maybe that would make it stop. It didn't, but it did seem to silence some of the other noise of his head. He still saw her, but the beautiful woman he imagined was different. As he moved away from her, he could see her skin was more white than tan, wrinkles creasing her forehead and cheek. Her lips were not the luscious, full red lips he had felt pressing against him, but thin and chapped. Her eyes were dark, sunken. Her hair wasn't blonde, but thin strands of white barely covering a sickly bald head.

The woman didn't just look old. She was ancient. A fairy tale character reminiscent of a children's book. The beautiful woman had been replaced by the witch from *Hansel and Gretel*. Rob remembered the story. He used to read it to Jake when he put him to bed.

With the new image of her, he was able to take another mental step back, no longer seeing the perky breasts. He saw sagging white sacks that were nothing more than hideous ripples of flesh, disgusting him.

"*Expel out the darkness*," Father William whispered.

Before, the priest had told him to believe. Rob really wasn't sure he could do that just yet, but he did know one thing he believed in with every ounce of his heart. He believed in his family, knowing he loved them and they loved him in return. He believed in Robyn and he believed in Jake.

Rob could feel more of his body. He hadn't realized how numb and cut off from it he had become until he felt his knees, the stabbing pain from still being on the ground and having to move around in such an unnatural way. He wasn't in his twenties anymore, which his body loved to remind him of with different aches and pains, his knees and back just being part of the many.

He could feel ice against his chest. It was a powerful, intense feeling, like fire against his skin, burning at the hairs. As it spread deeper, he felt it touching his lungs. The cold forced a warmth to flood in, along with deep breaths of air.

The images drifted away, the fog lifting with them, allowing the world around him to refocus.

Rob opened his eyes to look up at the woman. He could now see her clearly. She was old. How had he not seen it before? She was dressed in the same clothes he had seen earlier, the tight shirt and jeans, but her skin was a pale, sickly color, and her face was a mass of wrinkles.

She wasn't paying any attention to him, and he was glad for it. He felt like he was coming out of a trance and didn't know when or if she would notice. Her eyes were transfixed on the darkness as it continued to flow into her athame. If he was going to do something to save himself and the boy, now was the time.

Damn. I know I'm going to regret this.

He rushed at her. Sure, he had played some football in high school, but that was a long time ago. Plus, he had never been good at it. No, this was just all out, going in for a tackle. Most days, he would have been worried about hurting someone, and himself in the process.

He didn't hold back, didn't hesitate. He hit her hard, wrapping his arms around her midsection, slamming her back into the far wall. He heard crashing all around him, glass falling from nearby shelves. He didn't look around as he reached his hand up to find hers. He had her against the wall, but didn't want her bringing that knife down to stab him in the back. He was glad to feel the knife wasn't in her hand.

"You idiot," she yelled, trying to push him away. She was strong, stronger than he expected a frail-looking woman to be.

Just because she didn't have the knife didn't mean she wasn't dangerous. She wasn't natural. Who knew of what she might be capable? He wanted to slam her down and ask where the kids were, wanted to arrest her and take her out among the parents, string her to a stake and burn her like the witch she was.

She was a witch, wasn't she? It made the most sense, and witches burned by fire. That's what the old stories always said. That's what the kids did in the fairy tale. They burned her in an oven.

He grabbed her wrists and pulled them down, not taking any chances with her flailing arms. When she struggled, he forced her against the wall, shifting to pin her to it. His muscle memory had taken control, years of police training guiding his motions. He spun her around, tugging her arms behind her. He needed to secure them long enough to pull out his handcuffs and subdue her.

The handcuffs he didn't have with him because he wasn't in uniform.

Damn it!

"You bloody fool! You have no idea what you are doing." He didn't recall the crisp English accent before, but ignored it as he pulled her from the wall and crashed her to the floor, positioning his knee in the small of her back. "I'm trying to stop it. I'm trying to—"

She stopped, no longer struggling to look at Rob. She looked across the room, her eyes focused on the knife, then the boy.

Rob turned. The black smoke, like essence, billowed out from the athame and swirled around the room. The boy just watched it. Rob couldn't see him clearly through the haze in the room, but he knew he just stood there.

"Get outta here!" Rob yelled as he pulled the witch back against his knee. When the boy didn't move, Rob looked back at her. "I don't know what you're doing, but stop it!"

The look of horror he had briefly seen in her face faded as she turned her head to glare up at him. Her lips peeled back into a snarl as she spat out, "Ventus."

Rob found himself on the floor across the room, his back against the wall. As he pushed away the cobwebs he suddenly felt in his mind, he realized his body hurt...and he was upside down. He had no idea how he had gone from being on top of her to where he was now, entangled with himself on the floor.

He wrestled to right himself. His arm was tucked under his leg and he had to shift his weight to pull it free.

291

She had somehow tossed him across the room like he was a rag doll. He knew he was lucky he felt no broken bones, although he didn't feel too lucky right now. Everything hurt.

He turned to look at the witch sauntering over to him, her smile smug. There was an air of confidence, the fear he had briefly seen before gone. Now she was a tigress stalking her prey.

He felt the earlier conversation with Father William trying to push in on him.

"Believe in good and the power of doing what is right. Believe, and He is a shield for all who take refuge in Him."

He couldn't remember when they had this particular conversation, but he could see the father sitting in the pew, Rob next to him. They were talking about beliefs and how much one could truly be devoted to God in today's world. Damn it, why couldn't he just understand what the priest wanted him to know? Why all these damn games?

Rob felt his body go limp, his muscles turning into jelly. His head flopped forward, not having strength to lift it. Then something else did. He looked up and watched as his body lifted and pushed back against the wall hard. It held him until he felt like he would be a permanent fixture on the wall, his feet dangling, hanging there like a piece of art.

"Pretty, pretty thing. I wanted you as my pet, but maybe I'll keep you as my art." She paused, reaching out to run her hand along his chest. "Although I may bloody you a little. I like my pets to be beau-t-ful." Her accent stretched the word as she worked to get it out. "I prefer my art to be a little macabre. Death is its own art, don't you think?"

She looked up at him so he could see her eyes. They had turned into feline slits—yellow, cat-like, and hungry. He tried to speak, but found he was frozen, not even able to scream. All he could do was gaze into those eyes.

"You shouldn't have interfered. I was fixing the darkness. Now I'll have to start over."

"You...are...the...darkness," Rob whispered. He didn't know how he got it out.

"No." She seemed to pout as she said it, although Rob wasn't sure. "I just woke it up. The power... It attracted me." She looked at his chest, her fingers cutting his shirt and into his flesh beneath, leaving long marks. He wished he didn't feel as aroused as he did, but there was an electricity pouring out of her. "Too bad." She looked back up at him, the brief wistful look she had disappearing, the smirk returning. "Too bad."

Then the look was gone, replaced by confusion. Rob could feel the pressure around him suddenly releasing. He dropped to his feet, staggering.

He stood just a few inches taller than she did. He saw her stagger slightly toward him, then turn away. The knife handle protruded from her back, the blade sunk deep. The black mist spilled out from around the wound.

Her legs gave out as she collapsed. When she hit the floor, the mist swirled, a cloud of black forming over her.

Rob looked up to see the boy standing there. The black fog wasn't just forming over her. It moved toward the boy. Rob could now see the tendrils flowing into him. He was electrified by it, his skin nearly glowing white as it entered him. A tornado of black tendrils swirled as the boy smiled.

He looked up at Rob, the black orbs looking into his eyes. Rob didn't know how long they stood there. Time disappeared as they tried to learn more about each other.

Then the boy was gone...

* * * *

293

Confused, Rob emerged from the little flower shop, not really sure what had just happened. He was alive. That was all that mattered. He could go home, be with his wife and see his son, and whatever that dark mist crap had been was gone. It had disappeared when the boy had, suddenly making everything in the room feel blindingly bright.

He had wasted no time getting out of there, nearly tripping over himself as he ran to the door. He felt like a little child running away from imaginary monsters, but the body on the floor proved this was all real.

He couldn't wait to feel the warm sun on his skin. The shop had been like an icebox. He hadn't realized just how cold he truly felt until he made it outside. The breeze, as brisk as it was, felt warm to his pale skin. He looked up. The sun was...

Dark, along with the sky. It was unnatural, not like an eclipse. He remembered part of the science behind what made the sky blue. Who could have a ten-year-old and not know? When Jake had learned about the sky, he came home, excited to share what he had learned. Of course, it was over Rob's head, but he caught the gist. Dust scattered in the atmosphere, blue light being shorter than red light and the like. These blue particles got scattered among the dust and mixed with particles in the sky, giving it a blue appearance.

But when he looked up, he couldn't see any blue sky or yellow sun. What he saw was the absence of color, the sky getting dark way too early in the day. It was faded, the sun pale, without a single cloud to explain it.

Rob looked around the street. He saw a few cars pass by and a couple going into a store the next block over. No one seemed to notice their world fading around them. Had he noticed before the priest said anything about it? The sky had just seemed cloudy. He hadn't thought it was anything out of the ordinary. It was October. The sky was overcast more often than not.

He didn't know quite how long he stood there, staring at the sky, before he felt the vibration in his pocket. He reached into it and grabbed his phone, feeling a momentary grogginess, like violently waking from a dream. It made him unsure if the darkness were real or not. If the witch had been real, was the boy?

"Hello?" He heard himself say into the phone, not really feeling attached to the voice. It sounded alien to his own ears, as if he talked from a long distance away.

"Officer Alletto?" He heard the panicked voice. His recognized it, but from where? Yesterday seemed like a lifetime ago. Everything before the flower shop affected another Rob Alletto, not this one.

"Yeah?" His voice was quiet, almost a whisper.

"This is David. Remember? I helped you walk the coal dump? You told me to call if, well... You just told me to, well... I..."

Rob took the last step down toward his car, the jarring sensation of moving down stairs helping shake some of the weirdness out of his head.

"What's wrong?" Rob asked, knowing something had to be wrong.

"Ally... Allison... She's gone."

CHAPTER 28

It didn't take long for the sinking feeling of dread to weigh down Rob's stomach. He had just survived the impossible, only to get a phone call slamming him back to reality. This wasn't over. The witch hadn't been the cause of it. What was it she had said? She had been trying to stop it? She had been capturing it. He guessed it could have looked that way when he had gotten involved.

No, that still wasn't right. If she had been doing a "Glenda, the good witch" impersonation, why had she gotten into his head? Why was she even there at all? No, he didn't buy into any of that. She may have been capturing whatever that darkness was, but she wasn't doing it altruistically. She was here for the power, trying to take it for herself, for her own ends. Rob had to trust his gut, and that was what it told him.

But there was still the darkness. He had no name for it. It was some force, something evil that had been here a while. She said it had only recently awakened, but that meant it had been here, dormant. For how long?

Rob wasn't familiar with the town's history, so there was no way for him to say if something like this had ever happened before. If he had time, he might try to do research, find out what he was up against, but he didn't. The sky made it apparent this was moving too fast. He had to do something, and he had to do it now.

No, he didn't have to do anything. He wasn't in charge now. The state was there, the trooper waiting for him. This was now his job, whether or not he was able to handle it.

When David had called, Rob told him about the state trooper. Rob knew this was all unfinished, but he wasn't officially part of it anymore. There really wasn't much he could do. David hadn't been happy. He wanted Rob to run off somewhere and save Ally. He was reminded of the boy missing from last year. The one who had never been found. Sure, last night they had gotten lucky and some of the kids had been found, but that wasn't always the case. The boy last year was proof of that. If they couldn't find Michael, or Mikey, last year, Rob wasn't sure how he was supposed to magically find him now just because David's girlfriend was missing. It didn't work that way.

Rob let out a long breath, feeling his shoulders slump as he opened the car door. He felt the wetness at the corner of his eye. He was getting so tired of not being able to help people. When was he going to win? When would he finally have that moment he could actually save someone, rather than inform loved ones they would never see their family member again?

In real life, there was no such thing as happy endings. He began to realize that as he eased his sore body into the small front seat of the squad car. He didn't know where he could go to look for the girl, but right now, he had an appointment to keep. He had kept the state trooper waiting far too long.

Just what the hell was he going to tell him? What could he tell him that wouldn't have the trooper calling for him to be put in for observation? He had to admit, if someone told him this story, he wouldn't believe any of it. How would he ever get the trooper to listen?

* * * *

Something wasn't right. That was evident the moment Rob pulled the squad car up behind one of the

297

state troopers' vehicles parked on the side of the road at the end of the side path. It was on the opposite side to where Rob had been last night when he found Jake and the rest of the missing children.

It was smart for the trooper and the rest of the CSI team to park their vehicles there, although they must have moved them sometime during the night because, yesterday, they were parked closer to where the chief's car had been. Over here, there was less chance the vehicles would damage any potential evidence. That suggested they expanded their crime scene to look through more of the coal dump.

It was smart, but that didn't explain why there was no one around. As Rob climbed out of the car, he didn't hear anyone, either. He would have expected at least one person to be nearby, keeping an eye out for someone. Where was the state trooper he was there to meet? The place was quiet. Too quiet.

That was it, wasn't it? Since he had pulled up, his back had stiffened and he had cautiously kept an eye on everything around him. His cop senses had gone into overdrive as he opened the door.

He realized there was more to the silence. It was quiet, but not just because he didn't hear the sounds of people working a crime scene, even if they were up the hill. He didn't hear people at all. He didn't hear any cars, even in the distance, either. There were no lawn mowers, no kids laughing, no people yelling at one another or calling out a quick hello.

There was something else. It was a wooded area. Where were the sounds of squirrels scurrying through the underbrush? Why didn't he hear any birds chirping or flying through the trees? He scanned the area around him. Nothing.

He took a step on the gravel shoulder, the crunch beneath his shoe like a shotgun blast in the silence. He slammed his car door behind him, just to feel the comfort of the sound.

"Hello?"

He heard the soft, tentative voice. It was followed a moment later by the sound of crunching footsteps, a young man appearing around the front of the CSI van. David. Rob had told him to meet him there, figuring the trooper would want to hear what he had to say. Rob still wasn't sure what he had meant on the phone. The kid had been a mess, talking over himself as he tried to tell Rob something about a missing girl and a little boy.

"Have you talked to the state trooper yet?" Rob thought he already knew the answer as the kid could have only just gotten there himself, the place seeming pretty deserted. He still figured he had to ask. The kid shook his head, not meeting Rob's eyes.

"Not yet. No one's here."

"How long have you been here?"

"Little over five minutes."

"Did you think about calling out or checking up the hill?"

Rob read the kid's mind as David looked into the woods. He was scared. Had it really been just yesterday the kid had been eager to take him up there and show him some hiding spots he knew? He barely resembled the person he had met then. His shoulders slumped and, as they talked, he never once looked up from a spot on the ground.

"Okay, well, I gotta go up there and find the state trooper. You are welcome to join me."

"Do you think he'll find her?"

"He might. The state guys are who they call in when we local guys can't solve the big mysteries. He's got more experience with it than I do."

David looked at him. "Really? Because I heard you used to work up in Chicago."

"True, but I was just a patrol officer. Just took the reports and let the detectives do all the big stuff."

"Okay."

Rob could hear defeat in his voice.

"Look. I'll walk you up there." He felt like he was talking to a five-year-old, but he had to keep in mind the kid had been through a lot. "If the trooper doesn't have any issues with it, I'll stick around after you make the report to see if I can help."

David nodded, and they started walking toward the entrance to the path.

David stopped at the edge of the woods, looking at them. "I know who took her."

Rob narrowed his eyes. "Who's that?"

"Mikey."

Mikey... Why did that name ring a bell? Rob could swear he recognized it.

The image of a boy in tattered clothing surrounded by wisps of dark tendrils billowing out from a black cloud came to mind. Those demonic appendages tearing apart the woman from the flower shop. A boy he had recognized, but wasn't sure from where. There had been a familiarity to him that he couldn't place. Something about it...

And then it clicked. He should have realized it before. It had been staring him in the face. The picture of the older brother he had used to search. He should have seen it. He should have placed it. He had looked for that boy last year.

That couldn't be. He had been missing for a year. There was no way Rob or David had seen him.

"Are you sure it was him?"

David nodded. They stood there, not wanting to enter the woods, stepping among the trees where it was obviously darker than around them. Not that it was bright out. The day was getting darker, the shadows in the trees deeper than they should be.

Rob wanted to dismiss what the kid had said because it sounded crazy, but how crazy would *he* sound?

When they found the trooper and David told him about his missing girlfriend, would Rob back up the story?

No matter how crazy it sounded, would he add his own input?

He was afraid of the answer.

"Is it just me or is it too quiet around here?" David asked.

Rob looked around the woods, not liking that the kid said what he felt. He didn't answer, not wanting to acknowledge the silence.

He took a step onto the path. He was a couple paces in when he heard David following.

"Where are we going?"

"I'm thinking the trooper is probably by where the body was found, checking in with the medical examiners. I figure we should check with them."

"Okay." Rob heard the tremble in the kid's voice, knowing he was frightened. Rob couldn't blame him. He was, too.

* * * *

Rob took a long, deep breath and looked at the crime scene tape floating on the breeze. Someone had ripped it from around one of the trees, leaving the other part attached to one. Rob saw a CSI kit sitting there, various baggies next to it. He noticed some were labeled and closed; others were partially open.

What had happened? There was no question now that something was wrong. The team would not walk away from a crime scene and leave remnants of their work. Even though Rob had very little experience with them, he knew they would have more professionalism than that. If it was ever found out that they left a scene unattended, their careers would be over.

It was just more evidence that there was something wrong. Maybe they had found the heart of it all. Did that mean something had to be down there? Was it waiting for them, or was it off taking more kids from the town? The thing seemed to have a taste for them. As far as Rob could tell, it mostly took children.

"Are you going down first?" the kid asked. Rob was pretty sure the kid's name was David, and he'd been thinking that was his name. He really needed to get better with names. He was becoming that old man who would call everyone "kid".

Yeah, well, he knew he wasn't going to change his habits now. He was just stalling anyway. They had to go down there. He just didn't want to, and he could tell the kid didn't want to, either.

"Nah, kid, you go down and I'll keep an eye out for you from up here," he wanted to say. Yeah, that would sit well with his conscience. If something happened to him, Rob knew that would just be one more face he'd see at night. He had enough demons when he closed his eyes. He didn't need another one.

Who was he kidding? He wouldn't have let the kid go down before him. He just wasn't wired that way.

"Give me the flashlight," Rob said, taking it from him.

"You sure you don't want me to hold it while you climb down?"

Rob looked at the kid, then flicked on the light, shining it into the pit. There was a ladder and some safety lines, which were tied to one of the trees. Since there was a ladder, it couldn't be all that deep, right?

"Nah. You'd just be shining it in my eyes."

The kid nodded, taking a step back from the hole. Rob looked at him as he started to step onto the ladder.

"What's wrong?"

"I…I just don't like heights."

Rob looked at him for a minute, doubting it had anything to do with the height of the pit. The kid was white as a sheet as he stared down into the hole. Rob understood why. It sounded like they'd both been through quite the ordeal, so the idea of climbing down into such a dark hole terrified Rob, as well.

He knew he really shouldn't take the kid down there with him, but what were his other options? He could call for backup from the county or state, but who knew how long until they would get there. Once they did, how much could he tell them? There were the missing CSI team and the trooper, but how much of that would be put on him?

So was he only covering his own ass?

No, because bringing the kid down there was probably only going to get him in more trouble in the end. However, the thought of going alone terrified him. He didn't want to admit it, but he was bringing the kid because of his own fears, not because he thought he'd be able to help. If something happened, though, Rob was going to be in a lot of shit.

In fact, Rob started to realize just how bad all of this looked for him. His boss killed, county officers all missing, and he was left holding the bag. Him, the one who looked to benefit the most from the chief's disappearance. Him, the cop with known psychological issues. Him, the one always in financial trouble and in desperate need for money and full-time work. Him, the guy who looked the other way while his coworkers did a shady job on the side, knowing it wasn't really one hundred percent legal.

So, yeah, taking the kid down there with him was just icing on the cake at this point. Every way he looked, he was fucked.

Then why are you still going down there?

Because, once again, he just wasn't wired any other way. It was the right thing to do, no matter how it would hurt him in the end. Sure, the kid shouldn't be going down there, but he doubted he could stop him. If Rob read it right, the kid had a thing for the missing girl. He wasn't going to stay up here while she might be down there. He was adamant she was down there, and Rob knew where he came from. He felt it, too. There was a pull, drawing him down. For good or bad, they were going down there. The kid was young, dumb, and stupid, but what was Rob's excuse?

So what does that make me? I am obviously old, dumb, and stupid. How else do I explain doing this, getting caught up in these messes time and time again?

He felt the ladder shift as he lowered his foot onto the first rung. His stomach lurched. He closed his eyes to calm his breathing.

Yeah, he wasn't a fan of heights, either.

He took another step into the pit.

CHAPTER 29

It was not easy to climb down. Each step was torture as the ladder shook, his grip tightening on the cold steel, his knuckles turning white. Even when he'd let go to grab the next rung, it was a quick motion. The ladder would shake and he'd tighten his hold until he caught his breath and the ladder steadied. He would wait a few seconds, his eyes closed, then repeat the process. It was nerve-wracking and took several minutes.

Once he felt the hard-packed earth under his boot, he let out a breath. However, the relief was short-lived as he felt the darkness around him, reminding him how cold it had been in the flower shop. The shaft smelled damp and musty, but he knew the chill didn't come from the dark. It wasn't cold enough for that and there was no movement to the air. Still, the hairs on the back of his neck raised, his shoulders stiffening.

This was where the remains of the chief had been found. Whether it was the darkness or the witch who killed him, he ended there. He could almost feel the cool touch of the dark, as if it were sneaking around him. It didn't move the air, but he sensed it was there. Dark hiding within dark, watching him, biding its time before it would take him like it had taken the others.

He quickly pulled out the flashlight and flipped it on, turning to see the small cavern around him. Shadows receded everywhere he aimed the light, not showing anything strange, although they returned when he moved.

Of course they did. That's how light works.

He pointed the light up toward the kid, momentarily feeling his chest tighten as the darkness enveloped him. He wasn't sure what he expected to see. Knowing part of the chief had been found hanging from the top, he hadn't expected to come down and find more bodies. Looking up the shaft, he didn't see how any part of him had been just hanging up there. He couldn't see a ledge or anything for the body to have gotten hung up on. It was a clean drop, no outcroppings large enough to have held it up there.

He turned one more time. The light wasn't as strong as it had been just a moment ago, and he hoped it wasn't due to the batteries going bad. As he turned, the beam seemed to soak into the rock walls around him. The area was not that wide, just large enough that if he were to hold his hands out, he wouldn't touch anything unless he moved a few inches. It felt very claustrophobic until he noticed the small circular opening dug into one of the walls at about knee level. The hole was just over shoulder width apart, which would be very cramped. If it were closed off at all, there would be no way he could make it back out.

He pushed away the thoughts of getting stuck in there and knelt down to examine it. He ran his fingers along the outline, then the wall. The surface felt rough. Who would have made it? It wasn't a mineshaft, which had been kind of what he expected. This was an old slag pile, right? Made from the days when this area had been heavy with coal? So there should be shafts. That was what he had always seen in the movies. Long, deep shafts that were prone to cave-ins and gave the miners lung cancer.

So who made this small tunnel? Maybe the better question was where did it go?

His fingers snagged on a rough edge of something wedged into the dirt. He pulled on it, wiggling it free before pulling out a long piece of red plastic. It had words on it, but those were faded. He had no way of knowing

307

what it was, but the color and the feel of the plastic made him assume it was from a toy.

He started to feel around for more, but couldn't find any. When he heard the sound of the kid jumping from the last rung of the ladder and onto solid earth, he pulled his hand back and turned to look at him.

When he saw how pale his face had become, he bit back his father's saying of, "I would have laughed if you fell through."

"Anything?" the kid asked. Rob stepped away from the hole and pointed his light at it. He heard his hard intake of air, knowing he had a dislike of tight spaces, too.

Don't we all.

Rob nodded at him and turned back to look at the hole, once again dreading the way he was wired.

Before thinking about it too much, he lowered himself down and into the hole.

"Are you sure you want to do that?" the kid asked, sounding worried.

"No. Now shut the fuck up," Rob hissed back at him.

He was only a few feet in before he realized this had probably been one of the dumbest things he had ever done. Why hadn't he let the boy go first? He was smaller, could easily have fit into the confined space. He was an old man. *Okay, I'm older than the kid. I shouldn't be doing this.*

His legs scraped against the surface, the rocks stabbing into that soft spot just below the knee. He tried to ignore the pain as he continued to inch forward. Even though he wore a long-sleeve shirt, he could feel the walls rubbing against him.

He tried to keep the flashlight beam trained in front of him, but it didn't cast much of a glow, and every time he moved his arms, the beam would slip off to the side.

Sweat dripped down his face. He could feel it rolling off him, the dirt and grime running in streaks. Chunks of dirt fell from the ceiling, collecting in his hair.

"Officer?" he heard the kid call. Rob didn't know if he had followed him into the tunnel or not, but he heard a slight echo to the voice. He assumed he had stayed back at the mouth of the hole. "Deputy, it's getting dark down here without the light."

What did you expect, kid? Next time, bring a flashlight of your own.

"I'll be back in a minute. I want to see where this leads."

His voice sounded loud, booming off the tight walls around him. It sounded like more dirt fell with the vibration of it, making him worry about what he would do if the tunnel collapsed behind him.

And have you thought about just what you are looking for? What are you going to do if you find it? You went up against it once, hotshot. What are you doing going down a cramped tunnel where you can't even reach for your gun if you need it? Even if you could, what would you do with it? What you saw back in the shop... Did that look like something you could just shoot and be done with it?

He already knew the answer. Just what in the hell was he supposed to do if he found anything?

He had started this, had come to the crime scene to find the state trooper. Never had he thought he would be climbing down there. This wasn't his concern anymore. He should just walk away, call the officer, although he knew the trooper wouldn't answer. If he wanted to do something actually useful, he could call county and report the disappearances. Why was he down there?

You're afraid of what you will find. Of what you had come down here to find.

He didn't want to actually find it. He wasn't ready for whatever it was. He didn't know if he would ever be ready.

309

Something rubbed against his face, a thread poking into his nose. It itched and burned as he breathed it in before he could catch himself. He stopped to tilt his head and reach up, pulling at what he had run into. His fingers touched the web, a chill running down his spine.

Spiders... He knew they had to be down there, but out of sight, out of mind. He sure as hell didn't want to think about them crawling on him. Eight legs scurrying across his skin, spinning their webs, hatching their eggs, eating his flesh before burrowing beneath. He couldn't go back there and be in that nightmare. Not after...

He refused to let his mind wander back to that time. He refused to think about the town that no longer existed. The town he never thought he would escape last year, just like he was never going to escape this tunnel.

It became harder to breathe. What had been a cool dirt catacomb began to stifle him. He had to take shorter breaths. Part of it was from the exhaustive effort of crawling inch by inch, and part was something else. Even though he wasn't wedged against the top of the cavern, he could feel a massive weight lowering onto him.

The fading light no longer pierced through the darkness. He looked down at the flashlight in his hand and saw the last of the glow fade. Then there was nothing but pitch black around him.

He stopped and closed his eyes. It didn't matter. Open or closed, there was nothing he could see around him anyway. All he had now was his sense of hearing to rely on, yet it still felt like he could hear better when his eyes were closed.

That's it. I'm done, he thought, on the verge of tears as he lay there. He didn't give a shit anymore. This was all too much. When did it ever quit? He moved his family to be safer, but something seemed to happen every day. When would he be safe? What would it take for all this to go away? Well, it was going away now because *he* was going away. He was going to back down the tunnel, then climb up the ladder and out of there. He would go home and pack up his family. It was the only thing left to do. Maybe the next place they went to would actually be safe and...

The kid moved up behind him. Rob could hear the dirt shifting as he shuffled. It sounded like the loose dirt above them fell on him, as well. There was a pattern. He moved a few inches, then stopped, the dirt falling, then he moved again. He felt the kid reach out and hit Rob's foot with his searching hands.

"Why'd you stop? Everything okay?"

Well, there was no way he could shuffle back now. Rob kept his eyes closed and tried to focus on everything around him. The darkness felt like it closed in, but he refused to open his eyes. That would only make everything seem that much more hopeless.

What was in front of them? Death, or even something worse than death, could be waiting beyond. Was that what they were going to find? Would they really find anything down there? This was an ancient cave. Who knew how long it had been there, or how long it had been since anything living had been down there. What reason did they have to think they would find something? This was all just crazy crap he had somehow allowed himself to think made sense. None of it made any sense.

What? Some ghost of a kid, who had gone missing over a year ago, just came and started taking people from the town, bringing them down here? How the hell did that make any sense? How would it get them down here? Why would it take them? Do you really believe in that garbage?

Did he have to ask? Hadn't he seen enough weird ass shit that would make a sane man's hair turn white? With some of this crazy he always seemed to wander into, how had he stayed sane? Or was he?

Yeah, I'm stalling.

He hadn't moved since the light had gone out. He just stayed there, listening to the sound of his own breathing echoing in the tiny space.

311

Right now, he wished he were a smoker because he'd have a lighter on him. He'd start thinking of offbeat funny one-liners, and it would eventually come out how he needed to "come to the coast and have a few laughs".

He sometimes felt like he watched way too many movies, but feeling like he was in an air conditioning shaft sure as hell felt better than knowing he was underground in a tunnel that could collapse any time.

Yippee ki-yay, motherfucker.

He closed his eyes to listen again, hearing nothing.

"What's wrong?"

He heard the wheezing of the boy behind him, knowing he was probably having a harder time than Rob. He hadn't forgotten the look of fear on the kid's face when he saw the small tunnel. He was probably having an anxiety attack back there. Maybe he would even be the one to suggest going back.

"Nothing. Flashlight went dead."

"Oh. You're still going to go on, though, right? Ally needs us."

Fuck's sake. Did he not hear him when he said the flashlight was dead? How did the kid expect him to see where he was going?

Screw this, Rob thought as he reached forward. The kid was right, but Rob wasn't about to acknowledge it. *Damn this all to hell.* He reached out and shuffled forward just a little more, then he heard it. It was faint and distant, but he knew he could hear crying.

* * * *

"Hello!?" he called out, wincing at the loud echo and the dirt falling into his eyes. He couldn't keep from inhaling it in, coughing. That only brought down more. He found himself covering his head to shield himself. His lungs burned as he fought against another surge of coughing threatening to burst from him. His eyes itched and demanded to be rubbed, tears trying to form.

"You okay? What's going on?" Rob heard as it echoed around him. He felt disoriented as the sound seemed to be everywhere, but he knew it was from the kid behind him.

Rob nodded into his arms before he realized there was no way the kid could see him in the dark.

"Yeah," he finally choked out in a harsh rasp that he couldn't recognize as his own voice. He swallowed back some dirty saliva, grimacing at its bitterness. "I hear crying."

"Yeah? Hello?! Ally?"

Damn the kid. Why the hell did the echo seem to reverberate through his skull? It was like the kid had yelled right at him. He wanted to yell back and tell him to shut up, but he didn't have the strength. He also didn't have the voice for it, fighting against the new wave of dirt shifting down on him. Was none of this crap coming down on the kid? Why the hell did it all have to fall on him?

That seemed like a loaded question as it wasn't just the literal dirt that seemed to fall on him. Just when would the figurative dirt stop? When would his family just have that moment of happiness and peace?

Blah! Something just went into my damn mouth. What the hell was that? He tried to spit it out as he felt it shifting around. *Phut. Phut. Ugh.*

He squirmed and couldn't help but push himself back. It was reflex, but as soon as he did, he could feel it was a mistake. More dirt fell and shifted around him. He could feel them now. Tiny legs crawling over his hand.

"What's going on?" he heard the kid call up to him, but he didn't respond. Bugs. Bugs were all around him. He couldn't deal with it.

Spiders. There have to be spiders down here. They are all around me. It has to be spiders.

They were in his mouth, under his shirt. He felt them on his skin. Thousands of tiny legs all over his body,

313

sneaking their way into his pants. They were in his hair, and he felt something long snaking its way around his ear. He couldn't shake hard enough or fast enough to get them all off. He was trapped in there with them.

"You okay? What's happening?"

He could hear fear in the kid's voice, but couldn't grasp it. He sounded scared, but why wasn't he more terrified? These things were all over him.

He wanted to just be out of there away from the damn things. As soon as he opened his mouth to shout back at him, something long with a lot of legs slithered in and straight down his throat. He felt the legs moving through his mouth, pushing the thing deeper. It gagged him. He wanted to writhe and cough, force it out, but it just kept moving. When he felt it make its way into his stomach, he lost it. He bit down, unable to bite through whatever the hell it was, but at least he was able to bite down hard enough to keep it from going any farther.

He just didn't care anymore. He didn't care if the whole tunnel caved in on him, he shimmied his way forward, deeper into the darkness. He had to keep moving. Stopping meant more bugs. He moved, now on a mission. He had to get to some opening that would allow him to reach up and pull this thing out of him.

The thing in his mouth shook back and forth violently. It didn't like to be held, wanting to get farther into him. It was vicious as it shook. Its body was hard, like he bit down on some kind of shell, but he could feel something underneath it pulsating against the pressure of his bite.

Out of mind. Force the thing of out of your mind. Don't think about it. Get somewhere wider and just pull the damn thing out. Come on. You can do this.

Although he didn't think he would ever truly be able to convince himself that he had anything under control.

Keep going. Keep go-
"*Fear no evil, for you are with me.*"

He heard the pastor's voice, like a beacon in his thoughts. If there were room, he could write it off that somebody had just spoken in his ear, but he was cramped in a dark tunnel. It was hard not to take in the man's words. Just...

He saw some kind of opening in front of him. He squirmed, focused, teeth clenched, as he moved as fast as he could. Then he was there, falling forward as the tunnel gave way to a drop. Thankfully, it wasn't deep, only falling a foot onto the hard-packed earth.

Wasting no time, he pulled his feet from the hole. He didn't know how large an area he was in or what was around him. He could be in a den of vipers for all he knew, but it didn't matter. As soon as he could twist his way to the side and get his weight off his arms, he reached up and grabbed at whatever was in his mouth, pulling hard.

He heard the pastor again. *"And the Lord said, 'I am the light in the world.'"*

He wasn't sure what was going on. His head swam, different thoughts came and went, and it hurt to even think. He tried to push them all away, focusing on the thing in his mouth and getting it out. The thing was slimy and hard as he tried to grip it. It slithered out of his grasp each time. The legs... He thought those should help, but instead, he just felt them along his hand, keeping it from his grasp. It was like it danced through his hands.

The thing was long. Rob could feel its tail thrashing around his waist, like it wasn't just happy with going down his throat. It also wanted to wrap around him. He fought as it curled up and wrapped around his neck. The mental image of the facehuggers from *Alien* tugged at the back of his mind, and there was no damn way he was going to have its damn love child. He'd shoot himself before having something burst through his stomach.

"Officer?" The kid had finally reached the end of the tunnel. He must have heard Rob fighting with the thing because he heard concern creeping into his voice. "Sir?"

Rob tried to answer, but his mouth was pulled tight around the pulsating thing, having to clench his jaw to keep it from getting farther inside him.

"What are you fighting?" he heard. It would be too dark down there for him to see anything, but could probably hear Rob thrashing in the dirt.

Rob tried to scream, but all he could get out was "hmm" as he screamed against clenched teeth and a full mouth. He repeated the sound over and over, trying to convey to the kid that he needed his help.

Having space, he was sure the kid could get his hands around whatever it was and yank it out of him. Then Rob would shoot the damn thing over and over again until there wasn't enough of it to stick to his boots.

"What?"

"Hmmhmmhmmhmm," Rob screamed, knowing the words were still in his mind. In there, he yelled, "Get this damn thing the hell out of me. Pull it out!"

"I don't see anything!"

Of course you don't see anything, you idiot. It's pitch black in here. The only way Rob knew the kid was in there was by the voice. How was he ever going to get him to see he needed his help?

Damn flashlight. Dead or not, where the hell had the thing fallen to?

Well, there was one way. Rob wasn't going to like it, but the kid was going to like it even less.

Rob rushed and slammed into him, forcing him back. There was no way the kid couldn't feel the thing now. It would be writhing against them both.

"What the hell!?"

The kid grabbed at him, but didn't reach for the thing. Instead, he fought against Rob, who concentrated all his strength into pushing the kid back. If he were lucky, maybe he could topple them over so Rob could be on top as the thing attacked them both.

Then he would have to help him.

The kid seemed to be trying to push him back. Rob couldn't be sure, but he could feel his hands trying to find purchase. The kid was trying to spin away from him.

"Hmmhmmmm!" Rob screamed, the mucus from the creature coating his throat in slime. He hoped the kid could hear what sounded like, "Help me!"

He still felt his hands on him, trying to push away from Rob's body. "What are you doing?"

Rob could almost imagine what this had to look like to the kid. Some crazed man coming after him for no apparent reason. If they had light, the kid would see the thing trying to crawl down Rob's throat. It had to be the size of a large snake. If it didn't have all the legs he could feel, he would have thought it was one.

It almost made Rob think of that incident last year when those things had attacked everyone. People became monsters, making it hard to tell who was infected until they started attacking one another.

He was sure that was how he now looked. Some crazed police officer trying to get this kid while they were hidden far from anyone ever seeing.

Did he have that dead look in his eyes like those things had? Was this how they felt? Something didn't feel right. He wasn't sure what it was, but there was something wrong. Something…

It hovered on the edge of his consciousness, like he was stuck in some dark and twisted dream. Something was there. He should be able to see it, but he just couldn't. Like how the flashlight had just died on him, the light fading away, the thought just seemed to fade, as well.

A pain shot through him so intense, he collapsed to his knees. He could see stars in the darkness as every synapse fired through his head, the pain impossible to endure. He couldn't think. His jaw clenched. He could feel fresh tears at the corner of his eyes. The top of his head felt like it started to peel away, his skin hot, like it was searing off. It was way too much.

317

And then it was gone. He was gone. His mind fell to the dark as he collapsed forward, crashing to the ground, unconscious.

CHAPTER 30

Rob was surprised to find himself standing in the entryway to a church similar to the Catholic one in Standard, but brighter. Every reflective surface glowed with the light filtering in through the large stained glass windows. The ceiling was far above him, and the windows rose high to greet it. The front of the church had a large scene that he recognized as what one would expect in a Christmas display. It was a depiction of the birth of Jesus with the barn, people gathered around a woman cradling a small child.

"We don't have much time."

Rob's attention was pulled away from the display and the windows to see Father William sitting in the second-to-last pew, facing him, resting his arms on the back of it.

"Come, Rob. Have a seat."

Is it ever real? Are you even real, or is this a dream? The last thing Rob remembered was being underground and fighting some creature that wanted to nest in his stomach.

"Rob, you're still there. Right now, we're in your head in what you consider a safe place. You need to listen to me. You should probably sit down."

Rob took a step toward the last pew, finding himself sitting and facing the young priest. He looked around quickly, not knowing how he had gone from the back of the church to the pew.

"Think of this place like being in a dream. However, unlike most dreams, there is more reality here than I'd like to admit."

"But it's not real," Rob said, hearing his voice echo around the cavernous church.

The priest nodded. "It's not, just like that thing you think is in your throat."

"What do you mean? I could feel it. I fought with it. I could feel the slime in my hands and throat."

"You only thought you did."

"Okay... If I didn't, what the hell is going on then?"

The priest winced. Rob realized he had raised his voice and had started swearing. He leaned back in the pew.

"The darkness is real...and not real. It's getting into your head. It is playing off your fears. For many people, the dark would be enough, but you've been through a lot. You have demons in there much worse than the dark."

"Huh? Break it down for me."

"I can't."

"You *have* to."

Rob could somehow still feel himself and knew that outside this place, this mental church, he writhed on the ground. He could feel the creature's grip as its tail moved up and wrapped around his arms and neck, squeezing him, suffocating him. He couldn't breathe, knowing he would soon pass out, never to wake again.

He looked at the priest, who nodded in return.

"As long as you think it is real, the damage it does is real. You are doing it to yourself."

"What is this thing? Will I be able to kill it?"

"It is a creature from before, back before time had begun and light had been created. It is a small part of something else, something that hides in the darkness. Will you be able to kill it? No. The best you will ever be able to do is stop it."

"Just what does that mean? How does *darkness...*" Rob's skepticism grew.

He could feel the creature gripping him tighter. The walls of the church shook, the light dimming around them. Rob looked around and noticed that while he couldn't make out the images in the stained glass because of the sheer amount of light shining through them, he could tell they were writhing. Outside, he could see dark shapes flying around, smashing against the glass.

"Father, how does the dark do any of this? You're not making any sense."

The priest took a deep breath and looked at the windows. He must have sensed he was losing him. Rob knew the priest was trying to tell him something. He obviously wasn't just a priest, or this representation of him wasn't anyway. Why didn't he just come out and tell Rob what he needed to know? Why dance around about it. Just spit it out. It was so damned frustrating.

"In the beginning, God created the heavens and the earth. Now, the earth was formless and empty, darkness was over the surface of the deep, and the Spirit of God hovered over the waters. And God said, 'Let there be light,' and there was light," Father William said.

Rob sat there for a moment, just looking at him, not quite sure what to say. He didn't want the answer to his next question, but felt himself asking before he could stop it.

"You're saying the darkness was here...before God created light?" The priest nodded. "To say that, you would have to definitely say there is a God. That the *Bible* isn't just some book."

"I say that to a full church every week. How would what I say now be any different?"

"Because that's what you just told me."

"Is it?"

Rob was frustrated, but he had the sense there was some kind of understanding.

"So what about me? You always seem to be around, coming to me, even when I don't go to your church. There was that thing a few years ago… You led me to finding it so I could stop it. You seem to just always be where I need you to be. There has to be a reason for that."

"Do you remember what your mother once told you?"

"What? That I needed to go to church more? My wife says the same thing. My mother was such a devout Catholic, it kinda turned me off from the whole Catholic church thing."

"No. What she said about angels watching over you."

"Well, yeah. She said we all had guardian angels watching over us. They keep us from getting into trouble."

"Does it make sense that each person would have their own angel? Think of how large the earth is, how many people there are."

"Not only that, but it takes away the consequences of ones actions if they do bad things, and there are way too many people who do bad things."

"Yes."

"So what are you saying?"

"That some people are chosen. They are watched over by guardian angels because these people are meant to do great things in the world. Some do more than others, but these people have good hearts and are protectors of others. Guardian angels help guide them so they can help guide and protect others. It is a trickle-down effect that is meant to create more good in the world."

"Does it work?"

"Not always."

"So where does that leave me? You're saying I'm one of these guardians? Because if that's what you're spreading, it stinks. I haven't helped too many people. They always seem to die around me."

"Do they?"

323

"There was a whole town massacred because I couldn't save them."

"You can't save everyone, and not everyone is meant to be saved. You can only do what you can. You have to have faith in yourself or you will fall to the dark. It has crept deeper inside you. Unless you can free yourself from the bonds you have created, you will never be able to stop it."

"But if I am this so-called guardian, shouldn't I be able to save them?"

"You save whom you can. You save when you can. You run to the fire when others run away."

"Yeah, it's called doing my duty. It's me being a cop, raised in a family of cops."

"I'm sure that is part of it. It is more than that, though. Deep down, you feel it. There is more to you, Robert Raymond Alletto, than you are willing to admit."

"Sure."

The church shook again. A large black shape blocked much of the outside light and shook the window violently. Cracks formed in the glass. When Rob looked back at the priest, he saw concern in his glare. A hardness crossed his face, then left just as quickly as the man turned back to look at Rob.

"I wish I could just make you believe in yourself, but I can't. I will ask one thing of you. Will you pray with me? Please."

Rob nodded, feeling like it couldn't hurt, maybe even helping a little. He needed something.

"Give me your hand."

Rob did, the priest taking it in both of his. He bowed his head and Rob followed suit.

"Lord, we know you look over all your children, especially those who fight dark things. Rob has found himself having to fight one of the end darknesses, and he needs your strength and blessing as he is about to go into battle with this creature. Lord… Father… Please be here with us today and give us strength. Help Rob find his.

Remind him for what he is fighting. Remind him from where his light comes. Let him shine bright."

Rob had a hard time paying attention to the priest. His mind kept wandering, and as much as he tried to focus, he could only think of Robyn and Jake. He felt a tightness in his chest, but it wasn't uncomfortable. It made him feel okay as he thought about how much he loved his wife and how amazing she was. She had always been there for him. There to hose him down when he came home smelling of sewage. There to help him smile when he needed it, to hold him when he was ready to fall. Then there was his son. He had promised Jake he would always be there for him. When Robyn was pregnant, he would read to her growing stomach. The child they never thought they would have after years of trying. Their miracle son whom they upended their lives for in the hopes to keeping him safe.

Fresh tears fell as he heard the priest say, "Amen."

Then the church was gone and Rob was back in the cave.

* * * *

Rob wasn't sure what had changed, but he could feel something different around him. It didn't take long for him to figure it out. He slammed hard against the wall of the cavern, then he landed on the ground. Light flashed all around him. He saw the shapes in the room, the kid shining some kind of object down at him while also holding his own flashlight, which was lit. More shapes were in the far corner, but he could barely see them on the edge of the illumination cast by the two lights in the kid's hands.

That was all he could see before unconsciousness took him.

CHAPTER 31

"Mister Alletto? Rob?"

Rob opened his eyes. It wasn't as bright as the room he had just been in, but it was still brighter than what he thought it should be. When he tried to move his head, a stab of pain hit, reminding him he had hit a rock before he blacked out.

"Are you okay?"

He closed his eyes as he reached out to push himself up. Not seeing anything seemed to help shove away some of the pain pulsating through his skull and vibrating off his spinal column. He had been hit in the head before, and he was certain it had been worse than this. He wasn't sure if he was thankful right then, but it seemed like a good thing he couldn't remember when.

He couldn't hide the groan that escaped him, but he made it to his knees before he stopped to steady himself.

"Yeah, I'm good."

"Really? You don't look it."

He opened his eyes to glare at the kid, but he couldn't hold it. He had to turn away and look at the far side of the room. The shadows were at the edge of the light, but what they were was unmistakable. It wasn't the first time he had seen a dead body, even those of a kid.

"What?" the kid said as he turned to see what Rob looked at.

"Don't..."

It was too late. The kid stumbled back, but Rob was still partially behind him. Legs tangling, he came down hard, falling on his ass. Rob's flashlight fell onto him. As it did, he could see the other source of light had been a cell phone. It had one of those lights that could be used as a flashlight, even though it wasn't that bright. In an area of pure darkness, even the smallest light was bright.

The jostling made another stab of pain streak through Rob's temple like lightning. In a way, it felt good as it pushed back something else. Some fog he hadn't known was there. He could suddenly clearly see more around him.

His flashlight… Hadn't that gone out on him in the tunnel? The batteries had died. How was it working now?

Because, you idiot, it hadn't died.

The fog…

Just as it had lifted, he could feel it pushing its way back in as Rob allowed himself to get distracted with more questions. He could feel it, like a weight trying to push against him. He felt the ground around him stirring, the bugs climbing into his pants. He knew they weren't real. Just like the darkness, they were in his mind.

So what was real? Whom could he trust? He knew he could trust the kid. Okay, so he didn't know for certain he could trust the kid, but he felt pretty damn sure he could. Besides, he liked him.

He reached out and grabbed the flashlight as he stood. His knees popped, another glorious reminder of the impending age creeping in on him. All of this seemed like so much, and it always just kept going on.

He shined the flashlight around. The kid groaned behind him, but other than a sore ass, he wasn't hurt. The walls were rough. Rob could see where his head had hit, and while the pain throbbed, that might also be the reason his brain had cleared.

The floor was dirt, packed solid and uneven, and may have once been heavily traveled. Overhead was cut out, rough like the walls, and he could now see it was held up by large, heavy wooden beams that looked relatively stable, even though they'd been down there for years. Not that he knew what the hell to look for if they weren't.

We're in a mineshaft. Huh... There really are old mineshafts down here.

It wasn't really what he would have expected. He shined his light down one tunnel that seemed to go somewhere, probably to some long-ago access that had since been blocked off. It now just disappeared into the black abyss past the point where his flashlight could shine.

When he turned back the other way, his stomach churned.

Bodies. Kids' bodies tangled upon each other. Their skin was white, all the color drained from them, and their eyes seemed to be looking at him, lifeless. It was something he had hoped to never see again.

His legs threatened to give out on him as he took a shaky step forward. From his count, there were five of them, their naked bodies in a heap and pushed off to the side, thrown there like trash.

Push past it. Push it out of your mind. Don't focus on it.

He closed his eyes and took a breath, turning away from them. He wondered why he was the one down there. How was he supposed to deal with this? Why him? What was in his power to stop this? This wasn't some murderer or child molester taking these kids. This was something else, and he was incapable of dealing with it. What was he going to do? Shoot it? Just what made him think a bullet was going to do any good against something like this.

Have faith.

This time, it wasn't the father's voice in his head. It was his own. He had to have faith.

He took another step, forcing the flashlight to not shine on the bodies, seeing another separated from the kids. Pastor Amery. His body wasn't just tossed aside like the rest with no signs of any physical harm. This man was tangled in on himself. His limbs were broken, wrapping around each other, and his genitals had been ripped free and crammed into his mouth. He was surrounded by blood soaking into the earth.

Rob couldn't help but think about the rumors he had heard about the man. He had just chalked it up to how unlikeable he was. Looking at how the body was broken, though, made Rob think there must have been something to the rumors about this man and boys.

Rob couldn't feel sorry for him. He just wished he had gotten the chance to hit the man himself. He almost had. He wished he'd taken it.

He moved the light past the man, landing on someone sitting.

"Ally!"

The kid scrambled to his feet and rushed past him to the girl sitting against the far wall where the tunnel came to an end. She had her legs pulled up, her head buried in her knees. She was clothed and alive. *Thank God.* Rob could hear her crying as he walked toward her.

"David?" Rob heard her say as he neared. David kneeled down next to her, pulling her to him, her head on his chest.

"I got you Ally. I got you," he said softly. When her tears welled up again, he pulled her tighter and whispered into her ear.

At least something was going right, although Rob didn't like being down there, didn't like that they hadn't found anything else. Should they be afraid of her? Something had done this to the kids. He wondered if maybe she were possessed by it. His life had sure changed where that could be a possibility. He wasn't sure why he even thought of it. It certainly felt like something that could happen.

He hadn't realized that as David had knelt down next to the girl, Rob rested his hand on the butt of his revolver, fingering its release, ready to pop the little leather strap and pull it.

Strange. Did I grab it out of the squad car when I had first pulled up? Wouldn't that have given the state trooper the wrong impression? I didn't have it back at the flower shop. So when did I grab it? Did I have it the whole time, but something in my head told me it wasn't there? That seems strange, but I can't remember when I put it on.

When Ally grabbed David's shirt, pulling him against her, it was pure muscle memory that had the pistol in Rob's hand, aiming it toward them.

"David, get away from her."

The two quickly separated and looked up at him, their fear evident, both staring at him with wide eyes. Seeing the gun, their eyes widened more.

"Deputy?" David asked, his voice trembling.

Rob looked at the girl, then motioned for her to move away. She looked at the gun, not looking into his eyes, and there was a moment of hesitation. She glanced quickly at David, then looked back to the gun and shuffled away.

Rob focused his attention back on David, then motioned with his head for him to get behind him. The kid didn't move, though, looking up at him, as scared as the girl.

"Get behind me, David."

His mouth fell open. After a moment, he shook his head.

"David, trust me. Get up and get away from her."

"David?" When she reached out to him, Rob gave the gun a gentle shake for her to move away.

It took another moment of them all staring at each other in the silence before David finally found his voice. It sounded weak and confused.

"Deputy Alletto?" He spoke slow, pronouncing each syllable. The unsteadiness growing, he worked against it and stood, putting himself in front Ally.

"David, get over here...now."

David looked at the gun for a long time before he finally looked up to meet Rob's eyes. Rob would never know what he saw there, but whatever it was made the color drain from his face.

"Officer, please."

"It's not her."

"Officer."

Rob looked past the kid to the girl. With the boy's back turned, he had almost expected her to morph into something else, to show a new face. Her eyes would be black, and Rob would smell something he had feared smelling for nearly six months. A smell he had hoped he would never come across again.

And you still haven't.

There wasn't anything wrong with her. She was just some girl, looked like late high school, maybe early college. She might be a little nerdy, although it was getting harder and harder for him to tell with kids nowadays. She was dirty, her hair a mess, her face covered in soot of some kind, but it was definitely a girl.

She had grabbed David's shirt, but her grip wasn't like she was trying to take him, to do something with him, but just holding him. David had grabbed her, too. They'd been happy to see each other. How would he have grabbed Robyn if he had gone down into a hole to find her? How would she have pulled him to her? He had to imagine it would have been very similar.

But he had been fooled by a pretty face once already. Could this be another trick, something getting into his head again?

"Officer, please, put down the gun."

How could he know? How could he know if it were the real girl or something else?

What does your gut say?

His gut told him it was her. It had to be. There was no way something could do such a good job of looking normal.

And, my God, there are so many bodies. Please, let us find one alive. Please let the girl be okay. I need to save at least one of them.

He lowered the gun, watching it as he did, his eyes falling to the ground. At the rate he was going, there would be no way he could continue as a cop. Not if this was the way he'd handle every situation. He couldn't go on, especially in a small town, if he was going to pull his gun out all the time. That wouldn't go over well. Eventually, an accident would happen.

He was too scared of even his own shadow lately. Maybe Robyn was right and he should seek help. Would he ever admit that to her? God no. He would never live that one down.

"Officer?"

He heard the tremble in the kid's voice, but thought it had to be concern. Then he felt the cold surrounding him, the dimly lit room getting darker. Rob knew that any chance they had of getting out safely was disappearing with the light.

CHAPTER 32

Rob didn't turn around. He wasn't sure he wanted to see what was behind him. He had already seen the bodies, but now he knew there was something more. He felt the same feeling in the flower shop. It was that same darkness swirling around him. He already knew what was there. He wasn't ready to face it again.

Instead, he rushed forward into the little remaining light and grabbed David and Ally, pushing them up against the wall.

"Get low, stay quiet," he said, pushing them down. Right now, he didn't know what he was doing. It was more that he was going by instinct and the desire to protect the innocent. He pushed them down behind him, not knowing what else to do.

He had to face it. Turn around and face what was behind him. The evil that had tried to get inside him. The thing he had been trying to avoid seeing was now there. Every time the darkness came, the evil stayed hidden. He had to turn. He had to face it.

He wasn't ready.

He didn't think he would ever be ready.

Behind him, he heard something large and heavy plop against the bodies. It wasn't a hard thump, but more like the soft sound of flesh meeting flesh. Pictures of dead bodies piled on top of each other, bodies thrown on other bodies, entered his mind.

"Shit," Rob said under his breath as he heard the other two gasp.

"That's Tina," Allison whispered.

"Oh no," David said.

Rob glanced at them, seeing they looked behind him. They had seen a body fall onto the pile, obviously knowing who it was. Rob wasn't sure who Tina was. There were quite a few he had met in town, but it didn't really matter.

Rob followed their gaze, relieved at not seeing anything. There was nothing to see because there was nothing there. Everything was dark. Farther than a few feet in front of him, all he saw was a void.

He took an involuntary step back as he saw it moving toward them. It wasn't moving quickly, but he could see it slinking past a rock in the ground, slowly crawling over it, wrapping itself around it.

He didn't see any of the dark tentacles yet, but knew they could reach out for him at any time. He'd seen them once, had felt their icy touch. Not that it mattered. They were all trapped with the presence.

He took another step back, taking a brief glance over his shoulder to make sure he wasn't going to trip on the kids. He thought about the gun at his side, now feeling like a dead weight, making his arm go numb. It was useless, a relic of some other world that seemed archaic and pointless in the sight of true evil.

He holstered it as he took another step back. He could now feel the presence of the kids behind him. He didn't have to turn to see that they had stood back up. He could feel the warmth of their breath on the back of his neck.

"What is it?" David whispered.

"Mikey?" The girl's voice trembled.

Rob looked over his shoulder at Ally. She was afraid, they were all afraid, but there was something more. She was crying.

"Mikey?" she said again, a little louder than the soft whisper that had barely escaped before.

He had seen a little boy in the flower shop earlier, one he vaguely remembered. He had looked so damned familiar, but Rob couldn't place him. Of course, he had never seen the boy alive. He had only seen the pictures when he helped look for the boy last year.

It hadn't been the first missing kid he had searched for in this town. There seemed to be a rough history with kids going missing, although from a city perspective, it wasn't that unusual. But this one was different. There were stories around town about abusive parents, the pastor, and an older brother who liked to torture him. The kid had multiple broken bones throughout his early ears and, according to the stories, it was a "take your pick" of potential people who caused it.

So many suspects, but when Rob had looked at pictures of the kid, he seemed so innocent and sweet. It was a younger version of Jake. That smile… Different hair color, different eyes, but that smile… It was so pure and gentle. At the time, Rob had thought he could picture the kid holding the door open for him as he went in somewhere.

The apparition he saw standing in the midst of the dark void may have once been that child, but the innocence was gone. There was no smile. The eyes were recessed, black pupils hidden in the shadows. He was gaunt, the clothes hanging in tattered remains.

"Al-ly," it said slowly, the voice creaking as it spoke with a high-pitched whine…along with a dark growl. Two voices spoke, working together but against one another to make the words.

"Oh, Mikey."

Rob didn't turn, feeling her move up next to him. Just what the hell did she think she was doing? Was she really thinking about getting closer to that thing? She had to realize that whatever it was wasn't her brother.

No, he should know better. She'd been through a lot and was probably irrational. She'd been missing her little brother for over a year and had never given up hope. He could see that in the way she looked at the apparition. On any given day, she was probably a rational, run-of-the-mill college girl figuring out word problems and explaining away the strange. Today was not a regular day. The brother she had been desperate to find now stood before her. Rob had seen it before. He hoped he was wrong, but knew otherwise. She wasn't in her right frame of mind.

When she took another step forward, he reached out to place a gentle hand on her shoulder. It was enough to shock her and pull her out of her trance. She turned back to look at him.

"He's my brother."

Rob shook his head. "Whatever that is, it is not your brother."

"Look at him." She looked back at the thing in the dark. "Look at him! He's just been trapped down here. He's been all alone."

Sure, the bodies were now hidden by the darkness, but that didn't mean they weren't there. Could she really just forget about what she had been near when they found her? Damn, how was he going to get through to this girl?

She started to take another step when David stepped up next to Rob and reached out, putting his arms around her waist and moving up close behind her. It was subtle, but Rob thought he saw David pull her back a little. She seemed to pause for a moment before sinking back into him. Her eyes closed, a tear breaking free to leave a soot trail down her cheek.

"Al-ly," that wretched voice said again. It was hard to instill emotion on a sound that mangled upon itself, but he thought he recognized the subtle tone of a little boy in there. That soft voice calling out for a loved one. It was folded in on the sound, but he was fairly certain it was there.

Rob took a deep breath. "What do you want with her?"

The thing kept its soulless gaze on Ally, so Rob took a step to the side to get in front of her. He got closer to where the border just went off into nothing, and he couldn't help but take a quick glance at it. There was maybe a foot of ground before everything else was just gone.

"What do you want with her?" Rob repeated, forcing the nervousness out of his voice, sounding like a cop.

It slowly turned those black orbs on him, and he was lost in the endless darkness where there should have been eyes. It stared at him, through him, and he couldn't tell if he even existed in that gaze.

Something was wrong. He looked at those orbs, seeing no light in there. This wasn't some little boy anymore. This was pure evil in the shape of a child. So why was it acting like one? Why was it trying to talk to the little boy's sister?

This didn't make any sense…unless the boy was still in there somewhere. He guessed that made some kind of sense. Why else would it use the body of someone who had died nearly a year ago? It was almost like that creature he had faced years ago. What had it been called? Someone had told him the thing had been a Wendigo, but that never made sense to him. Since then, he had researched what was known about them. There was talk about possession, but nothing like what he had seen.

That was something completely different. That was taking a long-dead soul and using it to come back to earth, using it like an anchor. It used the soul and took life through it, but a Wendigo, from what he had read, possessed a living soul.

What happened then was much like now. A dead boy, his soul being used. That had to be what was happening now.

Rob had gotten lost in his own thoughts, not realizing he had stumbled out of the way of the child-like thing. He was no longer blocking its view of Ally, so its attention was now back on her.

She had to be the reason it hadn't killed all of them yet. It had some kind of bind to her.

Okay, the boy had been abused, maybe even sexually. What kind of monster did something like that to such a young child? That didn't matter right now. Focus. Boy was abused, then dies. His soul was given a way of coming back to... What? Get revenge? It made sense. He had one hell of a rough life. The spirit thing that possessed people allowed him to come back and get his revenge.

But how do thoughts like that get into such a young child? Michael...or Mikey, as everyone called him...was said to be one of the sweetest kids to have ever graced the town. How did that become this? How did a sweet, innocent child call to whatever this was and make a deal for revenge? And why wait a year?

Rob didn't think he would ever get all the answers, but he was starting to piece together some of it. Some came from what the witch had said and done. She came to the town for power. She knew the thing was here, which meant she probably tried to capture it, but something happened. Something like maybe the chief discovering her? His body was the one inconsistency. It would make sense if she got caught, then killed him, having to wait to try the spell again later. Maybe she had awakened it...

So how was Mikey involved? Maybe he hadn't called out to it. Maybe he had been *dropped* to it. The grate covering the entrance in what was Bobby's spot, and Bobby was said to be abusive toward his younger brother. Could he have done something? Pushed him down here or something? Maybe this creature found him...but what then?

Maybe it fed off his revenge as much as it fed off the bodies. Who knew how it worked. What the thing hadn't planned on was that no matter how tortured this young soul was, he still had a sister. Someone out there who had protected him. A sister he still loved.

Rob knew he made a lot of assumptions with his theory and there were still a lot of holes, but his gut told him he was right.

"Like a puppet on a string, the children sing. They do a little prance before they start to dance."

A children's rhyme, something he had heard long ago. He wasn't sure if it was one he read in a book or if another kid used to sing it in school. It felt childish and distant, another memory that felt more like a dream.

Much of his life felt like a dream lately. It was sometimes hard to tell distant memories from distant thoughts and daydreams. Maybe that was a side effect of these things getting into his head and playing around in there, or maybe he was just getting old.

He took another side step, then another. He could only watch as the little boy reached out to Ally and she lowered herself to him.

Rob couldn't let him touch her. Something screamed that if she did, he would have her, no matter what the little boy wanted. The thing that controlled him, his puppet master, would take her.

Something needed to change. There had to be a way to see through the darkness to find the creature pulling the strings. Rob wasn't going to accept that it was formless. If it had no form, it couldn't exist on this plane of existence.

"Now I lay me down to sleep. I pray the Lord my soul to keep. If I die before I wake, I pray the Lord my soul to take," Rob said aloud. It wasn't the best thing he could say, but it was all he could think of. A childhood prayer. He and Jake said it nearly every night, both of them on their knees as they prayed.

Jake and Robyn... He believed in their love so much. He wanted nothing more than to see them and hold them again. He believed in his love for them, wanting to have at least one more opportunity to tell them.

When Rob opened his eyes, he could see it just behind the boy. At first, Rob saw the dark man he had seen before, that toothy smile stretching from ear to ear, but then that shell was gone and Rob saw something else.

It stood tall, hunched over and gangly, its limbs long and multi-jointed. It didn't have skin, but had what looked like an insect's shell, the joints interlocking. Two long claws stretched high above the boy, coming together in a long body. It had many legs, but Rob wasn't going to count them. He didn't want to know. It was too large and too hideous. He had to close his eyes so he wouldn't see too much of it. The sight caused the pain in his temples to squeal with a new level of agony.

He kept his eyes shut, counting to ten, then fifty. He hadn't seen it. He had seen only the man. There wasn't that other thing.

Then he opened his eyes, seeing the man standing over the boy. He held his hands up, string running down, controlling the boy's movements.

It was what Rob wanted to see because it was what his mind could handle. In his heart, he knew it was just another shell, another mirage to hide the hideous beast. In order for him to face it, he had to see it for what it was and fight the darkness around him, as well as the darkness inside himself. He had to be the man he was meant to be. He had to become something more than what he was now.

He had to believe, but didn't know if he could.
Lord, give me strength.

He heard a prayer in his head and repeated the words. "And Jesus cried out and said, 'Whoever believes in me believes not in me, but in Him who sent me. And

341

whoever sees me sees Him who sent me. I have come into the world as light, so that whoever believes in me may not remain in darkness.'"

He felt a warmth swathe him in comfort as he opened his eyes. He saw the thing in its horrid state, controlling the boy as the boy prepared to reach out to his sister. The darkness that had been coming for Rob had backed away to form a circle of light around him. He was afraid, but the fear had lost its power over him.

He remembered another prayer and, with force behind his voice, recited what he remembered. "As I walk through the valley of the shadow of death, I will fear no evil, for thou art with me. Thy rod and thy staff, they comfort me..."

He could feel something happening as he spoke the words. *What was the rest of the prayer? He didn't think he was remembering it correctly. How did it go?* It was in his memories, just past the fog of darkness. He felt the fog lifting against his pressure.

"The Lord is my shepherd. I shall not want. He makes me lie down in green pastures. He leads me beside still waters. He restores my soul. He leads me in paths of righteousness for his name's sake. Yea, though I walk through the valley of the shadow of death, I will fear no evil. For you are with me. Your rod and your staff, they comfort me. You prepare a table before me in the presence of my enemies. You anoint my head with oil. My cup overflows. Surely goodness and mercy shall follow me all the days of my life, and I shall dwell in the house of the Lord forever."

The gun went off, startling him. Rob didn't remember drawing it, aiming it, or firing it. The sound of the shot woke him from some far away dream, painfully bringing him back to the present.

The thing rocked back as Rob's shot struck home.

The cloud in Rob's mind lifted more. He had the sudden sensation of being quickly pulled from consciousness without slowly attuning himself to reality.

He faltered, the world around him seeming to grow unsteady as it rocked back and forth.

He saw the creature again as it withdrew from the child. It fell back, unsteady, its multi-jointed legs nearly collapsing. They would start to give out, then it would catch itself for a brief second before it started falling again. Rob watched as it pulled itself deeper into the tunnel and away from them. The farther it moved, it recovered its speed, still shifting erratically. It spun around quickly, as though it weren't too sure of what was happening.

Rob started falling, but didn't know why. He had lost control, his legs not supporting him. They no longer understood how to hold him up. Pain shot through his chest as his heart struggled to keep a steady beat and his arms felt weak. He heard the gun as it fell to the ground.

The creature regained its balance and turned to glare at Rob. He could feel its anger. He couldn't see the eyes, but he felt the fire and knew it watched him.

It moved toward him, dropping onto all its legs, the claws outstretched. Rob watched as it approached, but he couldn't move. There was nothing he could do about it as he fell back. It felt like it took forever, like the world around him was just slowly moving to meet him.

Then the thing stood over him, hovering. Rob could see the claws and what he had thought was string. It looked like there were little free-floating tentacles reaching toward him.

No way. I'm not going to be next.

It felt like it was all part of a dream. None of this was real. He wasn't afraid. How could he be? He was still falling.

Then Rob felt a searing pain in his chest. It burned through his skin and his shirt. He saw a bright light suddenly fill the space, pushing away the darkness. He saw the room, the creature, all the bodies.

"The Lord is my rock, my fortress, my deliverer. My God, my rock in whom I take refuge, my shield, and the horn of my salvation, my stronghold. I call upon the Lord, who is worthy to be praised, and I am saved from my enemies. The cords of death encompassed me; the torrents of destruction assailed me; the cords of Sheol entangled me; the snares of death confronted me. In my distress, I called upon the Lord; to my God, I cried for help. From his temple, he heard my voice, and my cry to him reached his ears."

Rob heard himself as he shouted the words. He knew it as a verse, but not one he recognized. It seemed foreign to him, and he wasn't sure why or how he was able to scream it through his haze.

The creature stopped and stayed there, hovering over him.

The gun fired again, then another, and another. Had one of the kids picked it up? He would need to thank them later...if he lived through this.

The pain just kept burning him as the gun kept firing. He thought the clip should have been empty by now.

He should have been dead.

Then everything went black.

* * * *

He opened his eyes. Although the room was dark, it wasn't unnatural. He could see a faint glow not too far away.

"Michael," he heard a girl cry.

"You have to let him go. He's gone."

"No."

"Ally, you really have to. We need to get out of here. We need to check on the deputy."

"I'm not leaving him."

"Ally, he died a long time ago. That can't really be him."

"David, I don't care."

"Ally."

"David."

Rob drifted into his own darkness, the world slipping away from him.

CHAPTER 33

Rob woke up, blinded by the bright sun overhead. It was not just bright. The light was loud around him, screaming its intensity. He had to lift his arm to shield his eyes.

"He's awake!"

Rob turned his head to see David and Ally sitting on a fallen tree. David got up. Rob tried to give him a simple nod of acknowledgment, but the pain shooting through him told him he wasn't going to be moving his head too much in the near future.

"Yeah." His voice was dry and raspy. "We're out?"

"We've been out nearly an hour. We thought about going to your car to try and call for help, but neither of us wanted to leave the other alone."

"Yeah, I gotcha." And he did. He was already having a hard time remembering things, but what he did remember was something to fill nightmares. Tentacles and spider-like creatures hovering over him, darkness trying to grab him, a fire burning him. He was sure his old nightmares would try to intrude on all the new ones. In some ways, he wished one of his demons would just start killing off some of the other ones.

He looked at the kids hovering over him. They looked rough. Ally's eyes were red and puffy from crying. David looked ragged, his hair matted with dirt and debris, although he actually seemed a little taller than the kid he had met yesterday. Had it really only been yesterday, or was there another day in there somewhere that he just couldn't remember? Funny how hard it was to remember time, or anything else, over the last few days.

But David definitely looked like he stood taller. He hunched over Rob, checking him out. It looked like he had more confidence, his back straighter. The kid had been through a lot, but he seemed to be taking it well. He was a fighter. Rob liked that.

Ally was a fighter, too. She'd probably show more of it had she not faced down her little brother. The biggest, strongest of men would all weep when it came down to the person they loved the most being lost to them. Ally couldn't be asked to be stronger than she had already been.

"So how'd we get out?" Rob ground out.

The kids both looked at each other, then back at him.

"You got us out," David said. "After you kept shooting at that thing, it ran off to die in the tunnel. Then you started yelling for us to follow you out."

Rob glared at David, but he didn't see any sign that the kid was lying. Why would he? There wasn't any reason to. Rob had been the one to save them, to shoot the thing, but he didn't remember any of it.

"You got us up here, covered up the hole, and then you just passed out," Ally said. She tried to hold in the sniffle, but looked back at the grate, letting out a fresh sob.

Rob turned over and looked at the grate. He stood slowly and walked over to it, pulling it back.

Underneath it was dirt. The hole was gone.

He put the grate back, more confused now than he ever was.

347

EPILOGUE

In the last week, Rob had been left with more questions than answers. Everything went down last Friday. They had gone up there to find answers and save lives, but had come back with nothing but questions.

The question Rob had the hardest time dealing with was what did he tell the families. Allison was the lone survivor, but there had been other missing people. Rob felt they had the right to know that they would never see their loved one again. If they did, they should run away.

Rob was sure the thing down there wasn't dead. It had been alive for a long time. He doubted that shooting it or "praying" would make it disappear for eternity. It was gone for now, though. He wasn't sure if he needed to know more than that at the moment.

He was now the full-time police chief of Standard. It was a big position in a small town. The pay sucked for how many hours he put in, but it was enough to support his family. He figured that would be enough for him, although the new position had some issues when the state police and the medical examiners had never been heard from again. Rob didn't think they ever would be, even though they hadn't seen the bodies down below. He had a feeling they were definitely down there, but somewhere they hadn't seen.

When more state guys showed up to investigate their missing officers, Rob had been under an intense scrutiny, but he knew they wouldn't find anything to trace him to the disappearances. He agreed it was suspicious, but as he told them, all the officers were gone by the time he went up there.

Eventually, they backed off, although he doubted any future calls for help to the state troopers would be ignored.

Out of sight, out of mind. It was easy with the state guys because he didn't have to deal with them every day. The parents in town were different.

Joey's dad had become a regular at the bars since his wife and son were taken from his home. He had been home and hadn't seen anything. Other than Rob, no one in town believed him, but what could Rob tell him. The man was already on the brink of sanity and sobriety. Anything he said would only make it worse.

There was a pattern to the missing. Some Rob knew for sure, and some he could only guess at. Many had been bullies, picking on Mikey directly. Rob couldn't be sure about the others, but as the darkness grew hungrier, it might have pushed to target bullies and those who enabled them. That kid Joey… His mother definitely struck Rob as being an enabler.

Then there had been the pastor. Rob had his own theories about the guy, and they weren't pleasant. It wasn't much of a stretch to imagine him being up to dirty deeds. What they had been and what went on in that church, Rob didn't want to know. He just knew it wouldn't happen anymore.

Not that there weren't rumors spreading already. It was a small town, the local gossips doing their fair share of spreading all kinds of dirt. Some of it might have actually been true. The café boomed, having nearly a fifteen minute wait just to get a coffee at the counter. While Rob wasn't a frequent visitor, he knew it was definitely busier than usual, which meant everyone was trying to find out what happened.

349

Mr. Jenkins, who had run the grocery store in town until he retired, had asked Rob when he was going to track down the pastor and lock him up because he had to have been who kidnapped and killed all those kids. By now, most everyone had given up hope they would find the children alive. People were now angry, vowing revenge.

Maybe it was a good thing the pastor would never be found. If the town believed it was him, they wouldn't go on a witch hunt for someone else. That might just have saved an innocent life or two.

And the witch... Rob had been sure she was dead, but when he returned to the flower shop, she was gone. It was closed, empty. There was only a shell of what had been there earlier in the day, and where the witch had fallen was a spot of missing carpet. Even her blood hadn't been left behind.

She was gone, the evil she started was gone, and Rob doubted he would ever see her again. For that, he was thankful.

* * * *

Rob stepped into the church. He had put off coming here for weeks since the incident, not sure what he was going to say to the priest. The large wooden doors closed behind him as he stood in the small vestibule. In front of him, the doors for the chapel were open. He stepped into the long, high-ceilinged room.

The large stained glass windows immediately drew his attention. The images moved subtly. There was one that depicted a demon, shrouded in darkness, being driven back by an angel with a large sword. Another depicted Jesus standing over a soldier who knelt in front of him. Jesus was reaching down, placing his hand on the soldier's shoulder.

He walked a little farther down the outer aisle. The place was quiet, and he found the silence soothing after the noise of the last few weeks. So much craziness had gone on, people asking questions he wasn't sure how to answer. Was it over? He didn't know, but everyone wasn't content with that or any of his other answers.

They thought he was lying, but he knew there was no way he could ever tell anyone the truth. Not unless he wanted to find himself in a padded room somewhere, sitting alone in a straitjacket.

Where were the missing kids? Why couldn't anyone find the bodies? What happened to the county police, the CSI crew, all those people? What happened to the chief?

So many questions. He wished he could give someone an answer they would believe.

Who would believe something got into their minds, took them down into the earth, and that when Rob found them, they were lifeless shells. Who knew what had been done to them. Who would believe that, when they got out from down there, the tunnel seemed to be gone? It was filled in with dirt, but traces were still there. It looked like there had once been a hole in the ground. Why else would that grate be there?

He had no explanations for anyone, but they all still turned to him.

He watched as the next window shifted in its frame. Jesus faced a demon, darkness swirling behind it. A creature hovered over the demon, tendrils connecting the two, Jesus looking to be falling back from the thing. Above the demon, the darkness swirled, a ray of light flowing out of Jesus' chest. Depending on where Rob stood, it either looked like the darkness advanced on the Son of God or the light pushed it away.

The colors at the edges swirled red and orange, like fire around them, burning at them both. It reminded Rob of the sunset he had seen as he had entered the church. He was pretty sure it would be dark by the time he left. He wasn't sure why he was there, but time was already passing quickly.

351

The next window sent a chill down Rob's spine. It wasn't just a shiver. This was something he felt down to his core. Even his breath came out in a gasp when he saw the man depicted there. He was strung up, his arms outstretched. Fire burned around him, the flames licking, twisting. There was a dark man over him, strings flowing down, holding out the man's arms, as though he were a marionette.

The man's smile stretched from ear to ear. He had cold black eyes that when you looked into them, you saw the orange fires burning behind them. It was the man who filled many of his nightmares, and the man Rob didn't want to ever see again.

He couldn't look at any more. He turned, nearly running into Father William, who stood behind him. The father caught him, bringing him into his arms to keep him from falling.

"Whoa… You hurry like that and you might get mistaken for one of the altar boys we yell at about running up and down the pews."

Rob straightened and looked at the smiling face of Father William, noticing the sweet fragrance of cinnamon and roses for the first time. Such a strange combination, but in the chapel, under the cool air, the warm, flickering light of the candles burning around them, it fit with the calming nature of the place. It helped put Rob at ease as he pulled himself free from the man.

"Thank you, Father."

"No problem. I've been wondering when you would come see me."

"What have you heard?"

"Heard? Is there something to hear? I've heard more are missing, but no one…" The father paused, giving Rob an admonishing look, "has said anything more. Have you come to pray for help in finding the children?"

"No… No, I haven't."

Rob saw the surprised look on the priest's face, but it relaxed when he could see Rob working on saying something. Something that was hard for him to get out.

"I found the children."

"Really? I haven't heard about that. I guess everyone is too busy celebrating."

"I didn't find them alive."

Rob then told him about how he had found them. He watched the priest's reaction. The man seemed quite disturbed, but not about what Rob had seen. When he finished, Rob paused for a minute before he asked what he knew he had come there to ask.

"So… What was it?"

The priest gave Rob an appraising look. "Why ask me?"

"While I was down there, I heard your voice in my head. Then you brought me here while I was down there. I heard it earlier, too, when I thought I saw a witch trying to get into my head. I don't know why, but something tells me it all comes back to you."

The priest nodded. "And it might. I can't be certain what you saw down there, but I have heard of things. We have all heard of them, not thinking them real. They are old creatures that have been passed down. Some thought themselves angels, some demons, some gods, and some have called themselves devils. They have given birth to religions."

"Strange coming from a man of God."

"I am a man of the one *true* God. That doesn't mean there hasn't been things claiming the title."

"So what are they?"

"I'm not even certain they remember their own names or what they were. They probably only really remember what they have become. When they are awake, that is. Many of them sleep and don't pay much attention to man. They are there, though, occasionally mingling with us. It isn't spiritual, mind you. They are not celestial. They are ancient beings who do not die."

353

"Then how did I kill it?"

"Who's to say you did? Something had to fill in that hole you say is no longer there. You didn't kill it. You may have startled it, but if I'm right, I think the thing had just been awakened. When it was, it was hungry. It took the first child long ago, and had been enjoying that. When more came, it saw a food source and wanted to stock up. Now that something fought back, it went away. Not all these creatures want to be a part of this world. Like I said, they've lived a long time. Many are just tired and want to waste away quietly."

"But others don't. So you're saying there are more of these things?"

"Others don't. As to there being more, there are many things out there. Some have been around since before the heavens and the earth. Other things are more complicated to explain. I think this was one of the ancient ones, here before the heaven, and was tired, wanting to hibernate again."

"So how did I stop it? I felt this fire, then I could think clearly enough to stop it. How?"

The priest reached forward and grabbed the cross around Rob's neck. He held it up. It was an old cross, one Rob's grandmother had given to him when he had followed his dad's footsteps and become a CPD officer. He knew it had been his grandfather's before him. She had said it had protected him from many evils until there were just too many. Rob never knew what she meant by that. His grandfather had been an excellent cop. One night, he was gunned down on the streets of Chicago by Capone's men.

Rob stood and started walking to the door. He was halfway there when he turned to look back at the priest.

"When I was down there, I felt something. It used me to stop it."

"We are God's servants."

"I'm not sure I can believe in that."

"Rob, it doesn't take your belief, as God believes in you. You are part of this. The darkness has singled you out and is watching you, trying to get inside you. It is getting more aggressive. It wants you. You have to fight it before you find yourself pulled into the dark."

Father William stood and gave him a long, hard look, then that warm smile Rob had seen so many times returned. His eyes seemed to sparkle, and the church, even in the fading sun, seemed brighter than just a moment ago.

"Rob, I know you have so many doubts. You've seen so much, and many things in your life have been dark. Maybe that's why it looks for you and toys with you. I just want you to remember the good things in your life, as well. It will help you. You must find your own faith because I can only help you so much."

Rob turned away, hurrying to get out of there.

"Again, Jesus spoke to them, saying, 'I am the light of the world. Whoever follows me will not walk in darkness, but will have the light of life,'" the priest called out as Rob left the church.

Outside, the darkness had come, but the path to his car was lit by a single streetlight. The fall chill struck him, the coldness tingling his skin.

He had a wife and child waiting for him. It was time he went home.

AUTHOR'S NOTE

Hello. Thank you for reading *Into Darkness*. I hope you enjoyed it. I can't really say this was the tale I intended to tell when I started the journey. For me, I think the more terrifying story may have been a few revisions and ten years ago. That being said, I like this version a lot more and am happy to finally bring this book to publication.

I had the initial concept while I was in high school, not yet able to drive. The first draft was written before I finished school. We won't get into how long ago that was. What amazes me about the book you just read is how little has changed. The first chapter is nearly the same.

This book has been with me for a long time, shelved many times as I always felt it was missing...something.

Then Rob Alletto came along. When I finished *Inside the Mirrors*, he demanded to be a part of the *Invisible Spiders* trilogy. When I finished those first two novels, he pitched me an idea of adding him to *Into Darkness*, creating a trilogy with his character that would be parallel to the *Invisible Spiders* trilogy, but in a larger *Edge of Darkness* series. It took some convincing on his part, but when a character is as loud as Rob is, you eventually give in.

And then there is the other aspect of the story, which is how much of me I put into it. This book is dedicated to my grandmother as there are moments that remind me of her. I grew up in Wenona, Illinois, where we had a coal dump and a consolidated school. My grandmother always warned about "them hobos that sleep in the woods around the coal dump". I can tell you that I explored every inch of that slag pile, never finding any signs of anyone living up there.

I also feel this book represents three stages of my life. Bobby, the brat only child; David, the insecure and shy teenager who never felt like he fit in; Rob, the father who lives in constant fear that something will happen and he'll never see his family again.

So there is a lot to this book. I can't really say it was intended that way because Bobby and David were elements that remained unchanged from that first draft.

* * * *

So, I bet you are wondering where the idea originally came from. It partly came after the miniseries *It* premiered on television. I loved the idea of kids facing some hidden evil. I didn't want to do clowns, that had been done, but I wanted to explore a base fear that everyone has on some level. I wanted to write about the fear of the dark and what would happen when that fear came alive.

It was as I rode the bus home from school one day that I thought about having the evil presence live beneath the coal dump. At the time, my idea for the waking was an earthquake...which I hated because earthquakes didn't happen in Illinois. It was too easy an explanation...too clichéd. Interestingly enough, shortly after I wrote off that idea. Illinois had an earthquake.

I hope you enjoyed *Into Darkness*.

Until next time...